I0725381

CELAZAIN
Hipven
Cordance
Slanvai
Gredvin
Vinal
Graphak
Pullan
Chadain
Emlan
Thrisanna
Malora
Tymil
Zeyuse
Pullhiem
N
W
E
S

CHAPTER 1

The morning dust from a long-drawn dirt road kicked up behind a horse-drawn carriage before its handler pulled back on the reins. Ahead was a small country town. Wooden gates and houses spread out in random areas. A vast plain to one side and a field of green timber on the other end.

Trotting through the gates and into the town... inside of the carriage were two women, one older than the other.

"Are you nervous, Ebele?" asked the older woman.

"Of course not, Mother. If there's anyone better than me here, then that would be the surprise of the century."

"That arrogance," said her mother with a smile. "You really did get that from me, didn't you?"

"Is it really arrogance if it's true," replied Ebele as she slid her hand across a rifle spread over her lap. "I really don't understand why you insist on having me participate in these backwoods' competitions. I should be on a train right now, preparing for the Castle Trails."

"This is me preparing you." She shook her head. "You need to be aware of the tricks all essence welders can use. Not just the upper class."

She stared at her mother's clothing. "And why am I wearing a dress? Shouldn't I be wearing trousers like you?"

They were both dressed in matching outfits, red and black. But her mother wore a doublet and trouser set. A deep grey color, with red lining. A short shawl draped over the shoulders, tied in the front with a long back, white around the edges. The same at her waist in skirt form that sat over her trousers.

Her mother's hair was woven in coils that extended down her back when allowed to hang free. The red strands of hair mixing into the black, spiraling down her shoulders. Her hair was perhaps only a shade lighter, with the same red strands mixed in with the black coils. Although hers was only half as long since every few years it was cut.

"Of course not," said her mother as she patiently gazed out the window. "You never know if some high lord's son might be watching. You should put on a good showing, just in case."

Ebele frowned, the shine across the steel of the rifle reflecting the sunlight outside onto the ceiling of the carriage between them. Unlike her mother, she wore a long black and red blouse with similar white embroidery at the ends.

"You know that I plan to marry Saro. And if it's about appearing womanly, then why aren't you in a dress then? I understand that it helps manage my essence, but I'm long since needing that now. And besides, doesn't Father always say you should set a good example for me?"

Her mother laughed. "I set the example by marrying your father. So, I put on a good showing just by existing. But you, dear daughter, have yet to earn that right." She then looked down at the rifle. "And besides. If you are as good as you think you are, then I hardly think something as small as your clothing will be the deciding element of today's games."

The carriage bounced along the pothole-filled road as they went deeper into the town. From the window, Ebele could see other fancy carriages from other lesser houses.

Why do they even bother? They should just declare me the winner the moment I step foot out onto the field. No other highborns here. They all probably train by shooting at chickens in an open field.

Turning through one of the few gated homes inside the city, the carriage went up towards a manor before stopping at the half-oval stairs leading to the front door.

"We've arrived, madam," said a man from outside as he was heard leaping off the wagon to the ground below.

"I am aware," said her mother with a sigh and roll of her eyes. "Tell me." She said back to their driver. "Do you see any other houses to speak of out there?"

"The Branderbuilt's and the Turles. I see their house sigils. Oh, and I also see the Magnilia's."

"You see," said her mother with a smile at her daughter. "The Branderbuilts are here. You might be able to spend some time with Ervine."

Now it was Ebele's time to roll her eyes. "I'd rather not. And I thought you approved of Saro?"

"I do. He's a wonderful boy. But engagements are broken all the time, dear." She waved her hand at her daughter. "And it's not as if you have much experience with children your own age. So as a mother, I feel it is my duty to further along with your social skills. And keeping your options open is just one way of doing that."

Ebele raised a finger. "One, you hate people. When we're home, you spend all your time locked away with Father. And second, even if he was the last boy in Cela`Zain, Ervine will never be an option."

Her mother opened the door. "A bit overdramatic. But

perhaps one day you'll see how the world truly works."

Both mother and daughter stepped out of the carriage and stood before a large manor home, its white walls a stark contrast to the green forestry countryside behind it. Then, as if to announce their arrival, both women turned their heads to the sounds of gunfire. A single shot followed shortly after by another.

"Neekay," said a chipper old gentleman in a sir coat as he came out to greet them. Beside him were two white dogs, wagging their tails. He was fully bald but sported a thick mustache as he walked up with arms wide and a smile on his face. He embraced her mother with a hug and a kiss on both cheeks. "I'm glad you could make it."

"It's been a year since we've last seen each other, Curtis," said her mother with a smile. "How could I resist the invitation? And thank you for inviting us, by the way. She really could use the live practice. And from the sounds of things, it seems someone else thinks so as well."

"Ohhhh, that's just the Getten's testing out their rifles. They're a local family here. Moved in some years ago," said Curtis, adjusting his attention to Ebele. "Well, what do we have here? Haven't you grown since the last time I saw you? I think you were... humm... six the last time we met. How old are you now?"

"Seventeen, sir," said Ebele, being sure to mind her manners.

"Seventeen!" he repeated, wide-eyed. "Has it been over ten years since we last met?" He turned to her mother. "Neekay, you should have brought her more often. I bet she feels like I'm a stranger to her now."

Her mother sighed. "I would like to, but she's always being doted on by her father. A shame that he spoils her so."

"Don't be so down on old Arlan. Much like myself, the two of you only did have one child. You can't blame the man for being a bit overbearing. I was much the same when Danyella was born."

"Yes, but she doesn't have the gift. We both know it's a completely different scenario."

"Just so, but I did well by her and found her a spouse who does have the gift," he smiled and puffed out his chest a bit. "Along with a sizable dowry, I think that my grandchildren might have the fortune of essence."

"Let us both hope so," she looked up at the large manor. "For your own house's sake, at the very least."

"Yes…" said Curtis, adjusting his collar adherent of the subject, before turning back to Ebele. "I remember when you used to follow Danyella around, always tugging at her skirt in our garden. It's a shame she's not here. I'm sure she would have loved to see you."

"It's okay," said Ebele. "We actually were able to meet each other during last season's mid-wonders game. I think she was with her fiancé at the time. We spent the day talking and shopping throughout the city."

"That's good to hear," said Curtis. "I'm so glad that she kept you as a friend." He looked around for a moment, letting a small pause linger in the air before continuing. "Well, come along. I'll show you both to your rooms. You will be staying the night with me, won't you?"

"Thank you," said her mother before turning to their driver. "Kayin, see that our things are brought in safely."

"Yes, Ma`am," said her driver and came over, extending his arm to Ebele. He was a rather large man, pale skin with brownish-blonde hair and gray in his beard. Ebele knew him all her life, and the man was never what anyone would call a stylish dresser. Pants, button-up shirt, with his sleeves rolled up to his elbows, and suspenders to finish the 'Kayin' look. His defining trait was that he was one of the more muscular men she'd ever seen and always looked as if he would bust out of his shirt. Which did sometime happen when he began training Saro in fisticuffs.

"I can take the rifle inside," replied Ebele with a smile. "Don't worry yourself. Besides, that trunk seems heavy. No need to burden yourself unnecessarily."

"Yes, Ma`am," he repeated, as he then turned around and began unloading the cargo along with another servant from the house.

Her mother and she then went up the steps at the front of the manor with Ebele looking over the building. As they went inside, she tried to remember Curtis's words about her being here before, but the age of three didn't exactly hold such permanent memories for her. The home seemed quiet for such a large building as there weren't many servants about. She only saw the two, three if you counted the man helping Kayin with the luggage. Several of the rooms they passed had scattered clothing across the furniture and seemed as if they could use a proper dusting.

"Okay," said Curtis, after they ascended another flight of stairs and progressed down the hall, stopping at one of the doors. "Here's your room. It's the largest of the guest rooms." He opened the door for them.

"Thank you," said her mother. "You've always taken good care of us."

"Of course, we're old friends after all," he said, pointing towards the window at the back of the room. "From there you can see the competition grounds." The sound of another gunshot pierced the room. "We have a lively bunch this year."

"Good, Ebele can watch. Maybe she'll learn something."

"I doubt that," said Ebele as she stepped past her mother and Curtis into the room and began inspecting it. Unlike what she saw in the other rooms, this room seemed recently well kept. A large, lavish bed for her and her mother to sleep in and a tub for them to bathe in if they decided not to take a trip to the town bath. The furniture seemed fine and soft, with a carpet at the foot of the bed that had the embroidery of a rabbit eating a carrot. Ebele smiled at the sight of the embroidered bunny, for some reason her memory did recall that vividly.

"I'd hate to leave you both, but I have to see to the preparations for the competition," said Curtis as he turned to leave, but paused at the door before turning back to them. "And Neekay, do thank Arlan for me. This means a lot."

Her mother waved her hand dismissively. "Think nothing of it. I know how close you and Arlan are. If needed, I would have even participated myself."

Curtis smiled before nodding his head. "Right… right, I best be off then. Make yourselves at home."

A few seconds later, their bags were brought in by Kayin and a member of the household staff.

"Here you are, m'lady," he said, laying the trunk down in the center of the floor. "Let me know if you need anything else."

"Kayin," said her mother. "You should enjoy yourself as well. Go on and have a good look around. I think Ebele and I will be fine, and it will give us a bit of mother-daughter bonding time."

"Yes, ma`am," said Kayin before closing the door.

"Really?" said Ebele after Kayin had left. "Mother-daughter time? I thought we'd have gotten plenty of that in the week we spent on that carriage ride to get to this backwater tournament."

"Come now. A mother can never really know the inner workings of her child's mind. Sometimes it is best to be blunt and question the children directly," she said as she removed one of her gloves and walked to the window seal, sliding a finger across and inspecting it for dust. She then raised a finger to show her daughter. "Very clean."

"Yes, that's more than can be said for the rest of the manor. Did you really come here often? It doesn't seem like somewhere you would visit. Especially not for holidays."

"Good. You noticed the state of disrepair. But do you know why?"

"Lazy servants would be my guess."

"Humph, that so?" She flicked her finger before sliding

back on her glove and peering out the window. "Come here and take a look at your competition."

Ebele raised a brow. "Really?"

"What?"

"You're calling them my competition? That's a bit of a stretch, isn't it?"

"Oh, stop your sulking and come over here."

Ebele sighed as she placed her rifle down on the bed next to her, then stood up to join her mother. At the window, she could see a field ahead of her where dozens of large wooden logs were scattered across the green grass. Some logs stood tall while others were laid out on the ground. One man stood watch over the field as two boys next to him sat, loading their rifles. Each had a sling of bullets strapped across their chest.

The man that was watching them reached into his pocket and pulled out a round object, holding it up in front of his face. He stared at it for a moment before tossing it into the air. It came down, and he caught it. He tossed it twice more and then on the third time, on its way down, the ball stopped midair in front of his face and began to hover.

"Took him a while to get it started," said her mother. "So not the strongest blood. But for out here, I guess it's adequate."

The ball then began to float around the man several times before it let out a little puff of white smoke and took off into the meadow ahead, weaving through the wooden logs as it did so.

"You never did get me one of those for my birthday, like you promised."

"And even if I did, how long would it take before you and your father turned it into some type of flying death contraption?" asked her mother with a chuckle. "No, I chose the wellbeing of the house and the servants over your father's experimental whims."

After a few more twists and turns, the orb paused in the

air behind one of the logs. The man then raised his hand, giving a signal, and the boys took aim with their rifles. And then, with a drop of his hand, the orb dashed out from behind the log and began sporadically weaving in and out of sight between the logs as the boys fired their rifles, trying to hit it.

"They're terrible," said Ebele as she witnessed the boys tearing chucks from the standing logs as the floating ball zipped through the field. "They're just firing. They don't have any patience; just shooting, hoping that they hit something."

"I remember you being much the same," said her mother with a smirk on her lips.

"Yes, when I was ten, maybe," she shook her head. "But this... this is just painful to watch." She threw up her hand and walked back to the bed and grabbed her rifle.

"And where do you think you're going?"

"To teach them how it's done. Obviously, that instructor down there isn't up to the task."

Her mother laughed. "You do realize that they're your competition."

"Even if I was blind, I wouldn't lose to whatever that is out there."

"No." said her mother with a hand on her cheek as she smiled down at the display of terrible shooting. "I suppose not." She herself then turned from the window and walked toward the door. "But leave them to their own devices. I'm going to have you join me for a trip into town."

"What? Why? Shouldn't we rest? We just got here."

"No need for rest yet. After that carriage ride, I suddenly feel the need to go out and stretch my legs," said her mother, opening the door. "Come along."

Ebele frowned, placing the rifle's strap over her shoulder, and followed her mother out of the door. Together, the two women left the building and headed down the walkway and out of the gate into the town.

Upon exiting the gate, Ebele could see down the main street. It seemed a lot busier than she would have expected from her previous view coming from the carriage when they entered. The town mostly consisted of people in worn clothing. It was an old trade town that didn't have much in terms of trade anymore. Instead, its people seemed to just go about living their lives, perhaps hoping for a string of luck that would whisk them away from their own existence here.

"Don't you think we should have had Kayin accompany us?" asked Ebele, her eyes keenly aware of the looks that she and her mother were getting from the people as they strolled through the town.

"Why? I don't think we'd buy anything so heavy that we'd need him to carry it for us," said her mother as she stopped by a small wooden shop. It had some fairly cheap-looking ornaments that the shopkeeper was trying to hawk to any of the visitors to the town.

"No," said Ebele before picking up a pair of small, jeweled earrings and holding them up to her ear. "The people here. The way they look at us. I don't like it."

"It's called garnering attention, and of course we would. I mean, look at how we're dressed. And you, a young, beautiful woman in the spring of her life wearing a very fashionable dress. I can't imagine many men here not stealing a second or third look at you."

"It's not just lust. It's more than that."

"Yes, that would probably be their intent to rob us. But I doubt anyone here would be stupid enough to try." She nodded her head toward the surrounding street. "Pay better attention to your surroundings, Ebele. There's more in this world besides a rifle and a target."

Ebele frowned but did as her mother asked and took another look around the street. There were more than a few others who also walked around with rifles strapped to their backs. She wasn't sure or not how many of them would be her competition. *Surely not the older ones. So, they must be...* She thought as she noticed a few men with their backs against the walls of some nearby houses and stalls. Because of their posture, she didn't notice their rifles before, but they were there now that she was paying more attention. "Security, maybe?"

"Good eye," said her mother.

"But whose guards are they, then? They aren't wearing the uniforms of the kingdom."

"Probably a few mercenaries who've been given a bit of powder and gold to keep things neat here. Curtis has more than a few things at stake for this event to go well," said her mother, before turning and continuing to walk down the street.

"But why?"

"Do you remember what Curtis said about his daughter?"

"Yes, that she's married?"

"No, he said that he managed to find her a husband."

"What?" asked Ebele, her eyes narrowing as her lip twitched. "Isn't that the same thing?"

Her mother rolled her eyes. "This is why I was so against your father spoiling you so much." She turned down a street, rubbing her gloved fingers against the side of one of the wooden houses. "And have you seen her mother since we arrived?"

"Well, no... but we were only there for—"

"Good, now think on that for a while." Her mother shook her head. "I'd be doing you a disservice to just give you all the answers."

Ebele frowned as she followed behind her mother, turning a corner and passing by a stagecoach. *I don't get it. She always likes this. It's not like I'm stupid. And Danyella seemed happy enough about her marriage. And she's pretty, so it probably wasn't hard to marry her.*

"Ah, there it is," said her mother as she pointed ahead to a powder shop. "Just what I was looking for."

Together, both she and Ebele went on some old wooden steps and entered the building, the sound of a bell signaling their arrival. Instantly, the smell of soot and earth filled Ebele's nose as she took in a deep breath. She sighed with relief, savoring it as the aroma filled her senses. The richness of it was so thick, she felt as if she could taste it. *Even the low-quality powder here smells good.*

Ahead was an old man fiddling with broken down rifle pieces scattered across his countertop. He gave them a nod as they entered, but kept to his tinkering.

"Excuse me, shopkeep," said her mother as she picked up a vial of black dust. "What different powder do you have on hand today?"

"What?" asked the shopkeeper, as he gave them a look over. "Look, I know you fancy types are looking for some Hipven or Emlan power, but I only have the basic stuff round here."

"On quite the contrary," said her mother. "I'm actually looking for the worst powder you have. Something less grainy and refined. The more raw, the better."

The man raised a brow at her, looking a bit skeptical, but pointed to the second shelf on the left side of the room. "I got some Chadain. That shits barely usable as it is. But if you want low quality, that'd be it."

"Good," said her mother as she stepped to the other side of the room and examined the jars, till she picked up the ine named Chadain. "I'll take two vials then."

The man shook his head. "It's your money." He then held out his hand. That'll be ten silver pieces, please.

"Yes," said her mother as she stepped forward, reached into her pocket, and pulled out two gold pieces and placed them in the shopkeeper's hand. "Keep the change. But if anyone comes asking about us. Please tell them that we purchased two vials of Chadain powder from you today."

The shopkeeper looked down at his hand and then at her mother for a moment. Ebele felt as if she could see his mind trying to comprehend something behind his eyes. "So... ya want that I... tell them the truth?"

"Yes, exactly."

The old man twisted his head at her mother but then shook whatever thoughts he had away, seeming to give up trying to comprehend her, and pocketed the gold coins. "Aye, I'll do just that. Ya know, if someone comes ah` asking."

"Who should I tell them bought my cheapest powder?"

"Yes. my manners," said her mother. "My name is Neekay Pilsworth and that young woman there is my daughter, Ebele Pilsworth."

"Nee..." said the man before his eyes went wide. "The Warbird?"

Her mother laughed. "An old name. Nowadays, I am merely a bored housewife, who prefers to spend her days in the countryside with her daughter." She then turned to leave and waved a hand at the shopkeeper on her way. "Don't forget. If anyone asks, tell them what we bought here."

Ebele stepped out of the building, followed by her mother, allowing the door to close behind them.

"You're going to make me use that trash powder for this tournament, aren't you?"

"Of course, I am," said their mother as they went back up the street together. "I told you, your father spoils you with our family's powder. But in some cases, you won't be able to have fine powder on hand. So, you must get used to how other powders function."

"Even if that's true, I doubt I'll ever need to know how the worst possible powder reacts to me."

"Let's hope you're right about that," said her mother. "But it's my job to ensure that in case the worst happens; that you are."

As they continued, Ebele noticed two men lounging at either side of the corner leading back towards the main road. *They weren't there before.* Instinctively, her hand tightened around the strap of her rifle that was draped over her shoulder. But before they reached the two men, a shabbily dressed woman in rags came around the corner.

"Hey there," said one of the men, stepping out and impeding her path. "What ya got there?"

"Nothing. I... I was just sent by Lord Turles to fetch some powder for the tournament," said the young woman, looking a bit nervously at the two men. "I... I should hurry." She tried to step past, but the other man blocked her path.

"Ahhh, don't be unfriendly. We's just looking out for ya. You said Lord Turles, right?" asked the man as he tossed his arm over the shoulder of the woman, looking down at the small purse in her hand. "I know of a better powder shop across town. What say we show you the way? It'll only take a minute."

"No... I... I was told to go to this powder shop. I... I must follow m`Lord's words exactly.

"Don't be like that. Who's gonna know? You might even be able to share some of that leftover gold with us if ya—"

"Excuse me gentlemen," said the Warbird as she stepped to the group with a smile. "It doesn't seem like the young lady wishes to be bothered."

Both men turned towards her mother with sour faces.

"Whaddaya want? Mind your own business," said the one with his arm around the younger woman, still clutched onto her.

"Why, that's exactly what I'm doing," said her mother. "I have decided that the woman you two are currently accosting is interesting, and as such, she has become my business."

The woman struggled and broke free of the men and ran ahead, taking shelter behind the Warbird, only peeking her head out from behind her to ensure she was now safe.

"I'm sorry to bother you," said the young woman.,

"Oh, it's no bother at all," said her mother, looking back at the woman, still wearing her smile. She then turned back to the men. "I think I'll escort her to the powder shop. I'm sure you young men have better things to do. So, you best be off. I'd hate to keep you from your errands."

One of the men shook his head before looking at Neekay and cracking his knuckles as he stepped forward. "Ya shoulda minded your own business. Now ya done went and found ya'self some trouble." The man took another step forward along with his partner before a loud bang sound exploded and he looked down to see a hole in the ground near his right foot.

Ebele stood with her rifle drawn and her eyes glowing red. She peered down the sight at one of the two men. "You get one warning. I don't like wasting bullets. And I hate missing, even if it's intentional."

The Warbird turned her head back to her daughter and then sighed before turning back towards the men. "It seems my daughter is in a foul mood. I would suggest you two go on about your business before the town guards arrive and find your dead bodies."

The man twisted his lips with a snarl before he turned to his partner, patting him on the chest with the back of his hand. "Come, let's get out here. We can always catch up with that one later. They can't protect her forever."

The other man nodded before turning back to the woman with a grin. "Be seeing ya."

And with that, both men hurried off around the corner.

Ebele gave a sigh of relief as her eyes turned back brown. She then lowered the rifle, pulling back on the lock, dislodging the loaded round, before placing the weapon back over her shoulder.

"Well, that was fun," said her mother, before turning back to the woman cowering behind her. "I take it you know those gentlemen?"

"Yeah," said the woman, stepping out from behind Neekay. "They're Mitchell and Oswald. They hang around the city sometimes." The woman's eyes went wide as she took another step back and bowed her head. "I'm sorry. I forgot my manners. Thank you for helping me."

"Think nothing of it," said Neekay. "I doubt you really needed our assistance. Should we accompany you back to the powder house?"

"What? Oh, ahh... thank you. No, if you wouldn't mind. I mean... I'll be right back, if it's okay with you?"

"Go on then. We'll wait here for you."

"Yes, thank you," said the woman as she hurried off down the street and into the powder house.

"I should have shot them," said Ebele.

"It'd be a waste either way. I'm afraid there's not enough bullets for people like that. They always seem to appear in the places you least expect." She looked at her daughter with a smirk. "You didn't need to shoot, by the way. I'm fairly sure I could have talked them down without incident."

"My way was quicker."

Neekay gave a small laugh. "True, but it sadly spoiled the game."

"Game? You think those men were playing around?"

"Of course, they were. And should just admit that you just wanted to fire my rifle."

"I swear I will never understand you. How are you seriously, my mother?" asked Ebele as she stepped up beside the Warbird. She then nodded to where the men were. "What are we going to do about them? Perhaps tell the town guards? I mean, she did give us their names. They probably won't be hard to find."

"Humm. We could do that. But if we were to have them arrested, remember we are only in town for the tournament. What do you think would happen to a girl like that after we leave, and those men are released?"

A few seconds later, the girl came outside holding onto two vials of gunpowder.

"Thank you," said the woman.

"Don't worry about it. We're about to head back to Rivington manor. Will you be accompanying us? I think the

16

Turles will also be there."

"Yes, that is where I'm headed."

"Good, then let's be off, shall we?" said her mother and all three ladies turned the corner, walking back towards the manor. "Tell me, dear, what is your name?"

"Ah... it's Aretta, m'lady."

"Aretta? That's a fairly old name in this day and age."

"Yes m'lady. My mom, she... she named me after her grandmother." She shook her head. "I never liked it much. But I can't do much about it, seeing that's what everyone calls me after all."

"My mother decided to give the name of my grandmother," said Ebele. "Trust me, it wouldn't have been my first choice either."

"Always the ungrateful daughter," said her mother, before turning back to their new companion. "How old are you, dear? You seem to be around the age of my daughter here."

"I'm fifteen... or sixteen... I think. But I'm sure I'll be having a name day soon. My family wasn't much for keeping up with dates and such." Aretta turned toward Ebele, eyeing the rifle at her shoulder. "What's it like holding that? Doesn't it get heavy?"

"Not really," said Ebele, adjusting the strap on her shoulder. "I never thought about it much. My mother's been training me since I was a baby, so maybe I'm just used to it." She looked Aretta over, noticing her disheveled hair and holes in her garb. "How long have you been working for... who was it you said? The Turles?"

"Oh... I don't really work for him. He saw me in the kitchen with Miss. Landry and bid me to go and buy him some Tymit powder." She smiled, clutching the metal in her hand. "He gave me a gold coin."

"So, you're... a cook?"

"Yes, m'lady, or at least I will be when I'm done with my training. Miss Landry has taught me many things. I can make mutton, roasted lamb, rabbit stew, and I can cut some chicken, and make breakfast along with eggs or a porridge."

"Well then," said her mother, humoring the girl. "Sounds like you're well on your way to becoming a fantastic cook."

"Do... do you have a home in need of a cook? If you do, I wouldn't mind. I... I've never been out of the city before."

"Well now," said Neekay. "It seems you're not shy about going after what you want. But unfortunately for you, our kitchens are fully staffed. Perhaps there are some other lords or ladies at the tournament who're in need of a good cook."

"Yes, m'lady," said Aretta, looking dejected. "Perhaps it is as you say."

"Do you not like working for Mr. Rivington?"

"Huh? Oh, no. I... I enjoy it well enough. It's just... well, ever since Mrs. Rivington left. Mr. Rivington... well, some nights he.... He looks at me kinda funny, is all."

"Oh, I see," said Ebele, taking a quick glance at her mother. *Our kitchen isn't filled. Why, just two weeks ago, one of them was married off. Surely, we can hire another. Sure, she's of low station and those rags she's wearing are terrible, but it shouldn't be much trouble to clean her up a bit.*

"Well, thank you so much for ahh, walking me back. I should go and give Mr. Turles his powder." She smiled back at them. "Maybe he's in need of a good cook." And with a wave, Aretta went ahead of them, headed off towards the side of the estate.

"She seems like an interesting girl?" said Neekay, as she watched Aretta wander off.

"It's a shame," said Ebele. "I kind of wish we could help her. Especially since we recently lost someone."

"Don't worry. A girl like that. I'm sure she's not done with us."

"What do you mean?" asked Ebele, confused.

"That young woman is wise for her age. Seeking out opportunities where she can. I'm sure if I were to have her in my kitchen, then it wouldn't be long before she tried to find her way into your father's and my bed."

"What?" asked Ebele as she went back up the steps of the manor. "You can't be serious."

Her mother stepped to her side, opening the door for her. "My poor, innocent daughter. You really only know about guns, don't you? Maybe it'd do you well to have a friend such as her around, so you can see how the rest of the world truly operates."

"Or… maybe… you're just being paranoid. She's a year younger than me, maybe. Father would never touch her."

"I'm not sure your father would have a say in the matter. A little moonlight oil in his food at night and your father wouldn't know his cock from his finger. Or, for that matter, his wife from an entrepreneurial young cook with a hunger for a rise at her station in life. All it takes is for her to have a child with the gift for high essence and she'd do fairly well for herself, I'd imagine."

Suddenly, her mind pictured Aretta with a large stomach and her father standing behind her. Ebele shook her head. "I'd prefer not to think about this."

"Humph," moaned her mother with a smirk. "Then tell me. Would you still be so interested in that Saro boy if he didn't have a pension for powder?"

"What? Of course, I would."

"And would he still be interested in you if you didn't?"

Ebele frowned. "Yes. Life isn't just about having essence. There's more to it than that."

"Says my wonderful daughter, who apparently fell in love at a marksmanship tournament." Her mother threw up her hands and shook her head. "And now she says that her gift has nothing to do with their infatuation with one another."

Her mother's words seeped into her mind like they always did. *I'm sure he'd love me without my essence. He's said so. Even if I never placed a bullet into a rifle again.* She gripped the strap of her rifle harder, as if looking for security in her own way from its presence. *Yes. I'm sure he would. It's not like mother is always right.*

"Well, that was an exciting time about the town," said her mother after they entered back into their room. She then pointed towards the window. "Go take a look over the field and then take your rest. You should have fresh eyes for when the tournament starts."

"Alright," said Ebele as she walked back to the window, peering out over the field. The man and the two boys who were there earlier had left, and the course was empty. Ebele studied the field, committing as much of it to her memory as possible. Then she closed her eyes and tried to visualize it. The spaces between the logs. The small hill at the top. The mounds of dirt that had been piled up near the left side. The bundles of hay that were stood up between the logs. Everything that she noticed, she tried to create and organize it into a memory in her head. Then finally, when she was sure had it all, she turned around and stepped towards the bed.

"Wait," said her mother. "Aren't you forgetting something?"

Ebele turned back to her mother, who had moved over to a small table, and in a small tray, she had poured the powder that she had bought. Ebele sighed. "You really are going to make me use that underdeveloped powder?"

"Of course," said her mother as she extended her hand. "Now, hurry up. I'll get everything ready while you rest."

Ebele shook her head, but then reluctantly removed her rifle from her shoulder, handing it to her mother. She then leaned downward, staring at the powder as her eyes turned red. Then, in response, the black powder on the tray also glowed as a reddish mist seeped out from it and floated into the air. After a few seconds, Ebele's eyes stopped glowing, turning back to brown. "There," she said, leaning back up and turning toward the bed. "Let's hope that it actually fires.

I'm the best one here, but that doesn't mean anything if the rifle doesn't even work."

"Don't worry," said her mother as she pulled out a device from her suitcase along with a few empty bullet housings. "I'll be sure to pack well."

"I hope so," said Ebele as she removed her dress, letting it fall to the floor, then crawling into bed. The cool softness on her skin felt as if it were calling to her the moment she touched it. Her body instinctively slipped under the covers as her eyes closed just as soon as her head hit the pillow.

In the darkness of her mind, she envisioned the course. The routes the target could take. The ups and downs, the over and unders, and how she would aim for it.

And interrupting her thoughts in the darkness was the sound of her mother loading and pressing the bullets. The clicking, the sharp ping after every one was sealed. It reminded her of her childhood. How she would sit as a child, watching her mother load her own armaments for her soldiers or her family. Hundreds of times a night for dozens of nights, she would sit there and watch.

And with thoughts of days gone by, Ebele's mind drifted off into a hazy dream as the world went black.

CHAPTER 2

Ebele awoke to the sound of a gunshot. Her vision blurry, she rubbed at her eyes before turning over to see her mother holding a candle as she stood by the window.

"Oh good, you're awake. I was afraid I'd have to rouse you myself. I suppose the wagon ride and the excitement with that cook wore you out."

Ebele slid over to the side of the bed before sitting up, waiting for her senses to come back to her. "This is why I hate infusing low-quality powder. It makes me tired." She squinted at the candle as her mother turned towards her. "Wait." She looked around, noticing the shadows in the room and the star filled sky outside the window. "It's night-time. Did I sleep through the tournament?" she asked as she hopped to her feet, looking for her mother's rifle.

"Oh, did I not mention this tournament would be held at night? It must have slipped my mind," said her mother as Ebele grabbed the rifle from the foot of the bed before turning back with a frown. "Don't worry. You still have around an hour before it starts."

Ebele's shoulders slumped as she dropped her head. "You know I haven't had enough practice with night targets."

Neekay clapped her hands. "My, weren't you the one claiming how undefeatable you were just some time ago?"

"You know what I meant."

"And thus, the reason why we are here. You might be good at shooting simple targets in the middle of the day. But nighttime is something else entirely. And out here, away from the comfort of home, these country riflemen have developed their own skills to compensate for their lack of powder potency."

"Fine, I get it. This is your way of trying to get me to focus," said Ebele, noticing the ammunition round across the table. Stepping over, she picked it up, examining its bright red tip. She then looked down in her mother's ammo bag and saw all the bullets she made all had bright red tips. "They gave us our house colors for the tournament?"

"Yes," said her mother. "Although that was only after I urged them to. They tried to give us yellow, but I personally think that's bad luck. Yellow has never been a good omen for us. So, I had them swap the color with another family."

"With or without our house color, I still believe that I'll be able to out-gun them. Even if they are used to the environment."

"Of course. Confidence has never been something you lack. It's the humility that I plan on having you work on," said her mother as she reached over and pulled out an ammo belt and four orange sticks with netted cloth tied to the top. "Now go on and get dressed. I've loaded enough powder sticks for you. These should be enough to last through the tournament."

"How many parts does it have?" asked Ebele before reaching over and grabbing her garbs.

"This tournament has just two parts," said her mother as she began inspecting one of the bullets she had made. "One is a basic marksmanship with disks that will be launched into the air and the other will be with the powder ball that you saw earlier. For the first part, I asked that you be the final shooter."

"Why?"

"Well, even in the dead of night, I still expect you not to miss."

"Didn't you just say that I needed to be humbled?"

"Yes, and that's why I want you to struggle under a new scenario. You were trained by your father and I, so of course I'm still expecting you to go out there and show these would be marksmen how it's done."

Ebele frowned. "You're terrible," she said, but still felt a bit of pride in knowing that her mother had faith in her skills.

There was a knock at the door.

"I've come to fetch the madams for the tournament," said Kayin from outside their room.

"It's open, Kayin," said Ebele as she reached for her corset and placed it around her waist.

Kayin opened the door to see Ebele in her bloomers as she fiddled with the strings of her corset. He then closed the door behind himself before coming in. "I can handle that for you, m'lady," he said as he walked over to her and knelt, taking in the strings as Ebele held the garment to her sides. "If you're going to be moving around, you shouldn't keep it so tight. So maybe we leave it loose, so you feel comfortable."

"I was thinking the same," said Ebele as she felt it tighten around her waist. "Okay, just there. That will do fine." Kayin then reached for the bottom half of her dress and spread it out on the floor for her to step in. Once inside, he brought it up to her waist and began tying it into the corners until it was snug on her hips. "You're always helpful, Kayin."

"Yes m'lady. I'm very happy to be of assistance," he said as he then took the matching blouse from the bed and helped Ebele into it before buttoning it up for her. "There, now you look like a proper lady."

"I guess we can head to the proceedings now," said her mother as she walked over, handing Kayin the rifle. "Carry this for us, won't you?" She then handed the four sticks to Ebele. "Always remember to check your powder before going into battle. Even if I am your mother. You should always be the last one holding your powder before use."

"Yes mother," said Ebele, her voice now more serious as she pocketed the powder sticks in little straps alongside the waist.

Together, they all left the room, heading downstairs and outside into the nighttime air. Around the back of the house they went, where Ebele saw a large gathering of people standing around several tents. Illuminated by sparsely placed lamps, she gazed over the obstacle field.

It's going to be hard to see the powder ball if it spends a lot of time in the shadows. I'll have to hit it early and keep track of it.

"Neekay," said Curtis as they approached. "There you are." He stepped over from the group of men he was chatting with. "I was wondering what was keeping you. I was just about to send one of the maids up to fetch you all."

"We had to powder our noses," said Neekay with a smile. "We're not at war anymore. Us ladies can afford that luxury nowadays."

"Quite so. Well, you both look lovely," said Curtis, gesturing to his companions. "Come, let me introduce you. This is Mrs. Hamlington, Mr. Fortorn, and Mr. Gregory. They're all locals to this area, and each of them has a child or grandchild in tonight's games."

"I'm pleased to meet you all. I'm Neekay—"

"Oh, please dear," said an older man who Ebele assumed would be having his grandchild participate. "We've known of you for a while. Many of us are here purely because the

25

invitation announced that you would be making an appearance along with your prodigy of a daughter." He looked at Ebele. "I assume that's her behind you."

"You would be correct. While visiting my dear, dear friend Curtis here…" She locked arms with Curtis, giving him a kiss on the cheek. "I thought it would be a learning experience for her to compete against the many skilled marksmen residing in the countryside."

"Oh," said a blond woman who Ebele assumed to be Mrs. Hamlington since she was the only woman in the group. She wore an elegant green evening gown, while waving a matching fan at her face. "My daughter will be participating. She is also very skillful; making it so far as to come in second at the last tournament held in Gredvin."

"I think I've heard about that tournament," said the Warbird. "I was told they used a new tournament device there."

"Yes," said Mrs. Hamlington, shaking her head as if saddened. "They called it 'The Pelter.' It was much like the powder ball. But instead of just being a target, the ball itself could fire on the participants. It was a ghastly device. Not to mention that they debuted it with twelve other powder balls. The poor children had to run around the course trying not to get hit while also shooting the other less offensive ones while they did so. The whole thing was a mess to watch."

"That sounds intriguing," said her mother. "Tell me, how did they aim that 'Pelter?' Who was controlling it?"

"I haven't the slightest clue. It could have been a single person or a dozen for all I know. I've never seen anything like it before."

"I'm intrigued. Perhaps I shall inquire about it when we return. It may be the perfect thing to—"

"Okay, everyone," said a loud voice over the crowd. "All those participating in the tournament. Please come over to the front tables with your ammunition."

"Go on and get ready, dear," said her mother with a pat

to her side. "From here on out. It's all up to you."

Ebele nodded as she accepted back her rifle and ammunition from Kayin.

"Give'em a good showing, m'lady."

Ebele smiled at her attendant. "Don't I always?"

She walked over to where the other participants were. She counted seven other boys and girls who looked to be around her age. *Thought there were supposed to be ten of us. Where are the other two?* She panned around and spotted a boy and girl coming around the corner holding hands with rifles strapped to their backs. They hurriedly ran over and joined the rest of the group.

"Well, since we're all here," said one of the men around the group as he looked over at the couple who had just arrived. "Let me go over the rules."

Ebele couldn't help but stare over at the boy and girl as they seemed a bit out of breath in their disheveled clothing, with the boy tucking his undershirt back into his trousers.

"You and your little girlfriend are late, Pepper," said one of the boys near her. "Don't you think you should have waited until after the competition before one of your little romps? I don't think you'd have any stamina left at this point."

The boy who was late smiled back at him. "Some things just can't wait. And besides, if I'm a little tired and unfocused this round, then I'd say that probably makes us about even."

They all laughed, but the girl that was late just merely began looking over the field. And after a few seconds, she turned to the boy, saying something that Ebele couldn't make out. The boy beside her just smiled, before kissing her on the forehead and running a hand over her head, messing up her hair a bit.

"Quiet, all of you," said the competition host. "There will be plenty of time for snide remarks after you've earned them. Now, I'm sure you've heard that there will be two parts to this competition. The first will be speed shooting.

We will send out several loops and the ones to shoot them will be awarded five points per direct hit. I'll explain the second part when we get there. So go on and load up your rifles."

Following the instruction, Ebele reached into her pocket, pulled out an empty clip, and began removing bullets from the strap across her chest. One by one, she slid them in, on top of each other. Left side, right side, until it was filled with eight casings. She then repeated the action with another clip, which she then placed between the vest on her chest, wedging it between the bullets.

She never liked the power necessary to load the rifle; always feeling a bit self-conscious as she had to place the butt of the rifle against her thigh as she pulled back on the locking mechanism before sliding the clip into place and then releasing it to load a round into the chamber. She could use her essence to enhance her stretch, but that seems like a waste when she would need it for firing.

Kayin and her father, ever since she could remember, had been so strong that they could hold the rifle with one hand and reload with the other. Although she did feel a bit better seeing some of the other participants doing the same. But she noticed that a few of them were using different varieties of rifles. Some of them had small revolving drums that spun after every shot and could be detached to load in longer drum.

Most of them had a mix of the drum type, magazine type, and her own. But she did notice that the girl who had come late with the previous boy had an older model rifle that she wasn't too sure about. It had some type of lever that protruded out the bottom of it, which she guessed opened the loading chamber.

"So, this is how this works," spoke the event planner. "Those special bullets we gave you all have a fluorescent powder attached at the tip that when your round strikes true, it will explode in a bunch of sparkles that will illuminate the night sky in your colors." He stepped to the side. "Who wants to go first?"

"I will," said one of the boys holding a drum rifle. "It's best to get things started, right?"

"Alright," said the man. "There are several of our men out in the nearby woods and will send out five disks. You only get one shot per disk, so pay attention to the night sky and make every shot count."

The boy took a breath and raised the rifle to the side of his face, placing the butt on his shoulder. "I'm ready."

The man nodded his head and then raised a torch. A few seconds later, they all heard it. Something dashing out of the woods, a slight whistle as it cut through the air. Ebele squinted her eyes over the skyline as she tried to notice any changes. It took a moment, but it was there, something moving fast and obscuring the stars in the sky.

Then came a loud bang as the boy shot the rifle and instantly there was a small purple explosion of color overhead in the distance.

"Woo, I got it," said the boy.

"Pay attention, son," said the man. "There's still four more to go."

"Right... right," said the boy, as he flexed his shoulders, trying to loosen them a bit for the next shot.

Again, they all heard the whistling sound of another disk being loosed into the air. This time, Ebele felt it was somewhat louder. Squinting her eyes again, she saw it moving lower to the ground than before and from a differ-ent direction. The boy spotted it too, and he fired. But this time there was no explosion of color, and the whistling sound slowly faded into the background as it floated off into the distance.

"Damn," said the boy as he shook his head, preparing for the next.

Out of the next three, he only hit one more and Ebele guessed that was more of a panicked lucky shot, rather than a heightened sense of skill. The next few participants didn't really fare any better, with each of them getting two or three rounds to hit the target with all of them missing the final shot.

Then came the boy who had rushed in late with the girl. When he brought the rifle up to his shoulders, Ebele could see that he had more muscle than the other boys. A trait that was ever more present with the way that his suspenders pressed tightly against his shirt, showing the outline of a broad chest. He used a rifle much like the one she used, a long barrel with metal low profile sight.

They released the first plate. The whistling only lasted a moment before the distance exploded in a small white light. It was an impressive shot for how fast he achieved it, but Ebele saw that he didn't celebrate. Instead, his eyes stayed on the sights of the rifle, waiting for the next target. And then came the whistling sound, followed again by an explosion of white light in the distance after the bang of his rifle.

Quick and accurate, Ebele was impressed by his concentration. Again, the wish of the disk came, but this time, the boy waited, before firing. The swirling sound drifted slightly and before he fired again, but this time there was no explosion of light, only silence. But the boy stayed focused on his target. The whistling came twice more as they released the disks and once again the boy fired and both times there was silence and no explosion.

"Well, you almost had it," said one of the boys from before. "You managed two like the rest of us. Even if you did show up looking like a farmer covered in sweat."

The boy lowered his rifle, the serious look of concentration leaving his face as he turned to the other boys and girls with a smile. "I'll do better next time. I just need to catch my breath, is all."

"Yes. I imagine you both do," said the boy, laughing.

Following behind him came the girl he had come in late

with. She took her placement and raised her rifle before pulling out a small circular stick. She held it up, looking at it as it began to glow red and was infused with essence, then she inserted it into a slot at the side of the rifle at a slant.

What's that? Is that her fuse stick? I've never seen one like that before, thought Ebele as she watched the girl's eyes narrow and focus on the distance in front of her; her face looking just as serious as her apparent lover.

Once again, the man raised his torch and a few seconds later the whistling sound returned, only to be immediately blown out of the sky in a small purple explosion.

That was fast, thought Ebele, surprised by the girl's quick reflexes. *I barely heard it, let alone saw it.*

The girl pushed and pulled back on her lever of the rifle ejecting the empty shell casing and pulled another bullet from a pouch at her slide, placing it into the chamber followed behind with another small red disk that she held up to infuse with magic before inserting it.

She's going to reload after every shot? Does that rifle not have a round chamber?

The girl once again assumed her gunner's posture. Again, came the whisper and once again it was shot down almost instantly.

How is she doing that? Ebele wasn't able to analyze anything the girl was doing. It felt like it was almost instant. She looked around, wondering if anyone else found this odd, and was surprised to see the girl named Aretta from earlier that day standing off to the side, looking on. She was still in her ragged clothing and boots, but in her hand; she held two empty vials. *She came to watch? I guess that makes sense. I did say that I would be participating.* Ebele then shook her head and turned back to the other girl. *I need to focus. There has to be some trick to it. I just don't know it... yet.*

And as the other three disks were launched, unlike her partner, she repeated the process, blowing them out of the sky almost before they even got fully into the air. *I'm not even sure the last one had a chance to whistle. Is she cheating or does she know some type of trick to it?*

"That's my girl," said the boy she arrived with.

The girl sighed with relief when it was over, lowering her rifle as she then walked over, giving the boy a hug and burying her face in his chest as he patted her on the back of the head. The rest of the group could only stand there looking stunned for a moment, much the same as Ebele.

"What in all the Kingdoms was that, Pepper?" said one of the other boys. "I thought you both were tired. Your woman's not fazed at all. I'm starting to question your manhood if she can come out here and do that."

Pepper laughed. "What can I say? I'm a gentle lover." He then opened his arms wide towards two other girls that were nearby. "Or maybe my love can enhance a woman's skills. Come over here for a hug and find out."

"Humph," moaned one of the girls. "More like enhance our stupidity. Put those arms down."

I'm glad to see I'm not the only one who thinks what just happened is weird. Is it even possible to be that good? I mean, maybe mother's that good, perhaps father too. But she's around my age. There's no way she's that skilled. I would have heard of her, surely.

"Alright, next up. Come on," said the host of the event as he stood at the shooting stand. Two more women and another boy took turns with. each of them hitting between two and three. of their shots Then it was Ebele's turn. She would be going on last, just like her mother had said. Although after that one girl's performance, the idea of showing them how it's done didn't seem as guaranteed as before.

She walked forward, stepping up onto the shooting podium. She had already loaded her rifle, so she raised the butt to her shoulder, placing the stock against her cheek and took aim down its sight. She took a deep breath as the man raised his torch to give the single to release a disk. And just like many times before, came the whistling sound.

While her rifle was steady in her arms, her eyes darted from left to right over the night sky, looking for disturbances in the crystalline void above. Then she saw it, a star vanishing, then reappearing, then another and another. She channeled her essence, feeling it seep into her flesh and through her clothing as her eyes grew a crimson red. Quickly, she raised her gun, following the trail, taking careful aim where she knew it would be and pulled the trigger. Then came the bang, the recoil pressing into her shoulders, causing her to grit her teeth. A piece of the sky erupted in red light as the smoking shell casing ejected past her eyes. She'd hit the first target.

And before she'd even got another chance to relax, the man next to her raised the torch again and Ebele as she took aim, her eyes peering out in anticipation.

This whistling sound came in low, but this time she was ready. She'd heard it enough to know the distance. She fired and an explosion of red light appeared near the trees. A frown came across her lips as the gathers of the competition ooh'ed at the display of skill. *I'm still slower than she was. And she did it consecutively.*

The third disk was released, and it flew for a few moments before she fired. Her aim was spot on again and it exploded like those before it.

Trying to force everything from her mind as the shell ejected from the rifle, she focused on the field ahead. But there was a tingle at the back of her neck. And then on the side of her check as a loose strand of her hair curled upward, teasing the side of her lip as she heard the trees begin to rustle. Suddenly a large gust of wind emerged, and in that breeze, they would choose to send out the next disk; its whistling sound muffled by the wind and shaking of the leaves.

Her eyes quickly began scanning the field and sky ahead of her. *Where did it come from? From the left? From the right? Damnable wind, I can't hear it, and I don't know where to look.* Frantically her eyes darted back and forth, her fingers twitched on the base of the rifle nervously. Seconds. She only had seconds before she knew it would be gone. *Where are you? I know you're out there some…*

There in the distance. She squinted her eyes. The night sky, part of it flicked for a moment. There, somewhere in that small space. It was far off; she needed another sighting of it. Something to be sure that she wasn't imagining it. And then again, low to the ground, the patch of grass appearing black for only a moment. She pulled the trigger.

The sound of it ringing in her ear, piercing the quiet of the night. But the field stayed silent until she saw it. A bright red burst of light just above the ground, far out into the field. The nervousness she had, now swallowed before a sigh of relief.

"Good shot," said the man with the torch. "Even I'd lost track of it out there. You cut it kinda close, though. It had almost landed."

Ebele could feel a bead of sweat drop down her neck. "Did it still count?"

"Yeah. A shot like that. You bet it did."

"Good," said Ebele, never taking her eyes off the field. "Send the next one."

The man nodded his head with a smile and raised the torch once more. And a few seconds later, that piercing whistling sound emerged once again. It howled for a few seconds at first as she started to look for it. But then it hit her that this time it was different. This time, instead of growing weaker, it was like the sound was appearing weaker in different places. Different side of the field. *What's going on? Where's it coming from?* First it was to the left, then it was to the right. But unlike before, instead of growing softer, the whistling was growing stronger, as it was coming closer from multiple directions.

This has to be some trick. There's something I need to look for. She closed her eyes. *Focus, Ebele. You can do this. Where is it coming from?* She tried focusing more, the humming of multiple whistles coming to her as she tried sorting them out in her mind. *One is low... no, it's two that are low. They're not changing, but one is growing louder. Where's the louder one? Where's that sound coming...*

Her eyelids tightened. *No, not coming. What is the sound doing? Three whistling sounds. Only one growing stronger. It's... it's moving toward the other two? Where are the other two?* She listened more intently, putting aside the louder noise and isolating the two smaller whistles to the brush on either side of the field ahead of her.

If the louder one is the only one moving, then it must be behind me. The bastards are shooting it over my head. So instead of finding it off in the distance, floating from left to right, she knew she'd have to catch it when it passed them. *Don't look for it. Wait for it to come to me.* Focusing in on the moment, she waited for the whistling sound to reach its apex.

It came as she knew it would, almost feeling as if it would sting her ears. She caught the moment when the sound had just started to drop and raised her rifle, spotting it come into view and fired. A sparkle of red light exploded down upon them all as a piece of the disk crashed onto the field ahead of them only a few yards away.

The crowd covered their heads for a moment but looked on in amazement as Ebele heard the sound of applause.

"Well done, little lady," came the sound of Curtis as he stepped into the gathering alongside her mother. "I must say, I was a bit skeptical of using such a trick, but Neekay, you and Arlan sure have trained her well."

"Of course we have," said her mother, a smirk across her lips. "She has to live up to my name, after all."

Ebele put on a smile and bowed to the crowd as her mother walked up and stood beside her. *You always make things so difficult,* she thought, casting a side glance at her mother. But beyond her mother, she could see the girl in ragged clothing with a bright smile on her face and she looked on. *What was her name again?* She thought back. *Aretta, I think.* She smiled back at the girl. *It really is a horrible name.*

"Okay, everyone," said Curtis. "I've prepared some food for you all and we can let our young champions rest for the night. The second part of the competition will take place tomorrow evening."

Ebele was surprised. *Tomorrow. I thought both parts would be tonight.*

Her mother took her hand and helped her back down from the podium as Kayin came over to her with his hand out.

"I'll take your rifle, m`lady, and see that it's taken care of."

"Yes," said Ebele, removing her armament and rounds, handing them both to her aid. "Thank you."

"Now come along, daughter," said her mother. "I shall introduce you to the parents of your competitors. I think you might find this interesting."

Her mother was right. Ebele was very interested in learning more about the other competitors. But more specifically, there was one girl she certainly had an interest in. So, she allowed her mother to usher her around the festivities as the participants linked back up with their sponsors.

She learned a few of their names and which house they were from. If they were the child or adopted child and what not. But Ebele quickly noticed as she went along with the conversations beside her mother. She was never introduced to the boy and the girl, who had appeared late and disheveled.

"Mother," said Ebele after they had stepped away from the crowd for a moment. "There was another girl. One who also hit all the targets. Do you know what family she's from... or her name?"

"No," said her mother. "I was off in the tent conversing.

I wasn't particularly interested in the other contestants and had Kayin come and inform me when it was near your time. So, there was another girl who managed to tie with you?"

Ebele looked dejected but began looking around the grounds. She didn't see the person of her interest, but did see a few people up around the house. "I'm going to go and look for her," she said, taking off up towards the house before her mother might object.

I need to know how she did it. Was it really just skill or is there a trick to it?

Beside the house, she saw some people sitting down on a few barrels, sharing ale as they chatted amongst themselves. Getting closer, she saw Kayin was with them, enjoying himself a drink.

"Excuse me?"

"Oh, m'lady. Have you come to retrieve your weapon? I have it locked in your room, but I can go a and retrieve it if—"

"No, no need Kayin. Ah... actually, you were there to watch the competition. Did you happen to see the other girl who hit all the targets and where she went?"

"Why, yes. They just recently left through the gate and into the town. I assume they'd be staying at one of the ins."

"So, she won't be staying here?" asked Ebele, nodding toward the house. "I thought all the contestants would be staying?"

"Sorry miss," said another gentleman sitting on a barrel. "That's only for rich folks like yourself. For those of lesser stations, they're going to have to fend for themselves. And that's only if they have houses."

"What? I don't... do some of them not belong to a house?"

"Of course," said the man with a laugh. "Not everyone is as rich as them nobles back there, possessing enough essence to supply an entire brigade. Some of the lower ranks gotta manage for themselves. And seeing as this was an open tournament, some might not have houses at all.

Gunpowder Dolls

Ebele stared at the torch lit open gates at the end of the road ahead. *There's no way a lower rank is as good as she was.*

CHAPTER 3

The next morning, Ebele awoke in the bed beside her mother, who was already sitting up and reading a book.

"Oh, welcome to the morning. You certainly seemed to have a rough sleep."

"Yes," said Ebele, her eyes squinted, trying to block out the sun. "I couldn't sleep well last night."

"Yes. I saw that."

She rolled over, looking up at Neekay. "Mother, can we go back into town today?"

"Let me guess. You wish to search for that apparent mystery girl who seemed to be as good as you?"

"Wha... how did you know?"

Her mother gave a small laugh. "Please child. You're just a smaller version of me. Of course, I'd know what kept you up."

"Fine," said Ebele with a frown. "You're right, you're

always right. But I've never seen someone shoot like that. Is that so wrong for me to be curious?"

"No, we all must have our rivals. I myself had more than a few. But why bother now? You're undoubtedly going to see her again at the second part of today's competition."

"No. I don't want to wait. She might disappear again, and I might never get to see her. I… I wish to speak with her."

Her mother just smiled for a moment as she stared at her daughter.

"What? You're thinking that I'm being silly, aren't you?" She pouted, folding her arms over her chest.

"No," said her mother, her smile unwavering as she watched her daughter roll out of bed, placing her feet on the floor. "I'm just remembering things, is all. Fine, we will pursue your rival in town. But only after we've had our breakfast." She then stood and walked toward the opposite side of the room and began knocking on the wall. "Kayin… are you awake?"

"Yes, m'lady," came Kayin's muffled voice through the wall. "Do you need anything?"

"Please have someone bring us up some breakfast."

"Yes, at once, m'lady. I'll put on my clothes and head down to the kitchen."

There was a second's pause, before they heard Kayin mucking about in his quarters before the sound of his door opening and closing was heard.

"Right," said her mother as she turned back to her. "We didn't get the chance to properly discuss last night. How did you find the first part of the games?"

Ebele shook her head. "I hated it. Can I assume that you set up that stunt with the whistling coming from different places?"

"You would be correct. I thought you might find that interesting. It was a little trick the enemy used to use on me when I was in battle. It confused my senses for quite some time. But you only had two. Imagine being in a forest and there'd be somewhere north of fifty of them. That, mixed in with other gunfire, the stomping of horses, and whatever else was out there made for a terrible march."

"Fifty," said Ebele as she raised her hand to her face and began rubbing at her eyelids. Just the thought of it made her frustrated. "Were the war's really that bad?"

"Worse." Her mother sat down on the cough grabbing at one of the leftover rifle rounds and twirling it between her fingers. "Now imagine doing all of that while being rained on and covered in dirt and mud."

"I'm surprised you allowed me to become a gunner then, if it's that bad."

"Everyone of high powder proficiency must submit an heir to be tested by the kingdom. And you're my daughter. So that means you will probably be as strong as I am... or your father, of course, although he's not exactly the same as I. There was simply no way out of it. If I didn't train you, annoying as King Harlan is, this tradition precedes him. So, he must follow it."

"Why do you never talk much about the king? When people talk about the battle of Fairyorun, they always talk about how you rescued him from the enemy camp."

"That was a long time ago," said her mother, raising the bullet up to the window's morning light. While her eyes were focused on the shimmer of the metal, her mind seemed to be drifting back somewhere else. "And he was just a prince then. A young, idiotic prince. Now he's a grown man with sons of his own."

"You know, in school. They would often tease me by saying that you and he were lovers and that I'm actually a princess."

She placed the bullet down on the windowsill. "Unfortunately for you and his royal highness. I was in love with your father by then. And a heated escape from an enemy encampment wasn't enough to convince me to call off my engagement."

"I don't know," said Ebele, as she closed her eyes, a small smile across her lips, as she relaxed back into the bed. "I wouldn't mind living a life of pampered comfort like a princess."

"If that's the case, then you can take the road I didn't, and marry one of his sons."

Now it was Ebele's time to laugh as she waved a hand. "Like you. I've already found someone. So, the royal family will miss out on the women of our family twice." She let out a small chuckle. "Perhaps they're cursed."

There came a knock at the door.

"Kayin?" asked her mother. "Is that you?"

"Ah... no mam," came the meek but familiar voice of a woman from behind the door. "I was asked to bring your meal. Is that alright?"

"I do think our enterprising young friend has come to visit us again," said her mother. "Yes, don't be shy. Come in."

"Yes," said the voice, and the door slowly opened, revealing Aretta holding the handles of a large wooden tray with an assortment of food spread across the top. "Your manservant asked that I bring your meal, as he had some matters to attend to."

"Did he now?" asked her mother with a raised brown. "Well, place it there." She pointed to the table where across the top housed some powder and a few loose rounds of ammunition.

The smell of cooked meat and spices did their best at rousing Ebele from her bed; the flavor quickly filling the room as she began sliding from under the sheets.

"Well, I suppose it's good fellowship to eat with company," she said, looking at Aretta. "Why don't you have a piece as well?"

"Huh?" asked Aretta, seeming surprised. She shook her head. "No ma'am, I can't. It would be improper."

"Don't worry about improprieties now," said her mother as she reached down, picking up a small piece of meat between her fingers. "We're all friends here." She then lifted the piece to Aretta's lips.

"No. I can't. It would be..." Aretta's words paused as Neekay playfully placed her hands on the girl's cheeks, holding her mouth open, and inserted the meat inside.

"There we go," said Neekay, with a smile at the young woman. "Now chew and enjoy the food with us." The surprise of the situation was evident on Aretta's face as she began to chew the meat as Neekay released her face. "Now tell me. How does it taste?"

"It... gaud." Aretta finished chewing and swallowed. "It's good ma'am."

"There. You see. That wasn't so hard, was it?"

"No, ma'am."

"Such a polite thing," said Neekay, before sitting down, patting the chair beside her. "Now sit. You're going to eat with us, and afterwards you are going to show my daughter and I more of the city. It'll be easier to have you guide us around. I'll get permission from the lord after we've eaten."

"Yes, ma'am," said Aretta, reluctantly taking a seat beside Neekay. "As you say."

Ebele couldn't help but smile as she watched her mother take control of the poor girl. "Don't worry. She does that to everyone," she said as she walked over, joining the two for breakfast. "I'm afraid she just simply doesn't understand boundaries." She then sat down beside the two and they enjoyed themselves a good breakfast.

A little over an hour later, the three were dressed and headed out, with Aretta telling them small tidbits about the city. Not so much was spent eating, but the other hour was her mother coaxing Aretta into one of Ebele's dresses and doing her hair. While not a fan of the idea originally, Ebele had to admit that she found an odd pleasure in doting on the lowborn girl.

"Those two men? They haven't harassed you since yesterday, have they?" asked Ebele as they headed down the town streets.

"Two men?" asked Aretta, looking confused.

"The ones that were in the alley when we met you," said Ebele.

"Oh, no ma'am. But I mostly keep myself inside the manor when I can. They won't come into the property where they got them guards. So, I'm safe as long as I don't leave for a while and give them time to cool down, I think." She nodded. "If you two had not asked. I'd have waited another week or so, or asked one of the guards to come to the city with me in case they sent for anything."

"Well, since the tournament will be here till tomorrow," Neekay looked at the few riflemen around the town. "I think you'll be safe till then."

"Yes ma'am," said Aretta, looking at Ebele. "This girl you say you're looking for. You said that she's a local?"

"Well, I'm not sure. You were there that night. Did you see the other girl who hit all the targets?"

"Ah, no ma'am. I was serving the guests, mostly. I just happened to sneak away for a moment to watch one or two shots. Otherwise, I might've gotten in trouble."

"Well, there was this guy and girl who came there. Ah, they were late, and I think they were a couple. The boy was an alright shot, but the girl. It was like she was hitting the targets the moment they released the disks."

"Have you ever fired a rifle before Aretta?" asked Neekay.

"Ah, no ma'am. Never. I haven't the gift of essence."

"Really? So, no young nobleman has tried tempting you with a shot from their rifle in hopes of getting under your skirts? You're a fairly attractive thing. Tell me, are there any boys you find yourself interested in?"

"Some of the young lords have tried, but..." she lowered her head a bit, looking down at the road. "Well, I'm not naive to the ways of the men. So, I usually go and hide in the kitchen or the stables till they leave. I've seen what happens to Low Town girls. They get with child and no one's there to help them. And the young lords, they leave or pretend the baby ain't theirs."

"Smart girl. If you're going to get knocked up. At least make it profitable, right?"

"Ma'am?" said Aretta, looking confused.

"Don't worry about my mother. Her mind is always suspicious of everyone," said Ebele with a sigh. "I used to always wonder if my father had other children. A lot of lords have bastards. But with my mother, I don't think that's possible. She'd probably hunt them down and shoot them."

"I... I see," said Aretta, looking a bit nervous as she glanced back up at Neekay.

"Ahh!" said Ebele, pointing a finger ahead of her. "That's him. That's the boy, the one who was with the girl." He had just exited a building and turned a corner. Quickly, Ebele picked up the pace, with Aretta trailing behind. Her mother, in contrast, kept her same leisurely stroll, allowing the young women to go off ahead.

Ebele turned the corner, but didn't see him. "Damn. Where'd he go?" There were several other houses and roads along with a horse-drawn wooden carriage. But she didn't get an image of where he might have gone. She hurriedly stepped down the street, looking between the small alleys for him, but didn't see him anywhere.

"Are you sure it was him?" asked Aretta, catching up with her.

"I'm sure of it."

"Well, I've seen him around the town sometimes. Maybe once or twice a month or two. You wish to try and split up to find him?"

Ebele looked around again, feeling a bit disheartened by the apparent disappearance of the boy.

"It's not nice to follow someone like that," came a voice from above.

Ebele and Aretta turned their heads upward and spotted the boy squatting, and looking down at them from a rooftop.

"Wha... how'd you get up there?"

"I climbed. Now you answer my question. Why ya looking for me?"

Ebele stepped forward a bit. "Ah... it's about the girl you were with. I'd like... I'd like to speak with her if I could."

"Yeah? And why's that?" He eyed her for a minute. "You were at that tournament the other day. You're the other girl who hit all the targets."

"Yes," said Ebele, pointing up to him. "And you only hit two. I wouldn't mind giving you some pointers if you came down here and answered some questions."

"Yeah, no. I think I'm fine up here." He then looked over to Aretta. "Who're you then?"

"I work for one of the noble houses. I'm their cook."

"I ain't never seen no cook dress like that before." The boy shook his head and then stood up to leave, turning to go.

"Wait. Don't go."

"I don't know what you both want, but I know it won't do me no good to find out either."

"Please," said Ebele, her voice softening a bit. "Can you... can you at least give her a message for me?"

The boy turned around, staring down at them again before sighing. "Fine. What's the message?"

A little surprised by the whole situation, Ebele realized she didn't know what to say. "Tell her... tell her that shooting was... well, it was beautiful. And that I look forward to seeing it again at the second part of the tournament."

"Fine," said the boy. "I'll make sure she gets your message." And with that, the boy above them disappeared behind the rooftop.

"What do we do now?" asked Aretta, stepping in beside Ebele. "Should we keep looking for her?"

Ebele shook her head. "No, this is fine. I probably should have just waited for this evening. It'll be enough if he tells her."

Both girls walked past the rickety cart and down to the street where Ebele found her mother talking to another well-dressed man. *That's one of the men from before. It was his son... or maybe his nephew that was there.* She looked around, spotting the boy nearby, a rifle slung over his shoulders as he walked over to them. She remembered him now. *He wasn't that good. Another boy who only managed to hit two targets.* A smirk came over her lips. *I can't wait to see her shoot again. I just know there's a trick to it.*

"Hey," said the boy. "Your mother tells us that she's been training you. It's no wonder you're so good."

"Huh," said Ebele, taken out of her thoughts as she looked at her mother. "Yes, she thinks that me being out here will make me a better gunner." She rubbed her mother's shoulder. "I was skeptical at first. But it looks like she was right."

"Well," said her mother. "How rare it is for you to admit your mother was right. I suppose you got what you wanted?"

"Not yet. But it's starting to look like I will."

"Ebele," said her mother, introducing the man and the young boy. "This is Mr. Farrenhowl and his nephew Mavil. They've come from a nearby town to attend."

"Yes," said Ebele, nodding to the two. "I saw him shoot yesterday." She smiled at Mavil. "He managed to hit three targets."

"Yes," said the boy. "Perhaps I should have tried harder. But I didn't want any contention from the other marksmen. Although you don't seem to have such fears."

"No, but everything is a learning process."

"Well, if you feel that way," said the boy with a smile as he swung his rifle off his shoulder to show her. "I wouldn't mind showing you a few things. Maybe we can meet up later."

A blank stare came over Ebele's face as she watched the boy try to flirt with her. Giving him a quick look over, she admitted he was somewhat attractive. Half a head taller than her. *They're always the same.* Ebele thought back to the balls or public outings where her mother would try to introduce her to a host of would-be suitors. *Clean hair. Taught to speak like they actually care about me. But half of them just want to inherit my family's wealth and the others just want to fuck me. And worst, they shoot like shit.*

"See," said her mother with a smile. "He wants to teach you. Isn't that why we came out here?"

Ebele looked up at her mother with narrowed eyes and a frown. *You can't be serious.*

"Go on," said her mother with a nod of her head. "You two go on and entertain each other. There's plenty of time left before the competition. You both can have a little game before the final event."

Ebele wanted to sigh but held it in before reaching over and grabbing Aretta by the arm. "Of course. I think that's a wonderful idea. And we can show Aretta too, since she's never held a rifle before." *There's no way I'm suffering through this alone.*

"Oh," said the boy, looking a bit disappointed. "Yes, of course. I'd love to show the both of you. Ah, what house were you from again?"

"House?" said Aretta. "I'm in Mr. Curtis' house. I work—"

"Yes, she's working there as a scholar," chimed in Ebele. "Examining our weapons and the different ways we all use them."

"That sounds interesting," said the boy. "Do you have the gift as well?"

"Gift? You mean that essence stuff?"

"No," said Ebele, cutting in again. "She doesn't. But someone has to document the details of riflework for the future. Being a scribe is a noble profession."

"Huh? Yes, of course. Forgive me m'lady, I didn't mean to offend."

"No. I am... I'm not offended."

"Good," said the boy. "Come on then, there's actually a

small field on the outskirts of town where a shooting range has been setup. I can show you how a field-man shoots."

Do I really have to go along with this? Ebele looked up at her mother and saw that she did. "Yes, I'm sure the gunnery skills of the countryside can teach me a few things," she said, turning back to the boy. "But aren't you afraid that you might be giving away your secrets? It might make it easy to beat you in today's competition."

He laughed, "It'll take you more than a day to learn all I know."

No, I'm pretty sure the sum of it would take less than an hour. And thats being generous.

"But either way, I hardly think it matters out here at such a small event. And besides, better riflemen make a better nation is what my father always says." He extended his elbow to her. "Come along. I'll escort you like a proper gentleman."

Reluctantly, she accepted her fate as this boy's chaperone and linked arms with him. "Come along Aretta. It seems we're in for a rousing lesson in countryside marksmanship." With well wishes, her mother and her companion watched them leave with Aretta tagging along behind them as they headed through the small town.

"So," said Mavil. "What's it like being the daughter of a legend? Your mother's war stories were taught in history classes at my school."

"Oh, about the same as you I'd imagine. I wake up in her shadow, then I go to sleep in her shadow. People expect me to be like her. She expects me to be better than her."

"And what do you want?"

"Honestly? To be better than her?" Ebele laughed. "I guess in that way we do want the same thing. We just have different ideas on what is the best way to pursue it."

"And what of you, Miss. Aretta? Do you come from a long line of scholars? Your father and mother putting parchment in your hand since you were a child?"

"Me? No. My Father... I was told he was a brick mason. But he passed away when I was little."

"Oh, I'm sorry to hear that."

"It's fine. I have my older brothers. We take care of each other."

"I see. And what of your mother?"

"My mother? Well, she... she's busy a lot, I guess."

The sound of gunfire interrupted their conversation as they got closer to the outskirts of the town. The powerful echoing sound was rhythmic as one round set was followed by another. Piercing, like the sound of a whip cracking, but less sharp, pounding like a drum. It was as if she could feel the waves of it invisibly roaming over her clothing and skin.

"That's a lot of practice," said Ebele. "I hear several different rifles."

"What?" asked Mavil, as they got closer. "You can tell different rifle sounds?"

"I mean... somewhat. Shorter barrels have a short snap when they shoot, while longer barrels have a more pronounced firing sound."

Mavil shook his head skeptically. "Okay, then tell me. How many different rifles do you hear? Because we heard six shots. Are you going to tell me you heard six different rifles?"

Ebele stopped, her arm still linked in Mavil's as they halted and listened as several more rounds went off. *Loud, louder, loud, dull, dull and short, loud.* She then slowly tilted her head left to right in thought. "I think they have four different rifles. I'm not sure of their models. I'm not good enough to know that yet."

"Okay then," said Mavil as they resumed their steps and turned the corner to see a man instructing several young children on how to shoot. "Jimmy, don't let that rifle sag. Brace it against you. I don't want to see any slack between your shoulder and the butt of that rifle."

"I don't think you're going to get the chance to show me

anything," said Ebele with a smirk. "It looks like this range is full."

"Yeah," said Mavil, a clear frown across his lips.

"What are you three doing here?" asked the instructor, after spotting them and stepping over.

"Sir Mavil here had asked me to come so he could show us girls his skills with his rifle. But it seems like this space is occupied."

The man looked at Mavil with a frown on his own face. "If you're trying to show off to the girls, do it somewhere else. Go shoot a tree or a bottle or something."

"We were just having a discussion while on our way over," said Mavil, before patting the hand of Ebele. "My friends here are from far away and I had hoped to show them a variety of different types of rifles."

The man took a look at the two girls. "Rifles aren't toys for high society girls. You'd be better off going back to manors and sipping tea or something."

Ebele gave the man a playful smirk and reached up to her shoulder, only to remember that she didn't bring her rifle with her. She then looked over to Aretta, who seemed to be looking around much like a curious cat. *I guess we do seem like that.* She turned back to the instructor. "Please humor us. A lady must have curiosity, after all. I'm sure a man such as yourself understands this."

The man stared at Ebele for a moment before rolling his eyes and sighing, then pointed towards his young students. "We have eight different types of rifles here. But this group is only allowed to use three since they're so young."

"Ah-ha," said Mavil, triumphantly. "So just three, not four."

"What?" asked the instructor, looking confused.

"Oh, sorry. Nothing. You've simply satisfied my curiosity, that's all."

"Sir," said one of the girls, holding a rifle. "My rifle won't shoot."

The instructor shook his head before turning around. "Dang it, Jalise. Did I not tell you not to wait so long before firing? Now you've let the resonance run out of your powder again."

"Is that all?" said Ebele, as she stepped forward, walking past the instructor and over to the girl. "Hello there. May I have a look?"

The girl appeared unsure for a moment before handing Ebele her rifle. It was a lever model Hashkitay single round shot. Ebele pulled back the lever, exposing the round and pulling out the fuse chip behind it. She could see a small amount of resonance still in it, but was sure it wasn't enough power to ignite.

"Are you any good?"

The girl nodded. "Yep, I can even beat some of the boys. But they say I take too long to shoot, so my powder runs out."

"Let's see what we can do, shall we?" Ebele's eyes began to glow red, a soft crimson hue enveloping her pupils. She began channeling her essence into the fuse chip, the stiff black powder quickly beginning to match the color of her eyes. Then with a slide of her hand, the chip lodged back into its slot behind the round, pushing the lever up, and sliding the round back into the place. She handed the rifle back to the girl. "Now go on, take as long as you like."

The girl smiled, struggled a bit to lift the rifle up, and then planted it against her shoulder. She pressed the side of it against her cheek and she focused down the sight. Ebele watched as she steadied her breathing. And finally, when she was ready, she pulled the trigger. The recoil sent the girl stumbling back, the tip of the rifle swinging upwards, while the target's straw head burst open, splitting cleanly down the center.

"What the?" said the instructor.

"Wow?" said the girl. "That's never happened before. It felt different."

"Yes. I might have added a little something special in there," said Ebele as the girl smiled back up at her.

"Just what…" said the instructor, taking a step towards Ebele. "Who are you?"

Ebele stood back up and bowed to the instructor. "I am Ebele Pilsworth, daughter of Neekay Pilsworth. But you may know of her as 'the Warbird.'"

CHAPTER 4

Ebele, her mother, and Aretta arrived back at the manor, where they found Kayin helping the workers move a barrel of hay. They were laughing with each other as they went about their work, but Ebele saw that even while working, he still had her rifle strapped over his shoulder, keeping it safe.

"This was a fun outing, don't you think?" asked her mother.

"No, I don't," said Ebele. "If anything, it was annoying having to listen to that boy boast about his make-believe accomplishments."

Her mother laughed. "Yes, but that's all high society is. I've let you abandon the courts for too long. You're of the age now where you should understand the necessity of brown-nosing."

"I understand it. I just don't like it?"

"No one likes it. But it's part of the game," said her

mother before raising her hand to their attendant. "Kayin, we require you."

"Yes, m'lady," said Kayin as he dropped the hay on a wagon before making his way over to them. "How can I help?"

"We've sweated a bit walking out in the sun. Can you see to it that a bath is brought up so that we—"

"Already done, m'lady. I assumed you'd want that and had two tubs brought in for you and Ebele there. They're in your room with heated essence rocks keeping the water hot for you."

"I swear," said Neekay with a smile as. "There's no one better than you is there?"

"There might be," said Kayin with a smirk. "But I'd imagine you'd be hard pressed to find them." He then reached into his coat pocket and pulled out two clear vials of a reddish white liquid. "And I made my way into town earlier and picked up some bathing oils. This will have you both smelling like sweet melons after you all washed up, or you can just mix them with your bath. I think it works the same."

Neekay took the vials in her hand before leaning in and giving Kayin a kiss on the cheek. "If I hadn't married, then perhaps it would have been you sharing my bed at night. Capable man that you are."

Kayin chucked. "Perhaps, but then I wouldn't have married Frohail. And I've grown quite partial to her and the kids." He then turned and went back towards the other workers. "I'll bring you and the young mistress up some towels when I'm done here."

"Yes. You do that," said Neekay, and she turned and led the girls back into the house.

"Is it normal to talk to your servants like that?' asked Aretta, looking surprised as Kayin went back to work.

"No," said Ebele. "But Kayin and my mother were both in the war together. After it was over, he came to live with us." Ebele rubbed her chin. "Well... with them, I guess, seeing as I wasn't born yet."

"Yes," said Neekay. "But Kayin is a special case. Calling him a servant is a bit of an exaggeration. He's more of a curious assistant."

"A curious assistant?" said Aretta, making a face as they entered the house and headed up the stairs. "I don't understand."

"Kayin comes from a good family," said Neekay. "He doesn't need to work for us. Honestly, I sometimes wonder why he does it."

"Oh?" said Aretta. "Do you often let him keep your rifle like that? I mean. Isn't it valuable? You never think someone might steal it?"

"From Kayin? Oh, I'd love to see them try," said Ebele as her mother opened the door to the room and they saw two steaming baths waiting for them. "Oh, thank goodness." The door closing behind them, Ebele began unbuttoning her blouse and fidgeting with the connectors of her skirt, anxious for a soak in the water.

"Thank you for the clothing," said Aretta as she began taking off the dress that they had loaned her and walked back over to her rags, which were folded neatly on the couch. "I'll be gone just as soon as—"

"Non-sense," said her mother as she stepped over and began pouring the vials into the water. "Go on and take a bath and wash yourself. You can take mine, since I need to head back downstairs and speak with Curtis before the competition today."

"Wait," said Ebele. "You're not planning another surprise for me again like last time, are you?"

"No surprise, just a bit of housekeeping that needs to be done."

"Oh, I couldn't," said Aretta. "I mean, that was meant for you."

"Yes, it was, and I won't be using it. Now go and help my

daughter undress. She seems to be fidgeting a bit too much over there."

"It's these dang hooks," said Ebele. "They always get stuck. This is why dresses are so annoying."

"Right," said her mother, placing her hand on Aretta's shoulder. "I'll leave you to it then." And before another word could be spoken, she walked out the door, closing it behind her.

Aretta frowned at the closed door before turning around and seeing a sympathetic and understanding Ebele holding out two of the hooks of her dress.

"A little help, please."

She sighed before coming over and the two young women helped each other disrobe before soaking their bodies into the water.

"I swear, there's nothing better than this," said Ebele as she slid down deeper until only her head was visible, her hair draped over the side. "It's like it washes all the problems away." There was a moment of quietness that felt odd, as she didn't receive any response, so she opened an eye to see Aretta staring at her. "Is everything alright Aretta?"

"What? Oh, ahh... yes m'lady?"

"You're staring at me. Why?"

"Oh, ahh, well. Your hair..."

"My hair?"

"Some parts of it are red. I was just curious as to why, is all."

"Oh. I guess you would be. Well, it's nothing too special. I'm told that those that have a high abundance of essence have a color change in their hair."

"Is that why only you and your mother here have it? No one else here has... high essence?"

"Yes, I suppose so. But that's just one way it appears. And apparently, it only manifests after long periods using essence. Up until last year, my hair was pure black. Then, after a particularly hard day of training, I went to sleep with a fever and woke to find my hair had changed a bit."

"Oh. I guess that makes sense," said Aretta as she picked up a bar of soap beside the tub and began inspecting it as if it were a foreign object.

"You act as if you've never had a bath before? Do you really not know what soap is?"

"No, I have. I've used the bathing house in town a few times. It's just none of them have soap that smells this good," said Aretta, before leaning over the tub at Ebele. "Do... do you mind if I ask you something?"

"Not at all. This is probably the best time, actually."

"Do you like having that essence stuff?"

"What? What do you mean?"

"I mean. Like having it. The way people look at you for having it. You don't find it odd?"

"I don't understand. What's odd about it? I have it, so I use it. Not many people have essence and if they do, then it's probably not enough worth mentioning. Why? Do you wish you had essence?" She laughed. "Do you wish for colorful hair? Although there's no guarantee it'll be red."

"No, I guess it's just different is all. Do you know what you're gonna do? Don't you have to join the military or something?"

"Some do? But I just like shooting."

"Oh... well, have you ever shot anyone?"

"No. Just targets. Thankfully, the kingdom is pretty quiet except for a few random muggings you hear about," said Ebele as she ran a wet cloth down her arm. "We're not living through a rebellion like my mother did."

"There's more than muggings. They have bandit parties and things. They like to capture those that have essence and try to sell them back to their families. Either that or auction them off to mercenary camps."

"I've never heard of that," said Ebele. "You've seen that happen before?"

"Yeah, I have. It mostly happens north of here. There

were more battles up there. The reason we came down here was to escape all that."

"Oh, I thought all the fighting had ended up north."

"The big ones did, but when they lost the war beyond the mountains, that's when the little ones started going."

"That's weird. I was walking to my mother about it on the way here and she…"

Suddenly, came a knock at the door.

"Miss. Ebele, I've… I've brought the towels for you and the other young lady."

"Good, come in Kayin."

The sound of the key unlatching the lock was heard, and the door opened with Kayin stepping in, holding a set of drying clothes with her mother's rifle still on his back. He closed the door and locked it behind him. As Aretta quickly covered herself, Ebele rose from the water to greet him.

"You're right on time, as always," said Ebele as she stepped out of the water onto the floor, opening and stretching her arms around for him.

"You could have waited till I brought the towel over to you," said Kayin as he placed one towel to the side on a chair and opened up the other. He then stepped forward, patting the towel over her skin before wrapping it around and under the arms of Ebele. "Now you're getting the floor wet."

"I take it you spoke with Mother."

"I did. The event will be in a few hours. You are to rest here until then. If you're going to strain your eyes looking down the barrel of a rifle, then it'd do you good to have your eyes rested."

"Of course," said Ebele, adjusting the towel and patting it against herself to soak up the last bits of moisture. "You know I take this seriously. And I think there's someone here who will give me a reason to do so."

"Yes, Neekay told me about your fascination with a certain girl you met yesterday. I assume that was the girl you asked me about last night."

"That's correct. I'm looking forward to seeing her again."

Kayin sighed. "Well, you've always been the stubborn type. Try not to impose on her too much."

"You make it sound as if I can be overbearing."

Kayin's eyes slid over to Aretta, who was doing her best to keep herself covered by the water. "Why don't we just leave it there, shall we?" He then fully turned to Aretta. "I'll leave your towel over on the chair, miss. Use it when you're ready." He then turned around and left the room, closing the door behind him, the clicking of the lock announcing the closing of the door.

"Are you... are you not embarrassed to be seen like that by him?" asked Aretta, finally turning back towards Ebele.

"Like what?"

"Like... like that," she pointed at her nakedness under the towel.

"For Kayin? Why? He used to dress me and change my undergarments as a baby." She laughed. "I'm more embarrassed to be seen naked by you than I am by him." After removing the towel and drying herself, she crawled into the cover and placed her head on the pillow and rested her eyes. She then patted the space beside her. "Come sleep with me. Having you near will keep me calm until the moment of the competition."

She heard Aretta get out of the water, along with the sound of her towel being unraveled.

"You're very close with people," said Aretta.

"Am I?" asked Ebele, eyes still closed, as she rested. "You said you have brothers. Have you not bathed with them before, in a lake or a stream?"

"That's different. They are my family."

"And Kayin is like family to me," said Ebele as she felt Aretta crawl into bed beside her." She then rolled over, wrapping an arm around her waist, feeling peaceful as the comfort and the cold chill against her skin was soon replaced with the maid's body's heat. "See, we're the same."

"No," said Aretta. "I really don't think we are."

***

Ebele awoke in bed sometime later. The mid-morning sun of her previous outing was now replaced by an evening overcast. Her bed was empty and across the couch, ahead of her lay the dress that Aretta had worn. Her ragged clothing, like the woman herself now gone.

A little groggy, she slid over across the bed, standing to her feet and stepping over to peer out the window to the grounds below where she saw a small amount of the previous day's participants gathering. She felt a small jolt of excitement come over her in anticipation of competing against the girl from the night before.

She then walked back to the clothing that had been laid out for her and started to dress herself. Once again, a blouse and dress in her family's colors lay over a nearby table for her. *I swear, a pair of trousers would be much simpler than this,* she thought as she fiddled with the links of the dress, connecting them to the corset piece over the blouse. It took a little longer than was comfortable, but she finished dressing and headed for the door, stepping out into the hallway.

Just as before, there were no maids or servants, and Aretta was nowhere in sight. With the lack of company, she started feeling more conscious of the sounds around her. The squeaky floorboards beneath her feet or the silence of the long hallway, all things when in the company of Kayin or her mother, she never had to pay any attention to.

"Aretta, are you here?" she asked when she reached the steps, but still there was no response. She did smell the scent of food coming from the kitchen and decided to follow it. There she found an older woman in the kitchen chopping some vegetables. "Excuse me? Have you seen Aretta?"

"Yes, she left around an hour ago. I'm sorry you missed

your chance to say goodbye."

"That's fine. I just wanted to check on her. I'm sure I'll see her around or after the—"

"No, I'm sorry, child. I meant she's gone. She's resigned."

"What?" asked Ebele, her eyes fluttering in disbelief as her fingers pinched the side of the door frame. "But that can't... did she say why?"

"No, it was the darnedest thing, considering how hard she'd worked to get the job. Why, she even stood at the gate out there for two days. Master Curtis finally took pity on the poor thing and invited her in. For her to quit like this, must have been something fierce that spooked her so bad."

"Oh... well... thank you," said Ebele, turning her back to the woman and walking away. *Was it something I did?* She shook her head at the thought. *Or course not. I made an effort to share a bed with her. I even allowed her to adorn one of my dresses. Yes, that's right. I've been the model of generosity.* A sour look came over her. *I'm sure it must have been something Mother said. What would she do that would be so egregious to send her running away without so much as goodbye? I mean, she was washed and given good clothes.* She raised her hand to her mouth, biting lightly down on her thumb. *But she did leave the clothing... and I didn't notice her take anything.*

Her random thoughts on the sudden disappearance of the maid led her outside and towards the gathering for the competition. But out here she wouldn't be allowed to be alone with her thoughts as her presence garnered the attention of the attendees.

"Hey there," said Mavil, who had previously escorted her to the shooting grounds. "You're ready to lose to me today?"

"Huh... oh, ahh... I think I'll win."

"The powder ball will be controlled by someone experienced. Apparently, he was a scout in the war. You know, the one your mother was in. So, he's bound to have some tricks up his sleeve."

"Hey, did you see the girl I was with yesterday?"

"No," said the boy, looking a little confused. "I mean, I thought I did earlier, but that was just some girl in rags."

Ebele's eyes opened with a bit of hope. "Did you speak with her? Did she say where she was going?"

"No, I just so happened to glance at her when I entered through the gate earlier. I didn't actually speak with her."

"Right... of course not." *Well, he's certainly useless. No surprise there, I guess.*

"Excuse me, young man," said her mother as she approached. "I would like to have a word with my daughter." Her mother then took Ebele by the arm and began leading her away. "Alright, what's wrong?"

"What?"

"That look on your face. Obviously, something is bothering you."

"Aretta. Did you know she quit? Did you say anything to her?"

"No," said Neekay. "Humph, but I guess it's not that surprising. Did she take anything?"

"No... I mean, I don't think so. I didn't really go back to check. But she even left her maid's garb in the room, lying out over our bed. Isn't that odd?"

"That is odd. Perhaps being around us caused her to reconsider her life choices?"

"What? What would..." said Ebele, confused. "Do you really think we did anything to cause it? I mean, I know we may have taken up a lot of her time. But I just assumed Curtis wouldn't mind, since you and he are old friends."

"Please, dear. He didn't mind at all that we monopolized that girl's time. In fact, he was quite pleased about it."

"Then why'd she quit?"

Neekay placed her hand on her daughter's shoulder and turned her around, having her face the group of people huddled under the tents. "Tell me. What do you see?"

Ebele was confused by the question but knew how her

mother never liked to give the immediate answer. So, with a sigh, she looked ahead of her and saw the same people from yesterday. "I don't understand. It's just the same people for the tournament."

"Yes, but haven't you noticed that there are particularly fewer people than there were yesterday?"

Ebele looked again and noticed that her mother was right. She saw only seven of the contestants out of the dozen or so from yesterday. "Why... where have they gone?"

"Apparently there's been some ruckus up north and they all decided to head back to see to their homes."

"Up north?" said Ebele, remembering her conversation with Aretta. "She did say she was from the north."

"And seeing as she was asking us for a job away from here. I'd imagine she asked the other lords as well. I'd guess one of them accepted her and she's now gone off to work at their manors."

That makes sense, thought Ebele as she made a soured face. "But she could have at least woken me up and told me."

"She probably thought it'd be too much of a pain, seeing as you two seemed to be becoming friends." Her mother shook her head. "I guess that's the price to be paid for sheltering you so much. The loss of a new friend can be hurtful. But no need to be lonely. Life will always invite—"

"I'm not lonely," said Ebele, frowning at her mother. "I'm not."

"Of course not, dear. Why else would you go whisking through the town looking for a girl you've barely even known?" She patted her on the shoulder. "Now get that cook out of your mind. You should focus on the game ahead of you. It will start soon."

Ebele began rubbing her fingers together in a fist, trying to calm the anxiety she was feeling, and took a deep breath. *Mother's right. I need to focus. And that girl's coming. If I'm going to beat her, then I'll need to focus.* "Okay... where's Kayin?"

"He's doing the final inspection of my rifle. I told him it was fine as I did it myself yesterday, but he insisted." She nodded to a man who was coming around the corner of the house. "Ah, there he is. Right on time."

"Good, you're here. I was afraid that I would have to come and wake you," said Kayin as he walked up to them, taking the rifle from his shoulder and extending it to Ebele. "I've adjusted the sights a bit and oiled it for you. You shouldn't have to worry about it jamming anytime soon."

"Thank you," said Ebele, taking the rifle and looking it over. She could see that he also polished the wooden stock. She ran her hand over it, ensuring that there wasn't any slippage, then brought it up to her face as she checked the sights. She could smell the oil he used to polish it, an oak scent that reminded her of her time in the woods training with her mother.

"How's it feel?" asked Kayin.

"As good as it ever does," said Ebele. "You really are the only one I trust with her outside of Mother.

He laughed. "And what about your father?"

She frowned. "I would trust him if he'd stop trying to make modifications to it. She's fine just the way she is."

"Your father has always been the tinkering type," said her mother. "He sees a toy and away he goes. Thankfully, that nature of his has only ever been with machines and weapons. I'd have locked him away long ago if that pertained to women as well."

"Okay, young ladies and gentlemen," said their host, Curtis as he stepped out of the small crowd. "All who have gathered, take your positions at the range and we will start while we still have some daytime left."

Ebele nodded to her mother and Kayin before heading over to the field. As the rest of the participants lined up, she eagerly began looking around for the girl from the day before. There were only eight participants, including herself. But she was a little confused to see that the girl from before wasn't among them. She looked around again, wondering if she and the boy were going to be late again.

"You looking for someone?" asked the girl next to her.

"The girl from yesterday who hit all the targets. I don't see her."

"Oh," said the boy with a laugh. "They've probably gone already. They do this all the time. They show up, hit their first targets and then disappear. They've never completed any tournaments so far."

"What?"

"I think they just do it to show off."

Ebele felt as if the wind had been taken away from her. She had looked forward to competing against the girl. *So, Aretta's gone and now...* She shook her head. *I don't even know her name.*

"Okay," said one of the older men as he walked ahead and stood before them. "Today you're going to try to shoot this powder ball." He reached behind himself, dislodging a white ball the size of a melon from a holder strapped to his back. Opening a hatched in the ball, Ebele watched as the man's eyes turned green as he infused the powder inside the ball with his essence. Then, closing the hatch, he began tossing the ball in the air with one hand, catching it as it came down and bouncing it again. On the fourth bounce, the ball stopped above his palm and began floating in the air.

He took longer than the last time. Is his resonance with powder that low? She looked around the field again at her competitors and sighed. *Of course, it is. If not for the chance to see her again, I wouldn't even care to do this anymore. Most of them can barely shoot.*

"Now listen up," said the man. "I'm going to be sending this ball all over this field for two minutes. In those two minutes, your job is to target and hit it as much as you can. Each of you have been given eight rounds, and each person has a set of different colors, same as yesterday. If you hit the powder ball, your color will mark it, indicating you have a point when all this is over. Keep in mind the ball will only take ten hits, then it will fall to the ground and the game will be over. So, the goal is to score the most hits out of the eight of you who are left."

"What if someone hits the same spot as me after I take my shot?"

"Unlikely, but if that does happen, then tough luck. And besides, this ball will be at a distance, and I doubt even the Warbird herself is that good. Any other questions?"

Ebele was only half paying attention as her eyes went back and forth between her supposed competition. Her spirit and any expectations she had for the tournament were crushed when she didn't see the girl from before who had managed to tie her. *First Aretta and now she's gone. And I'm here stuck showing off to these country bumpkins.*

The man holding the powder ball looked at the contestants' faces and was met with silence. "Good." He then turned and sent the floating ball off into the field. It was surprisingly fast as it zipped around some of the wood pillars before hiding somewhere out of sight. The man turned back around to them. "When I give the signal, you will raise your weapons."

She sighed before trying to refocus her mind on the task at hand. *Calm down, Ebele. Even though I'm most certainly better than everyone here. I still need to pay attention,* she thought as the man walked back to the participants, passing them so that he would not be in front of their line of fire. *What a waste of my time.*

"Alright, raise your weapons," said the man when he was clear.

Ebele followed the direction, then ensured a round was loaded. Placed the stock against her shoulder, she focused on where she last saw where the ball had hidden.

"Okay. start."

The powder ball zipped out of an entirely different place

than where she had last seen it. And there were several loud bangs that rang out.

Probably some underground tunnel or something, thought Ebele as the white orb went zooming through the field. *Probably more than one.* She focused on the powder ball, trying her best to keep it in sight as it zipped and zagged. Behind a wooden pillar, around the over a hanging bale of hay. She hadn't heard a hit yet; a fact that seemed to make the others hesitant now.

Don't shoot where it is, shoot where it's going to be. It came out of hiding from another pillar, then down under a log. The sight of her gun matching its speed as she followed it, and as it went down and came back up again, she tilted her gun upward just enough before firing. The kick on her shoulder, making her clench her teeth as a metal ping was heard and the powder ball went spinning, bouncing off one of the wooden pillars, before quickly resuming its sporadic ongoings.

She sighed again, before taking a deep breath and focusing again. *Of course, I would be the first to hit it.* Her eyes glanced over as the sound of another missed shot rang out. *And given this crowd, I'll probably be the only one to hit the target.*

Focusing again, her eyes tried following the ball. Up and down before disappearing again and appearing on the opposite side of the target field. *Another one of those tunnels. Are they connected? Let's see...* taking her attention off the powder ball, her eyes looked to where the first time the ball disappeared. *So, there first, and it came out over to the left of it. So, four holes so far.*

Feeling confident, she focused on the orb again, as it looped high into the air. Now it was visible for all to see and clearly being telegraphed. *Making it easy for them since no one else has been able to hit it, huh?* She quickly took aim. *Then they should get better.* Her finger danced over the trigger before pulling back. There was an almost synchronized explosion *sound of her and someone else.* Then the powder ball spun out of control for a second before dropping down. But this time, before it gained full control again, another loud bang sound came as it went spinning out of control again.

Ebele narrowed her eyes as a bit of frustration seeped into her. She'd been around rifles long enough; she knew it was her rifle that went off second. And that the first shot that spun the powder ball had caused her to miss her own shot. And to add to the insult was the sound of a girl shouting '*I hit it,*' as if she needed confirmation.

If mother's watching, I'm sure I'm going to hear about that later. She adjusted her shoulder, titling her neck in a stretch as she pressed the side of the rifle harder against her cheek. *Don't think. Just focus.*

The powder ball zipped out from behind a wooden pillar again. Now her competitors started feeling more confident after the two connecting shots that weren't hers. Their eagerness was signaled by the letting loose of thunder in attempts to hit the target. The missed attempts tearing chucks away from the wooden logs. Kindling exploded into the air as the powder ball zoomed through the debris.

They're using good powder, thought Ebele as she witnessed the wooden carnage. *But they're still terrible shots. What's the use of all that power if you still can't hit anything? They should practice with low-quality powder until they understand... no, stop. Who cares about them? It's their own fault for not training enough. If that girl was here, she'd probably know that. Dammit, why didn't she show up?*

The ball emerged through the last cloud of exploding wood, and she pulled the trigger. Her shot connected just as it emerged and sent the ball spiraling back, bouncing off the side of one of the broken pillars and then taking off again. *Well, fine. It's not like I could have learned much from her, anyway. In fact, yes... I most likely would have taught her some things. Yes, she's lucky I took an interest in her. So, it's her loss, really. She could have learned from the daughter of the*

Warbird.

She fired again. *And Aretta too, she could have... No. She doesn't have the essence. She's just a cook.* She fired once more. *Given the war to the north, maybe she was worried about those brothers she said she had. If I had brothers, perhaps I would have left too.* Again, she pulled the trigger, her eyes on the powder ball as it grazed the side of a barrel of hay. *Still... Yes, I was sleeping. But would a goodbye have been too much to ask for?*

"Okay," shouted the host. "Eight shots have landed. Two more before the competition is over."

Eight? Thought Ebele, the man's voice snapping her out of her thoughts. *When did they hit eight? No... I've hit three or four, right? So, I also have half, it's eight of us, so some of them have just gotten lucky shots. I... I just need to focus. Clear your mind, Ebele.*

Taking in a deep breath, she held it, her eyes narrowing down the sights. It was a second later that the powder ball appeared from behind a bricked arch before taking a sharp turn and heading back down near another pillar. Ebele tilted her rifle, aiming carefully, and fired just as others did. The pillar beside it exploded and the powder ball went spinning out of control, disappearing behind a stack of hay.

She exhaled, counting her hits. *That's nine. So, we all have one more shot.* She waited, but the powder ball didn't reappear. There was a moment of silence as they all stood with their rifles pointed out over the field, waiting. *It's in one of those tunnels again. I know it. But which one? It landed to the left, near where it had exited before. So, if I'm right, then that means...* She pointed her rifle over to where she remembered the powder ball disappearing before. *Hear. Somewhere over here.*

Focusing hard, she could feel a bead of sweat dancing just above her brow. Her finger kneaded the stock of the rifle. *You're in there. I know you are.* She felt as if she could hear it whooshing down there in its little tunnel, waiting to come back up; the edges of it grazing against the dirt or metal it was housed in. But like a bullet in the chamber, it was ready to explode from the end of its chamber. *Come on. I know...*

She saw the tip of it appear before the hay. Raising her rifle to match its speed, she pulled the trigger, and a loud bang roared. Through the round smoke, they could see the powder ball dash off into the air. She had missed. And to celebrate her failure, came the applause of the gunfire of the others as they all fired, trying to hit the target.

"I hit it again," came the sound of the girl from before, as the powder ball went spiraling through air, before falling back down to the ground. "That's two. I hit it twice."

"Okay, that's it," said the man from before. "Everyone, lower your rifles."

Ebele did as instructed. Trying to hide the snarl on her lips, she bit the inside of her mouth as she took a deep breath to calm herself. One of the men around went to retrieve the powder ball from the field.

"How many did you get?" asked one of the boys.

"Probably none," said another boy. "Did you see the way that thing was zipping around? Charlotte thinks she got two."

"I know I hit it twice. I can feel it."

"Here you go sir," said the man, who retrieved the ball, bringing it back to the host.

"Thank you," said the host as he took the ball and held it to his face to inspect it as everyone gathered around. "Now let's see here." Rotating it, he began looking at the impact marks. "So first it seems we have four single shots. House Rihal, Singva, Pascal, and Juniper, all Singles."

There was a nice round of applause for the group.

"Next, we have Houses Mecali, with two imprints."

"See. I told you I hit it twice," said Charlotte, as another round of applause came.

"And finally, and probably to no one's surprise. We have

House Pilsworth with four imprints on the powder ball. Almost half. Absolutely wonderful, from the little warbird in training."

A final round of applause came for her. Ebele knew that this moment was not meant to show herself sulking. So, she took her eyes off the ground and looked out at her peers and gave them a large smile and a nod.

"Come up here darling," said the man. Gesturing for her to stand beside him on the podium. "Come get your prize."

Prize? Thought Ebele as she stepped forward. *What prize?* She took her place beside the man and told the other gentlemen to bring something forward. And to Ebele's horror, she saw a man holding what looked to be the statue of a golden chicken.

"Ladies and Gentlemen, I'm proud to be awarding this year's trophy of the Seqineal Rooster to Ebele Pilsworth. And we all can't wait to see what she does in the future. I, for one, am sure that she will become an expert markswoman, just like her mother." They all cheered for her, and Ebele continued to put on her best smile. Although she was screaming inside, it was all she could manage to not smash the thing on the ground and go running away.

After getting the admiration of her peers, Ebele was allowed to step down and walk over to where Kayin and her mother were waiting for her.

"Congratulations, young lady," said Kayin as he reached out, taking the golden rooster from her. "I'll take this up to your room. Shall I also take your weapon?"

"No," said Neekay. "I'd like to take a look at it."

Kayin nodded. "Right..." He gave Ebele a worrying look that she'd seen many times in her life when she'd gotten in trouble. "Well, I'll go ahead and take this up, then." He then patted Neekay on the shoulder and headed off.

"Go on," said Ebele, lowering her head. "You're going to say how badly I messed up and how I need to focus more."

Her mother nodded her nod before sighing, "Well,

seeing as you can read my mind. Then perhaps this time I don't need to say it. Hand me the rifle." Ebele did as asked and her mother took it, opening the chamber. "Tell me," she said as she slid her finger inside, ejecting the clip with the few remaining rounds. "Has today's event been so distracting for you that you would miss so many?"

"What do you mean?" asked Ebele, looking back at her mother. "I only missed two sho..." Ebele's eyes went wide as she looked at the clip in her mother's hand. It was her standard for eight round clips, but none were left. *What? When did I fire two more shots? I don't understand.*

"I can see by the look in your eyes that you didn't realize it," said her mother as she placed the butt of the rifle on the ground and shook her head. "Well, you did win. So, I guess I should be satisfied with that. But think about this lesson. Distractions like this can lead to dire situations."

"Yes, mother."

"I still have a few other things that I need to discuss with Curtis. You can chat with your new friends if you like." She reached out, placing a finger under her daughter's chin, lifting it so she would see into her eyes. "You'll do no good sulking, dear. Whatever you're looking for, there will be more in the future. There always is. Now go on."

Ebele looked at her mother for a moment before nodding her head and walking off towards the manor ahead. On the way, she took a look back at the other young man and women as they chatted and celebrated. There was a short moment where she thought that she should join them, but that interest left her just as quickly as it came.

The trek back up to the manor didn't take long, and she was glad to once again be away from everyone. Although when she entered, she wasn't exactly happy to see the statue of the golden chicken sitting prominently on a table in the center of the room.

There's no way we're taking this home with us. If Mother insists on leaving this town with it, then I'll just have to toss it on the side of the road after we've gotten far enough away. She shook her head, disgusted by it, then looked over the room. *I can't wait to get out of here.* With downtrodden thoughts weighing on her mind, she sat at the end of the bed and began sliding off her boots, when she noticed something sticking out under the base of the chicken.

Curious and tossing her boots to the side, she reached forward, sliding it from under the statue. It was an envelope with her name crudely written on it. Or what she thought was her name, it was written E-bell- ah. She looked around the room again, before opening it and pulled out a piece of parchment. It read:

Hello, sorry, I not come to shoot rifle with you. Buddy said you came to see me. We had to go. You shot good. Very good shots. Never seen another girl shoot good like me. I want to shoot with you again. You Warbird. If get the chance, I come visit if buddy lets me. I think he will if I ask.

Till then, Mallory.

Her finger gripped the parchment hard, causing it to crinkle at the edges. *Oh goodness, she really can't spell, can she?* Her lip began to tremble a bit. *Well, of course. I mean, look where we are.* Her trembling lips turned into a smile. *Mallory. Her name is Mallory.*

The door to the room opened as her mother entered the room. "Ebele, I've come to retrieve a sample of our powder." She placed the rifle against the wall beside the door. "Not to my surprise, the locals here have yet to sample any of the Pilsworth powder. Since they are our gracious hosts, I figure why wouldn't..." Lifting back up, her mother stared at her for a moment before giving her daughter a suspicious look and folding her arms. "Okay, something happened. What is it?"

"What... what do you mean?" asked Ebele.

"What do I mean? A minute ago, you were just sulking, as if you've lost a puppy. Now look at you, grinning from ear to ear."

CHAPTER 5

The sun cast its light over a peaceful morning. A long fog hung over the ground outside of Curtis's manor as Ebele and her mother stood saying their goodbyes.

"Thank you for having us," said Neekay to Curtis as she leaned in, giving him a kiss on the cheek.

"Speak nothing of it," said Curtis, a hearty smile on his lips as he patted her on the shoulder. "I should be thanking you. Even with many guests leaving after meeting you, I don't think this would have been such a success without announcing that you would be coming." He looked at Ebele. "And to you, your shooting is just as remarkable as your mothers."

"Thank you. I hope to get better," said Ebele, her eyes wandering over to Kayin as he walked past them, holding the statue of the golden chicken. *I'll either find a way to get rid of it, or that thing is going to find itself mysteriously in our fireplace come wintertime.*

After all was said, Ebele stepped toward the carriage and opened the door. To her dismay, she saw the golden chicken was perched in between the two seats in the middle of the floor. She frowned.

"Sorry, my lady," said Kayin with a laugh as he spotted the look on Ebele's face. "Wasn't enough room in the back. Do try your best to deal with it."

"You're doing this to tease me, aren't you?"

"Of course, not my lady," said Kayin and he took hold of the door for her to step inside. "But if you're curious, I must admit, I do find your repugnance of that item somewhat amusing."

Ebele frowned. "If it's making you so happy. Perhaps you would like to take it when we get back. I'm sure it would look lovely in your home."

"Sadly, my lady, I'm afraid my tastes aren't as refined as yours and the great people out here. My simple mind finds the item impressively gaudy."

"If refined tastes are what it takes to appreciate that. Then I'd gladly be called simple-minded."

Kayin smiled and nodded his head before patting Ebele on the back. "Rightfully so, m`lady. Okay now, in you go. We best be on our way if we wish to reach Thrisanna by tomorrow's end."

Ebele stepped into the wagon, the metal squeaking as she did so. More squeaks came as she was followed in by her mother, who took a seat adjacent to her, the golden chicken between them. A little while later, she heard the sound of snapping reins before the wagon lurched forward and they headed off.

"This was a pleasant time out in the countryside, don't you agree?" asked her mother.

"No. I still don't understand why you insisted I accompany you out here. You certainly can't say that I learned anything."

"Oh?" said her mother, placing a hand to her chin. "I distinctly remember you boasting about how you'd found some girl who shot in a fashion you'd never seen."

"And then she disappeared, leaving nothing more than a letter."

"A letter that promised a future visitation." She waved a hand dismissively. "Don't put on airs about it. You're excited to see her."

"Perhaps... a little bit," said Ebele, folding her arms and turning her head out the window. "But I could have met her anywhere. She and her companion seemed to be some type of travelers. Who's to say I wouldn't have met them if they visited Tyrill."

"My poor daughter. I'm sure you get that stubbornness from your father."

"He says I get it from you."

"I'm sure he does. I married a delusional man, after all."

Both women continued their conversation until finally the rhythm of the rocking wagon caused them both to prepare for a midmorning nap; their eyes closing as the sun rose over their heads. Ebele's mind was filled with thoughts of the two girls she had met. One a barely literate markswoman and one a cook heading north.

"Mother," said Ebele, her eyes still closed and the softness of inevitable sleep lowering her tone.

Her mother breathed deep before sighing it out slowly. "What is it, dear?"

"The north. Is the fighting truly as bad as they say?"

"Yes, but ask me again after a rest. I'd prefer not to think of war before a nap. It poisons the dreams."

"Yes, mother."

And with that, both women let sleep overtake them as their visions of the world went dark.

***

Sometime later, Ebele was startled out of her sleep by the sound of gunfire. Her eyes struggling to focus, but still reached up for where she knew the rifle to be. Only beforehand, she caught a glimpse of her mother already having it in her arms.

"Is everything alright?"

"I don't know," said her mother before shouting. "Kayin! What's the situation?"

"No situation, mam? Just seems to be a carriage up ahead, perhaps signaling for help."

"Or a trap. This area isn't foreign to bandits."

"Rightly so, madam. There's a wagon up ahead. Perhaps a signal for distress. Should we not stop?"

"How many?"

"Appears to be four?"

"Any trees near them?"

"No mam, just open road? Tree lines are a few yards out."

The sound of another rifle shot came, and her mother frowned before looking over at Ebele. "Fine, stop for them. But be weary." She then handed Ebele the rifle. "Hold this for me, dear."

"Yes, ma'am."

Ebele felt it as the wagon began to slow down, with her mother standing up and opening the carriage to look ahead. Neekay clutched the railing above as she leaned out the door. Ebele gazed out at the tree line in the distance.

There, she heard the sound of a few riders on horses heading off.

"Hello there, good sir, how may... Why Mr. Harsetti, what are you doing here?" asked her mother before hopping down to the ground as the carriage stopped. She then nodded at Ebele to come out.

A little on guard, Ebele peaked her head outside of the wagon to see one of the men who were at the competition standing beside a wagon with a broken wheel.

"Damn bitch tricked me," said Mr. Harsetti. "You have to help me. She and her cohorts robbed me and took off."

"Calm down, Mr. Harsetti," said her mother. "Who robbed you? Were you not armed?"

"Yes, I was armed. But I was ambushed from the inside of my own wagon."

"Ambushed?"

"Yes. By that damned cook from Curtis's manor or whatever she was."

Ebele's eyes went wide. "Cook, you mean Aretta?"

"Yes, that was what she called herself. She requested work in my kitchen saying how she was being mistreated and since Curetis was falling on hard times; how she would soon be let go." He began patting the side of his coat for dust and trying his best to look less flustered in front of the ladies. "I thought I was simply doing the girl a boon. I wasn't aware that Curtis had in his employ would be bandits."

"Yes," said her mother, giving a small smirk and glance to Ebele before continuing with Harsetti. "Well, she did appear to be such a young and pretty thing. I'm sure you were feeling bad for the poor girl."

"Exactly," huffed Mr. Harsetti. "And look where such sentiment has gotten me. I knew I should have ridden with more than two guards. It was only a day's ride away, so I assumed the roads would be safe. A fool I was."

"Now, now," said her mother, kneeling and inspecting the broken wheel. "The spokes are shattered, so no use for this. Do you have a spare?"

"Aye, I did, but they broke those to."

"When you say they, how many were there?"

"Four. When they approached, she pulled out a blade and held it to my neck, ordering me to have my driver and guards stand down. They took our powder, munitions, and my purse, and made a beeline towards the woods. I had my rifle under my seat. But by the time I made it back to my carriage, they were already too far away for me to hit them."

"Well, I imagine they can sell the powder and the jewels. We can report them once we reach Thrisanna, and with luck, you may recover some of your stolen goods."

"Knowing my luck, they may have had a raft ready and are at this very moment sailing to Pillan or Matora."

"We won't know until we arrive," said her mother, looking up at the sky. "Rather than leave you and your man out here. I offer you passage with me and my daughter. It'd do us well to have another man around to protect us fair ladies."

"Why yes," said Mr. Harsetti, nodding to his man. "Willis, stay with the wagon and watch over what few items they didn't take. Once I reach Thrisanna, I'll come back with men and supplies to retrieve you."

"Yes, sir. Will do."

Mr. Harsetti grabbed his rifle and smiled at the two women before beginning to step into the wagon.

"Ah, excuse Mr. Harsetti."

"Yes."

"I fail to see how you would protect us while inside the wagon," her mother said while nodding ahead of the carriage where Kayin sat.

"Huh…" said Mr. Harsetti, realization hitting him a moment later. "Oh yes… yes, you're right. Forgive me, I've seemed to have lost my wits. Apologies, I wasn't thinking." He then stepped off and headed to the front of the wagon before coming back. "Ah… Miss. Pilsworth. If I may continue to impose on you a bit more. The bandits… well, they took the last of my powder and munitions. May I procure some from you? To be reimbursed or returned as soon as possible, of course."

Her mother looked down at the man's rifle and smiled. "Of course. Your rifle, it seems to be a modified Barrington. Is that correct?"

"Why yes, that is correct."

"So, standard Archon shells will do fine?" she said as she

reached into the side of her vest and pulled out a sleeve of eight rounds, handing it to him along with a vial of powder. "Please do protect us well."

"Yes. Will do. Thank you," said Mr. Harsetti, taking the supplies and then climbing into the passenger's side beside Kayin.

Her mother then turned back to Mr. Harsetti's driver. "Well, try to get to town as soon as we can."

"Appreciated, Mistress," replied the man with a nod.

Her mother then gestured back towards the carriage as she and Ebele entered, retaking their seats.

"Well, that was certainly interesting," said her mother as the carriage retook to the road.

"Do you think the girl that was with him might have been Aretta?" asked Ebele, with little hope in her heart that it wasn't.

"Oh, I imagine so," said her mother with a laugh. "I do remember saying that she seemed the entrepreneurial type. Although I must admit. I assumed her to be more of a seductress. Imagine my surprise when it turns out that robbery was her forte." She then covered her mouth as she tried to hold back her giggles.

"You laugh," said Ebele, a bit annoyed at her mother's apparent joy. "But we spent a large amount of time with her. What if we'd have picked her up? What if that blade Mr. Harsetti mentioned was placed against my neck?"

"Yes. It does beg the question. Why didn't she try to rob us? I mean, it's not as if she didn't have ample opportunity. You and her even shared a bath and bed together. Perhaps you should think on that."

Ebele narrowed her eyes. "You did something. Didn't you?"

"Or..." she raised a finger. "Maybe you did. Maybe she didn't want to rob her new friend."

Ebele stared at her mother for a moment, looking at her facial expressions. *She's always so hard to read. I swear she's like a child. What aren't you telling me?* But these questions would linger throughout the day and deep into the night after they had rested their horses. She did, however, hold out hope that perhaps there might have been another young woman who was also a cook in that lord's manor. Even if such hope felt fleeting by the hour.

*****

Much to Ebele's relief, they reached Thrisanna by mid-afternoon the following day. Unlike the city of Chadain, Thrisanna was a more mid-level city. Less woodwork architecture and more stone and mortar cabins and homes. On an average day, they would see many people from the surrounding villages with smiles on their faces as they entered for commerce. But instead, they were greeted to a line outside of the city's gates that stretched for half a mile at least.

"It seems something has occured since our departure from here," said Neekay, opening the door while peering outside. "At this rate, we won't make the inn until nightfall."

"What could have happened?" asked Ebele. "I imagine if it were serious, don't you think the travelers we passed on the road would have mentioned it?"

"Perhaps its fairly recent," said her mother, hopping down from the carriage as it slowed to a halt. "I guess I should go and find out the situation." She turned to Ebele. "You stay here with the carriage. I shouldn't be long."

Ebele stood from her seat and watched as her mother took one of the horses from Mr. Harsetti's guards and headed off, galloping down the road towards the city. "Is it alright to let her go alone?"

"It's fine, m`lady," said Kayin. "She probably has some business to attend to. I'm sure she'll be back soon."

Mr. Harsetti lowered himself down from the wagon's front to stand beside Ebele. He then began stretching, his joints popping so loud Ebele could hear them. "Tell me, dear. You're getting up in age. Will you be joining the military as your mother did?"

"No, mother and father are against that. Instead, they wish for me to get married or pursue more scholarly trades."

"Really? Then why learn the rifle? You obviously have your mother's talent for it. And you were gifted with resonance. Seems to be a waste."

"I always wanted to learn. Mother was against it at first, but father and Kayin convinced her to train me."

"Yes," said Kayin with a laugh. "We simply reminded her of how reckless she was in her youth. And if Ebele was anything like her, she'd find her way to a rifle one way or another. But it was up to her if she would be trained by her of someone else."

"That's splendid. I think it's wonderful that you and your mother have that shared interest. And do forgive my rudeness earlier. One need not have a wish to kill people just to enjoy the art of marksmanship."

"What of you, Mr. Harsetti? Were you in the military?"

"In fact, I was. But being the valued lone son in my family, my position was more clerical. Not on the front lines, like your mother and your chaperone there." He looked off into the sky as if looking upon a distant memory. "I used to receive reports on the war on how we were fairing. Strategic wins, losses, and the like. But one name continued to come across my desk: Neekay Pilsworth. You call her mother. We called her the Warbird. The enemy, after a few campaigns, began to refer to her as the Warbi—" He coughed, before halting his words. "Well, let's say it wasn't a pleasant name."

"Mother doesn't tell me much about her time at war. She just says that's where she met father."

"Yes. Your father," shaking his head as if in disapproval. "It's a wonder of the world that those two managed to get together and conceive a child." He then turned back to Ebele. "Tell me. Has your father or mother ever told you who pursued who? I'm fairly curious as to who waved the white flag first."

"White Flag?" asked Ebele, confused.

"Well, while I never truly got to know your mother during the war outside of her reputation. I did, however, have many opportunities to interact with your father."

"Really? What was father like back then?"

"Humm. Sporadic, I'd say, would be the right word. Always focused on his research. Always going over budget in his theories and tinkering with armaments. I imagine the prince... well, the king now, was quite relieved when your mother took him away. The kingdom's coffers were lifted from his heavy burden."

Ebele frowned. "Then he hasn't changed much. He's always in his lab breaking things and trying to put them back together."

Mr. Harsetti laughed. "Yes. Rightfully so."

The conversation continued with Ebele asking Mr. Harsetti about his own affairs of family and country before heading back into the carriage to rest. It was near nightfall when her mother arrived back at the wagon.

"Okay, I've managed to get us entry into the city," said Neekay, pulling on the reins as the horses clopped to a halt. "There's apparently been the murder of several prominent members of the city. So, they have it locked until the culprits are found."

"What?" asked Harsetti. "But I've only been gone four days. Did they say who the victims were? Surely not someone of true note."

"I didn't ask. I was preoccupied with getting us passage. But the Maquis has asked for us to visit him when we arrive, so I'm sure he'll inform us."

"Yes, let's hurry then, shall we?" asserted Mr. Harsetti. "I need to know if my house is still in order."

Neekay dismounted her horse, handing it over to a guard, electing to ride inside of the coach with Ebele as they were escorted through the crowd of people towards the front gate. She could see that some of the people had elected to pitch tents for the night near the walls of the town as they wouldn't be let in for the night.

"How long have they been out here?" asked Ebele, feeling a bit sorry for the people.

"I imagine ever since the first body was found, or perhaps the second. Two, maybe three days."

The city was more on alert than when she had first passed through with her mother some weeks ago. At the top of walls were stationed with several guards on both sides looking down over the city and its people.

"Feeling nervous?" asked her mother as Ebele peered out into the city.

"It would be weird if I wasn't," said Ebele. "Not all of us here are like you."

"Fear is good. It's what keeps you alive."

The people of the city seemed to be going about their day, as you would expect. Unlike the hungry and disheveled appearance of the people outside. The further into the city they went; the wooden houses were starting to be replaced with stone buildings. Dirt roads transitioned into brick as they entered the high-class section of the city.

Here is where the city felt different. Nobles were still gathered along the side of the streets, going about their day. Many could be seen shopping, while maids walked around holding bags of groceries. She even saw someone behind the cloth of a powder photograph machine taking the picture of a couple holding wooden rifles against what looked to be the painted silhouette of a shadowy male figure.

"Maybe I shouldn't feel scared if people are out doing things like that," she said, nodding just before the powder puffed up in smoke.

"That's the same with many nobles, my dear. Even if death was around the corner, many would treat it as if it was miles away. I never figured out why, though. Whether they do it out of fear or ignorance is truly a wonder."

Afterwards, it wasn't long before they found themselves at the steps of the marquis's manor.

Stepping out of the carriage, Ebele was greeted to the sight of a large stone building with two guards at the entrance.

"Good," said Mr. Harsetti as he adjusted his Surcoat, trying to look presentable after a day on the road. "Usually, I would insist on making myself more regal before a meeting with the marquis. But I must get permission to go and retrieve my man." He then headed up the stairs towards the door as if forgetting he was accompanied by Ebele and her mother.

"Stay here with the guards, Kayin. Hopefully, this won't take too long."

"Seeing that it's nightfall," said Kayin. "I think I should go and secure our dwelling for the night."

"Nonsense," said Neekay, looking ahead to Mr. Harsetti as he conversed with the guards at the top of the steps. "I intend to make use of a certain noble's hospitality, especially since we ensured his safe passage here."

"Rightfully so," said Kayin with a smirk.

"Come Ebele, let's go and see to it that our benefactor there doesn't get pushed back down those steps."

"What's going on here? The Marquis is expecting us."

"No," said one of the guards. "He's expecting her." The guard nodded to Neekay as she and Ebele came up beside Mr. Harsetti. "He specifically said, just the Warbird."

"Don't worry," said Neekay. "Mr. Harsetti here is accompanying me today. He may have some information on the killer. He's an invaluable part of my investigation."

"I do?" said Mr. Harsetti with surprise. "Wait, what investigation?"

The guard frowned before standing to the side. "Alright. Whatever you say, Mrs. Warbird." he nodded to Ebele. "I assume that girl is with you as well."

"My daughter. And yes. I'm training her. So, she follows me as my second."

After the guards stood to the side, they all were allowed access to the building and stepped inside. Ebele had been through the city many times, but this was the first time she'd ever been in the home of the Marquis. It was just as massive as it appeared from the outside. The main hall's ceiling reached up fifty feet into the air and the floors were made of marble that looked to reflect the light of the candles that had been lit throughout.

Soon the echo of footsteps was heard inside of the empty space and a man appeared ahead of them at the top of the steps wearing a servant's garbs.

"Hello there," said the man. "I take it you are the Warbird."

"I am."

"Good. The master has been awaiting your arrival. Please, follow me."

"How nice," said Neekay, as she stepped forward, walking up the steps with Ebele and Mr. Harsetti behind her. "How hospitable of him. I do hope he's prepared something to eat for us. The road was long, and I haven't eaten yet."

"If you would like, I can have the chef prepare something for you," said the servant as he waited for them at the top of the steps.

"Thank you," said Neekay as they all were ushered through the candle lit building.

Even with the light, the stone walls felt cold to her. Whereas her home also had stone floors, it felt warm. There was always a fire going in each of the rooms at night, not to mention the guards' chatter could always be heard if you were nearby. But here there weren't many guards and no jovial banter to listen to. Only the cold silence and the echo of their footsteps as headed towards their destination.

"Master," said the servant as he opened the door. "You guests have arrived."

"I see. Please come in," said an older gray-haired man sitting at a desk illuminated by candlelight. "I've been expecting you ever since I was informed of your arrival."

"I shall go and see about procuring something edible for you all," said the servant, as he turned to leave.

"Just some wine and bread if you have and a few pieces of meat. Nothing too fancy."

"Yes, ma'am."

Ebele stepped into the room, continuing to follow behind her mother. She looked over the room, noting the paintings of not just people, but also there was a larger painting of the entire Cela`Zain Island. Every major city was named, including those of the offset smaller islands. Even Pillan, Ebele saw the small image of the Goo Goo creature that had been known to attack ships. Her mother used to tell her stories about it as a child to scare her during the night festivals.

"Have a seat," said the Marquis, folding his hands together and resting them above the pieces of parchment over his desk. "I was told that you also arrived at this city some time ago. Right before the mess we have started. It would have been courteous if you would have come and introduced yourself beforehand."

"We were in a hurry and just needed to restock on supplies. There was no need for introductions then."

"And you think now is?"

"Not especially. We surely would have even skipped past your city on the way home if not for the escorting of Mr. Harsetti to his home estate."

"I see," said the man, glancing past her to Mr. Harsetti standing behind them.

"It seems you're having a bit of trouble," said Neekay, taking a seat and gesturing to the other for her daughter, leaving Mr. Harsetti to stand. "I hear you're having a bit of a murder problem."

The Marquis chuckled at the remark. "Yes, I suppose

you can say that I have that problem." He pointed a finger toward Mr. Harsetti. "You're very lucky to have been out and away during all this. Some nights ago, one of your servants reported to the town guard that they saw someone inside your home."

"What?" shouted Mr. Harsetti. "What of my wife, the children, are they—"

"They're fine. She locked herself inside the servants' quarters, along with some others. Your guards managed to chase the figure away. But my guess would be that the assassins were unaware of your recent travels."

"Yes, well... I did leave in somewhat short fashion. Since it was only a days' ride, I figured, I need not inform everyone, since I would be back within the week."

"So," said Neekay. "How many are dead?"

"Four. Lord Hetchel and his wife, Lord Prescel, and as of this morning Lady Elliot was found dead in her bed with a blade plunged into her throat."

"Four high nobles in as little as three days?" said Mr. Harsetti. "By the grace of graces, what are the town guards doing?"

"Searching. But with no one having a description of the perpetrator... well, you can see why some in this city might be a bit on edge."

"How did the others die?" asked Ebele. "Were they also stabbed?"

The Marquis turned to Ebele, seeming a bit surprised that she had spoken. "And you are?"

"Oh, where are my manners?" asked her mother. "Marquis, allow me to introduce you to my daughter, Ebele. I'm in the process of training her and as such have been taking her around the local land to several of the tournaments."

"Ahh, I see," said the Maquis as he gave Ebele another look. "Well, to answer your question. The usual blade to the chest. Apparently, one night, the murderer appeared holding a rifle, but no sounds of gunfire were heard. One of the bodies, Lady Elliot, I believe; we haven't exactly figured out how she died. Her body was searched, but we haven't found any wounds that we can consider to be the cause of her death."

"Was she an older woman?" asked Ebele, turning to her mother. "A heart attack, perhaps? Or some type of poison?"

"Oh, are you taking an interest in the dead? I'm sure the Marquis would let us look at the body ourselves."

"Ebele frowned while thinking of touching a dead body. She was curious, but she hadn't gotten to the point where dead bodies weren't creepy. "No... I don't think I want to do that."

"Shame. Your father loves cutting into the dead."

"Ahem," coughed the Magistrate to regain the attention, then glancing over at Neekay. "We are hoping your mother might be able to assist in the matter, since she was quite the skilled tracker during the war."

Neekay smiled. "True, in the past I was as much. But these days, I am nothing more than a wife and a loving mother. Plus, I have my daughter with me, and with a noble murdering fiend on the loose, you might imagine my reluctance to stay here and have her at risk."

"Oh," said the Marquis. "Then perhaps you shouldn't have entered." He smiled. "The city is on lockdown. No one leaves until the culprit is found."

Neekay stared coldly at the Marquis. "And yet I was allowed to leave to retrieve my daughter and Mr. Harsetti from outside the walls."

"An oversight by the guards. I'll see that they are reprimanded for it."

"And if I were to force my way out of here?"

"Then we'd have no choice but to brand you and your daughter here as the murderers. Why else would you be so passionate about escaping the city? I'm sure the king would be saddened to strip you of your home, land, and access to your powder mines."

"Of course," said Neekay, the smirk on her lips never fading. "Saddened, you said. Humph, I can just imagine his dismay as he signed the parchment for our arrest."

"Yes... I've heard of his particular fondness for you."

Her mother sighed. "Well, then." Standing from her seat, she turned to Ebele. "Let's go. I guess we should rest for the night."

"Wait," said Mr. Harsetti. "My man is out on the road because of a robbery perpetrated against myself. My wagon is broken. I would like to send supplies to have it fixed and have him returned to me."

"Unfortunately, your man will need to fend for himself till the matter is resolved," said the Marquis.

"Surely, you can send one of your guards to..."

"Mr. Harsetti, must I repeat myself?"

"No... No Marquis. I... I will wait until the matter is solved."

"Good. I will have my men bring over parchment with all the details of the murders for you to look over, Warbird. And if you need any assistance, please do ask. There are others in the city looking for the murderer as well. Perhaps you will collaborate with them."

"Perhaps I shall," said Neekay. "Come, Mr. Harsetti. It seems we shall be in your care for more time than we anticipated." She then opened the door to leave and found the servant standing before her, holding a plate of wine and food for them. She took a piece of meat and bread into her hand. "You can drink the wine. I'm sure you need it more than I do working here." She then headed down the hall, munching on the food.

Ebele could see that her mother was annoyed as they left the building, but as they reached the top of the steps, she couldn't help but look over the city, which had now become her pseudo-home until the situation had been sorted out.

High arched buildings, candle lights seen through

half-closed windows, cobbled streets and in between them somewhere was a killer who was hungry for the blood of nobles, which outside of her mother she just happened to be the most famous one in the city.

CHAPTER 6

The next morning, Ebele sat on a bed looking out the window over the City of Thrisanna. She had been given a room to share with her mother at the estate of Mr. Harsetti. She had felt a bit anxious about sleeping there with a murderer on the loose, but Mr. Harsetti felt secure after doubling the guards at his estate.

Now that we're here. What are we going to do? He can't honestly expect us to find some murderer, can he?

Still in her shift, she left the room and headed downstairs. The house was impressively large with Ebele, having to walk down two separate hallways before she reached the steps that lead to the first floor.

She caught the smell of cooking meat, and her empty stomach compelled her to follow the scent. It was in the kitchen that she found her mother sitting down on a stool, chewing on a piece of chicken with a glass of wine before her.

"Humm," she moaned before swallowing the meat after seeing her daughter. "I was wondering when you might wake up?"

"I had trouble sleeping," Ebele said as she stepped into the kitchen, taking a seat beside her mother and picking a piece of roasted chicken from her plate. "You always did like getting up early. Are we going to go out today and look for the killer?" She then plopped the chicken in her mouth. It was soft and moist; the juices flowing over her tongue, causing her to close her eyes and savor the taste. *Oh, that's good.*

"I have already been out scouting. I'll rest first before I go back out again. But you, young lady, will stay here where it's safe."

"What? There's no way I'm going to stay locked..." She looked her mother over, finally noticing that she was still in the same clothes as yesterday. "Wait, have you even gone to sleep? No... You were out all night in the city, weren't you?'

"Of course. I needed to handle some things, and I sent Kayin to go and inform your father as to the happenings with us. If we didn't come home. I'd hate to think what he'd do if his mind were left to wander for too long."

"Wait? Kayin's gone. But the city's been locked off? How?"

"No place this large is truly locked off. There's an old service tunnel through the sewers. I once used it during the war when the city was in threat of being ransacked. Not many know of it, since it's in a rotted-out part of town. But it's there."

"And you didn't think that it might be a good idea for me to go with him, rather than be locked in here?"

"Well, I didn't think you'd find it particularly pleasant to go wading through the shit and piss of the people here," said her mother as Ebele frowned at the sheer thought of such an action. "Exactly, I figured as much. But I'd also have to worry about the marquis getting word of your escape. That could lead to more uncertain action on his part."

Ebele's shoulders slumped as she shook her head. "So, what? I'm supposed to be a good little girl and hide here while you go off and possibly get killed by some shadowy figure you haven't even seen yet?"

Her mother laughed. "No, I know you better than that. I know by day three of being locked up here. You'll slip away and be out exploring the city."

"And how do you know that?"

"Because that's what I would do if I were you and my mother tried to house me up like this." A smirk came across her lips as she shook her head. "And unfortunately for me, you are the spitting image of me, just with a few less scares."

"Okay. So, what now, then?"

"Now?" said her mother as she stood up with a yawn. "I'm going to get some sleep. When I wake up, I'll take you out into the city and give you your first lesson in gathering intel." She placed her arm above her shoulder and began stretching her neck and she headed for the door. There, she turned back around to her daughter. "Don't leave the estate until then. Is that clear?"

"Yes. Mother."

"Good. Get to know Mr. Harsetti's children and wife while you're here. You might end up enjoying yourself."

Ebele watched her mother disappear in the doorway as she popped another piece of meat into her mouth. *Great, so now I'm supposed to act like a babysitter.* She looked around the cold, empty kitchen before thinking back to her room, where she remembered seeing her mother's rifle leaning against the wall next to the window. *Wait. We didn't bring any other weapons, did we? Did Kayin go back without one? Will... will he be okay?*

"Why hello, dear," said a maid as she entered the kitchen. "I see you made your way down and cooked yourself something to eat. Mr. Harsetti informed me earlier that we had guests, and I thought I'd come in to fix you all something to eat, but it seems to beat me to it."

"No. It was… no, never mind. Where is Mr. Harsetti now?"

"Oh, he's out back tending to the horses. He does that when he's nervous. And he's been out there all morning. I guess hearing about that person some night ago has got him fretting something fierce."

"You want me to go out and tell him you wish to see him?"

"No," said Ebele, standing up from her seat. "I'll go back and get dressed first and then I'll go and see him." She then headed out of the kitchen and back up the stairs. *Maybe I should ask for a space closer to the stairs,* the thought as she traversed the long corridors back to her room. When she got there, even though the door was closed, she could hear the sounds of rummaging and voices coming from inside.

Instantly a jolt of fear creeped down her spine as she took a step back, but then remembered that her rifle was still in the room. Quickly, she looked around for anything and saw a nearby metal candle holder atop a table. She grabbed it, letting the candles fall free from their perch to the table before falling to the floor. Steeling her resolve, she crept forward, placing her hand on the door and slowly sliding it open. Gripping the base of the candle holder as straight as she could, she peered inside, hoping to catch whoever was inside by surprise. But she was shocked to see two children rummaging through her truck, her clothing scattered over the floor.

"What's going on here?" said Ebele as sternly as she could, stepping to the room. "Stop that, both of you."

"Why?' asked the young boy defiantly. "This is our home. We don't have to listen to you."

"Yeah!" said the young girl with a laugh as she tossed around more clothing. "Our home."

"Now you both listen here," said Ebele, as she stepped in and began picking up her clothing from the floor. "I swear, if you both don't stop right now. I'm going to tell your father and you're both going to get spanked, and I don't think you…" She spotted the boy picking up her mother's rifle. "Oh, no, you put that back. That's not something a child should play with."

"I'm not a child. I'm the man of the house when my father's away. So, you have to listen to me."

Ebele slowly rested on her knee, letting the clothing fall to the floor. "I'm tell you to put that down or you—"

"Stop trying to tell us what to do," yelled the boy as he slammed the rifle to the floor with a thud, the metal pieces clanking off the floor as it settled down. "I'm the man of the house and we want to play here."

Upon seeing her mother's precious rifle thrown to the floor, Ebele's body shook for just a slight second before she silently stood up and headed for the door.

"Hey, I didn't give you permission to leave," said the boy. "You have to listen to me.

"Yes," said the girl. "All the servants have to listen to us because we're the young masters."

Ebele reached the door and placed her hand on the knob, closing it before locking it. She then turned around to face the children, her eyes narrowed as all the pity she might have had for them left her body. She then took a deep breath and stared at the children silently for a moment.

And just as a prey that had noticed that it had caught its predator's eye, the children froze, and the room grew silent. What happened next was an eruption of chaos as Ebele leaped forward at the young boy. He jumped on the bed to dodge her, crawling away as fast as he could toward the door. But just as he was about to leap off the bed to the floor, Ebele caught hold of his leg, yanking him back down on the mattress. His finger dug into sheets as he yelled before Ebele climbed on top of him and pulled down the back of his plants, exposing his bum.

"I'll show you who I have to listen to," said Ebele as she reached over and grabbed the strap of her rifle that she used to hold it over her shoulder. She then pointed it at the girl who was cowering near the down as she couldn't unlock it. "And when I'm done with him, you're going to get yours."

For the next several minutes, only the sound of slaps and crying children could be heard through the walls of the house.

When it was all said and done, both the boy and the girl sat on their knees on the floor being quiet while Ebele sat in a chair in front of them, her legs crossed as she stared at them, the strap dangling from her hand.

Soon, there came a knock at the door.

"It's unlocked," said Ebele, her eyes keen on the children, just hoping they would try moving toward the door.

"Sorry to bother you, dear," came Mr. Harsetti's voice as the door slowly opened. "I'm curious if you've seen... oh there they are. What are you two doing here on the floor?" He looked toward Ebele. "I do hope they haven't been in too much trouble."

"Oh no," said Ebele. "They've been behaving themselves well. Why, they even helped me clean the room, and it was in such a mess."

"Really? I thought I asked the maid to clean it when we arrived. They must have misheard me." He clapped his hands. "Well, come on, children. Your breakfast is ready and after that, it'll be time for your lessons."

The two children glanced up at Ebele for approval, and after a nod of her head towards the door. Both children stood up and began rubbing at their knees before heading over to their father to be comforted by pats on the head.

"Now, go on downstairs. Your mother has just arrived back from the Wellingtons. I'm sure she can't wait to see you."

Both the children quickly hurried off down the hall,

their little feet pounding the floor until it was just a distant drum in Ebele's ear. A smirk of satisfaction in the discipline that she'd given.

"Ahem," coughed Mr. Harsetti. "I didn't just arrive here. I've been standing outside the door for some time. One of my servants came and got after hearing the whaling of my children from inside."

"Then you should have come in and joined me," said Ebele, raising her strap and looking down at the belt at his waist. "It wasn't easy with... I think you called them the tiny terrors before."

Mr. Harsetti smirked. "My wife prohibits any form of physical discipline on them. She believes they will just grow out of their respective rambunctiousness."

"And you?"

"I and the servants found ourselves enjoying a bit of cathartic joy in listening outside the door."

Ebele shook her head. "And you're going to leave me to deal with the wrath of their mother when she finds out?"

"I hardly think that will be a matter of concern soon. Their mother and your mother haven't exactly seen eye to eye over the years. Those two were in the academy together. So, I expect Neekay will manage it when she awakens."

"All the same. I think I'll just wait in my room until then."

"A fair choice. I shall go and explain the situation to their mother, not that I'll imagine that it'll do us any good."

Ebele closed the door behind Mr. Harsetti, locking it again and then headed over to a dresser where she had placed her mother's rifle across. She then took a seat and began inspecting it. *It doesn't look damaged;* she thought as she ran her hand over the empty chamber opening, the cold metal tingling her finger.

Pulling the trigger caused a satisfying click that she'd heard all through her life, reminding her of her childhood in her father's workshop as he tinkered with rifles for the military. A thousand clicks, and thousand rifles, a thousand days. Even the smell of the oil he and polished he used felt as if it was forever etched into her mind. She couldn't help but place her nose near the opening, the faint hint of powder still lingering inside of the chamber.

Looking down the sight of the barrel, she could see that it was off now. *Probably from the drop.* She tried twisting it with her finger, but it didn't budge at all. With a sigh, she placed the rifle back on the desk and went over to her trunk and began digging inside of it until she pulled out a small pouch. She then walked back over to her desk, flipping the flap of the pouch open and exposing a set of holstered tools that her father had given her.

I really don't want to take it apart. Powders kin, that'd take too long. I wish Kayin were still here. His eyes are better than mine. And if I asked my mother... well, that's a conversation I don't feel like having now. With a little hesitation, she began to dismantle the trigger and sight inspecting them to see if there was any damage. But there was nothing that stood out to her besides the sights being uneven, which was an easy fix. Taking her time, she would spend the next few hours dismantling pieces of the rifle for inspection.

Hours later, Ebele found herself being awoken by a knock at the door. The world was a bit hazy; it took her some time to come to her senses and realize that she'd fallen asleep while putting the rifle back together. Getting up, she wiped her eyes, and she walked over to the door.

"Hello there," said her mother as stepped inside. "I hope I'm not interrupting."

"No...no, I was just resting."

Neekay smiled. "I can see that. Your hair is a mess and judging by that mess on the dresser over there, I can see you've been busy. Have you taken a liking to tinkering like your father?"

"No, the twins here... they came in and did what children do. I was just making sure that they didn't damage it."

"I see," said her mother as she stepped over, picking

up the rifle, and began looking it over herself. "Humm, the spring has shifted for the clip. Not such a big deal."

"What? How could you know that?"

"The sound when you press down on it. The squeak is too loud. It probably shifted out of position. It's not so bad. Sight's also a bit off, but that's normal."

"But I just fixed the sight."

"Oh, don't worry. You'll get better. I've spent twenty years with this rifle. It makes sense that I would be accustomed to its little nuances. Now come on, and have a seat," said her mother as she turned the empty seat at the dresser towards her. "We're going out to search for the city's murdering problem and I need you looking your best."

"I didn't realize going around bothering the local towns-folk with questions required me to look pretty," said Ebele as she stepped over, plopping herself down in the seat as her mother grabbed a nearby hair lock.

"There's many ah` thing you don't realize. But do not worry your little heart, mother will teach you everything. I suppose I should have started earlier, but there's no sense in crying over the past."

Despite a bit of uneasiness about going out into the city. Ebele took some pleasure in this mother daughter moment as she felt her mother's finger gently glide over her head, parting her hair. *When was the last time she did my hair? Two... no, maybe three years ago?* Her mind flashed to the thought of some strange person murdering nobles and then she began to wonder just home many times she had left. "Do you think you can find the person doing all of this?"

"I don't know," said her mother with a sigh. "This will be different from hunting someone through trenches and over tree cover plains. And even so, how long and how many more bodies are going to pile up before I do." She stared at Ebele for a moment, her hand resting on her shoulder. "I'm going to need you to be careful, dear. I can't have anything happen to you."

The admission of worry was a surprise for Ebele as she reached up and patted her mother on the hand, before leaning over and kissing her on the finger. "I'll be careful mother."

After twisting her hair, her mother asked her to put on a more high-society dress that she had brought with her. Ebele was curious as to why but went along with it. But even more curious was that she also did her makeup and placed on her a bit of perfume.

"I look like I'm going to a ball," said Ebele as she looked over herself in the mirror with her hair tied back in braids.

"The people who were killed were nobles, dear," said her mother as she picked up the rifle, slinging it over her shoulder. "One of us at least needs to look the part."

"I guess," said Ebele as she fidgeted with the hymn of her dress. "If you say so. But that doesn't make it any more comfortable."

Together, they both left the room and headed downstairs, where they found Mrs. Harsetti and the twins waiting for them.

"There she is," said the boy twin. "She's the one who hit us."

"Yes," that's her, said the girl twin.

"Neekay," said Mrs. Harsetti in a stern voice. "How dare you invade my home and unleash your uncouth child upon my children. I want you both out of my home this instant."

"And there she is, if it isn't Darlene Hitchens. My old classmate," said her mother with a sarcastic joy to her voice. "How are you? Congratulations on the twins, by the way. I'm sure they're a lot to handle."

"A lot... who do you think you are?"

"Me?" said Neekay, placing a hand to her chest as she walked down the steps to greet her old classmate. "I'm the woman who's come to save my old friend from the noble murdering scum plaguing this town. I heard you awoke to find them on top of you in your bedroom. I'm sure that was a familiar sight."

"Don't you dare talk to me like that in front of my children."

"Hello children." Neekay looked down at the children as they clenched onto their mother's dress. "My daughter is going to be your new babysitter for the next few days. It's that great?"

"What?" said the boy, looking at Ebele as she scowled back at him. He then looked up to her mother. "No, mother. Make them go away."

"Oh, you don't want that," said her mother with a smile. "Because I'm sure that the only thing keeping you mother alive is the knowledge that I have taken up residence here. Assassins tend to get very perturbed about missing out on a kill. And the moment they hear I'm gone…" she shook her head. "Well, they might just decide that it's the perfect reason to come back."

"Don't you dare pretend that you're staying here because you care about me or my children. I know the Marquis has locked you in this city."

"Either way," said Neekay, as she headed for the door. "I'll be back after I do some investigating. And if our rooms aren't well prepared for us when we get back. Well… we might just decide to take up residence at another lord's home that actually enjoys not being attacked while he sleeps."

And before Darlene could utter another word, both Ebele and her mother exited the building, stepping out onto the road leading to the gate.

"Do you really think the assassin will come back?" asked Ebele as neared the gate.

"Depends on why they are doing it. If Mr. Harsetti has pissed off the wrong people enough, then perhaps. I often find that revenge is a far better motivator than just money."

As Ebele stepped past the manor gates where she could get a good look at the city down below her, she began to feel a tightness in her chest. She'd never been in a situation anywhere near like this. Searching for a killer. Sure, she'd shot mannequins before and learned targeting, but she'd never aimed at a real person. Taking a quick glance back at her mother and the rifle over her shoulder, she swallowed as much of the nervousness as she could.

That's probably why she has the rifle now. I mean, there's no way she's going to ask me to kill someone. The thought of killing someone begins to make her stomach feel a bit queasy.

"Are you ready?" asked her mother.

Ebele nodded, and they headed out into the city, which went as Ebele had pictured it would in her head. They would stop at random vendors in the city and ask random questions; mostly seeming to be idle gossip that danced around the topic of the killer, but not directly mentioning it themselves. Instead, she saw that her mother would wait for them to bring it up and if they didn't, then they would leave it be and move along.

"Are we not going to go to one of the noble's houses that were killed?" asked Ebele as they left another vendor and headed down the stoned streets.

"We will," said her mother as she looked up at the sky. "But we still have a bit of daylight left, and I want to get a feel for the city. It's hard to do that at night when everyone is stored away in their homes." She plucked an apple from a stall, tossing the worker a bronze coin before handing the apple to Ebele.

Ebele took a bit while looking over the crowd of the people they passed and trying to understand what her mother meant. "I don't get it. The people here don't seem to be worried about a killer. Most of them are just smiling and going about their day."

"That's because they aren't nobles," said her mother, nodding ahead to a few men with rifles over their shoulders. "Tell me about that one."

Ebele followed her mother's nod to see in between the men were a man and a woman in fine clothing. And while the rest of the crowd were jovial, they, on the other hand, seemed to be on high alert; their eyes constantly spanning over the crowd. Now, taking notice of this, she began to look for other finely dressed individuals as they walked alone. And sure enough, anyone that looked like they might be a noble had more weary and alert eyes than the average town go'er.

"Okay, I'm starting to get your..." Ebele stopped walking for a second as her mind began to process what that meant, and she then looked over her own dress and realized why her mother asked her to get dolled up today. "You... you're using me as bait."

"Oh," said her mother with a smile. "You figured it out on your own."

"Really, mother? I'm your daughter."

Neekay, still smiling, stepped beside her daughter, linking arms with her and led her away. "Oh stop. You're in the prime of your beauty. What good would it do if you weren't using it to lure unsuspecting men to their deaths?"

"How did you ever convince father to marry you?"

"Simple. After I was pregnant with you, he felt as if he didn't have a choice."

"What? But I thought you said you had me after you were married."

She patted her daughter on the shoulder. "Please dear, I think we're a little old for fairytales now, don't you think?"

Speechless, Ebele could only blink as her mother led her down the street. Eventually, they would walk past the stone-filled street into the lesser peasant's quarters of the town. Gone were the high garbs of nobles, now replaced by the ragged clothing of those who perhaps would have called it fortunate to own a secondary pair of boots.

Most women had disheveled hair and Ebele found herself getting more and more unsavory looks from the unshaved faces of the men she'd passed.

"What are we doing down here?" asked Ebele, feeling more nervous than she could remember.

"We need to cover all areas," said her mother. "As wonderful as it would be to just assume our target is of the high societal class and is at this very moment dining on the finest roast duck with a glass of wine. It's more likely that we'll find the information amongst the dredges of the city."

"And you think it's a good idea for me to be down here like this?" asked Ebele as she felt her nice boots squish the wet ground beneath. "For goodness' sakes, I have to lift the sides of my dress just to keep it out of the mud."

"Exactly the point, dear," said her mother as they reached a more worse-for-wear looking tavern. From the outside, they could hear the sounds of chatter and laughter from inside. But that was probably because of the obvious holes in small holes in the side of the building that had yet to be patched up. "Come on. I doubt there will be any accosting while it's still daylight outside."

They walked up the steps where they met a very large man standing at the entrance, a bit of suspicion clear across his face as he looked over at Ebele.

"Hello there," said Neekay. "Does Greggor still own the place?"

"Nahh, his son does. But that old fool's still inside."

"Oh, good," said Neekay as she turned back to Ebele. "Count to ten and follow me in." Then she turned back to the guard, patting him on the chest. "Look after her, will you?"

"What, but you can't..." said Ebele, but her mother swung open the door and stepped inside, giving a small glimpse of ragged men and ale filled air as the door closed back on her. She then slowly turned and looked up at the lumbering door guard, his eyes narrowing on her as if she were a fox and he were a wolf. "Ah... hello."

"Count," said the man in a short, stern voice.

Ebele nodded. *One... two... three... four... oh fuck this... nine, ten.* And in a hurry, she pushed open the door, stopped inside to look for her mother. Upon her arrival, half of the bar suddenly began to quiet down. The other half, who had their backs turned, needed to be tapped on shoulders and alerted to Ebele. By their stares, she realized that she was a mysterious noble who'd just entered their bar.

Bearded men stared at her as if she were out of a fairy-tale, and the few women of the establishment looked at her as if she were a lifelong enemy who had just reemerged from the depths. Either way, Ebele quickly searched the bar, but was unable to find her mother. Unsure what to do, she stepped forward as confidently as possible towards the bar. The room was so quiet that she could hear the sound of the squawking floorboards under her head as she stepped.

Still no sign of her mother in the crowd as she stepped through the center aisle and stopped at the bar. There was a rough-looking man with a scar on his right arm that stood behind it.

"May I have a water, please?"

"Miss... I don't know what you're here for. But ya might want to get your water somewhere else."

"I... I thank you for your concern, but... I'm right where I need to be."

The man stared at her for a moment, before shrugging it off. "Alright. Suit yourself."

Dammit, mother. Where did you go? You didn't just vanish into the air. She thought as her eyes roamed over the barrels of ale in front of her. She could hear the murmurs of the patrons behind her begin to start up. Questions of: Who is she? Why is she here? Hey, go talk to her. Maybe she's lost. None of which helped to alleviate her anxiety over the situation.

She was so grateful when the man plopped down a mug of water in front of her. Even if it did splash on the counter in front of her, she clasped it with both hands, bringing it up to her lips. It smelled and tasted of hints of ale.

"Hey there, little lady," said a man who walked over and stood beside her. "What brings you down here to this part of the city? You seem kinda young to be out and about by yourself exploring. You come here looking for your daddy?"

Ebele gave the man a glance out the side of her eye. She could see his yellow stained teeth as he grinned at her. The rancid breath coming out of that same mouth didn't help things either.

"Leave her alone," said the man behind the bar. "I don't need any trouble with the nobles just because one of their babies wandered down here on an adventure." He pointed a finger at Ebele. "And you. Finish your water and leave before the sun goes down. Or just leave and go to another tavern. As long as the last place you're seen isn't here, it don't make me no difference."

I'm not a baby, thought Ebele, but decided to keep her mouth closed as she slowly sipped her water. *Dammit, mother. Where are you?*

"Ahh," said the man, sliding a bit closer to Ebele. "Don't listen to him, darling. What say I show you around the slums? We can have ourselves a little adventure. You know, something to tell your little lady friends about."

Just keep calm, Ebele. Just wait and he'll go away and then you can— Her thoughts instantly paused as she felt a hand on her ass. Instinctively, her eyes began to glow red as gripped the handle much tighter, swinging it hard and smashing the man in the face. "Don't touch me."

The man went flying forward, as the wooden much shattered into splinters on his face and he went sliding across the floor of the tavern. Suddenly, the tavern went quiet as they all stared at her.

Shit. I messed up. What do I do now? Ebele froze as she stared out at the tavern. One man rose from his seat and stepped over and placed his hand on the man she sent playing to the floor. He then shook his head before turning his attention back to Ebele.

Okay, Ebele. Think. I don't have a rifle. I'm in this stupid dress and... and... fuck! She swallowed and prepared herself to run.

"That was a nice hit, missy," said the man with a laugh as the rest of the bar joined along, bursting into laughter. "He'd bet he'd get to at least grab one of your tits before ya whacked good." He placed his foot under the man and lifted it, rolling him over on his back. "Seems he lost that bet. Hey Ellis, gimme some water to wake him up."

"Yeah, yeah," said the man behind the bar as he placed another two mugs of water on the table. He then slapped Ebele on the shoulder. "You owe me for that mug."

"Huh?"

The man who kicked over the man she had knocked out came over beside her and took the mugs of water, before walking over and splashing them on the face of the unconscious man causing him to wake up gasping for air.

"Wake up, you damn idiot. You lost. You owe me five silver."

"Huh. What? What happened?" asked the man as he began wiping his face as the crowd roared with laughter again.

"What's going on here?" came the familiar voice of her mother from up above.

Ebele took a few steps back to look up on the top floor and saw her mother leaning over the balcony, looking down at her.

"Mother! Why did you leave me alone down here?"

"Warbird!" yelled the man behind the bar, leaning on the counter. "This brat belongs to you?"

"I am not a brat."

"Yes," said Neekay. "She's my daughter."

"Yeah, well. I probably should have guessed that from the man laid out on the floor. You owe me for the mug and that chair she damaged with his face."

"Put it on my tab."

"Fuck your tab. You disappeared for five years and expect to have a tab?"

"Fine. but wait till I'm done up here. Your old man and I are in the middle of negotiations." She waved her hand down at Ebele. "Come on up, dear. There's someone I'd like you to meet."

Ebele felt foolish as she slumped her shoulders and proceeded to the stairs. She took her time stepping up, annoyed by the whispers of how she was the Warbird's daughter. *If you all think it's so easy, why don't you try being her daughter? See how you like it.* She soon made it to the top, where with a pat on the back, she was ushered through a door into a large room where, at the center, sat an older man at a table.

"Well, hello there," said the man. "You must be Ebele."

Ebele looked at her confirmation before turning back to the man. "Ahh... yes, I am."

"Well, come on in and give this old fella twirl and let me have a good look at ya," said the old man, lifting a finger and swirling it around to illustrate his point.

Ebele looked to her mother again, who subsequently gave her a nod, gesturing for her to follow along. She frowned at her mother, but then turned back to the man with a smile and stepped forward and did a quick spin in her dress, letting the frills float around her.

"Well, don't you look absolutely lovely," said the older man, gesturing to one of the chairs in front of him. "Go on and have a seat. I'm sure you're tired from your trip down from the nobles' quarters. And not to mention having your mother drag you around must have been hard on the nerves."

"Oh, it's just the worst," said Ebele, the words escaping her mouth before she even realized. Instantly she regretted it and tried covering her mouth.

"Ha!" said the old man with a laugh. "I see that you're

still as impossible to deal with as always."

The man's words resonated in the heart of Ebele as a smile spread across her lips. "You mean she's always been like this?"

"Yes, Little Neekay has always been—"

"Little Neekay?" responded Ebele, unaccustomed to anyone speaking of her mother in such a way.

"Yes," said her mother as she took a seat beside her. "Emmie here was my outfitter during the war?"

"Outfitter? You mean he gave you weapons, right?"

"Well, yes," said Emmie. "But that was only part of it. I was also tasked with issuing out provisions and bandaging your mother back up every time she returned wounded. I'd imagine most of the wounds on her body were patched up by me with little more than a hot needle and some thread."

"Although you could have been more gentle," said Neekay. "I swear half the time you treated me like your own personal pin cushion."

"The pin cushion would have been easier to manage," said Emmie, pointing an accusing finger at her, before looking back at Ebele. "I imagine you're easier to get into a proper noble's clothing than she is. Every time we had a ceremony, it was my job to dress her up like you are now and drag her ass to the event." He shook his head. "Kicking and screaming all the way."

Ebele laughed. "I can't imagine that."

"Neither can I, and I had the unfortunate privilege of living it for five years."

"As wonderful as it is to have you whisk us down memory lane. I'd like for you to first answer my previous question."

The smile left Emmie's face as his eyes shifted back to Neekay. He sucked on his lip while he looked her over again, as if thinking about something. "What's this noble killing got to do with you, anyway?"

"Nothing. I got a contract to kill them."

"Uh-huh. And you decided to bring your daughter on

this so-called contract."

"She's actually a good shot. Not as good as myself, but fairly impressive for her age."

After another stare at the two, he tapped his finger on the desk and sighed. "Alright, fine. Killing started half a week's back. Guys of mine say they spotted someone roaming around the streets at night. Word is someone put out a bounty on members of the Regal society."

"Regal society?" said Neekay, with a disappointed look across her face. "What kind of name is that?"

"A stupid one to us normal folk. But to nobles, I'd fancy it makes them feel real important."

"Careful now." She wagged a finger. "I'm a noble now myself, and so is my lovely daughter here. Feeling self-important is kinda a requirement before you even step in the door."

Emmie laughed. "Yeah. I remember hearing about that. You running away with that damn tinkerer. I swear, everyone in the sixth up to the fifteenth were laughing their asses off the entire night after that fiasco."

Ebele made a confused face at the comment. *Was mother and father's marriage that much of a big deal?* She then frowned. *But this is the woman who just decided to reveal to her daughter that their marriage was just a marriage of convenience.*

"Well, anyway, back to the topic of your hunt. Word has it there's two of them, maybe three. One, for sure, is a man. One of the maids caught a glimpse of him as he was leaving their manor."

"How can you be so sure there's more than one?"

"Cause the night before, caught wind of one of a rumor where they shot one of em' off of a roof and fell to the ground. But when they finally reached the spot they fell at, all they found was a pool of blood. You ever meet anyone who could get up from that and go killing the next night?"

"I see your point. Anyone been visited by the town

doctors recently?"

"Don't didn't check. I figure he's killing nobles. So ain't got nothing to do with us down here. And if I looked around too much, it might give them a reason to start looking back."

"A smart man. I knew there was a reason you'd survived so long." She looked around the room. "Although one wonders why you chose this place as your retirement cottage."

"Why? So, I can go off and die on a farm somewhere?" He shook his head. "Give me a good ale and some conversation, and I'd gladly die with my throat slit in the middle of the night rather than with shit in my pants in my old age."

Neekay laughed before standing up from her seat. She placed both legs together and stood straight and placed a fist to her chest with two extended fingers. "Gunner Neekay, off on a hunt, sir."

"Humph," Emmie took two fingers, placing them across his neck, sliding them over his skin as he spoke: "Good hunting, Gunner."

Soon Ebele and her mother stepped outside of the tavern and back onto the dirt road.

"What were those hand signs you and him were doing?" said Ebele. "I've never seen you use those before."

"Just our fun way of parting. All of us in the third had our own way of saying goodbye."

"Wait. He was in the third?"

"Humm. Yes, and no. He supplied us without assignments. But he found himself trapped with us on more than one occasion. So, think of him as more of an honorary member." She then stepped forward, heading down the street. "Come on. It seems we still have a few other places to visit."

"Where are we headed?"

"There are probably a few doctors in this city. We're going to look for the ones who are willing to patch up a bullet wound in the middle of the night and not ask any questions."

Gathering the information on the city's doctors didn't take much effort. A coin from her mother to the pocket of several in need and they were able to find that only one such doctor resided in Low Town. The rest handled the affairs of nobles and those with the money to properly reward a physician.

From one murky looking street to another, she and her mother traveled through the lower quarters of the city. As their sunlight dimmed with her passage of time, Ebele continued to grow increasingly aware of her surroundings as she caught glimpses of people staring out at them from their windows.

"Mother. This isn't seeming like the type of place where we should be." She grimaced at the sight of a man giving them a toothless smile as they passed.

"Don't worry, dear. Just a few more stops before we can head back," she said as they stopped at another shack of a house near the edge of the city walls. Worn black lumber along with the shadows casted on it by the city's wall made the place look as if it were abandoned. On the wall next to the door, carved crudely into the wood was the word 'Doctor.'

"You're up, honey," said her mother, stepping to the side.

Ebele shook her head before lifting a leg as if she were hobbled. She then knocked on the door. "Excuse me," she knocked again. "I'm looking for a doctor."

"Go away. We're closed."

"I'm sorry to bother, but I simply can't walk anymore. I'm told you're a doctor." There was a moment of silence. "I... I have money."

Suddenly, the door squeaked open just enough for a man to peek out an eye at them.

"You don't look like you belong here, girl," he said, noting Ebele's appearance. "Why ya here?"

"You are right, I don't," said Ebele. "But I was out

exploring with my guard when I twisted my ankle on a mud patch. I tried to walk back, but the pain... please, it's too much."

The man looked back inside before turning back towards Ebele. "Fine." he said, opening the door. "But mind my other patients. I'll look you over, but then you'll be on your way."

Seeing him, Ebele was surprised to see a young man, not much older than her. From his eyes and his voice, she'd just assumed it'd be a much older man. But instead, it was a half shaven doctor, with a hoarse voice.

Ebele stepped inside, still pretending to favor her ankle, with her mother following behind.

"Take a seat on that stool and I will look you over."

Ebele looked around the room and saw two beds, both occupied with patients. But she could see their faces as they were covered by a hanging white cloth.

"Thank for... for taking a look," said Ebele as she took a seat on the stool.

"It's fine," said the man as he knelt in front of her. "Lift up your dress for me a little so I can check your leg."

Following his instructions. Ebele lifted the hem of her dress for him, exposing her ankle. From this position, she could see that one of the patients had his leg wrapped in a bandage. She then glanced at her mother, nodding to the individual behind the curtain. Her mother came to stand behind her, taking a look herself, and then patted her on the shoulder, as if to say, 'good job.'

Aware of the man's warm hands over her ankle, which perhaps were up just a bit to far, Ebele decided to investigate a bit further. "How old are you? You seem pretty young for a doctor. When I heard you speak, I thought you were an old man."

"I took over the shop when my father died," said the man. His voice broke a bit as he talked. "This voice is the result of me getting caught in the rain delivering medicine to the people around here. The cold I had is gone, but the voice still hasn't recovered."

"How old are you?"

"Twenty... why?"

"Nothing... just wondering where your wife might be."

The doctor's hand stopped as he looked up at Ebele to see her smiling back down at him.

"You got yourself a new girlfriend, Highgard," said a voice from the man behind the sheet with a busted leg. "How's she look?"

"Shut up, Fegan." said the doctor, looking annoyed. "You're lucky I'm letting you sleep off your stupidity here." He then looked back at Ebele. "Your leg's fine. Might be a slight sprain. I got some old crutches you can use to get you back to the high quarters."

"Okay. Do you... think it'll be too much if I asked you to walk me back?" asked Ebele in her most flirtatious tone.

"I like this," said Fegan with the busted leg. "It's about time you get yourself a woman."

"Shut up, Fegan. Before I—"

"So, you don't have a wife then?" asked Ebele, interrupting and adding to the confusion.

Doctor Highgard looked up at her with a look of confusion and sheer disbelief on his face. "What? No? I mean, I'm not looking for a wife at the moment."

"Doctor, do you think I'm beautiful?"

"What!"

Ebele had to admit that she was taking a sort of joy in seeing how twisted the doctor's face could get in his confused state.

"Please forgive the mistress here," said her mother. "It seems the pain in her leg has gone to her head."

"Ahh... yes, of course," said the doctor, finally releasing Ebele's leg and standing back to his feet. "I'll go get those crutches for you." Doctor Highland then walked off with the sound of laughing patients in the background.

"I see you're having fun," whispered her mother.

"You're the one who dragged me down here. I might as well enjoy some part of this... whatever this is," whispered back Ebele.

Neekay looked to the side. "You, in there laughing at all this. What happened to your leg? You fall off a wagon or something?"

"I won a fight," said Fegan with the busted leg. "Bastard got mad, and my prize was to have a pitchfork driven into my leg."

"Ha!" laughed Neekay. "Serves you right. Who told you to be a good fighter?"

The man behind the curtain also laughed as he reached his hand over the sheet and began pulling it back. "Don't you worry. When I get..." The man's words paused as he stared at the two of them for a moment.

As his eyes squinted in thought, Ebele could see his mind trying to recollect who they were. But Ebele instantly knew him. He was one of the two men that had harassed her at Aretta back in Chadain after visiting the powder shop.

"Well," said Neekay. "Hello again."

Suddenly the door opened and in stepped a young woman.

"Hey doc, I brought..." The young woman stopped in her tracks as she caught eyes with a very dolled up Ebele.

"Okay, I have the crutches," said the Doctor. Stepped back in from the back.

"Aretta!" yelped Ebele.

"Shit," said Aretta, dropping the items and turning and running out of the door.

Ebele looked confused for a moment, before the sound of her mother's voice snapped her out of it.

"Ebele, after her. Now!"

Her mother's words were like a lightning bolt in her veins. Ebele stood and dashed out the door, chasing after Aretta.

Out the door, Ebele leaped off the steps, her feet landing in the soggy dirt as she ran off down the street; the bottom of her elegant dress being caked with mud as she did so. Ebele could see Aretta ahead of her. She wasn't so far away, but her movements weren't being constricted by an overly cumbersome dress either.

Why is she here? Dammit. Why is she running? Wasn't that guy in the bed one of the men who tried to rob us back in Passala? Why is he... no wait, Mr. Harsetti's, why did she rob him? "Dammit Aretta. Get back here." Ebele's eyes began to glow a red and she could feel her muscles tighter and she began picking up pace.

"Go away. Leave me alone," yelled Aretta, as she turned down one of the corners.

Following behind her and through the alley, she went. Catching a glimpse of Aretta once again and she dashed into another street. But Ebele was gaining on the girl fast, her enhanced speed shortening the gap between the two fast. She could see there were nearing the nobles' quarters up and Aretta dashed off the main road again into another alley. Ebele followed, turning down the alley to see a wooden fence in front of her and Aretta halfway over, about to lift onto it.

"Oh, no you don't," said Ebele, running up and leaping up with all her might. Catching Aretta, she wrapped her arms around her waist and began to pull back. Unfortunately, she was still enhanced by her essence and instead of pulling the girl back down slowly, she snatched the girl from her perch and they both went falling back uncontrolled to the ground, landing in the soggy mud.

The impact caused Ebele to lose her concentration of her essence as she couched from the force of Aretta landing on top of her.

"Let me go," said Aretta, rolling off her onto the ground. "Why... are you chasing me?" She tried to pick herself up, but as she stood, her foot slipped, and she fell back down in the mud beside Ebele. "Ahhh, just look at this." She lifted her hand before flinging mud from her fingers.

"Why... are you running?" asked Ebele, as she lifted herself to her knees. "And why are you speaking differently?"

Aretta just stared at her for a moment. "Are you really that stupid?" She then shook her head. "Gods, I can't believe I didn't rob you when I had the chance," she said as she stood back up to her feet again, maintaining her balance. "Look, just... just stay away from me, okay. I gotta get..." She stopped her words when Ebele stepped in front of her to block her path.

"I can't let you go."

Aretta shook her head before lifting her leg and reaching into her boot and pulling out a knife. "Look, I don't want to hurt you. But I ain't gonna let you take me off to no jail to be locked up."

Ebele looked at the blade, the shimmer of the moon glimmering off its cold steel. "Is that the same blade you held to Mr. Harsetti's throat before you robbed him?"

"No, this is the blade I held to his neck after he slipped his hand up my skirt after trying to fuck me." She then waved the blade. "So..." She swallowed. "Let me pass, and then I won't have to use it on you."

Ebele stared at Aretta for a moment. The blade in her hand, the mud over her clothing. But she herself wasn't any better. Her dress was now much heavier with the dirty water soaked into it. Her face and arms, both covered in mud, she slipped her feet out of her slippers and into the mud to get as much of a solid feeling as she could. "I'm sorry, but I can't. Mother wants me to bring you back."

"Yeah," said Aretta. "And I really don't want to see her again." She then lowered her stance, placing the knife in front of her. "Sorry, but I like my freedom."

She then lunged at Ebele; the blade pointed slightly upward at her shoulder. Ebele's eyes glowed red again as she dashed to the slide, dodging the blade slash from Aretta, but the enhanced movement didn't help with her control. Because when she tried to stop, her feet carried the mud with her as she went flying to the left, slamming her elbow in the side of a house, cracking the wood. She winced at the impact before turning to see Aretta staring at her, confused.

"You really are a clumsy bitch, ain't ya?"

"Yeah, well…" said Ebele, pulling herself from the wall and standing face to face with Aretta again. "It's not easy, controlling essence in the mud like this." She dug her feet into the mud again, preparing for another attack. "Why didn't you try to run away just now?"

"Why? So, you can just chase me down again with your freaky magic feet?" She shook her head. "Nah, I figure if I cut you enough, then you'll leave me alone."

"And here I thought you were just a simple girl from the country. Is your name even Aretta?"

"Does it matter?"

Ebele sighed. "I hate it when mother's right," she said before her eyes started glowing red again.

"You still ain't learned your lesson yet," said

"We'll see," said Ebele, preparing for another attack.

Again, Aretta stabbed for her shoulder, and again Ebele dodged to the side, but this time Ebele parried, slapping Aretta's wrist before lunging forward again. This time, just like before, she knew she wouldn't be able to stop in the mud, so instead, she gripped Aretta's clothing, pulling as hard as she could. The young girl was lifted off her feet as Ebele went forward, out of control, and collided with the opposite wall.

Even with enhanced essence it hurt, but she grit her teeth and turned back to see Aretta back down in the mud after having been lifting off her feet. Ebele had pulled so hard that she had ripped a large piece of the fabric from her outfit which was now clutched in her hand.

Aretta moaned as she rolled over. "What… is… wrong with you? I swear that—"

Aretta's words were cut off as Ebele seized the opportunity, and hopped on the girl's back, wrapping her arms around her neck and began squeezing.

"Get... off," murmured Aretta as she began clawing at the skin of her arm and began trying to pull her away.

"It's okay... it's okay. Shh, shhh, just go to sleep," said Ebele as she cut off the girl's airway. As she straddled her back and tightened her grip on Aretta's neck, she could feel the girl's flailing begin to slow. Her body began to shake before finally her arm gave out and she fell back down into the mud. Ebele was sure to keep her grip in place a few moments longer to ensure the girl was out and also turn her head so that her mouth was in the mud.

When satisfied that she was out cold, Ebele released her grip, sliding off and turning her body over. Ebele then sat there, knee deep in mud for a moment, and regained herself. She then giggled a bit. *I'm glad Kayin isn't here to see this. He'd probably scold me with how sloppy I am.* She took a deep breath and began to stand when she noticed the knife under where the girl was; its once shimmering blade now covered in filth. Reaching down, she picked it up before standing and examining it. An average blade. A little dull, but she decided to hold on to it. She wiped it off on her dress before sliding it into the sash at her waist.

In the distance came the howling of a dog. Nighttime was here, and the moon hadn't reached its peak yet, so there was still a long night ahead of her. A little annoyed at her situation, she shook her head before stepping in front of Aretta's body, grabbing her by the arms. And with a heave, she began to drag her through the mud, back towards the main road.

I swear, Mother better appreciate me doing this.

CHAPTER 7

Aretta opened her eyes and found herself staring up at a wooden ceiling, the soft comfort of a pillow under her head as her eyes shifted from left to right, trying to gather a sense of where she was. In a bed somewhere, but she couldn't see anything as there were white privacy curtains all around the frame of the bed. It was daylight, that much was clear. How long had she been out since the crazy girl climbed atop her and strangled her half to death? She reached up pinching the skin of her neck, taking Dolls deep slow breaths as her heart stayed tight in her chest.

Okay, stay calm. They've captured me. But I'm not in chains, so maybe they don't know yet. I just need to escape. She took a deep breath, taking her hand from her neck and resting it on her chest, where she grazed the side of her nipple. Feeling a bit annoyed, she lifted the blanket covering her and saw her body. *Why the fuck am I naked! Where are my clothes?*

She took another moment to compose herself before she sat up in bed, sliding her head through the slit in the privacy curtain around the bed. Outside seemed like a normal enough room for some noble. Cabinets and dressers for clothing. Ahead she could see a rifle sitting on the dresser. She frowned instantly as she recognized it. It was the rifle of that weird girl who choked her half to death in that muddy alley. But she didn't see anyone in the room.

I've got to get out of here before she comes back. Her eyes took a keen interest in the window near the dresser. *They think I won't try to escape from here naked, then they've thought wrong.* Although thinking that, as she stepped out from the bedding, placing a foot on the cold stone floor, she left it with the bed linen wrapped around herself for what little modesty it afforded.

She stepped over to the dresser and began opening drawers, looking for anything she could use, but they were all empty. Everything was barren except for the rifle on the dresser. She frowned at it once again, but didn't touch it. Instead, she made her way over towards the window. There was a piece of green land ahead of her that ended with a wall and beyond it, the city she had come to. And to her surprise, the window was unlocked, but to her dismay, she could see she was on the second floor and there was a large gathering of men sitting on a group of barrels just below her. *Fuck. Do I wait? It's not like I can fight off five guys.*

Frustrated, she turned around to look for anything she might have missed that could help her escape. But from her new position in the room in front of the window. She had indeed missed something. In a chair near the end of the bed, there was the mother of the girl who she had fought. Her breath froze in her chest as the woman just stared at her. *Fuck! She was here the whole time. Is she a ghost? Now what do I do?* Her eyes glanced back over towards the rifle over on the dresser. When she looked back, she saw the mother looking at the rifle also, and then back at her as a smile slid across her lips. *Fuuuuuuuuuuuuck. There's no way I'm falling for that.*

The mother of the girl then gestured to a seat in front of her and then nodded over to the rifle as if giving her the option and seeing with one she'd choose.

She stood there for a moment, as if weighing her options, but she knew what the only real option she had was. So, with a weary mind, she slowly walked over, placing a hand on the top of the seat before sitting down, all the while never taking her eyes off the woman. She had expected the woman to say something or accuse her of something, but instead, she just stared at her continuously. Every moment grew increasingly more awkward and uncomfortable the longer it went on.

What is this? Say something, you stupid bitch. Another moment passed. *What? Are we just supposed to stare into each other's eyes till we die? Fuck off.* She lowered her head with a shake, before giving a long exhale while rubbing the back of her neck. "What do you want?" she asked in a low tone, choosing not to look her in the eye while she said it.

"I don't know," said the Warbird after a short moment. "Am I supposed to want something?"

"Everyone wants something," she gestured around the room. "You got me in here instead of in chains locked up in some dungeon. So, you must want something."

"No. I was just curious what you would do when you woke up." She flicked a finger towards the window behind her. "The window was my guess. Tell me, why didn't you go for the rifle?"

"Does it matter?"

"Not really. I'm just curious."

"Will me answering get me out of here?"

"No, but maybe it'll help towards getting you some clothing."

She stared back at the woman. "I don't like guns. My

father died because of them. And besides, it's not like I can shoot the thing anyway."

"Your father, was he shot by someone?"

"He was a smuggler. Some years back, he stole some supplies from the military. They hanged 'em for it."

"Then that was during the war," she laughed. "Not a good idea to steal war supplies."

"He knew. We told him." She frowned. "But he didn't listen."

"We?"

"My Brothers and I…" When she said the word 'brother,' she saw a slight smirk come across the woman's face and instantly her mind went back to her walking into the healer's cottage where her brother was laid up. "Wai…, where are my brothers?"

"I was wondering when we'd get around to that topic," said the Warbird as she waved a hand dismissively. "But don't worry. He's safe, and still getting his leg treated."

Oh, thank goodness, she thought as her body untensed.

"Although now," said the woman, finishing her statement. "He's doing his healing in a prison cell underneath the mall hall of the Magistrate's office."

"What!" yelped Aretta. Her hands clutched the armrest of the chair as she almost jumped out of her seat.

"Oh please, dear. You all robbed a prominent member of the city. Of course, he's going to be held there."

Her breathing caught in her chest as she started looking around the room, her mind frantically spiraling through thoughts and ideas on how to salvage the situation. *I need to leave. But if he really is there. How am I going to get him out? Wait, she said he, so does that mean they didn't catch Drogal?* In the middle of her thoughts, she caught the woman examining her, as if waiting for a reaction. Then, realizing and accepting the situation she was in, she exhaled and slumped back in the chair. She knew that look; it was a look that almost everyone had at one point in time. "You do want something from me."

"Oh? Do I? I could have sworn that I said that I didn't."

"That's why you have me in like this. You're gonna use my brother against me to make me do what you want."

"I see you're familiar with blackmail. Unfortunately for you, even though I'm sure it would have been fun on my part. As I watched you sleep in that bed over there, I couldn't think of a single thing to have you do for me." She then stood from her chair and straightened her blouse into her trousers. "I suppose I'll alert the guards outside to have you brought down to Mr. Harsetti. You remember him, I'm sure; the man you and your brothers robbed on the way here after he so kindly offered you a ride."

"Kindly? After offering me a lift, I had to deal with his grubby hands as he tried sliding them up my shift."

The woman rolled her eyes. "Yes, well. You are currently in his house. So, I guess you managed to find your way into one of his beds either way." She then turned back and stepped toward the door.

"Wait!" she yelped as she quickly stood up. "You can't just walk out. There's gotta be something you want."

"Honey, I had long time to think and nothing of worth came to—"

"Wha… what if I ahh…" Her mind quickly began running through thoughts of anything that could help. Skills that she may have. Anything that could keep her safe and perhaps get her brother out of his supposed prison. *Come on, think. Everyone wants something. And Powder's kin, she's my best chance rather than begging that pervy man for help. I already know what he wants. Anything that will get us out of here without people chasing us down.* Looking around the room, her eyes stopped on the rifle. "I can… I can carry your rifle for you."

She laughed. "Really? Is that your best attempt? And even though you just admitted that you hated guns." She shook her head. "It's not much trouble to carry my own rifle. And even if it was, I have my own servant for that." She turned to leave again.

"But what about your daughter? Does she have a servant? I can carry it for her?"

The woman turned around again, but her face held a tinge of amusement across it. "You wish to be the bearer for the girl who beat you unconscious and then dragged your body through the streets?"

"No, I don't want to do it. But I will if it'll keep me from having to beg that old perv we robbed, and that you promise to keep me and my brothers safe from him for as long as I'm under your employ."

This time the woman stared at her, and if she could see the plotting going on behind her eyes. *Okay, she's thinking about it. That's something.* "It's not a bad deal, right? I... I remember you and your daughter talking about how she doesn't have friends her own age. Well, we're bout the same age, then it works out for you, right?"

"And how long will you stay under my employ?"

"As... as long as you want." She said hastily, grasping onto the thread of hope she was seeing. "You take care of us and I'm yours. That's more than a fair deal, right?"

The woman rubbed at her chin, her lips twisting, and she considered the offer. "Fine, I accept."

With her words, she felt as if a weight had been lifted from her shoulders. *Yes. Thank the Kins.* She felt as if she could breathe again. But it was short-lived.

"But with a few caveats. One is that you listen to me completely. Is that understood? I won't have you robbing people while under my supervision."

She nodded her head. "I understand."

"Second, is that you will not inform my daughter of our little arrangement. For as much as she knows, that little scuffle last night was a way to reunite you two."

She nodded her head again. *What am I supposed to say? How I love to be beaten up?* "Ah... what about the robbing of that pervy old man? Does she know about that too? What am I to say to her about that?"

"You make up some sob story," said the woman. "Despite her brash nature and ability with a rifle, my daughter is terribly naive. And given that she has a fondness for you, I'd assume she'll accept any excuse you give her."

"Right..." she said, the sound of her voice doing nothing to hide how unsure she felt about the situation she was in or her daughter actually believing anything she made up. But she nodded her head just the same.

"Well then, I suppose we have an arrangement," said the woman, placing a hand on her hip. "So, tell me your name."

"My what?"

"Your name. Obviously, it's not really Aretta."

"Oh. My name is Marigold... Marigold Sprunster."

"Humph, not a bad name, I guess," said the Warbird before giving her another look over. "I should go and get you some clothing. It really is a good thing you and my daughter are around the same size. It seems you're going to be spending quite some time in her clothes." She then turned around one and headed toward the door, opening it, and closing it behind her.

She watched as the woman exited the room, feeling a weight lift itself from her chest as she did. *Okay.* She sighed. *Okay, I managed to talk my way through that.* She turned and stepped back towards the window and looked out of the city. *Now I just gotta play nice till I can find us a way out of this city. It doesn't look like they found Drogal. I just need to find him and tell him what's going on. Then we'll get Frovik out of that dungeon and find a way out of the city.* She shook her head. *As if it's really going to be that easy. There's something weird about that woman and her daughter. How am I going to escape them?*

She didn't get to stay in her own thoughts long before the door opened again, and the woman stepped back inside holding a set of clothing and undergarments in arms, along with a set of shoes.

"Well, let's say we get you dressed, shall we?" said the woman as the door closed behind her.

To her surprise, she wasn't given a dress like before. Instead, she was given a blouse and a pair of fitted trousers and a vest to match. It was much in the same vein of the clothing that the woman had on.

"What do you want me to do for you?" Marigold asked as she dropped the sheet from her body and began putting on the adornments.

"First, we will take a trip around the city together. I imagine you know far more about it than I do," said the woman as she stepped over to the window to look out at the surroundings. "A lot has changed since I was here last and even then, I didn't exactly get to know it very well. But I imagine you won't have that problem seeing as you do some business here."

"Business? What do you mean?"

"You rob a noble and then come here to sell his stolen goods in the same city that he resides in? No, you know people here. I'm going to need you to make use of that. There is a person here that I wish to find. Someone with a hole in their leg."

"Hole in the... is that how you found me? You thought my brother was the person you were looking for?"

"Exactly, and apparently, so does the magistrate. And he's quite keen on blaming your brother for this city's most recent woes unless we find the real person."

"What? I thought you said you'd release him if I helped you. You didn't say nothing about this other stuff and him taking the blame for someone else."

"Before, it didn't matter. I had thought to let him hang and be on my way." She turned back and gave a smile. "But you just were so convincing with your pleas and propositions. How could I say no?"

Powder's Kin I hate this bitch. I gotta get us outta here as fast as I can. The way she looks at me, there's something off about her, I can tell. "Fine," she said, finishing up the buttons on her blouse, before sliding into her vest. "What now?"

"Now," she said, heading toward the door and opening it for her. "We go for a walk."

Together, both women headed out of the room and down the hall. Marigold couldn't help but take in her surroundings. It wasn't just the room she was in that was nicely furnished, but it was the entire house. Even the floor of the hall had a center run that went down the middle and turned the corner. *Rich people.* She thought with disgust. *This house could hold how many families. How many rooms does a person need?*

"I see you're not used to having nice things," said the woman, noticing her eyes roaming.

She frowned. "I wasn't born into being some noble person. Me and my brothers have to work for whatever we get. Not like you, who just had everything handed to them since they were born."

"Oh, a sharp tongue," said the woman with a smile. "Yes, I suppose it's normal for you to see it that way. But keep in mind, most nobles come from poor families, that just so happened to get lucky with money."

"Well, my daddy didn't leave me no house to be set up in when he kicked the bucket. So please excuse me if I can't understand being born with money."

The woman laughed as she turned the corner to the stairs. As they took a step down, the front door opened and in walked her daughter.

"I'm back, mother. I hope every..." Ebele's words froze in her mouth as she spotted Marigold.

There was a slight moment when both the young woman froze, their eyes glued to each other, their lips not knowing what to say.

"Ah, there you are," said her mother. "Just in time. She has awoken and explained to me her horrible situation.

Why don't you two talk it over?"

"Shit. What am I supposed to say?" asked Marigold under her breath, so only the woman next to her could hear.

"I expect you to lie," said the woman, her tone just as low. "You don't need to be born wealthy to know how to spin a good lie." She then gave her a hard pat on the back, which sent her skipping down the steps, before clasping on the railing for support, her eyes wide in surprise. She wanted to turn around and curse the old bitch, but instead she looked ahead towards Ebele and put on her best humble expression and softened her voice. "I'm sorry about the other night."

A look of surprise overtook Ebele's face. "I'll... I'll forgive you if you forgive me. After all, I may have been a little too rough with you, Aretta."

Aretta? She's still... I guess that's who I am to her. She frowned. *And may have? I thought I was going to die with my face in that mud.* "I guess I deserved it really. I didn't really mean to trick you so. I just... well, you and your mother were kind to me, is all. And I didn't really feel so good about stealing from ya, so I left. You know, best be on my way and all that."

Ebele sighed as she came forward and took a step up before extending her hand out towards her. "I understand. I thought it might be something like that. I even said so to mother when you disappeared." She looked up at her mother with a smug smile. "See, not everything is as you say."

"So, it seems," said her mother as she stepped down while shaking her head dismissively. "Well, since we're all made up, I suppose we should—"

Suddenly the door to the manor opened again and two little children came running, making a beeline towards the kitchen. They were soon followed behind by their parents, Mr. Harsetti, and his wife Darlene. Unwelcome expressions appeared across both their faces, although the severity was vastly different. Whereas Darlene seemed displeased, Mr.

Harsetti seemed to be in pure disbelief.

"What... what is she doing here?" said Mr. Harsetti, pointing a finger at Aretta as she scowled back at him.

"Just in time," said Neekay as she stepped forward. "This girl here is my daughter's attendant and will be staying with us here until the matter at hand is solved."

"By Powder's Kin she will not," said Darlene, waving a finger at Neekay and Ebele. "It's bad enough to have you two in our beloved home. You can't just do as you please and invite another stranger."

"Stranger?" asked Neekay with a puzzled look. "Your husband here knows my friend very well. In fact, he was the one that offered her a ride to the city."

"Yes," said Aretta, her eyes lowering, but catching on to her mother's suggestive words. "Your husband was very adamant about offering that ride."

"What?" said Mr. Harsetti, before understanding the situation he was in with his wife standing next to him. "I mean, yes. You were supposed to be here days ago, darling girl. What kept you?"

"I'm sorry for my late arrival. I had to make sure it was safe. After all, a girl traveling alone. I'd hate to admit it, but I wasn't sure of your intentions."

"What?" said Darlene. "My husband isn't some savage. You'd be as safe around him as you would any other nobleman of class and high standing." She looked over at Neekay. "But given as you're in service to this family, I guess it's no wonder you'd think that way." She took another look at the three before turning back to her husband. "You finish with them, dear. I'm going to look after the children."

"Ah, yes, dear," said Mr. Harsetti as his wife left, headed into the kitchen. Then he turned back to Neekay. "Why isn't this woman in chains?" His voice was low but stern as he pointed to Aretta.

"She's become useful," said Neekay, matter-of-factly. "And I will use what is useful. And from the story she shared about your brief carriage ride, you very much tried to do the same."

"Come now," he laughed. "You can't believe the word of a beggar over me, can you? We've known each other for years."

Neekay laughed as she stepped forward and patted Mr. Harsetti on the cheek. "And I have known men much longer." She then stepped forward toward the door. "But don't worry, given who your wife is, I suppose it was inevitable." She reached her hand for the doorknob but stopped when she saw it creak open on its own and outside popped the head of a small child. It was one that she'd seen around the yard. He looked around for a moment cautiously before spotting Mr. Harsetti.

"Ah... excuse me, sir. You... you told me to come to you if..." he looked at Neekay and the girls and bit his lip. "Well, I mean... about the thing."

Mr. Harsetti's eyes went wide. "Yes, of course. Step in child. Don't worry about these ladies here. Tell me what you know. Has there been another one?"

The boy stepped fully into the house, the door closing behind him. "Yes, sir. It was... it was Sir. Richmond. They found him near his bed some time ago."

"Richmond!" replied Mr. Harsetti, a look of shock on his face, before placing a hand to his lip in contemplation. "I see. That doesn't bode well. Has it been announced yet?"

"No, sir. I only know because I'm friends with one of the young stable hands there. He says the guards are keeping things under wraps as to not cause any more panic in the city."

"You appear nervous, Harsetti," said Neekay, as she studied his reaction. "Are you afraid they'll come back here?"

"Of course, I am. I have children. How can I be sure of their safety with such things happening in this city?"

"Agreed," said Neekay, as she reached over, placing a

hand on Ebele. "I guess that means we now have a place to start. Shall we be off, then?"

And with those words, Neekay left the house with Aretta and Ebele following behind her.

A place to start? echo'd the Warbird's words in Aretta's mind. "What are you trying to find?" she asked, a small amount of fear in her voice for the answer.

"Oh, mother plans to find the person who has been killing all the nobles in this city and catch them."

"What?" said Aretta, halting in her steps for a moment, before quickly stepping forward to catch up to them again. "You can't be serious."

"What," said Neekay, "You wish to revoke the terms of our contract? Well, I'm sorry to say that it's a bit too late for that, dear."

"Yes, I mean no... I mean, what about the city guards? Isn't that their job?"

"It is. And I'm sure they have their own investigation. But as they haven't found the killer yet, that means the hunt is still on."

"The hunt?" replied Aretta, a look of disbelief on her face. "These aren't some petty bandits in the woods. These are real killers... targeting nobles... who have guards and stuff. And they probably have weird essence tricks."

"Yes," said Miranda with a smile. "It's going to be an interesting hunt."

Aretta looked towards Ebele for any type of solidarity but found nothing as the girl was busy staring off at a boy sitting on a bench fidgeting with some type of machine.

"Mother, have you ever thought of getting a photograph machine?"

"Your father has tried. But the material for it is rare. Whenever a photographer arrives in the city, he gets this look in his eye that..." The bitch shook her head as she turned to see that her daughter had stopped and was staring at the boy with the machine in his hand. "Yes, much like the look you have now." She clapped her hands to get her daughter's attention. "Ebele, come. There will be plenty of time for photographs when this is all over."

"Ahhh," said Ebele, apparently realizing she was left behind. "Yes, sorry mother."

"By the Grace of Graces, you are truly your father's daughter."

What is wrong with these people? How can they act like this when... no, never mind. I don't care. The moment I find a way out of this with my brothers, I swear I'm leaving this city as fast as I can. Let them both die here.

The trip through the city was simple. This time they needn't visit the lower quarters and instead traversed the noble's and prominent merchant areas of the city. Here in the morning hours of the day, with the sun still peaking just past the horizon, she saw many people in their high garbs shuffling through the city streets. Stone buildings, washed with lime to create a white vestige, littered the streets and corners.

Look at them all. I bet their purses are fat with gold. I swear, if we could just spend a day up here and blend in, we could really make out. But those damn guards are so strict about who they let in here. Gotta talk proper, gotta dress proper, everything's all gotta be just so... Stopping in the middle of her thoughts, she then realized that none of the nobles were staring at her with that typical look of disgust that she'd come accustomed to. Her eyes shifted back and forth in confusion for a moment before she looked down at her own self and remembered that she herself was wearing the noble's garb that the bitch had given her.

"What's wrong?" asked Ebele, as if noticing the confusion on Aretta's face.

"Huh?"

"The way you're looking. Did you forget something back at the house?"

"Oh! Ah... no, sorry. I was just thinking, is all. I'm still not used to wearing such fancy clothes."

"Really?" asked Neekay. "And here I thought you were just thinking how many of the people you could rob before you got caught?"

For a small moment Aretta sucked in her cheeks as her eyes went wide, but quickly turned the expression into a smile and she looked up at the woman. *What? Is this bitch a mind reader or something?* "No," she said, lowering her head. "I promised I'd behave. I'm just scared, is all. I mean, what are we supposed to do even if we find the killers?"

"Run, obviously," said the bitch with a smile. "Our job is to locate and identify them. Then we inform the magistrate and guards of who they are, where they are hiding, and what they look like. Afterwards, we let them clean up the mess of catching them."

"Oh," replied Aretta, feeling a small weight lift from her chest. "That... that doesn't sound as bad as I thought. I thought you were going to try to catch them."

"Please," said the bitch. "I have my daughter's wellbeing to think about." She shrugged her shoulders. "And you also, apparently. I won't have 'leading two young girls to their deaths eating away on my conscience."

The bitch led the way through the city to where the most recent murder had been placed.

"Hello, there," said the bitch upon reaching the gate. "There was only one guard at the gate. He was a regular house guard. Not a city guard, as they would have been in robes and armor."

"Sorry, The Lord isn't taking visitors today."

"Yes," said the bitch. "Being dead does tend to put a halt to the number of visitors one can take." Her words catching the guard by surprise as he began stumbling on what to say in response, but she cut him off before he could form another sentence through his bumbling. "His Lord Magistrate sent me to perform an investigation as to the death. So please be a dear and open the gate for us."

"What... are you the Warbitc... Warbird." He looked between Aretta and Ebele. "I was told there'd be only one of you."

"I'm sure you were." She placed a hand on the shoulders of the girls. "These are my assistants. But you're free to not let us in but do understand that I will just have to tell the magistrate that a guard decided that he knew better than him. Ahh... What was your name again?"

The guard frowned before opening the gates to them and escorting them to the front door of the manor house. From the outside, it looked just as fancy as any other lord's manor. The main thing she noticed was that all the window covers were shut. Atop the steps they went and through the halls. She could hear multiple voices from inside.

The guard then opened the door for them and as they stepped inside, Aretta saw a slew of guards standing around the lower levels of the house.

"What's this?" asked one of the men as the ladies walked in together. "What've you got there?"

"This is apparently the Warbird the captain's been waiting for, and get this, she's brought two little baby warbirds with her."

The man's eyes went wide with understanding before turning back to the other guard. "Thank you, soldier. You can return to the gate now."

"What? Don't you want me to take em' to the captain?"

"No, I'll escort them myself," he said curtly. "Please ensure no one else is allowed on the premises." The man looked confused for a moment before turning and heading back out the door. "Sorry about that. He's more of a local. Probably never served with the proper military. So, he wouldn't know to show you the proper respect, madam."

The bitch looked the new guard over. "Oh? And you do? Judging from the appearance, you don't seem much older than him."

"Aye, you're right. I'm not. But I ran munitions at the tail end of the war when I was younger. It's the only job they let me do at the time since I was only a child of seven or eight. You may not remember. But you came through our encampment once. I showed where our captain was back then as well, and you reached into your pocket and handed me some sweet rocks."

The bitch sighed. "Yes... well, the field is no place for children, yet we had far too many there, regardless." She then shook her head, nodding to the back rooms. "Since it seems we're old acquaintances, there's no need to be so proper. Instead, I'll yes have you repeat your last mission for me and show me to your new commanding office." She smiled. "Sorry to say, I didn't bring any sweet rocks with me this time."

The boy laughed. "It's fine. Jacoby Wiles, that's my name."

Aretta noticed that the bitch wasn't boastful or as confident sounding in front of this young man as she usually was. *Does she not like talking about her past?*

They were allowed through the building; their presence catching the stares of all the nearby guards as they were led through the building. Aretta couldn't help but notice the lavishness of the building. Through open doors she could see fine dining rooms, set with expensive tableware. Others had mannequins adorned with dresses. All things she could imagine getting a few pieces of silver for.

"Ah, Warbird," said an older gray-haired man as they entered a room where a body lay still on the floor. It was a bedroom, but instead of on the bed, the body lay at the foot of it. The sun piercing through the thin cloth drapes, casting its warm rays upon what must've surely been cold, lifeless skin.

His cheeks were already turning purple, and his face seemed sunken in. His clothes were ripped, but the thing that seemed the most peculiar about it was that his clothes were backwards. Or at least that was her first thought until

Aretta looked down and saw his feet were also pointed backwards. She then realized his clothes weren't being worn in reverse, instead his face was facing the opposite direction.

"I guess this one fought back," said the bitch as she stood before the body.

"Aye, it does seem that way," said the gray-haired man, extending a hand. "Lancer Grieves, captain of the city watch. And you must be the Warbird."

"Neekay Pilsworth and associated company," said the bitch, shaking the man's hand, before gesturing to the body. "Anything you can tell me besides the obvious?"

"A few things now. We assumed that all the murders had something in common, but to the best of knowledge, they seem random. One woman, three men. All around the same age, mid-fifthies to early sixties. All nobles, but they don't appear to have any business dealings with each other outside or something cordial."

The bitch knelt besides the body, placing her hand over the twisted skin of its neck before rubbing the side of his face. She then looked down at his fingers.

"The knuckles are red; guess he didn't have time to grab a blade or a rifle. Tell me, did he have a gift for essence?"

"Yes, his son also has it. I'm told he attends the academy. A shame for him to have to come back to something like this."

"Have you gotten reports from any other cities regarding mysterious murders?"

"No, I've reached out to Graphak and Pillan, but outside of your typical muggings, or bar brawls, there wasn't anything of note."

"And I assume, like the others," no one got a good look at the one who did this?"

"Not so much as a glance," said Lancer. "The maid claimed to have heard shouting, but the door was sealed and by the time they went and got the guards to break the door in, this is what they found."

"Have all the murders been this way? Lock rooms, then people vanishing into the night?"

"All except Ingleton. Bastard caught a bullet between the eyes while out in the garden with his daughter."

"First, I'm hearing of this."

"Decided to keep the case under wraps to prevent any hysteria." He shook his head in disapproval. "Granted, that was under the assumption that we'd have caught the killer by now. With this latest murder, I'm afraid that's seeming increasingly unlikely."

"Well," said the bitch, standing back to her feet. "If it helps, I'm fairly sure your assassin is male."

Lancer turned his face to the bitch with a curious look. "How so?"

"She pointed to the man," I'm sure you noticed his jawbone is broken.

"Yes, we assume he was struck by something."

"That would be the case, but I think his jaw was crushed by another man's hand. A very strong man." She smiled as she turned to the captain and reached down, grabbing his hand and bringing it up to her neck. "Now, take my face as if you were to say command the attention of a disobedient child."

A look of hesitance crossed the captain's face, but as a man who follows orders, he quickly did as asked, placing his hands on the bitch's face. Thumb on one side and fingers on the other, both on her cheeks. A look of disbelief came across his face as he looked between the bitch and the corpse.

"Seems similar, right?" asked the bitch as removed the man's hand from her face. "And I doubt our killer performed his head turning trick from the front, so my guess would be he was snuck from behind and in one motion..." The bitch gave herself a light tap on the cheek while turning her head to demonstrate a snapping motion. "And that's all it took."

"If that were the case, then it'd take a man of considerable size. I doubt that such a figure would be able to sneak in and out unnoticed."

"And yet they were," said the bitch as she began rubbing a torn piece of fabric on the dead body. "What about the ripped clothing, the turned over furniture? I imagine that was our killer deciding to toy with us a bit. The clothing is cut, but did you find any lashes on his body where he might have been slashed?"

"Hummm. Stab wounds, but not slash wounds."

The bitch began looking over the room. "So murders whose victims have no known links besides being nobles of this city." She shook her head. "Well, that's hardly revealing. Tell me, this other victim that survived, where are they?"

"You mean her. And we're not too sure she was attacked."

"You're not? I don't understand. Do you believe she's making it up?"

"No, it's just she's been known to see things that aren't there. She's an older woman, who lost her husband and children in a fire a little over decade ago. It's affected her mind. We sent someone to check on her when it was reported to us, but nothing ever came of it."

"I see," said the bitch. "And what is the widowed person's name? No harm in us taking an inquiry into them, I assume."

"Of course not. It's Mrs. Dainslief, who lives near midtown. If you ask about her, you won't have trouble finding directions. She's rarely seen. I imagine the maids are just waiting for her to die before they move on to further employment."

"Right, thank you for sharing your info with us. If we uncover anything, we'll be sure to share it with you," said the bitch with a smile as she turned to leave. "Come on, girls. I suppose we should be on our way then."

The three women left the room and were escorted back to the street.

"I suppose we should start asking around the city for

this old widow."

"Actually Mother, there's something else I wish to look into if you don't mind," said Ebele, looking off to the other side of the city.

"Really?" said the bitch. "Would you mind sharing as to what that is?"

"It's something that was said inside. I wish to go look into it," said Ebele as her mother gave her a look of suspicion. "Don't worry. It won't be long, I'm sure. I'll just catch up with you afterward."

"Humm," moaned her mother as she looked up towards the sky. "I'll allow you to wander off on your own, but only if you agree to return to the manor before darkfall. I and Aretta will meet you back there when we're done."

"Agreed," said Ebele before giving her mother a hug and going off into the city.

"Is it wise to let your daughter wander the city alone like that?" asked Aretta after finding herself feeling a bit sympathetic towards her. "Would it not have been wiser to send me along with her?"

"Wiser, yes," said Ebele's bitch-mother, the suspicious look never leaving her eyes. "But it seems that is not what she wanted." She then smiled. "And I find myself asking why?" She shook her head to clear her mind from the thoughts. "Either way, I guess that means that you're going to accompany me in the questioning of one supposed elderly widow."

***

Feeling a little hesitant, Ebele left her mother and Aretta, setting her sights on the city ahead of her. Reddish high stone rooftops littered her vision. Although nighttime was an hour or so away, she could see the smoke from several homes that had already begun setting their fireplaces. On the way back, she made sure to pass by where the boy with the photograph machine sat. But looking around for him was fruitless. By the time she returned, he had already gone. But seeing him again wasn't her true goal, only more of a distraction.

Since she'd entered the city, every day at five to six-hour intervals, she'd heard the sound of gunfire ring out and now, rather than meet up with some old woman and her high tales. She was more interested in finding out where that gunfire sound was coming from.

She looked up at the sky, placing where the sun was. "Now, If I'm correct, then it should happen." As if on cue, Ebele once again heard gunfire. One round and then another. The first shot caught her attention, and when the second followed, she knew exactly where to go. Over to her left, somewhere at the corner of the city, near its wall.

The sound is bouncing off the walls, but it's still from that direction. While not exactly running, she was moving at a hurried pace. The crowds of the city folk along her path were just now starting to die down as citizens began making their way back to their homes.

Alone this time, Ebele was more aware of her surroundings. She wasn't in fear of the city, but she knew the potential dangers that could arise from any corner. Especially when nighttime approached and the shots came from the lower quarters near the wall. *I should be fine. I mean, I have essence. I'm sure I can fight off a potential mugger or something, or at the very least, run away faster than they can catch me.* She gripped at the side of her dress, lifting it slightly as to measure its weight. *Even in this, I think.*

To her dissatisfaction, it took over half an hour to navigate the city streets and make it to the area where she thought the gunshots were from. Just as in the other slums she visited with her mother, this area seemed equally run down. The only difference was that it was warmer than the rest of the city. The chill of a creeping winter wasn't constantly pecking at the back of her neck here. Where the rest of the city was heading inside, here many of its patrons were still lounging about outside their dwellings and children were playing in the streets. Their ragged clothing would not do for a coming winter in any other place, but here it would hold if the heat stayed all winter long.

But why is it... She scanned the area, and saw steam emanating from three large pipes high over her head. They were leading into a house that was built into the city's wall. Originally coming here for the sound of gunfire, Ebele's attention was now squarely focused on the wooden shanty built into the stone wall. Stepping past the roughhousing children, she came closer and saw a bright light illumination from the house. There was no door and inside she could see shadowy figures moving about.

Suddenly, another round of gunfire sounded from above her head. The sound startled the crows as they took off from the raptors above her head, their cawing signaling their eviction from their perches.

As if heralded from the flurry of loose crow feathers falling to the mud below, a slew of male bodies began to exit the shanty building connected to the wall. Shirtless male figures, their figures drenched in sweat, stepping out of the wooden shack and on the muddied ground. Parts of their themselves were covered in dirt and black dust. They groaned while stretching their aching muscles and walked past her. Some of them gave her curious looks, but most didn't seem to pay her much mind, but out of the crowd, she spotted one boy staring at her.

Shirtless with his suspenders drawn over his shoulders, the sweat from what must have been intense heat dripping from his chin down to his chest. He stood there eyeing her as if she were a rare white elk and he was a huntsman studying his prey.

"Are you lost, miss?" he asked as he stepped towards her.

"Careful, boy," said an older man, walking by and placing a hand on his shoulder. "A girl like this down here.

Could cost ya your head." He then looked at Ebele with a smile. "No offense, m'lady."

"Oh... ah, no, it's fine," said Ebele, a little taken aback by the comments. "Why... I mean, am I not allowed to be here?"

"Don't worry about him," said the boy, patting the older man on the back with a smile. "He thinks you're here looking for someone to pin the blame on for those murders. There's been an increase in guards around here looking for suspects."

"Yeah," said the older man with narrowed eyes, looking over Ebele. "The guards failed with their swords and guns, so they switched to sending an innocent-looking girl instead. And they even dressed her up like a princess."

"What? No, I'm... I'm new to the city. My mother and I were traveling back home and stopped her for supplies when the city was locked down."

"There, ya see, old man," said the boy. "Nothing nefarious about that. She's just locked in here like everyone else."

"A likely story. And aren't you supposed to go see that Helheim fella?"

"And leave you here to accost this fine young lady," said the boy with a smile and a posh voice. "I think not, sir. I most certainly think not."

"Aca—What does accost mean?"

The boy laughed. "I actually don't know. I heard some noble say it while trying to defend a woman and figured it'd work here."

The older man shook his head. "By the Grace of the Graces, was I ever this dumb?"

"Hey. You don't know what it means either."

"Yeah, I wasn't talking about that," said the older man before turning back to Ebele. "Then tell us, then m'lady, what brings a girl like you to a place like this? Nobles don't often dwell in the filth, and hardly any young girls travel alone."

"What? I mean... is it dangerous? I keep hearing gunshots around the city at random times during the day and I decided to see what the cause was."

"Humm!" moaned the old man, still eyeing her with doubt.

"Okay, old man. You've asked your questions. Why don't you let me handle it from here," said the young man with a playful smile as he placed a hand on the old man's back and pushed him away.

"You say that now. But you'll see that I'm right when that cock of yours lands you in the dungeons," said the old man as he reluctantly went off on his way.

"Sorry about that," said the boy. "He means well. He just doesn't trust new people. When I joined the powder crew, he thought I was here to recruit all the essence users for the military." He reached out his hand. "I'm Tannor, by the way."

"Hello, Tannor. I'm Ebele," she said, shaking his hand, and getting a firm grip from him in response. It was only after that did she realize that he left her hand covered in black powder dust. She frowned before pulling out a handkerchief. "Powder crew? What's that?"

"Oh, that's just the term we call ourselves down here." His lips twisted as he saw the confusion on her face. "Oh, that's right. You said you weren't from here." He pointed up to the large pipes above them. "You see those. Well, there are six different places like it around the city, each one providing heat to different areas."

"Oh, so like a fireplace."

"Exactly, just a much larger one," he said as he turned and motioned for her to follow. "It'll be easier for me to show you."

Curiosity getting the better of her, she followed behind him till they stood outside the door. Here, closer to the light source, she could see a large flame ahead of her where men stood shirtless, and each one standing with a shovel in their hand as if waiting for something.

"What are they doing?"

"Just wait, it's almost time for another one."

It was only a moment later when a man from another group took his shovel and walked over to a large black pile of dirt. He then scooped his shovel in, lifting a large amount, before taking a deep breath. After staring at the dirt, his eyes began glowing, and she watched the dirt in the shovel resonate with him.

"Powder?" said Ebele, the surprise clear in her voice. "He's an essence user? Why..."

Before she could finish her words, she watched as the man then shoveled the powder into the furnace as the flames inside went from a light yellow to a bright burning orange.

"This is an interesting way to use powder. It makes sense given the heat, but seems like a waste."

"Yes, but it's mostly the lowest grade powder. You know, the left-over batch from mining. The junk that's not worth sorting from the dirt."

"But don't you get tired? That's a lot of..." Realization came to her quickly. "That's why there's so many of you. You take turns."

"Hey, you catch on quick," said the boy. "Come on, let's step away. The guys might wonder why a noblewoman is peaking in on them."

"Is it really that odd that I'm down here?"

He laughed. "The fact you don't know is probably the most amazing thing I've seen all year. A noblewoman searching out the sounds of gunfire. The idea itself is hilarious."

"I'm not afraid of rifle fire. I'm an essence user too. I could have joined the military if my mother would have let me." The thought of an essence user shoving low grade powder into a furnace made her curious. "Wait. If you can use essence, why haven't you all joined the military? I thought the king wanted all essence users."

"You really don't know?" asked the boy, as they stepped out down the street.

"Know what?"

"I guess, being a noble, you might not. Well, not all essence users are the same."

Ebele nodded her head, clearly understanding that she was more skilled than most essence users and could create a strong powder shot.

"Okay, well, did you know that some of us don't even have enough essence to be accepted by the military?"

"No... I thought... I never met anyone who..."

"And what do you think happens to older essence users who are no longer fit for the military, the ones who might have lost an arm or a leg? Not all the grunts in the military have noble families to rely on for a cushy retirement."

"I... I didn't... I mean, I never gave much thought to it."

"Don't worry," said the Tannor with a smile. "Most nobles treat us like we don't exist. So, it's not surprising that you wouldn't." He stretched his arms as they made their way down the street. "But since you're here. Have you eaten yet?"

"What?"

"Food. You know that thing that you eat when you're hungry? You want some? There's this place ahead. We can go to if you want." He smiled. "And we can get to know more about each other."

"Didn't that gentleman from before mention how you had to meet someone called Helheim?" asked Ebele, taking another look over the boy as he flirted with her. "Do you really have time for this?"

"Who? Him? He's slow anyway. He's always making me wait. I think it's time he waits for a change."

With a tilt of her head and slightly narrowed eyes, she stared at him for a moment. Here stood a shirtless boy covered in sweat with powder lines smeared all over his body. She thought back to Saro, her fiancé, for a moment. *Well, it's not as if this means anything.* His warm smile and green eyes did little to dissuade her from coming to the obvious conclusion. *This is for mother and her hunt. I'm doing this for her... perhaps, who knows... maybe he knows something.* "Is it far from here?"

"No, it's just up their hill there. Some nobles even come through every now and again, so you won't even attract much attention."

She looked up the hill where he pointed and then back to his bare-chested self. "Don't you think you should put on a shirt first? It is starting to get cold after all, and you'll really feel it when we leave this little trench area."

"Nahh, I work in a furnace. My body's always hot."

CHAPTER 8

With sunset appearing over the city, Aretta and Neekay approached the manor at the top of the hill near the northernmost wall of the city. From the gate, they could see that the area wasn't as run down as they'd thought. Instead, the property seemed well managed. It had a manicured lawn and a woman squatting before one of the rose bushes that sat on either side of the path leading up to the main house.

"Hello there," yelled Neekay through an old metal gate, getting the woman's attention.

Spotting them, the maid stood while patting some dirt and leaves from her lap before proceeding to make her way over to them. "Hello, may I help you?"

"Yes. I was directed here by the captain of the city watch. I am to speak with your mistress about the attack that supposedly happened to her some time ago."

"Oh," said the woman before looking around as if afraid.

"I'm... I'm not sure she wishes to have company. You'll have to make an appointment when she's in a better mood."

Neekay looked surprised for only a moment before smiling back at the woman. "No."

"No?"

"Yes. No. I'm going to visit your mistress right now," said Neekay, placing her hand on the latch lock of the gate. "So will you please go and inform her that Neekay Pilsworth, also referred to as the Warbird, has come to sit down and have a cup of tea?"

The maid stared blankly at them for a moment before blinking and shaking her head as if confused. "I'm sorry, but even if you are on orders from the city watch, I can't afford to let...."

Neekay gently pulled the gate back, opening it for herself. "Well, how nice of you to leave the gate open for us." She then stepped inside and stood before the maid. "Now I'm going to have a look at those wonderful roses you were tending to, and you can go and inform your mistress." She leaned forward, looking down into the maid's eyes before reaching forward and placing something in her hand. "Or must I go and find her first, myself?"

"What? How did you..." She looked ahead and then back towards the manor home. "I... I'll go and inform the mistress of your arrival." She looked shaken for a moment, before turning around and heading off and up the steps of the building.

"You can pick locks," said Aretta, a little surprised. It wasn't a question, but more of a realized statement.

"I can if I need to," said Neekay as they stepped forward, walking over to the rosebush. "But, if possible, I try to be as upfront as I can about certain things." She slid her finger across one of the leaves. "What about yourself? Are you going to tell me that you, thief, that you are, have never pried open a lock?"

"I have. But I have tools. I didn't see you use any tools."

"Anything can be a tool if you need it to be. But it's always up to you to decide its purpose," she said before plucking a rose from its limb and turning to place it in Aretta's hair. "There, you see. A tool to highlight the beauty of youth."

Aretta couldn't help but feel a chill come over her spin as the rose was placed atop her head. Because. in front of her was the cold smile that this evil bitch had worn since they had first met.

The door to the manor opened, and the maid popped her head out. "Ah… the lady of the house. She says you're free to come visit and to please not disturb her garden any more than you have."

"Good," said Neekay, patting Aretta on the back, allowing her to take the lead up the steps. "Good. Have you already gotten the tea ready? I prefer two scoops of sugar."

"I'll get right on that Madam," said the maid as they entered the building.

As they stepped inside the building, Aretta couldn't help but stare. The entire lower floor was bare. Just spotlessly shined wooden floors leading into each room. Ahead was a stairwell, and to her right, next to a fireplace, was a woman in a nightgown, sitting in a rocking chair with her back turned to them.

The maid closed the door behind them and stepped forward, leading them into the room, their footsteps providing small echoes in their approach.

"Here they are, madam. As you requested."

"Good, then you're free to go and retrieve that tea."

"Yes, m'lady."

"So…" said the older woman as her maid left the room. "What brings the great Warbird to my doorstep? Here to celebrate my misfortune at the loss of my family? Revel in my disgrace? Or to see if those damnable assassins managed to injure me in a manner that you'd find pleasing?"

"Surprisingly," said Neekay as she walked over and placed a hand on the top of the fireplace, leaning against it and looking down at the woman. "I've just come to make sure you're okay. And besides the gray hair, I suppose you look the same."

They know each other? thought Aretta as she stepped forward to get a look at the woman's face. She didn't seem like a frail older woman. Sure, there were crow's feet planted at the edge of her eyes, but as far as she could see, the woman seemed spry.

"I'd heard you had a daughter after running away with that researcher," said the old woman, after giving Aretta a glance over. "Humph, it seems she must take after her father. Suppose that might be for the best."

"No," said Aretta hurriedly. "I'm not her daughter. I'm…" Her mind began to scramble to think of anything else. "I'm her assistant. She's… she's teaching me things."

"Humph," moaned the old woman. "I see. So, you elected not to bring your daughter then."

"She elected not to bring herself. Said something about wanting to explore the city."

"And in this city of murderers, you let her?" asked the woman, her voice harsher than Aretta would have expected. She then shook her head, as if disappointed. "Between you and your mother, I'd imagine she has the same proclivity for chaos and finding her way into trouble."

Neekay shook her head before turning back to Aretta. "Allow me to introduce you to Analyse Dainslief, the former lead researcher of the King's army."

"Yes…" sighed the woman. "And apparent target of a group of assassins."

"Group? So, it is more than one. You've seen them?"

"Yes, but I only saw the two. If there's more, then I'm not aware. Assassins, to my knowledge, usually work in pairs, so perhaps not. Anymore and they'd draw attention if moving as a group." She looked at Neekay. "I take it you're here to hunt them."

"It is what I was trained to do."

"And you would bring that daughter of yours into such a business?" She gave out a small laugh. "Yet you've called me a monster."

"I assure you; the situation isn't one of my choosing. But I'd rather her stay beside me where she'd be safe."

"Says a mother who allowed her to go gallivanting in the city as dusk approaches."

Neekay waved a hand dismissively. "We're just going in circles. Just tell us what you can about the assassins, and we'll be on our way."

"A man, and a woman. Of course, I didn't see their faces. The man, fairly large, or at least his hands felt that way when they were around my neck. The woman, petite, somewhat young, I'd guess. Perhaps a little shorter than your assistant. Her hair was brown. I could see it poking out from under her cowl."

"How did you survive, anyway?" asked Neekay. "Considering everyone else is dead, I suppose I should congratulate you. Did you have a hidden trap? Considering your past, that wouldn't be a surprise."

"No, I'm ashamed to say I wasn't as well prepared as I should have been. I had lit a candle by my bed to read, and after fiddling around a bit, I had decided to rest for the night. Well, when he approached me, I would guess he'd thought I was to be as frail as I appear. So instead of a blade against my neck, the fool tried to strangle me with his bare hands. Even lifted me into the air. Sadly, for him, a bout of hot candle wax to an orbital socket does wonders for making one choose self-preservation. And as such, I was unceremoniously dropped to the floor."

Neekay leaned forward and placed a finger at the cloth below the woman's chin, sliding it over to reveal the skin beneath. There, she exposed the reddish bruise from her apparent strangulation. "Yes. I suppose that wasn't pleasant. And what happened afterwards? I can't imagine they'd stop just because of that."

"No, but after hearing of the other murders and how they could be related to myself, I had two armed guards standing outside of my door. I imagine the thud from me being dropped to the floor and my deep gasping for air alerted them. And the rifle-toting guards didn't seem to please them, so they broke my window and escaped."

"Did they leave anything behind?"

"No. Nothing."

"Wait, you said there was a connection between those that were killed and yourself. I know that you and Harsetti were on the research board. But the other two. I don't remember them in the war."

"No. You wouldn't. They were part of the earlier development process. The king, during our great victory, granted us our noblehood and some land here in this city together. I assumed he'd done us a kindness by allowing us to grow old while staring into each other's faces, justifying the things that were done."

"What research?" asked Aretta, disturbing the conversation they were having as if she weren't there. "Do you mean with the powder? Things like that?"

Analyse looked at the girl oddly for a moment and then to Neekay. Her lip twitched as if she were thinking. "Yes... powder, among other things. There are a great many services that go into war, dear. New weapons projects. Transportation projects. Chemical poisoning projects. Anything that the king found might be useful, we researched, and often completed for him." She shook her head. "But with you being so young, you wouldn't have felt the effects of war."

"No," said Aretta. "I was only just born when the war was near its end. But I know what happened after the war. The sadness that takes over the villages when all the men are gone, and the women are forced to work the fields."

"Yes," said Analyse. "Then perhaps you do understand war. Then tell me, girl. From which war-torn village do you hail?"

"Fara'dwell. You wouldn't know it. It's betw—"

"It's on the Qalack path... over the Trolan mountainside. Mostly cold weather there," she looked the girl over again. "And what would you be doing so far south? I assumed those in the north still hated us."

"Her brother became ill during my travels near the border mountains," replied Neekay. "He's currently under my care and she is working as my assistant to pay off the debt."

"You? Taking it upon yourself to use people again," said Analyse. "Yes, you always had a knack for turning others into war assets." She reached over and patted Aretta on the shoulder. "Don't worry, dear. She'll use you and release you like she's done to untold dozens before."

"Excuse me," said the maid, re-entering the room. "Sorry for the wait, but I've returned with the tea you've asked for."

"Good," said Analyse. "Our guests were just about to leave, and it'd be a shame for them to not have some tea before they venture back off into the cold."

They reached over and took a cup of from the saucer. Aretta could feel the warmth as she slid her fingers across its porcelain shell. It was a warmth that seemed to fill her body as she took her first sip. In fact, it was certainly the most delicious sip of tea she ever had. The realization making her stare down at it as if she were holding a miracle in her hand.

"This... this is amazing."

"Of course it is. It was my daughter's favorite blend," said Analyse with a smile. "My research does sometime spill over into the more domestic affairs." She nodded towards the window. "It will do you well on your walk home, especially on a night like this."

Following her gaze, Aretta turned to see the moon clear in the night sky, a foggy film on the window as its light shone in.

"Well then," said Neekay, after finishing her tea. "Shall we be going?"

"Ahh… yes," said Aretta, placing the cup back on its tray and turning to leave.

"And don't worry," said Neekay. "I'll be sure to send my daughter this way before we leave the city."

"No need," said Analyse, choosing to stare out the window rather than watch them go. "I doubt you share such affection for me. And I'd prefer not to be pitied."

"True, but my daughter doesn't know you," said Neekay, as she walked into the main hall. "If you wish to sour another relationship, then simply turn her away. I wouldn't be surprised if you did." She then threw a hand of farewell as she stepped towards the door. "So, accept her in the coming days, will you? And treat her to tea if you decide to see her."

Afterwards, she and Aretta exited the building, leaving the grounds, back into the street. Making their way down the hill, Aretta could feel the cold nipping at her skin as she began rubbing at her shoulders. The wind whirled over the rooftops and between the alleys, making the night feel eerily uncomfortable.

"Are we headed back now?"

"Yes," said Neekay. "We have enough information to go off of now. Knowing that all those murdered were a part of the kingdom's research group just means that the assassins are either disgruntled former victims of their crimes or were hired by those that were. A lot of people vanished during the war, and that doesn't exactly mean that all of them died."

"I still don't understand why you're doing all this," said Aretta, shaking her head. "And aren't you afraid? You were in the military, too. Why didn't you bring your rifle?"

"Really?" asked Neekay as she continued down the street. "Do you think I'd need it? We really aren't too far from Harsetti's manor. Just another few—" Her words paused in her throat as they spotted a man standing ahead, appearing out of the fog, in the center of the street. Fully clothed, his face covered, and in his hand, a rifle, barrel tilted over the ground.

"Yes," said the man ahead, his voice thick and deep, seemingly piercing through the wind. "A fitting question on a night where two women would walk the dangerous streets alone."

"Well then," said Neekay. "Since we are such damsels. Would it be your job as a chivalrous man to escort us home?"

The words sounded ridiculous in Aretta's ears. Clearly, this man had no interest in their 'best' interest. Slowly, she brought her hand down to her side, only to remember that The Warbitch had placed her in this ridiculous dress, and she didn't have her blade at her side like she usually would. *Shit! What do we do?* Her eyes scanned the area to realize they were between buildings now. *Should we turn and run? Maybe duck into an alley?* She gnashed her teeth at the idea. *But then he'd just shoot one of us in the back.* Then the chill of a growing fear tingled on her neck. From the shadows, footsteps, slow and steady came from behind her out of an alley. Then appeared another man, also draped in a cowl and mask that covered his face.

"So... more than two then," said Neekay. "How many?"

"Enough."

"Apparently not, if an old woman managed to save herself from the likes of you. But maybe it just proves how capable she still is. Tell me. The people you've killed you far, is there a reason or is this just for sport?"

"They died because they were guilty. And so are you... Warbird."

"Oh, of a great many things, I am sure. But tell me which ones specifically?" She raised her palm with a smile before rolling her fingers at the man. "It's so very hard to keep track as the bodies continue to pile up."

The man picked up his rifle, drawing it down on her.

Aretta jolted with fear as she stared down at its muzzle. Instinctively, she reached out, her hands clutching the fabric of Neekay's blouse.

"Really?" said Neekay. "Are you going to risk it? Here?"

The gun hovered in the man's hand as he steadied his aim. To Aretta, it felt as if she couldn't breathe, her breath catching in her throat. Her chest feeling tight as if the weight of the world pressed against her.

There was a long wait, as the two stared at each other. But after what felt like forever, the man lowered his weapon.

"That's better," said Neekay, as the man knelt, placing his rifle flat against the ground.

But Aretta could see as he did, from his boot, he removed something that shined in the moonlight. He stood back to his feet, showing a dagger, before twirling it in his hand and pointing it at the Warbird.

"A challenge," said the man. Not given as a question but spoken as a declaration.

"An acceptance," said Neekay, spoken as a declaration as well, before nodding to Aretta. "And the girl beside me?"

"Safe. As long as she does not interfere."

"Then a challenge is welcomed," said Neekay, before looking over at Aretta while patting her on the hand that clenched her blouse. "It's okay, dear. They will not hurt you."

"What!" said Aretta, still somewhat shaking. "You can't... you don't."

"I do," said Neekay, as she gently pressed against the back of Aretta's hand, causing her to release her grip.

She then pulled a loose ribbon from the cuff of her blouse, using it to tie her hair into a ponytail. "If their word is given, it will be kept. They have no reason to harbor any ill will against you."

In the cold, Aretta could feel the tears welling up at the side of her eyes. Sure, she didn't like the woman, but she didn't wish to see her die or have to report it back to her daughter, who she admittedly may have some fondness for.

Neekay stepped forward while lifting the front of her blouse and vest, revealing the top of a sheath housing a blade. Grabbing the hilt, she pulled it out before taking a stance Aretta had to assume was meant for knife dueling. Squatted, just slightly, so the knees were bent, one arm turned in towards her face, palm relaxed, while the other held the dagger pointing forward towards her aggressor as he slowly approached with his own weapon.

She looked around for any help, a useless gesture as the street was empty, all except for the two who would engage and the other assassin that stood behind her. She couldn't hear him. But his presence, it was as if she could feel his eyes on the back of her neck.

Then came a clash and her attention immediately fixated back on the two ahead of her. They were only a foot apart, their blades bouncing rhythmically in their hands. Their bodies beginning to radiate heat in the frosty night. The man stepped in, and from under, brought his blade up, aiming it at Neekay's face. With a grunt, she parried it with her own; the block forcing her off one foot, causing her to lean back as she tried to maintain balance. But the man, relentless in his efforts, rotated his arm and proceeded to drive the blade back down.

But this time, she didn't parry the blade. Instead, while off balance, she planted her foot into the man's chest, letting his body and movement bring her down to the stone ground. The moment her back hit the road, she adjusted her weight, pushing off and sliding herself out of the way as the blade pieced the ground between the stones of the cobbled road.

Taking advantage of the mistake, she lunged her blade at his neck. Reflexively, he blocked the blade with the wrist of his off hand. But Neekay was fast and brought the blade back around. Gripping the hilt of the blade he had previously stuck into the ground, he turned on his side, pulling it free, and then quickly rolled away.

Neekay, rising to her hands and knees, made a few quick strikes. But his movements were fast and with a push-up off the ground, he carried the momentum back up to his feet. Then, with a few reversed steps, his back was pressed against the wall of a house, his blade drawn defensively.

Neekay knelt, staring ahead at the man, her eyes focused on him through the small slit between his mask and cowl. Then, with a sigh, she placed a hand on her knee, lifting to her feet.

"I suppose I'm out of practice," said Neekay, tilting her head as she pointed her blade at the man. Her eyes glanced down toward the man's hand that was now dripping blood across his finger. "But apparently not as unready as you would have preferred."

A small laugh emerged from under the mask. "No," said the man, twiddling his fingers as if to test and see if any tendons had been cut. "But this is good. This will make for more sport. An easy kill is not a kill that is earned."

"And killing old research nobles is... earned kills?"

"Orders. I would prefer more hunts like you."

"And am I... an order?"

"No, you are a trophy."

"Well, then... aren't I flattered," said Neekay, before taking the time to slide her tongue over her lips. "Get your back off that wall and come over here and dance with this lady-in-waiting."

Pride perhaps hurt by the remark, the man took himself from the side of the house and stepped forward. To Aretta, it seemed as if the steam off his body began to grow heavier, rising above his head, distorting the surrounding area.

Aretta thought her eyes were deceiving her. Neekay was still there waiting in front of him. Her knife extended in her hand. Everyone seemed to be holding their breath, waiting to see who would strike first.

To her surprise, it was Neekay who lunged in first; the man parrying her blade. She went straight; the dagger aimed at his chest, but her quickness was met with his own. The sound of metal clashing was sharp as the blades clashed.

With a quick twist, he turned, guiding the blade down. And Neekay, taking advantage, aimed it at his knee. But this time, he drew his leg back, shifting his stance and letting her pass him.

Trying to recover from her missed attack, she twisted, bringing the blade back up, but he was faster and brought down his forearm on her side. The blow hit with such force that Neekay lurched back as her mouth went agape. A small shriek escaped from her lips as she crashed down on the road.

Not wasting a moment's time, the man pounced on his advantage, driving the blade down towards her. But as if in unison, she rolled over, bringing her own blade back up towards the man's face.

Seeing it, the man shifted his weight; the blade sliding around the side of his mask, cutting the string holding it in place. The Warbird, not relenting, dug her fingers into the dirt, leaping back up, and slashing at the man as his mask fell to the ground.

His quickness provided him with another advantage. For her near miss, she was rewarded with a kick to the stomach that was so strong it lifted her off her feet and sent her drifting backwards. She managed to catch herself, landing on the ground, sliding in the mud until she came to a stop, her free hand clutching at her stomach.

The scene was a shock for Aretta. Here stood the proud woman who had forced her into servitude now standing hunched over, hand clutching her ribs with half of her face covered in mud. And from where she could see, there was a loose piece of fabric on her back, now drifting freely in the night air.

The man had indeed cut her while she was on the ground, slicing a large area of her back. She couldn't see it fully, but it must have been bleeding well. The dangling piece of the blouse that escaped from the vest was stained crimson.

The Warbird's breath was heavy from her lips as she tried composing herself while looking up at the man. "So… that's what you look like… under that mask." The man's face seemed odd, his skin was pale, and it appeared as if there were red marks that covered his neck and cheek. She stood back up, seeming a little wobbly on her feet. "Not much to look at. But I'm sure there's a lady out there who'll have you." She nodded towards Aretta. "Not that one, though. I still have use of her."

The man rubbed at the side of his face, noting the blood on his hand. "Yes. The rumors said you were good. But the rumors never said you talk so much."

"Yes," said the Warbird, shaking off the fatigue and resuming her attacking stance. "Funny thing about rumors. They're usually made by the living, which no one who I ever hunted, is. Can you say the same? Clearly not, as I'm still here."

A scowl drew across the assassin's lips as he lowered his stance.

There has to be something I can do. Right? Thought Aretta as she watched the two square off again. *Of course not. I can't fight like that. How are they even moving so fast? I didn't even bring my blade with me. I'm in this stupid outfit.* Her eyes shifted to the corner of her eye as she tried to make out where the man was behind her. The moon was ahead of them, so she couldn't see his shadow and was forced to try listening to any footsteps. But no matter how hard she tried; she couldn't hear him. But he was there; she was sure of it. She could feel that he was there.

That was until she felt a hand across the back of her neck that sent a shiver up her spine, freezing her stiff as her eyes went wide with fear.

"Whatever you're thinking," came the man's voice. His masked face creeping up beside hers as his fingers twiddled over the skin. "I suggest you stop, or you won't live to see another sunrise. The hunt is ours tonight."

The fear almost petrifying her. She couldn't help but stare ahead. A slash left, a slash right, it was as if their blades cut the wind so clean that it was changing the air around them. Their feet maneuvered over the muddy stone road. The heat of the fight being exposed through the breaths leaving their bodies.

She wasn't able to tell who was winning the battle between the two. Each blade seemed to be so close to the other that all it would take was just an inch of a mistake and everything would be over.

Where do people even learn to fight like this? The only blade fights she'd ever seen were between drunk patrons at the taverns that she had managed to be hired on at. Drunk flailing idiots with ale was a far cry away from the display ahead of her. Parrying, weaving between each other's strikes, it was all like a dance. A dance that had to end soon.

And just as she knew it would, the end of the fight came just a sudden as it started. The Warbird thrust at the man's neck and once again he dogged, but this time grabbed her by the arm and while doing so, swung his leg out kicking her in the side of the ribs. She gritted her teeth as blood seeped over her lips.

But the hand she had lunged at him with held a broken piece of wood from the cart that she was knocked into earlier. And with that distraction, her true blade had firmly lodged into the man's leg. He winced, and she brought the blade up the man's thigh as he shifted his weight, preventing it from going up into his abdomen as it cleared his flesh.

Releasing her hand, he hopped back on one leg, falling onto a box of crates with a loud crash.

"It seems... your hunt... ends here," said the Warbird, trying to catch her breath as she stood over his body with him looking up at her.

A bit of relief came over Aretta as she watched the end

of the display. The two of them were speaking to each other, but she couldn't hear their words. Only small whispers in the cold. But even so, she couldn't help but focus on the hand at the back of her neck. It seemed to grow hotter as the man who held her captive watched. From beneath his cowl, she could hear his breathing. Slow and purposeful, his own body tensing as he placed his shoulder on her hers, leaning in as if trying to listen to their words.

But that thought was naive. He wasn't listening. He was preparing. In a split second, the grip on the back of her neck vanished, and all she saw was a blur dashing forward. Within a second, he was on Neekay, his blade lunging at her neck. But Neekay was quick, turning around and parrying the blade. But while the first was blocked, she didn't expect the second. She winced with gritted teeth as the man's other hand drove a hidden blade into her abdomen.

She reached down, grabbing his hand, struggling to free herself only for the final blow to come from behind as the man she just been standing over pulled himself from the wreckage and lunged back up, driving his own blade into her back. But this time, immobilized by the other assassin, she had no choice but to accept the blow as it pierced her back.

Neekay's head jerked back as blood coughed out of her mouth. Her last gesture was her eyes glancing over at Aretta. The assassin from behind removed his blade, and he lifted himself back up as Neckay's limp body fell in his place, crashing into the broken pieces of wood.

"You took too long," said the assassin with the scar on his face as he wiped his bloody dagger on his cloak.

"It was the Warbird. I had to wait till she let her guard down," said the other assassin, wiping off his blade in a similar manner. "How was it? Fighting a legend of the old war?"

"Fast, she was faster than me. Even with essence. I think she was getting faster."

"She's got a kid here, too. We should take care of..."

"No!" Yelped Aretta without thinking. This was an action that she instantly regretted as both men stopped in their conversation, turning back to her as if they'd forgotten she even existed. "You... I mean, she's not... you don't have to."

"Ahh, but we do," said the assassin with his cowl removed. "And you, you've seen my face." He rotated the blade in his hand as he and his companion stepped back towards her. The look in his eyes told Aretta she wouldn't live much longer. She wanted to run, but her legs wouldn't move. Her body jerked as her fingers began to shake. Petrified by fear, she tried forcing herself to move. A step, an inch, anything to survive. Her only thoughts were of the broken body of Neekay ahead, her arms and legs hanging out of the crate.

Move... please move, she thought as her body slowly began to listen to her.

"Hey, what's going on down there?" came a voice from down the alley. The body hidden by steam arising from a nearby pipe.

"Hel... help," muttered Aretta, her voice barely a whisper, and she pleaded with herself for a sound, any sound, to emerge from her lips. Anything that would alert someone to her distress. "Hel..." But the effort was moot, because out of the corner of her eye, she saw the assassin that was previously locked in battle with Neekay, now leaping off one leg back to her, his knife drawn at his side, ready to slice her. Giving away her final sight, she closed her eyes and tried to yell. But once again, nothing came out. *Dead in the street. Serves me right*, she thought as she accepted her end.

But after one second, then another, she realized that the killing blow did not come. Instead, she heard a thud, and something was now against her feet. Slowly, and with a grimace on her face, she opened her eyes and looked down. There, to her surprise, she saw the assassin that had charged at her, flat with his face in the dirt, shoulders over her feet. And to her astonishment, a blade protruding from the base of his skull.

Quickly, she looked up to see the other assassin looking down, the hilt of his blade now shared by Neekay. But now she appeared different. The same red lines that were on the neck and jaw of the uncowled assassin on the ground before her were now on her. Except her lines were more prominent. Instead of just the neck and jawline, hers covered her face, even coming through the top of her hairline and down by her eyes.

To her surprise, the assassin released his blade to her as he leaped back, distancing himself from Neekay as she flipped the blade around in her hand while standing up to meet the man.

"You're from the tests too?" said the man, the surprise clear in his voice. He titled his head as if trying to understand. "But why... which group were you?"

Neekay didn't say anything, just lowered her stance, as if preparing to attack.

"Who's there?" asked a man appearing from the alley in a city guard uniform alongside two other men holding rifles.

The other assassin looked over at the guards, and then to his companion, who was now dead at the feet of Aretta, the lines on his face receding back into his skin. He then took a few steps back until he was off into an alley and out of sight, never taking his eyes off Neekay before finally disappearing into the shadows.

"Ma'am," said the guard. "Ma'am." he repeated louder as he grabbed Aretta by the shoulder. "Are you okay?"

"Huh," said Aretta, still a little in shock. "Yes." Then, being forced to take her eyes off Neekay and focus on the guard, she realized it was the boy guard from earlier. The one who had led them into the house to meet the commander of the city watch.

"Well, this one's dead," said one of the other guards,

kneeling at her feet and inspecting the assassin's body. "But I guess with the blade sticking out the back of his skull, that's fairly obvious."

Then came the sound of another thud as Neekay crashed back down into the mud on her ass.

"What?" asked the male guard, turning and spotting Neekay up ahead. "Madam, madam Warbird, are you okay?" he asked as he stepped towards her.

"Yes," said Neekay. "We were attacked by two assassins that we think are responsible for the murders in your city." She raised an arm, pointing to the assassin on the ground. "Can you help me up? And walk me over to that one. It seems I've gone a bit weak in the legs."

"Ahh, yes. Of course," said the boy before spotting her injury still bleeding. "Shouldn't we get you to a doctor?"

"Perhaps later, Ugh," she moaned as she was helped back to her feet, and with assistance, stumbled over to where Aretta was. It was there. She knelt, placing her hands on the blade and drove it deeper into the man before twisting it inside of him before pulling it back out. "There, that should be enough." She then looked back up at Aretta. "Are you okay?"

At this point, Aretta wasn't even sure anymore. But she managed a nod of the head.

"Good," she turned to the young male guard. Can you take the body to the magistrate?

"What? Ahh, yes, of course. But what about you? I really think we should escort you to a doctor."

"Oh, don't worry about me. Have your commander come visit me in the morning after you report this. We will have a lot to talk about, I'm sure." She looked the young boy over. "But until then. Would you mind if I borrowed your cloak? And if it's not too much, would you have one of your men escort us home? I'm afraid I don't think I could fend off another attack tonight."

"Yes," said the young man before removing a cloak and

handing it to her. He then nodded to his men. "Escort these two to their home and return to me with a wagon so we can transport the body back to the barracks."

Aretta watched as the once proud woman leaned heavily on the support of the men around her as they escorted them down the street and back towards the gate. She could see the strain it was having on her as sweat dripped down her face. Her breathing stayed laborious, as if staying conscious was a struggle.

A little later, they arrived at the gate to Mr. Harsetti's manor, where Neekay loosed herself from the support of the guards and rested with her shoulder against the stone pillar that housed the gate to the in-ground.

"That... will be all gentlemen," she said as she rested, trying to compose herself. The men looked at each other as if they weren't sure they should leave them, or more accurately, Neekay in her condition. To which Neekay just smiled. "It's nice to see chivalry isn't lost amongst the soldiers of this city. But don't worry about me. You have done your job and escorted us back, and... I am mere steps away from a warm bath and a bed." She nodded back towards the city. "Go and find a wagon and return to your superior."

Still a little hesitant, but obliging, both soldiers nodded to Neekay and then turned, headed back towards the inner city.

"Ugh," she moaned as she shifted her weight so that her back was pressed against the stone before turning her head toward Aretta. "And you, my thieving friend, you are not to mention a word of this to my daughter."

"What?" said Aretta, confused. "Why?"

"Because that... is the deal you made, remember? You do what I tell you, and I keep your brother from being executed."

"But... I mean, look at you. You can barely stand. If you walk in there like this, she's going to ask questions."

"You... let me worry about that," said Neekay as she

shifted her back against the wall again. Except this time, Aretta could see the red veins appear again over the neck and face of Neekay. Her mouth opened and jaw locked in place as her face illustrated something akin to a silent pain. And after a moment, she pulled herself from the wall, standing up and breathing normally as if she wasn't just in a fight for her life just a little while earlier.

"What is that?" asked Aretta, her eyes narrowed in confusion. "That… that other assassin. He did it too."

"Yes, that was a surprise," said Neekay, as she opened the gate and started walking toward the manor. "Let's just call it a trick of the trade for assassins."

Aretta shook her head. She was too tired to pursue the questions and instead went back to a previous problem. "How do you expect me not to say anything when your face looks like that?"

Neekay smiled. "You let me worry about that." When they reached the door, she placed her hands on the knob, and then began stretching her neck and if she was stiff from a long night's sleep. So much so that there was an audible crack. Then, as if like magic, the red veins on her neck vanished back into her skin as if they'd never been there just a second ago.

She opened the door and walked inside, and as if being summoned by their presence, out stepped Mr. Harsetti's twin children, who ran in to see who was at the door, followed by Ebele holding a replica wooden gun in her hand.

"I thought I told you not to go…" said Ebele, before spotting her mother. "Oh, Mother, welcome back."

"Thank you," said Neekay, glancing down at the wooden rifle in her hand. "I see you're having fun."

"Oh, yes. Well, they were curious as to the parts of a rifle, and I was explaining it to them…" Ebele tilted her head and was silent for a moment, as if studying her mother. "Is everything okay? Why are you wearing a police robe, and your hair is pulled back."

"Yes, we had an eventful night. The assassins appeared again tonight and came after me."

"What!"

"Oh, don't be alarmed. We were safe, since the town guards were around us." She fluttered the left side of the cloak. "And it was cold, so I borrowed one of their cloaks. A good thing you came home when you did, perhaps they may have come after you. Tell me, did you find whatever it was you were looking for when you ran off?"

"What? No... I mean yes. But don't skim over how an assassin came after you. Are you okay?"

"Of course. Safe as can be. Although I think the cold weather has me coming down with a bit of a fever. And as such, I'll procure my own room for tonight. You can sleep with Aretta."

"But... I mean, the assassin, what did they look like? Was there more than one? Did they have rifles?"

Neekay laughed. "All questions I'm sure Aretta will be happy to answer later tonight. For now, I am going to take a bath, since Kayin isn't here. I'll have Aretta do the honors of helping me. You can pester her after she's helped me out of my clothes." Her mother then walked over to the steps. "You can continue on with your teaching lessons to the children."

The two then continued up the stairs, with Aretta stopping mid-way up to glance back down at a bewildered-looking Ebele. *And you expect me to not say anything? Look at her, she's clearly worried.* She forced herself to give a smile; knowing it didn't convince anyone, but still, she followed behind the Warbird. On the way, they stopped by her and Ebele's shared room, grabbing a large satchel, then walked out towards and into an empty room.

Once inside, she locked the door behind them before handing the satchel to Aretta and walked over to a chair underneath a table. Shen then began dragging it to the center of the room.

"Why didn't you tell her everything that happened? Surely you know there's a chance of her becoming curious and questioning the guards?"

"Perhaps, but that's a bridge to cross when I arrive at it," said the Warbird, while removing the cloak and letting it drop to the floor and exposing the large gash across her back. It was still bleeding well. She then sat down, straddling the chair and facing the bed. "No, child should have to see their parents in such a state if one can help it. She idolizes me. I wish for her to continue doing so for a little bit longer. Call it a mother's pride."

"But still... you could—"

"Inside the satchel, you will find ointments to stop the bleeding and bandages to wrap around me. I'll be leaving the rest to you. Remember our agreement."

Aretta frowned before flipping open the hood of the satchel, reaching in, and grabbing a vial of ointment. She didn't see any others, so assumed it had to be the right one. "I swear, I regret that I even got involved with you people," she said as she stepped over to her. The Warbird didn't say anything, which only added to her frustration. "Fine, take off your top so we can get this over with."

Still, the Warbird didn't answer.

"What do you expect me to..." Aretta's words froze in her mouth as she stepped in front of the woman, only to find that she had passed out, slumped over the back of her seat.

CHAPTER 9

The next morning, the sun rose in a room where Aretta sat in a chair overlooking the bed where Neekay lay breathing heavily. The night was rough on Aretta. Spending it undressing and bandaging an unconscious woman wasn't something she could ever have planned for. She never left the room for fear of the questions Ebele would ask and instead slept next to her benefactor. But beyond any questions Ebele might have, she had questions of her own.

How did she survive getting stabbed like that? I mean, I understand her having skill with a blade. She's their war hero. She thought about these things through the night, but there was one other question that plagued her mind. *What were those red lines across her face? That other assassin had them too. Is that something essence users can do? I've never heard about it before.* She thought back to the contest at the manor of the past day's tournament. *I don't remember any other gunners doing that.*

Taking her away from her thoughts came a moan from the bed as Neekay shifted her head. Her face twisted in displeasure as she tried opening her eyes to the sunlight that had filled the room.

"Emmm, close the shades. I'm not in the mood for much sunlight."

"I was worried you wouldn't wake up," said Aretta as she stood from seat and went about closing the curtains of the room.

"How long was I out?"

"Just the night. Were you expecting it to be longer?"

"Yes, but I suppose I will be resting for some time now," she said as she sat up in bed, noticing that she had been bandaged and was wearing a gown. "Did you do this?"

"It's not like I had much of a choice. I had them bring some water so I could bathe you as well. The satchel you gave me had some ointment, so I think that should stop any infection."

"You knew it was ointment? Did I tell you that?"

"No, but I have two brothers. I've spent my life patching them up after one scuffle or another. So, I know what higgenflock smells like."

"Yes. Well, I suppose it did serve me well to take you under my employ. Then what of my daughter? Has she come by?"

"Yes, but I told her you were still asleep and that I'd given you some medicine for a night fever. She peaked her head in to make sure you were alright but left afterwards. Said something about meeting someone in the city."

"Humph," laughed Neekay. "Of course she did. Always in search of whatever interests her."

"Are you not worried about the assassins going after her? I mean, you did kill one of theirs. Wouldn't that—"

"She knows to be back before dark. So far, all the attacks have happened at night. I doubt a loss of a member will cause them to deviate from that. At least not yet. Plus, I'm the one that's famous. There's no guarantee that they even know what she looks like."

"Can I ask you a question?"

"Humm?"

"How are you… I mean… are you immortal? Is that what powder does?"

"What?"

"I saw you… they stabbed you… twice. And then you did that neck thing with the red lines on your face. What was that?"

"Oh, I suppose you would have questions about that," said Neekay with a sigh as she smoothed out the blanket at her legs. "Well, dear, I can assure you I am not immortal. Special perhaps, but I can certainly be killed."

"Then… can Ebele… can she do that?"

"No, thank goodness. She may have gotten my looks, but that seems to be about it. And you, my dear ward, will not mention to her anything you saw that night about my fight with that assassin."

"Why? I'm sure she'd—" Suddenly a knock came at the door interrupting their conversation "Coming," said Aretta, walking over and unlocking it, sliding it open a crack to see Jacob, the guard from the previous night standing outside.

"Hello, there. I've brought the chief. Are we allowed to come in?"

"Let them in," said Neekay. "I suppose we might as well get this over with."

Aretta fully opened the door and in walked the head of the town's guardsmen. He looked as solemn and regal as he did days before as he stepped inside and stood before the bed, looking down at Neekay.

"I was told you had an eventful night, even managed to add a new body to our morgue."

"Yes, well, unfortunately, doing your job has left me in such a state as you can see."

"May I," he said, gesturing to the chair beside the bed where Aretta previously sat.

"Be my guest."

He took the seat. "Yes, well, perhaps any information you can give us will help us alleviate you of the troublesome burden we've managed to force upon you."

Neekay smiled. "Well spoken." She then turned her attention towards her ward. "Aretta, go out and find my daughter and try to keep her from getting into too much trouble. The head town guardsman here and I have a few things to discuss."

"And Jacob," said the head town's guardsman. "Go downstairs and fetch us some tea."

Aretta looked confused for a moment. *Something private between the two of them? Fine, let them have their secrets. I just need them to find my brother and I can escape.* She then nodded to Neekay before heading out of the door with Jacob.

"Is everything alright?" asked Jacob as they headed down the hall.

"What do you mean?"

"I mean with the Warbird. The cut on her back, it looked quite bad. I was surprised to see her awake."

"So was I," said Aretta, turning to face him. "Jacob, right? Ahh, do you have the gift of essence?"

"Me? Yes," he said as he turned the corner and began heading down the steps. "Everyone in the town's guard has a gift for essence. We're all riflemen here."

"Does essence allow you to heal faster than those that don't have it?"

"No. I mean, I've never heard of it before. I've heard that in some cases it can enhance a person's strength, but that's only for the elite guards and they surround the king or some high-ranking nobles. Not even the magistrate has someone like that. Do you think the Warbird has it?"

"It would make sense," said Aretta with a smile as they made their way towards the door. "Well, I'll be on my way then. I have to go and find her daughter."

"Yes, and I guess I'll go and fetch that tea."

***

Outside in the city, surrounded by the townsfolk, Ebele sat near a city fountain, raking her hands down into the cold water. The ripples parted as she watched her reflection distort. *Telling me it was just a night fever. To think I wouldn't know she was in pain by just how she was breathing. And the look in Aretta's eyes. I understand she doesn't want me to worry. And I'm not. She is okay, and that's all that matters, but I'm not blind. I saw those sprinkles of blood on the floor leading to our room.*

"Hey, down there," came the voice of Tannor from above as he leaned over a railing, smiling down at her. As she waved at him and stood from her seat, she could see that he acquired a rifle from somewhere as the strap was over his shoulder. Unlike before, this time he had elected to wear a shirt. Although, the clothing was rather battered-looking which signaled his lesser class very obviously. But Ebele didn't mind so much. He was fun and entertained her. He then gestured to a brown-haired boy beside him. "Hope you don't mind. I brought a friend along."

"No, it's fine," said Ebele as she stepped forward, making her way through the crowd to meet them. *Put it out of your mind, Ebele. You promised to be out with him today. This will be a good chance to learn more about the city.* She met them at the turn and saw that the friend Tannor had brought with him was using a cane to support himself.

"Ebele," said Tannor, "this is my friend Helheim."

"Hello," she said, before staring at his cane for a moment, then narrowing her eyes at Tannor. "This is the friend you said was always late?"

"Yes, but I never said that he didn't have a good reason for it."

"You are just terrible," said Helheim, slapping his friend on the shoulder. "You try walking around with a cane everywhere and tell me how fast you are."

Tannor laughed and stepped forward, leading them along. "Come, my friends. I'm excited to get a move on... well, slowly, of course."

Ebele shook her head before taking a closer look at Helheim. He didn't wear the rags that were common in the lower areas of the city. Instead, his clothing was more midtown or city dweller. She couldn't guess whether he was a noble or not. But not wanting to pry so early, she turned her attention back towards Tannor. "And where did you get that rifle? Did you borrow it from your friend here?"

Helheim sighed. "Unfortunately, no. Tannor here has this nasty habit of finding his way into trouble and asking me to be a lookout for him."

"Lookout? Wait... you mean you stole it?"

"Nah, of course not. I nicked it off the guard's pile during their morning outings. Fucker went to take a piss and left it alone."

"You what! You stole a guard's rifle? Won't they come looking for it?"

"Nahh, bastard would be too embarrassed. Upper man would have to hide if he'd reported it. I'll slip in back in the barracks tonight or tomorrow and he'll be so thankful he won't even question it," he said while handing her the rifle. "Now, would the sweet noble woman be so gracious as to show this lowly peasant boy how it's done?" He said while leaning forward, and bowing his head as he extended the rifle out with both hands.

Ebele frowned. "You're mocking me."

"A little bit. I mean, you are a noble lady, ain't ya." He then lifted his head and gave her a suggestive look as he bit the side of his lip. "As for the sweet part. Well, I have to admit, I haven't tasted you yet."

"Oh, just shut up," said Ebele, enjoying the playful

banter. "Helheim, how did you ever become friends with a person like this?"

"I assume the same way you did. He's actually kind of persistent... and of course, there's a certain charm to his foolishness."

In response, Tannor spun the rifle around from his arm to his neck and off to the other arm, catching it as if it were a stick. "I prefer to think of myself as a man with the playful essence of a child. Unlike you two serious people. I don't think either of you understands what fun is."

"Well, either way. I appreciate you both taking the time to show me around the city," said Ebele. "I just followed the sound of the rifles before, but it is much nicer with company."

"You are very welcome, my noble lady," said Tannor, as he stopped in the middle of the street with a mock bow.

"Stop that," said Ebele, being conscious of the people who began to stare at them. "You're embarrassing me."

"Fine, fine," said Tannor, standing beside them as they turned a corner through the city streets.

"But I must say, I'm surprised. I didn't really expect you to show."

"Really?" asked Ebele, a bit offended. "Why not? I did say I would."

"Yeah, ya did, but after yesterday, and how ya ran away? I'd thought I'd offended you or something."

"No. It's just that it was getting dark, and I was instructed to be back before the sun went down."

Tannor shook his head. "That sounds strict. Is that what a noble's life is like? You, following orders down to the letter?"

"That's easy for you to say. This city has a killer on the loose, and it looks like he's only attacking nobles. So, it's not like you're in any danger."

"I agree with her," said Helheim, pointing a finger at Tannor. "Your selfish request could lead to putting her in danger. By the Graces, they've certainly put me in precarious situations for the short time that we've known each other."

"Oh, yeah?" he said with a flex of his arm. "Then she just needs to rely on me to protect her." He then twirled the rifle a little half-hazardly to the point Ebele thought he might drop it.

"Protect me? Didn't you ask me out here so that I could teach you how to shoot?"

"Yeah," he nodded. "So that I can protect you."

Ebele frowned. "Your way of thinking is backwards."

Helheim immediately started laughing. "Oh, by the Graces, it's true. You've only known him a day and you've pegged him so well."

Tannor frowned. "Oh, laugh it up. But I've seen how women scream in the face of danger. So, if those assassins appeared now. You can't depend on my friend here." He patted his chest. "That means that I am your best choice."

"Most certainly not. If assassins appeared, I would most assuredly run away while screaming for the guards." Ebele thought back to her mother the night before. *She was trying to hide it, but mother was hurt. If they could hurt Mother, there's no way I'd even stand a chance.*

"Alright," said Tannor, after they entered a small open area near the wall of the city. "Now let's get this going and you can tell me how I should shoot this thing."

Ahead, Ebele saw a few circular practice targets made from straw. They were painted with blue circles on the outside and a red bullseye at the center. She couldn't help but stare at Tannor as he fiddled with the rifle. *He really is like a child.*

"Oh, just give it to me," she said as she took the rifle from his hands and turned her back to him. But on her own face was a slight grin at his crassness. Damned if she'd let him see it, though. Taking her time, she then began examining the rifle. It wasn't anything special, the stock was made of dark hardwood. The chamber and bolt handle were made out of a light silver metal. The barrel was a little shorter than her mother's rifle. She could feel the tradeoff. It was easier to swing in her hand due to the lesser weight.

Is it just that the barrel is shorter? Maybe the wood or the metal might also be lighter. When I get back, I should probably play around with some others. But it shouldn't affect my aim, should it?

"Everything okay?"

"Huh?"

"I'm just saying. I wish you'd look at me the same way you were looking at that thing."

"Oh, shut up. Did you bring the powder?"

"Aye," he said as he reached into a pocket and pulled out a small pouch.

"Good," said Ebele as she nodded over to a loading station under a canopy. Once there, she pulled out several shell casings, laying them across the workbench. "Now, fill the powder with your essence and then load several bullets with it. That way we can see how strong your essence is."

"Alright, I can do that," said Tannor as his eyes began to glow along with the essence that he placed on the table.

Ebele watched him go about loading the housing, and with a little instruction, didn't struggle much with the casings. But she had to admit it was fun watching him try to figure out how to properly load a cartridge. No, more than fun. Watching him figure out the mechanics of something. It was something close to intoxicating.

Why do I get like this sometimes? She asked herself with a lick on her lips as she looked him over. *I mean, it's not like it's him, is it?* She looked him over. Sure, he was somewhat attractive. Half-a-head taller than her, but that wasn't much since she didn't inherit her mother or father's height. Brown hair, dark eyes. She remembered the muscular body that hid underneath his clothing. *Fine, he has a nice body, but so does, my fiancé, Saro.*

"Okay, now what?" he asked as he handed the rifle back to her. "Did I put them in right?"

Pulled out of her thoughts, she took the rifle and inspected it again. Everything seemed in order, so she gave it back to him. "Now it's time for you to take your first shot."

"Finally. I've been waiting to try this," he said as he raised the gun up to eye level and pulled the trigger. It went click, and then nothing. He pulled the trigger again, it clicked, and then nothing, again. Frowning, he held the rifle in one hand and began shaking it up and down as if it were defective. "I think I swiped a broken one."

Ebele laughed and shook her head. "You can't be serious."

"What?" he asked, looking confused.

"Okay," she said as she stepped behind him. "Aim it again." He kept a sour expression on his lips, but did as asked, bringing the gun up to his eyesight. "Put the butt of the rifle firmly against your shoulder." *I sound like Mother. What has the world come to? If I have a child, is this what it would feel like?* She reached forward as she squeezed herself into him from behind, so that her hands could reach his fingers under the forestock.

The skin on his fingers was rough, and he smelled of something sweet. *Did he try to make himself smell better for me?* A smile appeared on her lips. "Okay, now use your essence. It will respond to anything nearby that you've infused with it."

He took a deep breath, and she could feel his chest rise and fall as she pressed against him.

"Good, now aim the rifle at what you wish to hit and then pull the trigger."

When he pulled the trigger, there came a click, then a boom sound as the end of the rifle exploded. The kick of the rifle wasn't as strong since he was taking most of the impact, but she could feel it. Ahead, she watched as the outer edge of the target popped, sending a small amount of the colored hay target falling to the ground.

"I hit it," said Tannor, with a smile as he raised the rifle above his head.

"Yes, you did. Now place the gun back against your shoulder and try again."

"Oh, sure. I guess this isn't as exciting for you as it is for me."

"I'm excited enough. Now aim again. We don't have much time."

"Why? You don't want to stay here with us?"

"I told you I have someplace to be today."

"Ahhh, yes; noblewoman business."

"Just shut up and aim properly. This time, don't just point and shoot. Close one eye and try to line up the sights with each other. That'll be your point of reference." Saying this, she could feel his body tensing up again. "Take a deep breath and try to keep your body loose. Tightening your shoulder will throw off your aim."

"Okay," he exhaled. "I got it."

Tannor pulled the trigger again, but this time there was no impact, only the sound of the bullet ricocheting off the stone wall of the city. "Shit."

"It's fine," said Ebele, squeezing herself into him tighter, her hand sliding over his arm and guiding him back to center. "We all miss. It's the practice that makes you a marksman. A thousand missed shots will guide you to your target."

Tannor let off a nervous chuckle. "That... that sounds somewhat poetic."

"When we were training, my father would tell me this when I missed. 'You're not failing, you're just learning.'"

"Sounds like a smart man."

"Smartest I know," she said with a bit of pride in her chest. Then she remembered why she really was out today. "Actually, I have a question for you?"

"What is it?"

"First shoot another shot," she said as she used a finger on his wrist to tilt the rifle to the left just ever so slightly. He shot again, and this time, he struck the target again, although now the strike was just a little right of the previous hit. "Good."

"Great, I hit it," he said as he lowered the rifle and turned back to her. When he turned, she was still in the position of having her hand on his wrist for guidance, and the two found each other staring directly into each other's eyes, their lips only an inch apart. "Thanks," he said in a low tone. His perfume drifted over her nose as his voice sweetly dripped into her ears.

"And suddenly I feel like I'm interrupting," said Helheim. "Should I leave?" He asked with a smile, as he gestured towards the gate.

"What?" she asked, a little confused as she was momentarily lost in Tannor's eyes. "Oh." She took a moment, regaining her faculties. "Sorry... ahhh... what of you Helheim? Do you... I mean I should have asked; do you have a gift for essence? Would you like to try?"

"Sadly no," said Helheim with a smile. "My life is just bad luck, it seems. No one to fawn over me, no essence, and also a bum leg." He shrugged his shoulders and shook his head. "The Graces have not been kind to me in this life."

"I... I wasn't fawning over him?"

"You sure? It certainly seems fawn'*ish,* if not fawn'*ing.*"

"Yes," said Tannor, nodding his head in agreement. "I do have that effect on women. Perhaps that is my curse from the Graces."

"Oh, shut up, both of you."

They all laughed in the moment before Tannor spoke. "Okay, okay. Now, what did you want to ask me?"

"Ask you?" replied Ebele, confused after being carried away in thought by their banter. But she quickly remembered. "You both were here when it started. I wanted to ask you if you've been hearing anything about why the assassins are killing people.

"Yeah," said Tannor as he began scratching his head. "I guessed you'd be keen on that, since you're a noble. Do you think they'll come after your family? I heard they haven't attacked for some time now. They might have even moved on."

No, that most certainly isn't the case. I'm sure it was them that has Mother in such a state. "I mean, they've killed so many, and I can't figure out why the guards haven't caught them yet."

He gave a small laugh. "Cause they ain't looking, that's probably why."

"Huh?" said Ebele with a curious look as she tilted her head. "What do you mean? They're the guards. Of course, they're looking for the murders. Don't you see them walking around the city with their guns?"

Tannor placed a hand on her shoulder while shaking his head. "No, you see them walking around the nobles' quarters. You don't see them walking around Old Town or the Dread Quarters."

"Dread Quarters?

"Yeah, I learned about that place when I first got here. Horrible place. Even then, I don't go down there that often unless I have to grab something and even then, I don't stay long. It's fairly normal to find someone dead face down in the dirt there. And their usually lcft there as a message. Heard once that a guard tried to go down there and extort one of the local slum lords. The next day, they found him and his friends naked and hanging by his necks. Their clothing and rifles neatly folded on a table placed under them."

"That's horrible."

"Yeah, it is," he said before turning back around to take aim. "And that's why I even make sure to stay away from there. There's no fun to be had in that place. At least not the kind I want."

Dread Quarters… maybe that is where they might be hiding. Either way, I should tell Mother about it when I get back. Her lips twisted a bit as she went deeper into thought. *Wait, Mother says she's been to the city before. Wouldn't she know about the Dread Quarters.* She shook her head. *Ah, what a horrible name. But I suppose it helps keep people away.*

"How do I look?" asked Tannor, once again dragging her out of her thoughts.

"Huh, Oh, ahh… let me check," she stepped to the side, checking his form. "Better. Just remember not to hold it too tight against your shoulder. Just enough so that it feels comfortable."

He pulled the trigger again, then came the crackle of rifle fire. Once again, he hit the area where he had previously struck twice.

"Again? Why always in the same area?"

"That's just because of how you hold the rifle. It's where you feel comfortable. Keep taking shots and slowly try making adjustments. You'll find your form over time."

Truthfully, she was happy for him that his first ever shot wasn't a miss and that he had some skill even if low. But what she didn't say was that she was somewhat disappointed in the damage that was caused by his shot. The target was barely impacted. He seemed proud enough of his skill, but in terms of efficiency, he was some of the lowest she'd ever seen. *I guess I should let him be proud of himself. He did hit the target, so I suppose that's something.* She looked down at the target again as her tongue ran over her lips. *Or I could just show him what a riflewoman with a lot of essence can do.*

"Maybe I can join the guards after all," he said as he took aim again.

"Wait, I thought you said you didn't want to be a rifleman."

"Well, I have to do something. I can't keep shoveling powder forever. Even Helheim has his photograph machine thingy. I figure I got to do something at least as—"

"Photograph machine?" yelped Ebele, turning back to a startled looking Helheim. "You were the one we saw when I first entered the city."

"I suppose," said Helheim. "I don't think anyone else in the city has one."

"Yeah," said Tannor. "Somehow this bastard managed to get his hands on something that rare and he charges nobles a pretty penny for their photographs."

"Don't make it sound like you don't benefit either," said Helheim. "You're the one who paints the murals for them."

"I remember that. The one with that creepy black shadowy thing on it."

"Well," said Tannor, looking a bit embarrassed. "It was supposed to be the assassins, but since I don't know what they look like, I just tried to make it look scary."

"We've been talking all this time, and how are you just now bringing this up in conversation?"

"What? I mean, is it important?"

"Huh... well... no, but it's interesting, to say the least."

"And what if I found myself a most appropriate profession?" asked Tannor, his eyes glancing over at her. "I might even find myself in the good graces of a certain dark-haired noble lady."

She smiled, knowing his words were meant for her. "Tell me. Are you always so brazen in your flirting?"

"I have to bc. Otherwise, you might run away and get snatched up by someone else. Probably, end up living in some big fancy castle, locked away. I mean, really. I've seen the noblemen of this city. They can't be that exciting, all of them walking like they're looking for a chamber pot to sit on."

She laughed. "Not all. Just some. And I'm sorry to inform you that I am engaged to someone back in Tymit." She placed a hand on her cheek as a grin came over her lips. "And I'll have you know, he's quite exciting."

"But not as exciting as me," he said as he closed an eye,

took aim, and pulled the trigger again. The shot tore into the target, although this time it was closer to the center. "Ha! See. I'm well on my way to winning over your heart. I get a little closer with each shot. A little more practice and you should refer to me as your Lord Husband. Much better than the dull noble life."

She shook her head as she stepped back over to him, watching as his eyes began to glow for another shot.

"Tell me then, my supposed future Lord Husband."

"Oh, I do like the sound of that."

"Would you rather wait till our wedding night, or would you prefer if I sucked your cock right now?"

The gun fired off and the sound of the bullet hitting the stone wall behind the target could be heard.

"What?"

"Oh, you missed," she said as she stepped to his side and began walking past him. "I guess we shan't be married after. And for the record. Not all nobles are as dull and unimaginative as you think we might be. But do go on and continue practicing. There are a few other things I need to see too in the city, so try not to get arrested when you return that rifle. And Helheim, the next time we meet, do bring along your photograph machine. I've always been interested in mechanical things."

She walked out of the training area with a smug look on her face. The outer roads weren't as filled as the main path. There she would see fine jewelry and clothing shops. She knew the city had an underbelly. Her mother had always said such about any large gathering of people. That's where the dregs and uncouth charlatans would be. And that's where she would most likely be able to find any information about the assassins.

Perhaps I should have asked him to show me around the Dread Quarters. He said it's dangerous, but.... She shook her head. *But that would bring up more questions, and I'd rather not deal with that.* She sighed. *I really want to go, but I suppose mother would be best suited for things like that.* She took a look down the street before clicking her heel against the stone walkway. *But perhaps Old Town can be explored with less risk of being accosted.*

With a nod of the head, as if making up her mind, she headed down the street in search of Old Town. While she did get a few curious looks from the nobles she pestered on her way, she was informed of the Old Town location on the other side of the city. Apparently, it wasn't too far from where she had met Tannor underneath the pipes.

Without the sounds of gunfire to guide her, she had to retrace her steps in her mind. Beautiful, well-maintained buildings slowly changed to less colorful and decrepit ones the lower she went towards the wall. The streets started to feel colder as she approached. But with another turn, she found herself beneath the same heating pipes from before. Being there, knowing that Tannor wasn't nearby made her feel a little anxious.

Stop this... The whole reason you even know him is because you came down here alone beforehand. She walked past the pipes and peered into the shack in the wall and saw, once again, the black shadows standing in front of a large flame. The silhouettes of the men seemed as if they were flickering in the strong light of the house. *Granted, the last time I was here, it was before mother had her run in with the assassins, so perhaps I am right to be a little apprehensive.*

With a stiffness in her chest, she stepped forward past the shack and into this unknown part of the city. Here, the dwelling areas once again turned back into mud and shanty houses. She clutched at the strap of her rifle tightly as she gathered in her surroundings step by step. *I'm not wearing a noble's dress. Surely, I blend in better than before.*

A wishful thought, but as she continued, she took notice of the citizens down in the dregs of the city. Some of the women she saw had holes in the clothing as they looked after children that ran about in garments no better.

Okay, so perhaps I am standing out more.

"Hey," said one of the children as they came running over from their group after eyeing her. "Are you one of the guards?"

"Me?" she said, looking down at the child. His disheveled hair and muddy face only being outdone by his two missing front teeth that brought more attention to his smile. "What do you think?"

"Humm. No, you don't dress like guards and your rifle looks funny," he said, pointing up to her weapon.

"Well, then. Maybe I'm a special guard."

"Special guard?" said the boy, looking unconvinced. "Why you special? Oh, is the rifle special? Does it shoot other things?"

"Other things?"

"Yeah, like sticks or... or like water."

"Boy, stop pestering her," said a woman, stepping out onto the street. "Now go back over there with your friends and play."

"But..." he looked up at the woman with a frown. "No, I don't wanna. I wanna see what makes it special." Ebele hadn't noticed her before in the few citizens that were out before. She seemed homely enough. She then pulled the boy on the arm. "Go on now, before I tell your mother, you're off playing near the Dread Quarters again."

"Owe," said the boy, before he pulled away. He then stuck his tongue out at her before running back over to his friends.

"Sorry bout that," said the woman, shaking her head. "Children got's lot of questions, is all."

"It's fine. I recently met two similar children who are the same."

"So," she said, looking Ebele over. "What ya looking for down here?"

"Who says that I'm looking for anything?"

"Not many people looking like you come down here

often and when they do, it's always for something. Noblemen come down here looking for whores. Noblewoman comes down here looking for... other things. Maybe big men whores too after they've given them awash." She pointed a finger at her rifle. "But with that, you're probably here looking for special powder."

Special powder? Her mind latched onto the words. *The only powder I've seen in this city was of such low-grade, I'd be surprised it could even launch a round past the barrel.* And despite her disbelief, her curious nature increased at the thought of what this low, unwashed place would consider to be 'special' powder. "And if I wanted to buy some. Where would I get it?"

"Daylon changes shops all the time to avoid the guards. The last time they found him, they confiscated what he had, so since then he's been hiding, only selling to certain people who come with an invited guest."

"And let me guess. You just happened to be that guest," said Ebele, very unconvinced by the woman's words. *This feels like the traveling salesmen who show up at our home claiming their tonics can cure blindness and impotency. Quick to leave town before one can open their eyes and the other can find a woman.*

"Me? No," said the woman, perhaps catching on to her skepticism. "But my handler, he..."

"Handler?"

The woman's eyes lowered. "I'm... Well, I belong to a Daylon you see... or at least I used to. We've been on the outs. Oh, but don't worry, it's just a spell. He gets like that sometimes. But I'm figuring that if I brought you to 'em that... well, that he'd forgive me."

That doesn't sound like any man I'd want to meet.

"Oh, but don't worry," said the woman. "He's a powerful man down here. He can get anything as long as you're paying."

Ebele looked at the woman and began to wonder if she

was telling the truth and if so, what exactly happened that would cause her to be in the bad graces of her supposed man? Curiosity be damned. She had learned many times not to pry into the affairs of men and women, regarding their relationships. "Fine. Where is this man? Is he near?"

"Oh, yes," said the woman. "He's a few corners down. He likes to gamble and is probably with the other men."

"Alright, take me to him."

"Yes, m'lady."

Keeping an eye on the environment, she walked beside the woman. *I have my rifle in case anything goes wrong and I'm pretty fast. And let's not forget that I'm not wearing an oversized dress today. So, I'm pretty confident that I'll be able to run away should things turn not in my favor.*

Following her guide, she was surprised to see that the shanty disheveled houses somehow managed to grow even more decrepit the deeper into Low Town she went. Up ahead she saw that the shanty houses were built on top of one another, forming an ominous wooden looking cave like crevice between both sides of the road.

"Is that where we're headed?" she said with the tightness of fear seeping into her chest.

"No." responded the woman quickly. "That's the dread quarters of Old Town. We don't wanna go there. My man stays near there but never goes in unless he has to." Taking a turn down the road, she found herself in front of a larger brick building amongst the wooden shanty homes. Inside, she could hear the sounds of chatter as men and women conversed with each other. "He's usually round back. Follow me."

"Can your man not come out here to meet me?"

"I don't think he would," she said with a solemn look in her eyes. "He's very proud and I can't go to him unless I bring you with me. Will you not come?"

Ebele frowned as she considered, but the look on the woman's face seemed to beg her to follow along. With a sigh, she flicked her wrist at the woman instructing her to lead the way inside. The building was, as she had guessed, a tavern. Inside, the air was stale with mead and the perfume of the unwashed. Whereas outside had the stench of perhaps feces and rotten food, inside was the cause of it. Her mouth twitched as she tried to slow her breathing.

The chatter amongst the patrons being the second thing to catch her attention. Rowdy men swinging mugs of ale, other's arm wrestling each other for coins as spectators cheered them on.

"Can't believe he expects me to find more of his apparent guests," came the voice of a nearby woman dressed in a maid's garb similar to that which Aretta wore before. In this area, she did stand out some, but even more than that, it was the man she was speaking to. He wasn't dressed oddly, but his clean-shaven face did seem out of place when compared to the rest here. "Searching here is like finding gold in the dirt."

The man she was with smiled before patting the woman on the head and giving her a kiss. "Don't worry. I'm sure you will find what you need. Just give it some time."

"Time? I barely have any of that."

"Hey there," said a nearby rough-looking man who had apparently taken an interest in Ebele. "Do I know you from somewhere?"

"Pardon?" said Ebele, confused by his statement. "I can't imagine you do."

"Then I think we should do something about that," he said with a smile and a laugh, exposing a set of yellow teeth, which made Ebele dread the thought of what his breath might smell like.

"This is my score, Hitcher," said her escort to the man. "You stay away. You hear me?"

The man laughed. "Fine by me. But bring her back around for a tour when ya done with her." He looked back up at Ebele with a wink that made her cringe inside. "That sound good, little lady?"

"No. I'd much rather not," said Ebele, not able to hide the look of disgust on her face, which apparently amused the man since his smile grew wider.

There were a few uncouth words directed at them from the patrons as they headed towards the bar. She was thankful that she had elected to wear pants and was in a more dressed down fashion today. *I'd hate to think of the reaction if I'd have chosen her to wear that frilly dress from before.* She thought about her tussle in the mud with Aretta. *I suppose they've washed it by now. I'll have to remember to check on it when I return.*

"Well, what do we have here? You return here to beg for Daylon to take ya back?"

"No," she said with a lying smile. "I just so happen to have brought him a customer. Someone who can pay real good."

"Best be some good pay if ya think he'll just take ya back after that stunt you pulled."

"Just tell me if he's here or if I gotta go someplace else."

"Yeah, he's here," said the man, gesturing with his thumb to a door at the back. "Him and..." A slight grin came over his lips. "His new and younger lady friend."

The woman frowned, then turned away. "Come on," she said as she headed toward the back, her fists balled at her sides.

"Good luck," said the man as he went back to his tasks, the smile still on his face.

Ebele gladly followed behind her guide, her mind anticipating the refreshingly rotten smell of the outside rather than the putrid stink inside. They went through the kitchen where an older homely woman was fixing a stew that smelled delicious. Although that feeling may have been her nose cherishing anything other than the previous environment.

Opening the door, they both stepped out into a shaded

opening facing the town wall. The ground was unkempt, with patches of grass scattered between the large swaths of dirt. Amongst it were a large number of dead tree logs where numerous men sat upon as they played some game involving stones. They shouted, cheered, and cursed at each other with each toss.

And while all of this was interesting to Ebele, as she warily took in her surroundings, her gazed fixated on a particular brown-haired man. He was talking to a woman that sat across his lap.

"Daylon," she said, just loud enough for the man in the chair to hear.

"Well, looky here," said the man as he patted the woman in his lap on the thigh. "If it isn't Lacy, and what's this? You brought a little friend with ya this time?" He wrapped one arm around the woman's waist. "Sorry, darling, but your position's been filled?"

"Oh, yeah?" said the woman, placing her hands on her hips. "This one brings ya any money? Cause she might look nice on your lap, but she ain't fattening ya pockets none, is she?"

"What?" said the woman. "You mean like you? Last I heard, your ideas only cost him money and even had three of his boys locked up for messing with that crippled." She rubbed his chin. "Don't worry, honey. I'm thinking up a plan that'll bring us a lot of money."

"Yeah, well," she placed a hand on Ebele's back and nudged her forward a step. "Well, I got a plan now. This noble here's willing to pay top coin for some rare powder. And she can pay too, you best believe that. I know you've been looking to get rid of something that recently fell into ya hands."

The man's eyes went wide, and he quickly stood up, sending the girl on his lap sliding off and stumbling forward until she caught her balance. He quickly walked over, reached out, and wrapped his hands around the woman's neck. "You dumb bitch. You bring a noble down here and tell them that I have… how you know she's not working for the town guard?"

The woman smiled while stretching neck upward to speak. "I know every noble woman in this city. And I ain't never seen her before today. She's one of them who got locked in after them murders started. That means she's clean. And if she's clean, then so is her money."

As his hands stroked on the woman's neck, his eyes darted over to Ebele and began focusing on the rifle at her back.

Should I say something? What would be the proper response in this situation? Point my gun at him and threaten him to let her go? She looked around, giving her environment another inspection and noticed the men who were throwing rocks beforehand were now standing up. A few of them even took a few steps closer. *Well, I can't shoot them all. So, I guess I should play along and see where it leads.* "I doubt I'm as wealthy as she proclaims, but I am here to pay if this is indeed special powder." *I don't really have much money. But he doesn't know that?*

The man frowned at her. "Please, I don't know you, and I sure as Powder's Kin don't trust this one after the money she's cost me. I ain't make it this far being too stupid enough to—"

"I can vouch for her?" came the voice of Aretta as she stepped over out from behind the gathering of men. "She's not part of the guards, or at least not the ones looking for what you got. Her mother's some big shot war hero. They got her here looking into the murders."

Daylon turned his head, looking at Aretta carefully, as if studying her face, before turning back to Ebele and the woman. He then quickly released the woman's neck and stepped back with his hands in the air and a big smile across his lips. "Okay then. If Harley says you're good, then you're good."

Harley? Is that her real name? Wait, no... not the time to think about that. She put on her best annoyed face and voice. "If I have to go through all this, I'm not even sure it was worth coming here."

"Oh, it was. If you're wanting something special, well, I'm currently the only place to get it. So, I'll be asking ya to forgive any misunderstanding. And since Harley has spoken for ya, we can get down to business and talk price."

"Before that, you're going to tell me what's so special about this powder. I can acquire top grade powder whenever I need. What makes yours so different?"

The man began nodding his head as he bit his lip and stared at Ebele for a moment. But then, apparently having made up his mind, he reached into a pocket in his vest and pulled out a small vial with a green sandy substance inside. "I usually just wouldn't hand over any product like this. But call it a gift in light of our little misunderstanding?"

Ebele took the vial and held it up to her face, tilting it slowly and watched as the grains of powder flowed back and forth. "Why's it green?"

"Don't know," said the man with a shrug of his shoulders. "I thought it was some type of spice or something at first."

"Then what makes it different from other powders I might find?"

"I heard gets hot?" said the man. "And it stays hot?"

"What? What do you mean, heard?" asked Ebele, confused by the statement.

"Stuffs rare. Apparently, not many can use it. But to those that can, I heard they'd be willing to fly to the moons and back for it."

"So, you haven't even tested it yet? How do you know it does what you say."

The man just laughed. "You got that little bit there. Go on and try it. Ya mom's that Warbird hero, yeah? Figure with a powerful momma like ya got there. She might be interested. I figure, if so. Then Harley knows where to find me."

A little annoyed by the man's nature, she pocketed the suspicious powder. "And where did this something special come from?"

"Best you not know," said the man as he turned back and took a seat in his chair. "The real question is, when ya come back for more, how much ya want and how much ya gonna pay."

"Wait!" said the woman who had escorted her. "What about me? I brought her. What about my cut?"

The man looked ahead to the previous woman, before reaching out and pulling her back down on his lap and then turning his head to her. "Fine, if ya want your spot back. Then ya better make sure ya little noble friend, there is the real thing, or should it be more precise, that her coin is."

Seeing that the negotiations had ended, Ebele turned to take her leave. She would have preferred to walk around the building, but that would mean walking through that mob of men ahead. So instead, she chose the disgusting stink of the tavern rather than risk any altercations. Although, whereas before she followed the woman, now it was the woman and Aretta that were following her.

She took a deep breath of the putrid air once she stepped outside. She had never been so thankful to smell something that she knew was unpleasant, but a far better alternative than the inside. "Okay," she said as she looked around the streets and found a path that would lead back to the nobles' quarters. "This way, I think." And proceeded to walk off.

"Wait," said the woman, as she hurried beside her. "You're going to buy his product, right? I mean, you do have the money?"

"That depends on what it does. Although, even if I do decide to buy it, I won't be able to get any money until the city opens back up. But do not worry, if your man or whatever he is to you has a word is as good as you claim, then you both shouldn't have any need to worry." The words left the woman a little speechless, and she stopped in the middle of the street as Ebele and Aretta carried on.

"Your mother sent me looking for you?" said Aretta, walking a bit faster to match her pace.

"Did she?" asked Ebele, her tone dismissive. "And you just knew I'd be in some place I'd never been before. In the slums?"

"No, of course not. It's that I had some business with them and figured I should take care of it while I had the chance. I'd rather them than deal with Brushwess."

"Brushwess?"

"The boss of Daylon, who gave you the powder." She waved at the street leading to the darkest part of town. "He's the king of Old Town and he's... well let's just say he's hard to deal with."

"Yes, well, I'm glad you were able to handle your business."

Aretta frowned. "Are you okay? Have I done something to upset you?"

Ebele sucked in her cheeks as she pouted a bit. "Harley. You... you didn't... well, you lied."

"Oh," said Aretta with a smile and a laugh. "Yes. Well, I guess I did."

"Why are you laughing? You think it's funny to laugh when you make a fool of someone with your lies?"

"Yes, sometimes," she said as she skipped forward a bit and turned around to Ebele while walking backwards. "I'm a thief, after all. I lie."

"Apparently."

"Why? Would you prefer to call me Harley from now on?"

"No... I mean, maybe." She shook her head. "I mean, why lie all this time? You could have told us the truth when we were brought back to Mr. Harsetti's. It's not like it would... wait, does Mother know?"

"Yes. She coaxed it out of me the morning after we arrived."

"Of course she did," said Ebele with a sigh.

"Cheer up," she stopped and let Ebele walk up to her, grabbing her by the shoulders to looking her in the face. "I'm sorry, okay? And besides... that woman has a way of bothering the truth out of someone."

Ebele looked down at the ground, still in a frumpy mood. A small smirk did creep over her lips at the description of her mother. "I guess she does do that. I admit, it is nice having someone else recognize it."

"See, now come on. Let's head back."

"Fine. But only if you promise not to lie to me anymore."

"Humm, no." She shook her head. "But I will promise not to lie to you unless I think it's to protect me or the people I care about. Deal?"

Ebele thought for a moment. "I guess that's fair."

"Good, now let's go get something to eat. I haven't had anything yet," she said as turned around and stepped forward. "And by the way. I saw you flirting with that man after you walked in."

"What? I did no such thing. What man?"

"Hitcher."

"Hitcher? I don't..." Then her mind went back to the disgusting man with yellow teeth from when she entered the tavern. "As if I would ever."

Aretta laughed as they went up the street with Ebele trying to defend herself against what she took as serious slander.

CHAPTER 10

"Well now," said Neekay, as she stood near the window in her nightgown, holding the vial of green powder in the morning light. "You certainly have been busy, haven't you?" She slowly rocked it back and forth between her fingers. "The world keeps on changing. Tell me. Is it poisonous?"

"Poisonous?" asked her daughter, making a confused face before understanding. "I didn't even consider that. I suppose it could have a smelling property or an irritation to the skin if touched."

She turned back to her daughter with a look of curiosity. "You mean you haven't opened it yet?"

"No? I was unsure. And I assumed perhaps you may have some knowledge of it. I mean, it's not as if you tell me everything."

"Wow, my daughter. Choosing not to instantly start experimenting. That certainly is a rare occurrence."

A frown slid across Ebele's lips as she folded her arms over her chest. "Must you always be so condescending?"

"The same can be asked of you, daughter," said her mother as she popped open the cork on the vial, to her daughter's dismay.

"Wait, but you just said—"

Neekay lowered the vial, then tilted it over before lightly tapping out a small portion onto the table. "Would you like to do the honors, or should I?"

Ebele stared at her mother for a moment, then down and a small amount of green powder in a mound on the table. She wanted to protest, but the excitement inside of her was building. All throughout the night, she couldn't help but stare at the vial, imagining what discoveries it could unfold. She even went so far as to sleep with it clutched in her hand. But now, with her mother's own recklessness adding to her own, she couldn't help herself but step forward. The gleeful smile spread across her visage.

"You do know, Father would never let us just do things like this."

"Well, it's a good thing he's not here, isn't it?" replied her mother, a smile across her own face, apparently enjoying the sight of her daughter's curiosity.

"Okay," said Ebele as she placed both hands on the table. "I'll just use a little at first. You know, just to see if it reacts. Apparently, not everyone has a reaction to it." Looking to her mother for acceptance and when given a nod, she turned back to the powder and began channeling the essence inside of her. Normally, she would notice a reaction in the powder when it where glow and change color in response to her. But for some reason nothing happened.

"Nothing?" her mother asked.

"I don't know. I thought I felt something. But... humm... maybe." She stared at the powder and thought back to the man who had given it to her. *What would be the point of tricking me? Or even giving me this.* She remembered the smile on his face. *Why was he so confident? No, there has to be something I'm missing. I mean, this nightgown is made for essence users, so it's not as if I'm being hindered in that way.* "I'll try again."

Taking in a deeper breath, she summoned more of the essence from within herself, and with the return of the redness of her eyes, she focused intently on the grains of powder. Something was there. It was slight, but she could feel it. Deeper, she focused on the grains until she saw it. A small amount of the top grain began to glow. But this glow wasn't red, it was somewhat golden. And then, as if being infected, the other grains of powder began to glow until the entire pile shone as if it were a tiny sun.

"Well," said her mother. "That's a new color."

But it wasn't finished. The small grains of golden sand began moving in on each other, almost fusing, eventually stopping when it had almost created a perfect sphere.

"That's weird," said Ebele, leaning in and inspecting it. Instinctively, she began reaching out a finger to touch it, only to have her mother reach over and grab her by the wrist, pulling it back. Ebele turned her head to look back at her mother with a frown, then realized what she had previously said. "Oh, yes. The poison thing."

"Yes," said her mother with a raised brow. "The poison thing. What say we leave anymore inquiries for your father? We'll purchase some to take home to him." She then narrowed her eyes as she looked around. "Do you hear that?"

"Hear wha…" Then came a slight popping sound. She then turned back to the table to see that the golden grains of powder that had clumped together had now sunken into the table and were slowly going deeper. "What is that?" she stared at, her eyes almost believing. Taking her other hand, she waved it over the gains. "It's not hot."

"Careful now," said Neekay. "I just—"

The clumped piece of grains plopped through the desk

and fell to the floor. It wasn't long before they could see that it was now making its way through the floor, and it was picking up speed.

"Amazing," said Ebele as she squatted down, observing it closer. "But it's not burning it. So, it must be more of an erosion effect or something of that nature."

Her mother grimaced. "I'm glad I stopped you from touching it, then. Wait... the room below us... What would happen if that... stuff, where to come into contact with a person?"

Ebele turned, looking up at her mother with a dreadful expression on her face. "I think I should go downstairs."

"Good idea. I think that would be prudent."

Instantly, Ebele ran to the door, swinging it open and headed frantically for the steps. *Oh, don't be standing below it. It's a big room. Surely, she wouldn't be standing below it.* Finally, making it to the stairs, she placed her hand on the railing as she clomped down the steps, the hem of her nightgown fluttering at her knees. Taking a step to the bottom floor, her heart pounding nervously in her chest as she ran and turned the corner just to see Aretta / Harley walking towards her room, holding a plate of food.

"Gretch... Harl... Oh, just stop, please."

The woman turned back, looking confused as Ebele ran up to her, out of breath, with her hands on her knees. "What are you doing? What's wrong?"

"Your room. You can't... well, you can't go in there just now, you see."

"What? Why?"

"Well, you see... mother and I... well, mostly I. It's about that odd powder I received the other day. It... we think it erodes and..."

"Wait. Slow down. Erodes? What does that even mean?"

"Oh, well, it means... it means that it breaks down—" Her words were cut off by the sound of a thunder that shook the entire house as the door behind them exploded, sending the wooden frame crashing against the outer wall. The force was so strong that both girls tumbled away with Aretta, dropping her plate of food to the floor.

There, caught between smoke, small pieces of wood and dust, Ebele blinked as she shook her head, trying and failing to clear the ringing sound that rattled her brain. She couldn't even think clearly as she crawled over to the wall and began pulling herself back up to her feet. Through the ringing, she could hear a voice. It was calling her name. Then, after a moment, she recognized it. It was her mother; her voice was coming from behind. Worried, she had apparently followed her.

"Ebele! Ebele! Are you there?" Her mother's voice was panicked. More frantic than she'd ever heard before.

"Mother!" She called back through the dust with what voice she could muster. "Mother, we're here. We're safe," she said as she saw Aretta rubbing her eyes and shaking her head. "We're both fine... I think."

"Oh, thank goodness," said her mother as she stepped in beside them. "What a horrible sound that was."

Ebele's shoulders rubbing against the wall, she slowly lurched forward to the open area where the door used to be and peeped her head inside the room. It was chaos. There was a large hole in the floor and the cieling and around it was broken chairs and tables shattered against the wall or on top of what was left of the bed.

***

A little less than half an hour later, Ebele and her mother sat at the main hall's dining table across from a very perturbed-looking Mr. Harsetti and his wife.

"I told you. I warned you that inviting this woman into our home was a mistake. Think, Husband. What if the children had been there?

"Calm down, Darlene. We both know the children's

rooms are next to ours, which is on the opposite side of the manor."

"Well, who's to say that they wouldn't have just blown up the whole thing altogether? Perhaps they'll try again. I tell you; you do not know this woman the way I do. There is nothing she won't do to get what she wants. And I promise you, her daughter is no different."

"Enough, Darlene!"

"We should kick them all out and be done with it."

"Enough, Woman!" he said, slamming a fist down on the table. "I wish to hear an explanation, rather than just assume the worst of them. And considering that the explosion happened in their own rooms, I highly doubt they were so eager to blow themselves up along with us."

Ebele watched the woman's cheeks redden as her eyes seemed to want to burrow into her mother if they could. *Why does she hate mother so? I mean, yes, we did accidentally destroy a part of her home. But there's something more.*

"How very logical of you," said her mother. "I assure you that we were investigating one of the leads to the murders. And it just so happens that there was an unexpected reaction to one of our leads."

Mr. Harsetti twisted his head while trying to understand. "A lead? What do you mean? How could a lead cause that much damage? Was it the assassins?"

"No, not personally. This time we were investigating something we happened to stumble upon while searching for them."

Mr. Harsetti began rubbing his face in frustration. By the look of the bags under his eyes and his unkempt hair, she could tell he was not having an easy time since his homecoming. "Warbird, please. I am in no mood for riddles or complex thoughts. Would you please be so kind as to explain it to me in simple terms?"

"That depends," said her mother, reaching into the pocket of her gown and pulling out a vial, placing it on the table. "I myself am having a hard time defining this in simple terms since I haven't quite caught a grasp of—"

Ebele watched a hint of recollection come over Mr. Harsetti's face before returning to a more curious look.

"Oh, perhaps not," said her mother, apparently catching on to the same tell on the man's face. "Tell me, Harsetti. Have you ever seen this before?"

"What? Why are you asking me? Why would I put my hands on anything involving you?" He frowned, but did take a moment to look at the vial in her hand. "And what is that, anyway? Some type of cooking spice?"

"I suppose to some it could be, but no. This is the substance that destroyed your home?"

"What? That small vial? Preposterous," chimed in Darlene in her usual annoyed tome, while shaking her head. "But that is like you, isn't it? Making up lies just so you might get what you want. Well, I won't have it."

"You won't? Then what of you?" asked Neekay, as she turned to Mr. Harsetti. A smirk on her face, she slid a finger over the side of her cheek. She then waggled a finger on the other hand toward him. "Won't you... have it."

With a look towards his wife, Mr. Harsetti lowered his head with a shake and a sigh before sliding his chair from the table and standing to his feet. "Follow me, Warbird. I think we should go for a walk and discuss things."

"Discuss?" said his wife in protest. "There's nothing to discuss. If you wish to walk, escort her to the gate and be done with her."

"Go see to the children, Darlene," his voice low and calm. "Warbird."

Neekay stood from the table. "I suppose it is nice outside. And seeing that my current room has a hole in the floor and shattered windows, I think it would be nice to get some fresh air. Ebele, come join your mother on her walk."

Standing from the table herself, they all headed for the door and out into the mid- morning air. There was still a light fog and dew on the ground from the night before.

"Shall we head for the garden?" asked Mr. Harsetti. He said this as a question but had no intention of hearing their answer as he stepped toward the side of the house. Ebele had only seen the garden from her window since they'd arrived. She'd only ever had a passing thought of coming here. A myriad of different plants and vegetables ran through the rows of the garden. Up close, she could see that each of the rows were very well kept.

"My wife is a sweet woman," said Mr. Harsetti as he knelt beside one of the plants and began rubbing a hand over its outer shell.

"Are you saying this as a way to convince yourself?" asked Neekay. "Because if it is me, you're trying to convince, I'm afraid your words are wasted. Our history is beyond you and the children she's given you."

Mr. Harsetti sighed. "Is there truly no road to peace for the two of you?"

"No," said Neekay as looked on to the horizon beyond the town. "But I think our dislike for each other has worked for your benefit. If not so much for her."

"My benefit?" he asked, looking back up at her curiously. "How does one even come to that conclusion?"

Neekay gave a small laugh. "You should ask your wife one day about her days visiting the military academy of Jerloin. She was never a student there, but she did spend quite a few of her days on the campus grounds."

"I am aware her father was one of your instructors. I assume you and he didn't get along either?"

"Quite the opposite, actually. Me, a promising military talent under his tutelage. We spent many a long night together as he trained me and taught me how to harness my essence." She patted him on the shoulder. "No, our hatred goes a little more personal. But that's a story you should hear from her." She dangled the vial of green powder over his shoulder for him to see. "I believe this should be our topic of discussion for now.”

“Yes,” said Mr. Harsetti, eyeing the vial. “Where did you acquire it?”

“Me. No, my daughter acquired it.” She shook her head. “I was just as unbeknownst to any of this when I arrived. But some pieces started coming together, and your response to seeing this just confirmed it. Tell me, does the king know of it?”

“Yes, the discovery was why we were all brought here.”

“So not just retirement then.”

“Wait,” said Ebele. “I don’t understand. What happened? What is it?”

“Oh, come now, daughter, think of the pieces. All the murders. What do they have in common?”

Ebele’s mind wandered for a moment, her mind spinning through the details of all the murders and the attempted ones. “They... all were older?”

“Very good. And why do you think they were all older?”

“Oh, so they all knew something,” she began tapping her fingers against her side as she remembered some of those that were attacked. “Wait, what about that old lady you went and visited? And then there’s Mr. Harsetti’s wife. What do they...” She shook her head, trying to further gather her thoughts. “No, the Assassins had no idea of knowing that he was away. He even said he snuck away. Soooo...emmmm... sooooo.” She switched from her fingers gently tapping at her side to her palm fully patting against her thigh. After a moment, her eyes opened. “The killers want revenge, perhaps. Or maybe to keep a secret. Although I couldn’t... wait, does this have something to do with that powder? Is that it?”

“Well done,” said her mother. “Although a little off, I think?”

Ebele frowned. “Well, it’s just assumptions, after all. But fine, what do you think it is?”

“I’m not exactly sure that this strange powder and the

murders are connected. Or at least not yet. I think our friend Mr. Harsetti just seems to have had a terrible run of luck lately."

"On that," said Mr. Harsetti as he stood up to his feet. "We are in complete agreement. And with the inclusion of you and your daughter stirring up my wife to no end, I'd swear that'd been cursed."

"So then, in efforts to bring this curse to its end, don't you think it would be prudent to stop withholding information from us?"

"I don't know anything about the killers. Except that all the targets had something to do with the Lazarus project during the war."

"Lazarus project?" replied Ebele.

"Yes, I wasn't privy to exactly what they were doing, but I know all who were involved. Well, almost all."

"Wait, so... you weren't involved?" asked Ebele, still trying to piece it all together. "Then why—"

"He was, and he wasn't," said her mother. "You see, Mr. Harsetti was an intern. A fresh young boy out of his training. The head of the project just had him shuffling supplies back and forth. He never really got to see what they were working on."

"Yes," said Mr. Harsetti, with a bitten lip. "I knew if I could get involved with a large research team, that it would hasten my rise amongst the nobles."

"Why?" asked Ebele. "Weren't you already a noble?"

Mr. Harsetti laughed. "I wouldn't expect you to understand." He then turned to Ebele. "But your mother. You can't pretend to be ignorant. Not considering she did the same thing as I, marrying someone of higher station."

Neekay smiled. "You are right in that regard." She raised her hands in resignation. "Amazing, isn't it? I can be sent off to war, murder for a kingdom, come back as a hero, and even after all that, it did little in raising my stock in noblehood when in comparison to simply taking my husband's cock from time to time."

"Mother!" yelped Ebele, aghast at the statement.

"Harsh truths," said her mother with a loving pat on her daughter's shoulder. "But don't worry, dear. Being the child of a war hero and a famous scientist means you won't have to pursue such means."

Shaken by her mother's words, her mind rushed through the hundreds of happy memories she had growing up as a child. *Was that all fake? Does she truly not like Father? No... no, that can't be true. They don't even argue. Well... at least I've never seen them argue.* Her mind rushed back to her mother's attendant. *Kayin, he'd know. And he's never lied to me. If I ask him directly, then...* Her eyes went back to her mother and Mr. Harsetti, and she saw their lips moving and realized she was missing out on more details of the murder.

"Exactly how much has your husband told you about the research he'd work on for the king during his days under their employ? I assume that's how you know all of this."

"You are correct. Men love to reveal things when laid up in bed with a woman. I think it's how they talk to the gods. Have you not let slip a few things to your wife under the cover of moonlight?"

Mr. Harsetti was silent.

"All men are the same in that regard. Let that be a lesson to you, daughter. A naked breast and a cup of the finest liquor often have the same effect when it comes to men revealing their secrets." She laughed a bit. "Ironic isn't it. Men have their gods, yet it's their wives who hold their secrets."

Mr. Harsetti shook his head.

"Oh, come now Harsetti. No need to hold a sour face." She wagged the green vial between her fingers. "Come now, tell us more on this."

He stared at the women for a moment and sighed. "Fine. Come sit down. I suppose if not now, then when?" He led the women to a nearby canopy, taking a seat, and gesturing for the women to do the same. "That powder that you're holding is Gatilope powder, or at least that's what we named it."

"Gatilope? An ominous name to give something as simple as powder."

"That powder is not simple. There are several complications when it comes to that powder, which makes it hard to replicate. It must be produced in a desert foliage environment and seasoned for no less than ten years."

"Desert?" replied Neekay. "But that would be in Burdock's kingdom."

"Exactly. During a recon mission some years ago, one of our spies stumbled upon it. We sent out a group to investigate, and the result is what you hold in your hand. The powder is a hundred times more explosive than anything we've seen before."

"A highly explosive new form of powder that only grows in an opposing kingdom," said Neekay with a laugh as a servant girl came, laid out a set of cups, and began pouring tea. "I don't assume his highness took kindly to hearing this information."

"No," said Mr. Harsetti when the servant girl had gone. "Especially since neither he nor one of his sons were able to use it."

"What do you mean?" asked Ebele.

"Apparently, to infuse this type of powder requires an extraordinarily large amount of essence summoning. So far, only two men that we know of have been able to use it. Sir Barrington and a young rifleman from Emlan."

"Sir Barrington. I assumed old age would have gotten to him by now." Neekay shook her head before taking a sip of her tea. "Even more so, I'd be impressed if the boy was still alive. His highness never liked being outdone. He's the type to think being the master of all essence is his birthright, as well as control over all who use it." She laughed. "Maybe he has the ability to control the sea beast they have near there."

"Yes... Well, I guess it's no wonder you were able to use it."

"Oh, no. I haven't tried yet. You have my daughter to thank for your mess of a house."

"You're daught..." His attention focused on Ebele so intently, it seemed as if his eyes were trying to figure out a complicated puzzle. "The odds. If you can use it too, then... then..."

"Oh, look dear. He's getting it in his head to try and fuck us for children. I've seen more than a few men with a lust for power have that exact same look. Who knows, perhaps I'm still fertile enough for another. The process is dreadful, though."

Mr. Harsetti's eyes went wide as he began coughing. "No... no... I mean. It's just so unlikely, is all."

"Yes, I agree. The likelihood of either me or my daughter finding our way into your bed does seem quite preposterous. But as they say, 'All men can dream,' and what not."

"Must you make light of everything?" he said with a firm hand on the table.

"That depends," said Neekay, placing a hand to her chest and staring at Mr. Harsetti. "I, a bloodthirsty hardened war veteran, just witnessed a man looking at my child, my only child... with less than noble intentions. How would you prefer I respond in this situation?"

Ebele watched as the words shuffled around in Mr. Harsetti's head, his cheeks sinking in as he swallowed nervously. She could hardly blame him; she knew what it sounded like when her mother was angry. That slow and low tone, even when she was a child, would send chills down her spine. Even now, she wanted to adjust her sitting posture to shake off the effect she was having on her.

"Look... Warbird," said Mr. Harsetti with his palm outstretched towards her. "You don't understand the significance of this. That powder you have could end this entire conflict with the North... forever. No more seasonal deaths when the cold thaws, no armed conflicts near the border walls."

"There will always be war. Those in power will always look for ways to kill one another. Whether over coin, or power, or whatever reason they can think of to justify it." She stood from the table. "But do not worry yourself too much, Harsetti. I will still fight your war and those of this city. After all, I've already killed one." She knocked her knuckles against the table and began leading Ebele away. "And it's best to not feel a job unfinished."

Her mother was often very well composed. Elegant when she was speaking to company, loving when she was around her husband. But on the rare occasions, those very rare occasions, so small that she could count them on one hand, she would see her mother's temper flare. Thankfully, today wasn't one of those days. But she was close enough to see the signs. A more pronounced sway when she walked, her arms stiff at her sides, a twitch of her neck along with just the slightest rotation of her left shoulder, all of these were things she'd noticed over the years. Rare amongst themselves but telling when together, chilling.

I wonder why that discussion made her upset. I mean, it's not as if I would sleep with him. She knows that, right? More or less, she followed behind her mother back into the house, through the kitchen, and up the stairs to their room. There she watched her mother walk around the hole in the floor and go over to the bed and reach under it, pulling out her truck, lifting it and placing it on the bed. Opening it, she lifted a myriad of clothing, revealing multiple vials of their own gunpowder and empty shell casing.

"Mother? Is everything okay?"

"Of course, dear," responded her mother, her normal voice returning to the confident and cheerful woman she knew. "I just think that now, with my health returned to me, I should continue my search for those assassins. It won't do me any good being trapped here in this house." She turned to her and smiled. "And if I am forced to hear another complaint from Darlene. Then gods only know what I will do."

Nodding her head, she stepped over. "Right, well, I can help. I can load the casing for you?"

"Oh, that would be helpful darling, but unfortunately for you. I have another assignment for you?"

"Really? I mean, okay. What can I do?"

"Remember the older woman I was supposed to have visited after our departure the other day?"

"Yes."

"Well, under these new revelations, I think she deserves another visit. And now, since I have a bit of clarity, I do remember saying to her that you might make a visit to her home."

Ebele looked confused. "I mean... I can, if you prefer. But why when you've already gone? She might not ever let me in."

"No, she will. She has plenty of reasons to allow you in. Probably the most is that she will be curious. But if you're worried, take Aretta with you. The maids at the gate will recognize her, I'm sure."

Ebele frowned, folding her arms over her chest as she stared at her mother.

"What?" asked her mother, noticing her daughters' ill-content

"Aretta... that's not her name."

"No, no, it's not."

"You knew, and you didn't tell me."

"That is correct. It was her secret to tell. Besides, there was no harm in you not knowing. I figured if you two became close enough, then she'd tell you of her own accord." She waved a shell casing at her. "And it seems she has."

"No, she didn't... well, not willingly, at least. Not at first."

"Then it still sounds like you and your little friend still have a ways to go. Remember, you were the one who wanted

a little friend. Well... this is what comes along with that."
She waved her hand towards the door. "Now hurry along.
We both have jobs to do."

"Fine."

"And be back before dark," said Neekay, as her daughter
left the room.

It took some time before she found her so-called new
friend outside by the well, taking a sip of water from a ladle
and bucket.

"There you are Gret... Harley."

"Just call me Aretta, if that's what makes you
comfortable."

"No... It's just. I don't know. I... maybe I will for now."

"Suit yourself. But I've had many different names in my
life. What makes you so sure that Harley is my real name?"

"Is it?"

"It is in this city."

Ebele frowned with narrowed eyes. "Fine, whatever.
Just come with me, Arettaaa." She said the name through
her teeth in annoyance. "Apparently, I have to go visit that
old lady you and Mother saw the other day. I would ask that
you guide me."

"Oh. And here I'd hoped I'd never have to see her again,
said Aretta as she lowered the bucket and ladle to the
ground, following off behind Ebele."

"Why? Was she unpleasant?"

"Not the world I would use," said Aretta as they exited
through the gate out onto the street. "Before your mother,
I'd never really seen her before. I'd just heard about her.
Some of her servants have said that she herself killed her
husband and children."

"Preposterous. Just the idle dribble from the servants."

"Probably. But as they say, 'A lie is just a different version
of the truth.'"

"Who in their right mind would say such a thing?"

"A man I know who's prone to lies," said Aretta with a

laugh as skipped a bit ahead. "But he always has the best stories to tell."

"Great. At least now I see where you acquired your proclivity for spouting half-truths." She said this with a spiteful tongue, but there was a hint of a smirk on her lip. She had to admit that the girl was fun to have around. More so that she'd thought she'd be in the beginning.

It took some time to traverse the city, but eventually they arrived at the gate to the older woman's house. There at the gate, she waved to one of the maids that was ahead of the gate. Curious, she noticed Aretta fiddling with the locked latch.

"What are you doing? You shouldn't need to pick it. Mother said we would be invited in."

"No," said Aretta. "It's just... it's a new lock?"

"Yes? And what about it? Perhaps the previous one rusted."

"Hello there," said the maid, walking up to them. "I'm sorry, but the mistress isn't receiving any company today."

"Yes," said Aretta, "That's what was you said last time. And how'd that work out for you?"

"What?" said the maid, confused.

"Just tell your master that the daughter of the Warbird is here to see her. Apparently, that should be enough."

The maid stared at them for a moment before looking back at the house. "Wait here, please." Doing as asked, the maid went into the house and sooner than expected came back out, hurrying to unlatch the gate. "Please come inside. She is apparently expecting you."

"Ahh... thank you," replied Ebele, a little surprised by the expediency of the maid. Up the stairs and inside, she was greeted by an empty house with a lack of any type of furniture. Not a table nor a chair to sit, except an old rocker by an unlit fireplace.

"The madam is this way," said the maid as she continued through the walkway alongside the stairs. Ebele studied the wooden planks along the wall. No pictures or paintings, just candle holders of modest metal design. The wood itself was of a blackish gray that gave the atmosphere inside a haughty presence, along with the screeching of the board underneath their feet as they walked.

Through the house they went until finally they were led outside to be graced with a startling contrast. Amongst the cold weather and the light patch of snow that had covered the ground. She and Aretta stood amazed by a large rose garden that somehow hadn't withered, even in the chilled climate. The bright red petals amongst the snow; the green stems with their prickly thorns along the side. It seemed somewhat ethereal, as small pieces of snow melting amongst the leaves.

"They were my late husband's favorites," came a voice adjacent to them. Ebele turned to her side to see an older woman sitting in a small gazebo overlooking the rose garden. "He was always so picky about them too," she continued, not looking over at them. "It really was a wonder I chose to marry such a man."

"Ahhh, hello there. My name is Ebele. My mother, she asked that I come and see you. You see, I have some questions."

She gave a small laugh. "Yes. I suppose you would." she finally turned to her and was silent for a moment, as if trying to take in her full measure. "Well, now. Come closer and take a seat. No need to stand out in the cold with the snow falling all around you."

A little cautious, Ebele walked over and took a seat opposite the woman with Aretta choosing to stand at its entrance, shoulder leaning against the wooden frame.

"Do you know why I'm here?"

"No," said the woman. "But I can imagine a few things. But seeing that you are here. I'm almost certain that the intention of your arrival will not be the same as your departure."

"What do you mean?"

"It's just that life is ever evolving and revolving, and all circumstances are just the same." She patted her lap. "So, go on then. Why don't you tell me the reason you think you're here."

Confused by her words, Ebele reached into her pocket and removed the vial of green powder and held it up for her.

The older woman raised a brow in surprised. "Well, I suppose I shouldn't have to wonder if the rumors were true anymore."

"Rumors? What rumors?"

"The rumors of a certain train hijacking. They reached my ears some time ago," said the woman as she stared at the young ladies. "Ah, I see you didn't know." She turned to Aretta. "But this one. This one did know about it." She rubbed a finger across her lip. "And yet the two of you came together. Wouldn't it be more productive to share information like this?"

"What? I mean... how? I just wanted to know if you knew about the origins of it. Well, I suppose there might have been a robbery of it. But... before then, I mean."

"Of course, I do. How could I not when I was the one called upon to synthesize it? Without me, that would merely be unusable dust."

"What? I mean..." Ebele's mind started to race with all the new information. Then, regaining herself, she spoke. "I'm sorry. I don't know anything about this stuff." She glanced over at Aretta. "And apparently, I don't know much about anything. Could you tell me about this?"

"Oh!" said the older woman, seeming a little disappointed. "Humility? Well, that's certainly not a trait you learned from your mother." She extended her palm toward the vial of powder. "Perhaps there's still hope for you then."

A little hesitant, she placed the vial into the woman's hand.

The woman turned to the maid. "Tell the driver to bring

the carriage around. I think I'd like to go for a ride."

"Yes, madam."

And within minutes. Ebele found herself in a carriage, riding through the streets of Thrisanna. The sound of squeaky wheels sloshing against the snow, mixing in with the clomping of the horse's hooves. Through the trip they were mostly silent, but she could help but notice the older woman staring at her from time to time, her eyes peering at her as if she was a picture. But whenever she would make eye contact, thinking she wanted to start a conversation, she would then turn away and look out the carriage window.

Well, that's a bit unsettling, she thought to herself after another moment of catching the woman staring at her. *But I'm here for answers. I want to know about this powder. If they found it near the mountains, why is it different? How did she make it usable?*

Soon she felt the carriage stop, and the driver opened the door for them. Stepping out, she found herself looking up at a large two-story building. It was near the outer rim of the wall and seemed to have been sectioned off from the rest of the city by another wall that encompassed it.

"Where is this?" asked Ebele as Aretta and the older woman exited the carriage behind her.

"This is... this was my research facility. It's the reason most of us came here." She walked past her and headed up to the door. "Not much to look at now," she said, waving a hand over the grass, weeds, and sticks that protruded up above the snow.

In the distance, she could see fallen target dummies and overturned wheelbarrows scattered amongst the yard. But the building didn't seem as if it was too derelict. The vines on the wall were barely halfway up to the first-floor windows.

"You said, 'was.' What made you stop?"

"We had finished." She slid in the key and opened the door, the squeaking on its hinges alerting the vermin inside to their arrival. "Well, or we at least we were told that we were finished." The woman walked forward, running a finger alongside a dusty table. She shook her head at the soot on her skin. "The end result was the powder you now have. We sent a large supply to the king some time ago. I suppose what you have there was some of the last shipment from the train robbery."

"You don't seem so upset about losing what you were working on," said Aretta as she stepped forward, looking over the lower level of the building. "I mean, shouldn't you be mad?"

"Mad?" she replied. "Yes, I supposed you would think so. But no, I've given enough. I miss the pursuit of knowledge. I miss the experimenting. Very rarely have I even cared for the outcome."

"My father is that way as well," said Ebele as she stepped towards the opening of one of the rooms. "He'd spend hours testing things, but the moment he figured anything out, he'd then get bored and look for something else to work on." She lifted a covering cloth from a table, revealing a workshop of flasks and beakers. "A diluting set."

"Oh, so you know your way around a lab?" asked the woman as she walked in beside Ebele. "Did you follow after your father, then?"

"No, but I'd often bother him while he was working as a child. I'd run in looking to play and he would just have me sit there and watch him work. Sometimes he'd even explain the things he was doing."

"Yes, that does sound like him," she said from the other room. "Well. Come along. Our goal is on the floor above us."

Ebele left the room, following the older woman and Aretta. But as she approached the steps, she heard the creaking of floorboards above her as small traces of dust fell from the ceiling.

"What's upstairs?" asked Aretta, placing her hands on the railing.

"More laboratories and some old research rooms. But there's something I wish to show you," she said as she led them up the stairs and down the left hall of the building. "This place is more or less just a storage area now."

"Storage?"

"Your mother. Did she really not tell you anything about me?"

"No, she just informed me that I should come and speak to you," she said, while stepping beside her. "But I'm assuming that you also knew her and father from the war. Mr. Harsetti is the same."

"Well, that part is certainly true," said the older woman as she turned the knob of one of the rooms and walked inside. This room was just as dusty as the rest, although unlike the others, she could see that it housed a considerable amount more than the others that she'd passed. There were tarps covering dozens of large and small items. She walked over to a few of the tarps, lifting them up as if looking for something specific.

"Is this all more research stuff?"

"No, these are my personal items," said the older woman as she continued to fiddle around. "You saw that I mostly live alone. But at one point in time my home was quite lively with the sounds of children. When they were taken from me...I... well, I didn't enjoy looking at the things that brought me memories."

"I'm sorry. I didn't know. But I don't understand why we've come—"

"Ahh, there we are," she said as she reached under one of the tarps and pulled out two large paintings. She rubbed off some small pieces of dust before bringing them over and handing it to Ebele. "Here, tell me what you think."

"Ahhh," said Ebele, confused, before taking the painting. "I don't understand. What do you want me to—"

"Oh, well looky," Analyse laughed, pointing at the painting. "It looks like you?"

"Wait. I thought you said you'd never been here before," said Aretta.

"I haven't," said Ebele, looking at the painting with confusion.

"Coulda fool me then," said Aretta. "I mean, look. It even has that rifle you're always carrying around."

"I don't…" She looked back towards the other portrait. "Why do you have a picture of me?"

"Do I?" asked the older woman with a smile before handing out the other painting.

Ebele handed the previous painting to Aretta before taking the other. On the new painting was a picture of her looking prim and proper in a stunning white dress with her hands resting in front of her.

"Wow," said Aretta. "How long did it take you to get into that? Were you meeting the king or something?"

"No," said Ebele, even more confused. "I've never worn something like that before in my life." She looked back at the older woman once again, who had a smile on her face as she stared at her. "What is this? Did my mother send you these?"

"No." said the older lady. "That picture you're holding. The one with the rifle is of your mother from when I'd guess she was around your age."

That revelation took Ebele by surprise as her eyes darted back to the portrait that Aretta was now holding. It was true that it looked like her, but she was stunned that her mother and her looked so similar in her youth. *Wait, does that mean I'll grow to look like her? Will I be as tall as her?*

Aretta nodded to the other painting. "Still though, it's hard to imagine your mom in something like that. But I guess you've known her longer than I have. You both go to a lot of fancy parties?"

"If she has, then she's never taken me? I can't remember the last time I've seen Mother wear a dress." She frowned. "Even though she is always forcing me into them. I mean, it's not as if I mind so much. But sometimes trousers are just more functional."

"Humm," moaned the older woman, placing a finger to her lip. "Perhaps that tomboy'ishness isn't as strong in you as it is in Neekay." She tapped her finger on the frame of the painting Ebele was holding. "Well, don't worry, that portrait there isn't of your mother. It is in fact a picture of my daughter, Rilistein. Her father and I picked out that dress for her seventeenth birthday. She was supposed to entertain suitors that day and we wanted her to look her best."

"What?" asked Ebele, looking at the portrait, this time even harder. Examining it as if she were looking for falsities. "But... but."

"Yes, it seems our family has strong genes. Even now, looking at you is like looking in a mirror and seeing my darling child. I suspect that our lifestyle choices alter our appearances somewhat. Perhaps because while we are sheltered in our parents' home, we all grow up with not so much hardship."

Ebele just continued to stare at the older woman. Her face did seem to share traits that she and her mother have. Slim nose, with high cheekbones. And her hair did have that blackish Auburn mixed in with the gray on her head, but it wasn't uncommon. She'd seen blackish Auburn from the occasional traveler that would come to visit their home. *Wait, does that mean the ones who came to my home... were they family? But... why wouldn't Mother say anything of it? She just has her meetings and then they'd just leave the next day.*

"It seems you are starting to believe me," said the older woman with a smile.

"I... I mean, then that would make you my..." she said, leaving the last word for the woman to answer.

"I am your great auntie. Meaning that I am your grandmother's sister. And aunt to your mother." She waved a hand dismissively as she turned back around, walking over to some other covered items. "Although it's not as if your mother would ever admit it. She likes to pretend I don't exist." She laughed. "Although if I were in her position, perhaps I'd do the same."

"Why?" she asked, the confusion clear on her face. "Why is this the first time I'm hearing of a Grand Auntie, or any other relative, for that matter? Surely—"

"Wait!" said the older woman, her eyes narrowing as she lowered an item in her hand back onto an uncovered table. She stared cautiously at Ebele. Not at her, but at the door behind her. Slowly, she took a step forward. "I know you're there; I can see your shadow in the door frame. You were silent but to miss such an obvious step, who are you? Come out or I shall be forced to scream for the guards."

There was a shuffle sound along with the flap of a cloth in the door frame before they heard the sound of footsteps hurdling away from them. Without another moment of thought, Ebele found herself dashing out into the hall and chasing the figure. By the build she could tell that it was a man. His head covered with a mask; he wore what looked to be worn overalls with a black shirt tucked inside.

The thought that this man or one of his associates was the one or ones who had hurt her mother fueled her in her chase. Down the hall, she caught up to him as he reached the steps to the first floor. She reached out for him, but he shifted his weight by grabbing on to the railing, pulling himself in and facing her as she glided past. Quickly planting her feet, she turned around and reached for him, but he dodged her arms again. He was quick. No matter how fast she grabbed at him, he would worm and weasel himself just out of her reach, if only by a hair.

She reached toward his face; he ducked under. A kick towards him. He shifted his weight and maneuvered behind her near the window. She spun around, swinging an arm, and he leaned back, just out of the way.

But the most frustrating part of it all was that he wasn't attempting to strike her back. It was as if he was playing with her. After every missed attack, she could see the outline of a smile behind the cloth mask on his face. The more she missed, the more he smiled, and the more irritated she became.

"Stay still, damn you," she said in frustration as she brought her hand down hard, desperate to grasp him. Unfortunately, she missed once again, this time her hand catching the window seal, and to her surprise, her grip shattered the wood into pieces.

Surprised, she stared at it, confused. But even more of a surprise was that her adversary now had wide eyes as he also stared down at the broken window seal. Brought back to her senses, she released the shattered board and reached for him again. He continued his evasive maneuvers, but this time, instead of staying in her vicinity, he stepped backwards down the canopy, now giving himself more room away from her.

"Stay still. Is that all you can do? Run?" She lunged at him, and he jumped into the air, and over the railing of the stairs, landing on the other side. He then turned and jumped through the air, grabbing the chandelier ahead, swinging on it only to release and land on the second floor of the other side. Ebele grabbed the railing and lifted herself off the floor as she stared daggers at her adversary. *If I had my rifle, I swear I'd shoot you in both those agile legs.*

As if sensing her hatred of him, the man took off running again and Ebele once again resumed the chase. Around the corner of the second floor she came, but he now had a much larger head start. But she was fast as she knew it. Feet pressing hard against the wooden floor, she dashed ahead, slamming her shoulder into the corner as she turned and saw him entering one of the rooms ahead. She dashed towards the door, entering the room only to see him in the window. He had just stepped out onto the ledge and with all her might; she leaped toward him. And as he stepped out on the ledge, she was finally able to crab him.

Or at least grab hold of his shirt.

The first of her grabbing a hold of his shirt caused him to lose his balance and go leaning forward over the ground from two stories high. Her hands waved as she tried to regain his balance. His weight pulled Ebele halfway out the window with him, her hand and thighs braced against the inside wall. The masked man reached behind him, grabbing a hold of her arm and pulled her back on the ledge. He then tried to pull away from her, tugging at his shirt, but Ebele had it held tightly in her arm.

"No, I'm not letting you get away, you're gonna…" Down below on the street, Ebele caught a glimpse of someone she knew. A crippled boy around her own age looking up at them. *Helheim? What's he… Nooooo.* "Tannor. Is that you?"

A familiar laugh came from under the mask before he reached for it and pulled it off, revealing his face. "I guess it was too much to ask for escape without you finding out."

"But… wait! Are you one of those assassins?"

"What? No. Look, I'll explain later. I gotta go before those guards see me."

"No, you're going to explain—" and before she could finish her words, head had already leaned down and planted his lips on hers. The shock of it caused her to freeze for a moment, and in that moment, he removed her grip from his shirt.

"I told you I was a good kisser," he said, after pulling away from her and stepping back on the ledge. "Come see me at the training place at noon tomorrow. I'll explain then, okay?" He said these words while walking back on the ledge before jumping down to boxes over a wagon and over a fence to the streets below, where he met up with Helheim and they went off, disappearing behind a building.

Ebele just stayed in the window and watched him, her mind racing with questions. Why was he there? He said he wasn't an assassin. And perhaps he really was a good kisser.

CHAPTER 11

The next day, Ebele lay in her bed with Aretta lying asleep beside her. Since their and the thief's room exploded the previous day, they were moved to a different, less damaged room that was only rattled by the combustion. The sun had risen an hour ago, but sleep continued to evade her. Her mind was anxious from the previous day. She didn't tell the old woman who was apparently her great auntie about who the mask man was. She didn't even inform Aretta, partly because she still wanted to talk to him and she didn't want Tannor locked up, but mostly because she was still angry at Aretta for her own secrets, and Ebele figured she could keep one as well.

The sound of guns shot rang throughout the air outside of her window, signaling the start of another workday for the town's citizens. *By now, Tannor should be on his way to where they burn the powder, where he will be there till mid-day.*

I just have to wait on him till then. Her fingers drummed on the fabric of the bed as she thought about him. *Why was he there? Looking for something? Perhaps I should inform mother.* A frown came over her lips as she thought of the consequences of doing such a thing. *That'd be a terrible idea. Look at how she treats Aretta. Her brother's locked in a prison. She'd undoubtedly do the same to him, perhaps even locking up Helheim. Born cripple and now thrown behind metal bars because of mother's whims.* She shook her head. *No, I'll get them to explain first.*

With a sigh, she rolled out of bed, placing her feet on the floor. *Maybe I should go look for Helheim, perhaps get some answers before meeting up with Tannor.* She nodded her head as if convincing herself. *Yes, that's exactly what I should do. It's best to do these things one on one, I think.*

Walking over to her trunk, she began searching through it for the clothing of the day. At first, she removed a set of walking pants and a blouse, but remembering that she would be seeing Tannor, she opted for more of a sundress. Nothing fancy, but something she could slip on and had a light bluish coloring. Fitting in some warm leggings and a coat, she felt ready for the day.

Who knows, maybe I will need to seduce him a bit. He does fancy me, after all. She examined herself in a standing mirror at the corner of the room. *Yes, this will do just fine, I think.*

Certain of herself, she exited the room, headed out into the hallway. Headed down the stairs, she saw the twins huddling around their mother as she adjusted their coats. Catching a glimpse of her, she frowned. Ebele had no intention of trying to warm up to a woman who clearly had disdain for her family, but she remembered that this woman had, in fact, attended the academy with her mother and might provide some information that she hadn't herself been privy to.

"Ah, how are you this morning?" Ebele asked, trying her best to put on a pleasant tone.

"We are fine," she said sharply. "Although we will be better when this whole assassin business is taken care of."

"Yes, mother and are doing our best—"

"I doubt that. If she were doing her best, she would be out of my house instead of gallivanting around town with that guard captain. The both of them, useless, a statement proven by the fact that those assassins are still at large."

Mother is out with the guard captain? Did she find something else out? But she didn't wake us. Would she have woken us? Certainly, if not me, then Aretta. She shook her head after realizing she was getting lost in thought and looked back at Mrs. Harsetti. "Mrs. Harsetti, this may be an odd question to ask, but you were enrolled at the academy along with my mother, correct?"

"Yes? What of it?"

"Well, you see, it's Mother. We've had a bit of a falling out. That speech you made earlier, about mother being reckless. Well, I often find myself pushing forward the same argument. Well, needless to say, I found myself yelling at her that we are nothing alike. But Mother, well... you know how she is. She seems to know just what buttons to push to dig into you. She claimed that not only are we similar, but in fact that I am the spitting image of her from her younger days. And seeing as you've known her, I would ask for your opinion on the matter."

The woman stared at Ebele. "Yes. I can see how being told you are anything like her could be vexing even to her own daughter." She then for a moment began accessing her, before nodding her head. "And as much as I absolutely dislike providing confirmation of anything that woman proclaims, I unfortunately must admit that she is correct. You indeed bear a striking resemblance to her at that age. Uncanny really, But I suppose if you try to at least not follow in her footsteps mentally, then the world will be better off for it."

"Mother," said the boy. "Come, we don't want to be late

for brunch with the Michelle family."

"Yes, yes, I know. Let's be on our way then," she said, opening the door for the children to exit, then turned back to Ebele. "We can't choose our bloodline dear, but if you can see the flaws in your mother, then perhaps there's hope for you yet." and with that remark, she left with the door closing behind her.

I guess that old woman was correct. Perhaps our family has strong genetics. She chuckled a bit. *A shame for Father. I hope he's okay with having a slew of daughters if he and mother do, in fact, try again. I wonder what the odds are of three generations of only females.* She looked ahead, reaching for the door. *Either way, a lesser mystery to be looked into later. Now I must see if I can find myself a cripple.*

Out of the house, she went. While still somewhat curious about her mother, she had her agenda. The problem for her was she hadn't any clue of the places Helheim would frequent or if he would even be out during mid-day. *I remember Tannor saying something about how Helheim would come down to the lower quarters to meet him. Does that mean he's a noble? He certainly doesn't dress like a noble. And would a noble use a beat-up stick as a cane to support himself? And if he were a noble; surely, he could pay for proper medicine.*

These thoughts and similar rummaged through her mind as she navigated her way through the nobles' quarters. Down the streets, winding roads between colorful houses and decorated lawns, she went hoping for a sighting. For an hour she walked, but amongst the well-dressed noble there was not a sign of him. She would even ask some passersby if there was the son of a noble who was a cripple in the city, but none knew of him.

Okay, so not a noble then. I guess that much should have been obvious. With a small amount of frustration scratched at her brow. *But all stones need to be uncovered before one can move on. I suppose I should try the town market next.*

The search through the town continued, and the market

was just the same as it had been before. More nobles walking and shopping, idle gossip from the women and men about the apparent assassins that were in the city and when the lock down would be lifted. She even passed by where she'd thought he'd his photograph shots before. But neither he nor the black shaped art Tannor made for him were there.

"Excuse me," said a young woman as Ebele stared into the window of one of the shops.

"Yes," she responded, turning her attention to the woman.

"I'm sorry to bother you, but you have the essence, do you not?"

"Ah, yes?"

"Wonderful. If you aren't terribly busy, may I bother you for your gift? We recently purchased a higher grade of powder from one of the local shops, and I'm ashamed to admit that we aren't strong enough to ignite it. So, we were wondering if you could, perhaps."

"Oh, sure. I could try."

"Wonder," she said as she reached into her pocket and pulled out a vial of grayish powder, handing it over.

Ebele held up the vial, examining it, and didn't judge it to be anything special. A mid-level powder type, at best. She summed her essence as her eyes glowed red. Instantly, the powder inside began to glow a dark red in response.

"Wonderful, just wonderful, thank you. Just hold it for one moment please," said the woman as she took the vial and led Ebele down the street and around a corner, where she saw a set of legs sticking out from behind the curtain of a photograph machine.

"Helheim," she said loudly as she began walking up the set of legs.

A second later, Helheim came out of the curtain, lifting it up, exposing his face. He smiled at Ebele. "Hey. I'm surprised to see you here."

"Oh," said the girl. "You two know each other?"

"Tannor likes her," he said nonchalantly to the girl. "I just hang around them."

"Oh. Well, she graciously decided to channel the powder for us."

"You're in luck then. I'm sure she'll provide an excellent picture. She's a noble who's been blessed with a high affinity for powder."

"Really?" said the girl excitedly as she turned to Ebele for confirmation.

"I... I suppose so," said Ebele, not sure about being caught up in anything Helheim had going on. But seeing the playful smile on his face. She just took the vial of powder back and channeled more of her essence into it. "Go on, get into place over there with your friend."

"Oh, yes, thank you," said the girl as she did just that. She and her friend posing under a new mural she assumed Tannor had made. This time it was of oddly shaped town soldiers holding their rifles in the air, forming an X. The girls struck a pose underneath the mural while holding their own mock wooden rifles.

"Just uncork the powder and place it in the tray," said Helheim to Ebele, pointing to the tray above his photograph machine. "I'll ignite it when ready."

Accepting that she was now just along for the ride, Ebele did as instructed and stepped over, uncorking the bottle, pouring it onto a tray at the top of his standing camera. She wasn't sure how much essence would be enough but decided on some that was a little less than she'd use when making rounds for her rifle.

Lowering himself into position at the perfect angle, Helheim stuck out a hand and began to count. "One the count of there. One, Two," There was a soft poof as the powder ignited, releasing a cloud of red smoke along with the camera's flash.

"Thank you so much," said the woman after placing down her wooden gun and coming back over to Ebele. "We didn't pay much mind to the grade of powder we purchased, and the powder shop is way over on the other end of the market. We'd not want to waste time on a trip back. And when I saw you with your rifle and not in a uniform, then I just knew you would do the trick."

But wouldn't the higher have been more expensive? Did you not care to look at the price? Thought Ebele, before responding. "Do not worry yourself. I'm just glad I could help." *And really, did you not have enough essence to enhance such a low grade of powder? Are the nobles of this city that weak?* "Are the nobles of this city who have essence not required to be riflemen?"

"Required?" responded the girl, looking a little confused. "Goodness, no, that hasn't been a thing since my father's time. I mean, sure, nowadays the young men enlist, but even then, it's more of just something to brag about before coming home during the winter months."

"I see."

"Come on," said the other young girl, coming up beside her friend to show her the picture. "It came out wonderful, come let's go and show the others."

And with a smile and a nod, the girl said their goodbyes and headed off up the street. As they passed the camera, Helheim emerged from behind the cloth.

"Thanks for that. It's hard to make any coin as a photographer when there's no essence for the powder."

"You know, I was curious if you had the gift for essence."

"Ha! I guess that would be convenient, wouldn't it?" He patted the photograph machine. "Usually, only nobles want their picture taken, so I just assume that they have essence because, well... you know... they're nobles. But every now and again, that isn't the case, so I have them search out someone nearby who does."

"A flawless plan if I've ever heard one," said Ebele, shaking her head. "Well, either way. It works out in my favor, since I've been looking everywhere for you."

"Me?" asked Helheim, a brown raised and a smirk on his lips. "Why me? I'm not sure I can help with anything."

"No, but you can explain to me why Tannor was in that research lab yesterday."

"Huh? What do you mean?"

"Don't try to play dumb. I saw you from the window. Tannor bounced his way down to you and you both disappeared together."

Helheim's face went through a couple of different emotions before he just shrugged his shoulders and looked up at the sky. "Ah, so that was you... in the window." He laughed. "It appeared for a moment if you were going to spill out of it and go tumbling to the ground below."

"Hey," she said, giving him a soft tap of the shoulder. "No laughing. Now explaining what you both were doing there."

"I," he said, trying to compose himself. "Was keeping watch outside." He reached into his pocket and pulled out a metal whistle. "If any guards came close, I was to blow this and hide. Then he'd know to get out of there."

"Guards? But there were plenty of guards outside the building."

"Yes, but not on the side of where the window you almost fell from was. I was inside the adjacent building, looking out. I could have opened the window and blown the whistle."

Ebele thought back to the houses that were nearby and indeed she did remember that area having tall buildings. She then looked down ted his leg. "You got down pretty fast, considering your leg."

"If you were in fear of being arrested, how fast do you think you could move?"

Ebele frowned. "That's a fair point." She shook her head, a little dejected by the non-revelations of their meeting. "So, you really have no idea why he was there?"

"Sorry, but he just asked me to look out for him. He

didn't even tell me that it was you in the window holding onto him. I just thought it was another guard."

Ebele sighed as she shook her head. "I guess nothing can be done about it if you don't know. I'll just have to wait until he is done shoveling powder."

"Well, if you have time, I'm done here," said Helheim as he began packing up his photograph machine, folding it into a small luggage case. She was surprised to see that one of the legs of the device detached and he used it as a cane.

She pointed to it. "Where's your stick?"

"At home. I try to look professional when I'm doing pictures," he said, showing her the detached leg on the camera. "I don't have to move much when I'm behind this thing, so often, they never even notice my limp." He nodded up ahead. "We can go and wait for Tannor if you like. Have you ever been up on the wall?"

"No… wait," said Ebele as they began to head off towards the wall. "They let you go up on the wall?"

"Of course, the guards know my father, plus sometimes I go up there to take pictures. When the sun is bright, I don't even need powder to get a good shot."

"How did you get that thing, anyway? I've only seen a handful of photographers in my life and all of them had essence. Is your father an essence user?"

"Yes, the reason I have it is because apparently my father saved some noblewoman and her son sometime back. He was a warrior back then, and the gift he received was this camera. I had taken an interest sometime back and imagine my surprise when he came home with it."

"Wow," said Ebele as she leaned over, looking at the luggage case. "I'm surprised no one has tried to steal it?"

He laughed again. "There has been the rare occasion, but Tannor was there and got them back off."

"How did you two meet? Are you childhood friends?"

"Hardly. Pretty much in the way you just said. I was new to the city and a trio of bullies decided I was an easy target.

They pushed me down and apparently Tannor didn't take too kindly to them picking on a cripple. And Tannor, being Tannor, we fought them off."

"We?" she asked with a smile.

He laughed. "I'll have you know my arms work just fine. And swinging around a big stick, I heard, hurts very much."

"I believe you," she said as they continued towards the wall.

True to his word, the guards smiled when he approached and stood aside, signaling for the elevator to be lifted. And before Ebele knew it, the gate had opened again, and she was fifty feet high, overlooking a wide and vast countryside as the wind blew over her face.

"It's beautiful," she said honestly as she stared over an open field to a sun setting horizon. The meeting of a green and blue line with the orange sun setting slowly off in the distance was a sight she had never gotten to experience before. Usually, she saw the smoke from houses or the movement of farmers and their animals off in the distance when she was home. But here, outside the city walls, there was just a serene feeling that seemed to wash over her.

"Yes," said Helheim, placing down his small luggage container, taking a seat on the walkway. "I find myself coming up here to think about things. It helps a lot when the world becomes a bit too much."

Ebele did the same, sitting beside him, and took a deep breath, embracing the moment. "I know what you mean. Sometimes, you just want to run away."

"Really?" he asked genuinely. "Even noble girls with rifles over their shoulders have problems? I thought your days might be filled with sweet cakes and servants singing your praises"

Ebele smiled and let out a light chuckle. "If only. I'm the daughter of a war hero. That apparently comes with expectations."

"Really? Do you not want to be a rifleman?"

"No, it's not that." She tilted her head back till she was looking directly up at the sky above. "You haven't met my mother."

He laughed. "You haven't met my father. Imagine a great warrior having a cripple for a son. I'm sure it wasn't his ideal plan."

She looked over at him. "You're right. I suppose we have that in common."

"Tell me. What about that rifle you have there? Were you forced to pick it up? I mean, you know... expectations and all that."

"This? No, thankfully, I love rifles. I love the smell of gunpowder." She took her rifle in her arms and ejected a round into her hand, holding it up in front of the sun. "I dream of one day being a better markswoman than my mother." She exhaled. "But at least I have Saro, I can always go to him when, as you said, 'the world becomes just a bit too much.'" She twirled the bullet around in her fingers before passing it to Helheim.

"Who's Saro? Your butler," he said as he held the round up and began examining the casing.

She laughed again. "No, my fiancé. But I'm sure he'd playfully regard himself as my butler for as much as I..." her words froze in her mouth after she realized what she had just said. She turned to him to see him just smile at her.

Helheim just reclined back, lowering his head to the walkway. "I think I remember mentioning that you had one of those. So... Saro. Sounds like a proper name for a proper fellow. I imagine Tannor is going to have a hard time if he expects to steal you away."

Ebele frowned, then just shrugged her shoulders. "You're a trickster. Has anyone ever told you that? I was the one who was supposed to get you to open up to me."

"You succeeded. It's just that here on these walls, you decided to let your walls down. The scenery has a way of doing that to people. They get up here and free their spirits."

"So, it seems."

"And don't worry, I won't tell Tannor. After all, you did say fiancé and not husband, right? And from the many before and after pictures I've taken of couples, I know that a lot can happen from between the wedding and the day you both join in with the fates."

"Sure. But I don't think anything about my fateful day will change. But what about you? Do you have a fateful day ahead of you? A woman waiting for you with cane in hand or a grand dream?"

"Nothing like that yet. But I'm sure I'll find my person and we will both travel the world taking pictures, drifting along the clouds in dirigibles."

She laughed. "Those sky ships they tried working on during the war. I heard those were a failure. Father said they never even managed to get them off the ground."

"I'm sure the same could be said for your rifle when it was first developed. How many explosions and broken fingers were sacrificed before it could be achieved? The same can be said for my camera. When building something new, you must always expect for it to break a few dozen or hundred times."

"Wow, how philosophical. An artist of the mind."

"Not really. I heard a blacksmith say it one time and thought it sounded good. A justification for all broken things," he said as he patted his leg.

"Is that how you see yourself, broken?"

"One thing's for sure," he said with a grunt, as he lifted himself to his feet. "I'm not what most people would consider whole." He held out the round for her to take back.

"Keep it. There's plenty more where that came from. It actually has my family powder in it."

"Your family's powder?"

"Oh, didn't that we own all the mines in Tymit?"

"No. I think I would have remembered something like that," he said, holding his hand out to assist her up. "Come on. It's almost time for Tannor to swap out. We can wait for him down below."

"Seems I forgot to mention that," she said with a smile. "Alright, come on." She accepted the assistance up to her feet and together, they walked over to the elevator and past the guard. The gate opened for them, and with a shout through the tube, it lurched and began to slowly descend back into the shadows.

"You said your father was a hero during the war, right? What was his name? Maybe I've heard of him. And if not me, surely my mother. Perhaps our parents even served together."

"Jacobs, Amber Jacobs. But I wouldn't be too sure of her knowing him. Apparently, he was—" His words were cut off by the sudden stoppage at one of the mid floors of the wall. Helheim lost his footing after the haulting and fell to his side, hitting his shoulder against the side of the cage. "Ah! Damnit," he said, banging his hand against the cage. "Hey, why'd it stop? Sorry, sir, shouted a voice from below. The gears, they jammed. We gotta go get a replacement."

Helheim shook his head, annoyed. "Of course, it has to happen when I'm on it."

Ebele looked ahead but was still in good spirits. "What were you saying about broken things having a purpose?" She pointed ahead into the darkened room. "What's in here?"

"Small barracks and munitions mostly," he said as he reached forward and slid the gate to the side with a sigh. "Come on. There are stairs on the other side. And even though I hate them, we can use them to get down."

"Are you sure? About the stairs, I mean. I don't mind waiting."

"No, but the blacksmith is over on the other side of town and there's no guarantee he will have the part needed. I'd rather not be here until dawn tomorrow." He reached over, grabbing an unlit torch and dipped it into a bucket of powder, before turning back to Ebele and holding it up for her to view. "If you would be so kind."

Understanding his meaning, her eyes glowed as she channeled her essence into the powder that had attached itself to the torch. As it glowed, he swiped it down as it contacted the stone floor, igniting the torch for them.

"You know a lot about essence users?"

"Of course, I've been bumming powder for my flashes for years," said Helheim as they began walking through the darkness. "You learn a few tricks along the way."

"I've actually never ignited a torch like that before. I mean, I knew it could be done, but I suppose I just never had the need."

"It's not so hard. Just strike it where it needs to be struck." He said as they passed by several sleeping cots and muskets that were illuminated by the shadows.

Ebele's lips curled up when she remembered her conversation with Tannor and the stolen muskets. *I guess this might be where he retrieved his.* "Are there any other interesting spots in—" Helheim stopped and began looking around. "What's wrong?"

"Did you hear that?"

"What?"

"I'm not sure, sounded like a click. Did you kick anything?"

"No, I don't think so." *Granted, I wasn't paying much attention... perhaps.* Then there came another click, but this time she heard it. "Okay. What was that?"

They both began looking around till Helheim turned back toward where they came from. "What's that?" he asked, extending the torch forward and squinting his eyes.

"What?" asked Ebele, following his gaze. For a moment, all she saw were the small shimmers of light from the elevator opening. But there, to its left, a flicker? No, a glimmer. Something green, just dim enough to... the realization came too late as she screamed. "Run!"

The next moment was a blur—a flash of light, followed

by a loud crack of thunder echoing in the darkness. The torch fell to the ground as blood splattered across the side of her face. Helheim went falling back. Instinctively, she raised her essence around her as several other shots rang out. Her shields guided the rounds away from her body as they struck the nearby furniture.

She felt her essence drain as each shot was deflected. Diving to her side, she hid behind one of the cots as one of the bullets tore the post above her head into splinters. Covering her face, her heart racing, she removed her rifle from her shoulder, clutching it to her chest. Taking quick breaths, she tried to remember her training. Checking the rounds, making sure they were secure, she pulled out a powder stick from her pocket. It shook in her hand as another shot rang out. But she stayed focused, channeling her essence into it, then loading it beside the rounds.

"*Okay, okay!*" she thought once loaded. *Near the door, left side, barely fifty yards, I think.* Taking a breath and holding it in, she waited until the next shot, before raising herself above the cot, taking a quick aim, and firing where she thought the shots came from. One round, then another to the left, then another even more adjacent. Uncertain due to the darkness and the lack of time to pinpoint her target, she had to assume she was still to the left. And she didn't see any shadow pass over the opening where the elevator was. But she could clearly see the spark where the two bullets hit the wall, so she knew it couldn't have been deflected by any essence.

It was only a second before she turned back around, lowering herself behind the cot again. She was at a disadvantage. The light from the torch gave her position away. What or who was there could see her and she only saw darkness. She felt something cold on her check and, reaching her finger to her face to rub her cheek, she saw the blood across her fingertips. Not hers, but across from her, was the lifeless body of Helheim, face down, the back of his head to her with blood across the stones.

She grit her teeth, fighting back tears despite wanting to wail. Instead, she lowered herself even more and crawled away from the light, merging herself into the nearby shadows. When then, stopping her in her tracks, came a clicking sound. It startled her until she heard tiny beads of something begin hitting the floor.

What's that sound? Is that something to find where I am? Confused, she began crawling forward, more into the darkness, but then came the same sound again of something light, sprinkling over the cold floor. As it happened more and more, it started to sound more familiar. It reminded her of being in the kitchen with the cooks.

Then a different sound came. But this sound she's heard a thousand times. It had a very distinct rattle sound. The metal chamber casing, being ejected from a rifle, clicking on the floor. Then the sound of a metal barrel as it slid on the stone.

That doesn't make any... Then she heard it. It was faint, but there was a muffled sound, as in some shifting. A small scrap as if someone picked something up off the floor, and she realized it was closer to her than she'd wished it to be. *The sounds, they only move when it lands. They're using the sounds to cover their movements.* She wanted to kick herself, and now, she was even more scared, because this whole time, she had been moving with her back to the torchlight, so she really hadn't any clue where he, she, or they could be. Annoyed with herself, she rolled over on her back and began frantically searching for any sign of anything in the darkness.

The sound came again, this time unmistakable—the same one that had reminded her of the kitchen. Except now she could somewhat see something ahead of her, peaking through the shadows. It floated in the air before disappearing and the light sprinkle sound followed. But she did have to wonder much longer as another could flow through the air, just this time in her direction and over her head before landing on everything, including her. Taking some between her fingers and bringing it to her nose. It wasn't long before she realized it was powder that came down raining on her. And with that realization, another came, and it was too late to stop it.

"Ignite," came a soft voice, as out of the shadows came a two green eyes.

Suddenly, the room erupted in small patches of green flames, the pain of which quickly began to burn her skin and clothing where it landed on her.

"Emmm," she moaned as she began squirming and trying to brush the powder off of her. A mistake, as more shots rang out in her direction. It was all she could do to bundle up, bring her knees to her chest and arms over her face and cast her essence in front of her, the sounds of the bullets crashing into the surrounding stone.

The room began to fade back into darkness as the small green flames didn't last long, but the flash of her rifle repeatedly brought white light back, over and over.

She had a strong essence, so she knew she could withstand some shots, but the frequency of his barrage, the bullet pounding against her outer essence, felt as if it was draining her, like small punches to her stomach. She was getting tired. And then it happened. A bullet made its way through, grazing her stomach as she let out a cry.

Her rifle clutched to her chest; she didn't know what to do. And then everything went silent. Freedom, a moment of respite, she wormed her way ahead, still clutching her rifle. Then, shaking, she sat up, her back against the wall, her eyes darting from left to right. Nothing but shadows and a dimming torch light over in the middle of the room. She bit her lip, looking down and seeing the blood leaking from her leg.

Don't think, listen. I can do that. They stopped. There must be a reason. Are they coming closer? Are they reloading? Deep breaths. Listen. I can do that. I am good at that. I can find them. I just need… As if responding to her thoughts, she heard it. A click, slow, low and muffled, but she heard it and knew what it was. The sound of someone emptying a cartridge. And that was all she needed. Her eyes glowing red, she grunted as she stood, aimed, and began firing where the sound came from.

The thunder of her rifle sounded out as she pulled the trigger. One, twice, three times. She would not waste the effort of reloading during their attacks. Consistently, she poured on. It was like her bullets were being eaten by the darkness. She couldn't even see where they hit the wall. Were they there? Was she hitting an upright cot, or a piece of wood? *I know you're there. You have to be. Come on… come… on. Over and over, she fired directly into the same spot.* Then, with another trigger pull, she saw it. A spark on the wall adjacent to where she had fired. Meaning it was deflected and since she didn't hear a ping other than it hitting the wall. That meant what deflected her bullet was someone's shield.

Again firing, same spot, same shot, again… again. And then it happened, movement from the shadows. The person dashed to the left. Her rifle stayed trained on them. Pulling the trigger and letting loose the thunder, she sent the person stumbling back. Fueled by adrenaline. She tried again, only to hear the sound of a click. No thunder, only the muffling of a figure in the shadows and her own footsteps.

Shit, she thought as she cursed the fact that she hadn't brought extra bullets with her. She had dressed for seduction, not combat. *What do I do? Should I run? Run where? I don't even know where the exit is. Helheim is the only… Helheim.* Instantly, she remembered the bullet she had given him. She turned around and saw its metal shell shining next to the torch. Dashing for it, she landed on the ground beside him, sliding along the floor, and grabbing it. She then lifted the chamber just enough to slide the bullet into place and slammed it back down inside. Crouched on her knee, she swung around to take aim at the shadows again, only to see and figure leaping at her from out of the shadows. She could see their face; it was a woman's face, and it was clear enough to aim for.

Their hand outstretched, she aimed right between their eyes and fired. It felt as if the world was in slow motion. The moment she pulled the trigger, there was a flash. The rifle kicked against her shoulder as she grit her teeth and the bullet let loose, flying through the air to thread the needle between her fingers and hit right between the eyes. That is what she expected to happen, but instead, the bullet stopped in midair for only a moment before the woman squeezed her hands over it, catching it in her fist.

The shock of what happened didn't even have time to register before the woman was on top of her, her head pinned to the floor as the stock of her own mother's rifle was pressed against her throat. She wormed under the weight of the woman who mounted her. Her hands on the rifle, trying to breathe. But even with her enhanced strength, the woman atop her was stronger, and she, having been exhausted from using her essence to protect from the hail of bullets before, was fading.

"Time to die, war princess," said the woman atop her.

Coughing, blood leaking from the side of her mouth. The world started to grow dark as the rifle slowly pressed deeper and her breath was taken away. The woman's face began to blend into the darkness as the shadow behind her began to grow. Larger and larger and then it twitched and suddenly Ebele found herself gasping, breath by the inches returning to her lungs. Through watery eyes, the world became bright as something metal began to appear clear. But what was surprising was where that metal appeared. Out from the shadows? No, not from the shadows. Through the shadows. Still coughing, the woman atop her eyes were wide and through her throat, Ebele saw a blade protruding towards her.

Now it was the woman who was gasping, her arm shaking before her finger clawed towards her own throat. She gave one final gasp, before falling over as Ebele saw a blood faced cripple stand over her.

"Are you... are you alright?" came his voice, hoarse as he reached a hand down towards her. Confused, she accepted it, allowing herself to be brought to her feet, although shakily as she grasped her mother's rifle in her other hand.

"Da... Do..." she tried to speak, but her voice wouldn't come out. Instead, there was only a pain so strong from her throat that it sent her crashing back down to her knees. In fact, just trying to breathe felt as if it was burning her. Helheim reached down under her shoulders, lifting her to her feet again.

"Don't... speak," he said with his own voice, barely audible as he struggled to get down and pick up the torch. Then, placing an arm around her waist, he pointed the torch ahead. "Stairs," was the only work he could shakily muster, and they both hobbled onward into the darkness ahead.

Eventually, they would find a spiral staircase and, given their situation, made it a dangerous endeavor to fall down. He, in front of her, one hand on the wall. She, behind him, one hand on his shoulder, slowly descended the stairs until they reached a door with a large wooden brace. They could see the slivers of sunlight through the wood. A sight Ebele never thought she would be so glad to see. The large wooden brace, on the other hand, wasn't pleasant. She knew if she could summon her strength, that it wouldn't be a problem, but in her current state, it would be impossible. And she watched as Helheim struggled to even make it twitch.

Instead, he lowered himself, placing it under his shoulder and with his legs, he began to lift. His crippled leg shook as his face twisted in pain. Ebele did the same, squatting in front of him, facing each other as they both tried raising the large wooden bar. It lurched upward and then they pushed hard, and finally managed to get it over the supports and the door swung open with them both tumbling out on the ground.

And there in the fresh air and sunlight, surrounded by a gathering crowd, she stared into the eyes of a bloody faced Helheim. The skin of his face was ripped, and she wanted to reach out for him, but the exhaustion finally took control, and her final view of the world was his twisted face before it all went black.

CHAPTER 12

Her eyes stayed closed when she awoke, as she breathed in short breaths. Very conscious not to expand her lungs more that she needed to with something like a yawn. Her stomach felt empty; arms, hands, and fingers exhausted. A thousand tiny needles inside of her lungs. It made her chest feel heavy. In this pained, half-asleep state, she unconsciously began exploring her own body. First a twiddle of the fingers, then a slight shift of her back in the bed. Then a deeper breath. It hurt, everything hurt. *Wha... what's happening? Why do I feel like this?*

She could feel a soft fabric over her body. It was light and cold on her. She moaned as she began to emerge from the drowsiness and into the light as her eyes opened. Blurry at first. There was the person hovering over her, but soon she recognized the face as Aretta. *Why am I so tired?*

"She's awake," said Aretta, a worried look in her eyes,

but still a smile of relief across her face. "Quickly, fetch the Warbird."

"Right away, madam," came the voice of a woman out of sight, followed by the sound of a door opening.

Her eyes surveyed the room they were in. She was back at Mr. Harsetti's, in the room she had acquired from them.

"We were worried about you," said Aretta, turning back to her. "Even Mr. Harsetti's wife. When you were brought in, she went and damn near dragged a doctor out of his home."

That's a surprise. That woman seemed to hate everything about us.

"Oh yes," said Aretta, as if reading her thoughts, or perhaps just her facial expressions. "You should have seen it. Your mother and her were at each other's throats for almost half an hour as they came back with the doctor."

"Hel... he..." she tried to say Helheim, but her voice wouldn't produce the word. The moment she opened her mouth, all she felt was fire. She then shuffled under the blanket, trying to raise herself up.

"It's okay..." said Aretta, placing a hand across her chest to keep her down. "Stay still. We removed your clothing so you could breathe better. And the doctor said you'd need a few days' rest."

Questions... how did we get back here? The assassins... were there anymore?

Suddenly the door swung open, and on the floor came several hard steps before her mother came into view. She didn't say anything, she just stared down at her for a moment. But Ebele could tell. Her Mother was angry. Her eyes were cold and watery. It was as if her mother was examining and carefully deciding what to say.

An unseettling feeling in the pit of her stomach, the anxiety wouldn't let her stand the atmosphere for long. So, she opened her mouth to try to explain again.

"I..."

"Silence," said her mother in a curt tone that implied no

arguments. She then lifted the sheets a bit and clasped one of her hands by the wrist, bringing it out from under the cover and laid it across her chest. "That hand is your words now and it can only speak two words: yes and no. You will display one finger for yes and two fingers for no. Do you understand?"

Her hand twitched shakily, whether from the trauma of the time before or of the fear of her mother, she wasn't sure. But with a little effort, she displayed one finger.

"Good," said her mother. "Now, did you purposely seek out those assassins without informing me?"

She displayed two fingers.

"So, it was purely a coincidence that you found them?"

One finger. *There was no 'them.' Only one, I think.*

Her mother sighed. "Good. I needed to make sure my daughter had better sense than that." She then reached over and pulled out a chair and took a seat before rubbing at her temples as if trying to relieve a large amount of frustration. "Fine. Next, there was a boy with a bullet wound in his mouth. They found you on top of him. He's still alive. Is he an enemy?"

Ebele's eyes went wide. As her finger twitched to display two shaky fingers.

"That's fine. Then tell me. Did you kill the assassin that was found in the crew quarters of the wall?"

Again, two fingers. As the thoughts of battle began to flood back into her mind, including the point where a blade pierced through the front of the assassin's neck.

"So, the boy killed her."

One finger.

"Now that's interesting," said her mother as she rubbed the side of her chin with her thumb and crossed her legs. "I would love to know what happened. But unfortunately, none of you are in any shape to speak. You with your throat halfway crushed and him with the side of his face almost blown off." She then stood. "But if he's no danger to you, I suppose it's fine to leave him there." She turned to the door. "Aretta, grab my rifle and meet me downstairs in a few minutes. We're going to examine the body of that assassin now that I know my daughter is safe."

Ebele watched as Aretta grimaced as she heard the door close.

"You know," said Aretta. "I had hoped you'd come back in better condition than you did. Following your mother around has been a pain in my ass."

Ebele rolled her eyes with a tilt of the head in hopes that she'd understand the gestures as a silent way of saying. "I know." But then came the sound of the door opening again, as she heard the sound of heels until she saw Mrs. Harsetti appear, holding a vial in her hand.

"Well, look at you two," said the woman. "And here I remember us having a conversation about the similarities between you and your mother. And it seems I was right, both of you are notoriously good and finding your way into mischief." She took a seat and raised a hand to her bedside while her lips trembled a bit as she tried to hide her emotion. "But... I did ask you to do something about those assassins. And... well. It appears you did. You and that lad. So... I've come to show my gratitude. I've brought some honey and herbs for you. It's a specific recipe my mother taught me, and I use it on my children, for when they have a sore throat. Seems to clear them up in a day or so, and I assume it might help with your affliction."

I'll take anything if it stops this burning in my throat. I wish I could ask what they did with Helheim. She closed her eyes and nodded. *But it's good as long as mother knows he's not an enemy. I shudder to think what she would have done if she thought he was working with the assassins.*

"Good," said Mrs. Harsetti, seeing Ebele nod her head before standing back up. Again, she tapped Ebele on the arm in an attempt to comfort her. "When you both are better, perhaps we can discuss more about preventing you from absorbing your mother's barbarous ways. And the children… they… they would like to see you well also." And with those words, she walked out of a sigh, the sound of the door closing behind her.

"I really don't think I will ever understand nobles," said Aretta as she picked up one of the vails and began inspecting it. "If she's worried, why can't she just say that?" She then uncorked it, placing it just beneath her nose to have a sniff. "Yes," she said while committing to a series of sharp blinks. "I can definitely tell it has honey in it. What other stuff it's mixed with, that… I'm not so sure." She then looked back at Ebele, holding it up for her, having it dangle from her fingers. "Your choice. You willing to risk it? One finger for yes, two fingers for no," she said with a smile.

Ebele stared at the vial for a moment. *If it will help with my throat, I'll try anything.* So, she gave a nod and Aretta smiled back at her before bringing the vial to her lips. Ebele opened her mouth and let contents slide in over her tongue. She knew she would only be able to manage one swallow, so she took in as much as she could and gulped it down her sore throat. Her body shook, and the taste was definitely honey, but also tart and greasy.

Then she felt it. The burning in her throat began getting hotter, and she could feel her body wanting to cough it back up. She tried fighting it, but the heat; it grew hotter and stronger the more she resisted. Until it was finally too much, and she began coughing uncontrollably, forcing her to sit up in the bed. Her hand flew to her chest, patting it as if she could push the fire out of her throat.

"Wait… don't," said Aretta before letting out a sigh. "Well, you're up now." She then began rubbing Ebele's back as she handed another vial of water. "Drink this."

Eagerly, she took another vial and began to gulp it down; the water leaking from the side of her mouth down her chin onto her stomach as she hurriedly swallowed. It was cold, and for the moment soothed the fire in her chest. But now, sitting up with her back against the headboard of the bed, she was able to see the rest of the room, albeit through water eyes, from the fit of coughing.

As it began to clear, she could see her mother's rifle leaning against the wall. She could also see herself in the mirror at the other end of the room. She was a mess, her hair tangled as she sat up topless in bed. She turned again to the other side of the room, and there she saw a lone chair in the corner. There was a person in it. She blinked at the sight, a little confused, before realizing it was Helheim. He had been gagged and his hands and feet were bound to the chair he was sitting in. But more than that, he was awake, and his eyes were intently staring at her.

Suddenly self-conscious, she tried to contain the last bit of coughing as she gripped the sheets and brought them up enough to cover her breasts.

"Well, I did say that I tried," said Aretta as she took the vial. "Are you okay now?"

Ebele turned to her with a nod of her head as she tried to blink away the water from her eyes from all the coughing and choking.

"Okay then. Well, your mother said I should untie him. Are you okay with that?"

Again, another nod from Ebele.

"Alright," said Aretta as she stood up and walked over to Helheim and began undoing his restraints. When freed, she went to undo the bandage over his mouth, but he turned away from her when she tried. "I'll just leave those on then. But when the maids come, you will have to have that cleaned."

He closed his eyes and nodded.

"So… I guess I will just leave you two be then," said Aretta and she walked over, picking up Neekay's rifle from the side of the wall. "Do try to rest."

Ebele watched as Aretta left the room, the door shutting behind her. Helheim sat in the chair for a moment, his eyes fixated on her. She could see his fingers clenching and unclenching as if he was trying to get a feel for his body again. Then, with a grunt through his bandages, he lifted himself up on wobbly legs. She could see the effort it took, hearing the wheezing of his breath under on the cloth. All the while, his eyes never leaving hers.

Is he angry at me... does he blame me for what happened to him? Is it my fault? Her mind went back to her struggles in the darkness of the wall. Him, lying lifeless on the floor, blood oozing from his face. She felt as if she would throw up. Just the thought of it made her senses recall the smell of the assassin's blood that splattered on her face as he pierced her throat. It's disgusting irony taste on her lips. Like a hot liquid metal. The feeling of powerlessness as the assassin mounted her, pushing her own mother's rifle into her throat.

Helheim took a step forward, his body shaking as she did so. Then, with a deep breath, he dragged his crippled leg forward and tried to place his weight on it only to collapse to the floor.

Forgetting her modesty, Ebele moaned with concern as she dropped her sheets, reaching out for him. But he lifted a hand, as if to say 'he was okay.' On his knees, he dragged himself to the bedpost and pulled himself up, the strain clear on his face as arms shook. Even then, he kept his eyes locked on hers, staring so intensely she thought he was peering into her soul.

With his hand on the bedsheets, he lifted himself onto the mattress and reached out towards her face. Feeling guilty and confused, she closed her eyes, not knowing what to expect. To her surprise, he gently pulled her head forward, pressing it against his chest. Atop her head, a bandaged mouth pressed against her hair. Slowly, he began to stroke the back of her head, trying to comfort her.

Ebele was confused at first by the gesture. *Why? Isn't he mad at me? He should... he should be mad at me. It's my fault.*

First a cripple and now his face. He wasn't a bad-looking boy. If it wasn't for me... then... then. Suddenly, the feeling and guilt began to well up inside her. The compassion he showed, even when she felt unworthy. It was almost too much to bear.

It was as if something inside her was about to break. Her arms found their way around him, gripping the back of his shirt as her eyes filled with tears once more. Silent cries escaped her lips, stirred by the memories of a horrific night and the gratefulness of having survived.

***

Aretta had left the room and headed down the stairs with the rifle over her shoulder. "There you are," said the Warbird upon noticing her, then adjusted her coat for the cold weather. "I was wondering how long you would take."

"You asked that I untie the boy," said Aretta as she stepped beside the woman. "Are you sure it's okay just to leave them in a room alone together?"

She laughed. "They both can't talk and have just gone through something very traumatic. They will need someone they can relate to. And I hardly think either of them is in a good place physically to get involved in any kind of bedroom mischief. So, I shall trust my daughter's judgment on the company she keeps."

"Wait..." said Aretta as she followed Neekay out into the cold. "I remember her saying something about—"

"Well, what do we have here?" said the Warbird as she approached the gate and saw a young man arguing with one of the guards.

"Please, can you at least tell me if they are in there?" said the boy.

"Young man, for the last time. You must remove yourself from the gate or else we will remove you."

"Oh, don't be so rude," she said, walking towards him

with interest. "What's your name, boy?"

"Tannor, Miss. My name is Tannor"

"Hello, Tannor. My name is Neekay. And you're here to see someone?"

"Yes. I'm here for Ebele...," his words paused as he noticed what Aretta was holding. "That's her mother's rifle. Are you her mother?"

She smiled as she unlatched the gate and stepped outside to meet Tannor, standing in front of him. "Well, now. You say you're looking for my daughter?"

"Yes ma'am. I know I may not be able to see her. But it will be enough just to know that she is okay. And anything about the cripple she was with, I'd be very appreciative. They're both friends of mine."

I already feel sorry for him, thought Aretta as she watched the Warbird examine the boy. It was the same look she had given her before she found herself as her attendant.

"Then rest assured, young man. Both my daughter and your friend are resting well inside that manor. After they have both healed somewhat, I'm sure they will be happy to see you."

"Thank you," said Tannor as he exhaled a sigh of relief. "Will you tell her that I came to visit?"

"Of course," she replied with a smile. "But we're actually on our way to pick up a few things for them, and you seem like a strapping young man."

And here it comes.

"Would it be too much of a bother to ask that you accompany us for a while? Perhaps even help us with the heavier objects."

"No ma'am, that'd be fine. I'd be happy to help."

"Good, come along with us then. We have a few stops to make along the way. And you can tell us how you met my daughter."

While Tannor explained the story of their meeting, they headed into the city. More than before, it seemed as if the snow was growing thicker by the day. A white blank was slowly beginning to cover the city, and Aretta was starting to feel the chill in her fingers.

Soon they arrived at the Magistrate's office, and Neekay led them up the steps.

"I thought you were going shopping," said Tannor, looking around. "Is it okay for me to come with you here?"

"Of course," said Neekay. "This is one of the places where I shall need you." She then turned to the guard. "The Warbird, to see the magistrate."

"Yes, ma'am," said one of the guards, before turning to push the door to open and beckoning for them to follow. Upon entering the main hall, they saw the magistrate in one of the main rooms with a few other nobles conversing.

"I shall inform the magistrate you here. His meetings just started, but I'm sure—"

"Oh, no need," said Neekay, taking the rifle from Aretta and handing it to Tannor. "Both of you follow me."

Both Aretta and Tannor looked confused but followed behind the Warbird as she stepped around the main hall and opened the door to the other room.

"Hello there, ladies and gentlemen. I do hope I'm not interrupting your morning meal," said Neekay, as she barged into the room. She then took an opportunity to take in all the faces of the people sitting at the table with their food spread out in front of them.

"Warbird," said the magistrate. "We were just in the middle of something. I'd ask you to wait outside and I'll be with you shortly."

"Warbird?" said one of the people in the room. "You mean she really was in the city?"

"Oh," said Neekay. "Yes, I suppose you all are deeply involved in city business." She then reached down, grabbing a piece of fruit, placing it between her lips. She then continued to walk past several of them until she was at the opposite end of the table from the magistrate where a noblewoman sat. Neekay then placed a hand on the seat and began staring down at the woman.

"Oh... ah... yes," said the woman. "I'm sure I wouldn't mind coming back later. Please, have a seat."

"Thank you," she said with a smile as she sat down in the chair and began staring at the magistrate.

Aretta could see the magistrate's tongue moving around between his cheeks as his lip turned into a snarl. "Everyone out. It seems the Warbird has some pressing business she wishes to share with me."

The squeaking of chairs sliding across the floor sounded in unison as the nobles of the city lifted out from their seats and exited the room.

"Are you satisfied?" asked the Magistrate, glowering up at her. "You wish to undermine my authority in such a petty display?"

"Not so much a display of power. Why would I covet yours when I have my own? I merely seek an audience with you and for a matter that I think you would much prefer to keep secret," she said as she reached into her bosom and pulled out the vial of green powder and tossed it into the magistrate, who caught it in his hand.

"Where'd you get this?"

"Does it really matter?" asked Neekay with a dismissive wave of the hand. "What I want to know is why didn't you inform me about it when I first entered the city?"

"Why would I? It has nothing to do with those assassins in the city."

"Really? So, you mean that the fact that every noble that was hunted down was also a researcher on the king's secret project has nothing to do with assassins? Calm me foolish, but that does seem a little shortsighted to me."

The magistrate began to run his hand over his mouth in contemplation.

"And now you're wondering just how much I know, aren't you?" said Neekay, placing an elbow on the table and resting chin on her thumb as a finger ran over her lips. "How we play a game to see just how much I know." She gestured the other hand towards Tannor. "Tannor, if you would be so kind. Point my rifle at the magistrate's head."

Tannor's eyes went wide as he looked at the Warbird confused.

"What? Now see here…" said the Magistrate, slamming his hands on the stable as he stood up. "I will not suffer any more of your indignations. War Hero not, this is—"

"Tannor if you would please."

The magistrate pointed a finger at Tannor. "Boy, if you so dare."

"That man is one of the many reasons why my daughter and your friend are in the condition that they are in."

Tannor's eyes went back and forth between the magistrate and the Warbird before his face turned into what seemed to be something resembling a painful expression, as if someone had pinched him at his side. Then with reluctance, he raised the rifle, pointing it at the Magistrate. "I'm sorry, sir."

"Not as sorry as you will be. Guards!" He yelled, and the door swung open with two guards entering. "Arrest that boy."

The guards looked at each other, confused.

"Do not touch that boy," said the Warbird, her eyes staring to glow a light red and in response out of the end of her barrel and chamber began leaking out a small red mist. "If you do, I swear on my name that I murder everyone in this building. Every guard and noble that I set eyes upon."

Now it was the guards that began looking between the Warbird and the Magistrate, their faces, not making the same painful expression that Tannor made, but they had in fact chosen not to move anymore.

The magistrate turned back to the Warbird. "You think you can—"

"The game continues, Magistrate. I'm sure your guards

have heard about what I can really do when I'm motivated. So now, I'll have you answer my questions. You answer truly, you live. You lie to me, you die."

While the words were terrifying, they did nothing when compared to the visage of seeing the glowie-eyed warbird now leaning over the front of the table, arms stretched out gripped at either side, while she had a smile so big that she could see the woman's fangs. To Aretta, she now seemed more demonic than any night terror she'd ever heard of as a child.

"You see, Magistrate. There is this trick those blessed with a large amount of essence can do. With enough essence, I can ignite the cartridge in the chamber without even having to pull the trigger myself." As she said this, her eyes glowed brighter and more of a pink-reddish mist poured out of the barrel of her rifle. "All I need is to think it and your brains will be blown to the other side of the room. And then, perhaps the next magistrate will be more applicable to my needs."

The Magistrate sucked in his cheeks before he looked around the room. Then, with a deep breath, he relaxed and sat back down in his seat.

"Good. Now, tell me. How much of this green powder have you shipped to the capital?"

"Forty Barrels," the last of which was to be transported to the rail yard a half-moon ago, but the cargo was taken."

"How many barrels were taken?"

"Eight."

"And of those in the capital, how many of whom have the power to resonate with the powder?"

The magistrate shook for a moment, surprised by the question. He stared at her for a moment before answering. "No one, besides Lord Harrington."

"Harrington? That old codger? Figured it would have to be him if anyone."

"I take it the king has been looking for those who can

harness the essence."

"Yes. He's been holding tournaments across the kingdom to find those that might be compatible with the new powder."

"The grand cardinal tournament," said the Warbird as she licked her lips. "Fine, the assassins. What link do they have with the powder?"

"I haven't a clue. They could be with some rebel group or from the Oblivion Kingdom. All I know is that they appeared shortly after the barrels were stolen and started slaughtering those that were involved in its production."

Neekay studied the Magistrate as if watching an animal watching its prey before she leaned back in her chair and the glow faded from her eyes. "Fine. I think we're done here. You can lower the weapon now, Tannor."

Tannor's shoulder dropped as he lowered the rifle to his side with a sigh of relief.

Neekay stood from the table and walked over to them as the guards stepped to the side. "Oh, and Magistrate, I'm sure you've heard that my daughter managed to kill one of your assassins two days ago. So together we have killed two. And I'm sure that knowledge must give the nobles of this city a sigh of relief. But let me tell you that if my daughter perishes in this mess you've dragged us into. Then you won't have to worry about the assassins getting to you. Because I will, and no high walls and no guards will save you from me."

CHAPTER 13

Exiting the room with Tannor, they followed behind the Warbird out into the main lobby; the guards staring at them as they walked by.

"You." The Warbird pointed out to one of the guards. "Where are they keeping the body of that assassin?"

"Ah... in the morgue near... the prison cells beneath us."

"Good, then we shouldn't have to travel far then," she said as she reached over and took her rifle back from Tannor and handed it back to Aretta. "You can go. I shall tell my daughter about you when she heals up. She and your other friend will find you in the coming days."

"Ah... yes, ma`am," said Tannor, looking a bit reluctant to go.

"That is, unless you're interested in helping me cut apart a dead body. I could always use another set of steady hands. The blood often makes it a slippery mess."

"No, ma`am," said Tannor. "I'll... I'll be on my way." And with a bow to ladies, he walked out of the building back into the snow, allowing a rush of cold air to drift over Aretta's skin.

"A good boy," she commented, before turning back to the guard. "Escort us to where the body is being kept."

And with a turn from the guard, they both followed him into the back of the magistrate's building and down several flights of steps. The steps squared off in levels, and at each a torch was mounted to the wall. Their footsteps echoed off the walls as they went deeper into the caverns of the magistrate's building.

That boy was the lucky one. I'm the one forced to obey this woman's every beck and call. I swear, befriending her daughter was the worst mistake I ever...

"Is everything okay?" asked the Warbird.

"Ma'am?" replied Aretta, confused as she was pulled from her thoughts.

"You seem as if something is troubling your mind."

"Oh... ah, I was just curious why you would need me here, when you were so thoughtful as to send that boy away."

"Simple. His innocent eyes had never seen a dead body before. Whereas you. I'd imagine you've seen your fair share."

Aretta halted for a moment as they reached the door at the base of the stairwell. "How..."

"The eyes, dear. They can tell you a lot. I can tell you've never really killed someone before. Maimed perhaps, but never murder. Unfortunately, it seems that the world hasn't been so kind as to allow you to miss out on the horrors of having a loved one die around you. Do not worry, you're not the first or the last. Always looking for an escape, but never having any place where you can escape to. Many a' war orphan has had those eyes."

Aretta's fist gripped the stock of the rifle tightly. The woman's words felt as if they were burrowing into her and pulling out pieces that she'd kept hidden. And to be laid bare and stripped of it in the middle of a cold stairwell by this uncompromising and just as cold woman was a punishment she no longer wished to suffer.

"Shall we go, madam?" asked the guard, perhaps sensing the uncomfortable mood.

"Yes, lead the way. Come along, girl. You should be glad. Your long-awaited reunion is also ahead of us," said the Warbird as she followed the guard.

Aretta bit down on the inside of her jaw with closed eyes, taking the moment to control herself before stepping down to the bottom floor and following through the door. Ahead, she found herself in a dank prison chamber with iron bars on each side. It was colder here, an arched passageway with wet floors.

"You don't know me as well as you think you do," said Aretta, the frustration building inside of her.

"Don't I?" responded the Warbird. "I always thought I was good at reading people."

"Well, you're wrong. I'm not used to death like you, and there's no way I'd wanna follow you down into some dank cavern with—"

"Sissy! That you?" came a familiar voice from ahead.

Aretta froze, her heart freezing in her chest. Her head darting left and right, searching the dimly lit cavern. "Fro… Frovik?"

"Hey, Sissy, it's me," came the voice. Up ahead Aretta could see a hand waving out from a cell.

Forgetting any of her concerns, Aretta hurried towards the cell bars. She stepped in front of them and could barely make out his face in the darkness. But she was sure it was her brother. "Are you okay? Are they taking care of you?"

Frovik laughed. "I'm in a jail, Sissy. I'm not too sure how much they'd be expected to take care of me. But they keep my leg bandaged. Doc's been coming here once a day to change 'em." He shook his head. "It's not the same for some others, in here."

The guard came closer with the torch and Aretta was able to see her brother's face. He looked well. No sunken in eyes and his clothes were the same he'd been captured in. The leg was bandaged like he'd said, but he looked to be in good spirits with a smile directed at her. But just as quick as she was able to see him, she also saw his eyes go wide as he stumbled back away from her, the fear and confusion clear on his face. He pointed a finger.

"Frovik?" said Aretta, worried.

"Why is she here?"

Instantly, Aretta knew who he meant. "It's... well... it's hard to explain?"

"Then allow me," she said, stepping in beside her. "Your...Sissy, is currently working with me. And after she's done, you and your brother will be free, and all charges dropped."

"Wor... Working?" He said as he leaned against the wall to support his weight. "What'dya mean working. What've you got her doing?"

"Don't you worry about that. Just know that your Sissy has been doing a wonderful job as my attendant." She stepped behind Aretta and placed her hands on the girls' shoulders with a smile. I've even come to think of her as something of a daughter in the short time we've been together."

"Ain't no way that's true," said Frovik. "No, Sissy, that woman ain't mean you no good."

The Warbird tossed her hand up beside her face and shook her head. "Why must everyone see me as the villain?" She sighed. "I guess we should continue on my guard. There is still a dead body that needs to be cut into."

"Ah... yes, ma`am," said the guard as he walked off, with the Warbird trailing behind.

"Sissy, look," said Frovik in a whisper before stumbling back to the iron bars. "You can't trust that woman. You gotta get outta the city."

"The city's on lockdown, Frovik. You know that. And I haven't found Drogal, yet."

"What. Why not... you think he's—"

"No, I just haven't been able to search for him. I've been wrapped up with that woman, her daughter, and those damned assassins in the city."

"Assassins? What they got to do with you?"

"Not me. Her. She's the one who's been hunting them?"

"What! And you're still hanging around her? Sissy, come on. You're smarter than that. You know this can only end badly for you, right? That's why we always moved on, remember? You know, never too long in one place."

"You think I don't know that? What am I supposed to do? Just let them hang you?"

"Better me than all three of us winding up dead on someone's noose."

"Girl," called the Warbird. "Come along."

"I gotta go. Look, I will be back for you as soon as I find Drogal, okay?" said Aretta before leaving the bars and heading towards them, her brother's whispering words of concern lofting over her ears.

"Sissy. Sisssssssy!"

"Oh," The Warbird asked, pointing a finger towards an adjacent cell. "What did they do?"

"Not too sure," said the guard. "Heard they caused some sort of ruckus in the town square a week or so back."

Aretta caught them, looking into the cell the Warbird had noticed and saw three young men shackled against wooden boards inside their cells. The light from the torch stirred one of them and his chains creaked as he tried shifting his weight. Instantly, she was grateful that Frovik was not in such a position.

"Through here," said the guard as he opened up another door.

Following them into the room, the smell of bile and rot accosted her nose. It wasn't so strong as to turn her stomach, but she did cover her nose with her hand.

"Here you are, child," said the Warbird, handing her a scarf.

Gratefully, she took it as she stepped ahead and saw the body of a woman lying down on the table.

The guard went around the room and began lighting torches at each corner. The body was injured with markings, but she didn't see any cuts outside of the wound at the woman's throat.

The Warbird unsheathed a blade, twirling it in her fingers before she placed it back at her side. Aretta was surprised as she didn't even see her unsheathe the blade or knew she had it on her.

"It seems she really is dead," she said, before gesturing to the guard. "You can leave us now. I'd prefer to be left alone with my ward."

"Yes, ma'am," said the guard. "There is an exit up ahead that will take you out to the courtyard." He then opened a forward door into another cavern area where she could see sunlight at the end before the door closed.

Afterward, The Warbird continued to examine the body, running her finger over the bruise marks. Then specifically on a large mark near the collarbone.

"What did you mean by 'she's really dead?' Did you think she wouldn't be?" asked Aretta, standing beside her, but still covering her face with the scarf.

The Warbird raised a brow. "Are you curious about the assassin? Well, let's just say in special cases. Sometimes dead doesn't mean fully dead."

Her words brought back the series of events in the alley with the other assassins. "You mean, like with you. I mean... I saw them... they stabbed you. You never said how you survived it. You didn't even need stitches." Then she remembered what the assassin had said before vanishing. "They called you one of them. What did he mean by that?"

"I'm curious about that myself. Since there aren't

supposed to be any more of me."

"Huh? What's that supposed... that doesn't answer my question."

"No, it doesn't," said the Warbird as she picked up the dead woman's hand and showed it to her. "What does this look like to you?"

Aretta stared at the palm of the assassin's hand. The flesh at the center and around the fingers were bruised as if they had been rubbed raw. "Why's it like that?"

"It seems our assassin was very skilled. Not many could focus their essence so much to slow the bullet down and catch it. She must have been desperate." She smiled. But not her usual mischievous smile. This smile seemed warmer and softer. "And my daughter drove her to it. Must have been mighty close, where she couldn't risk her essence not holding or deflecting it."

Okay, fine. She won't answer questions about herself. Then I just need to ask different questions. And I think I know just what to ask. "Ebele, do you think she's really going to be okay?"

"My daughter will be fine. A little bruising is a small price to pay for this kind of work," she said as she rolled dead body over and began checking the entry wound on its neck. "Clean and severed the spine."

"But she doesn't heal like you did in the alley. How long till you think she'll be, okay?"

"Perhaps a day or two. Which is good. She should understand what her limits are. I'm sure she'll be up and moving soon. You and her two young male friends will assist her while I finish this mess with the assassins."

"I... I don't understand you. Are you not scared?"

"Scared of what? A dead body? I hardly think—"

"No," said Aretta in frustration. "Don't pretend as if I'm the weird one here. I mean, of all the assassins, blades, and rifles around every corner. How are you always so calm? Does being some great war hero erase fear from your heart?" She found herself yelling the last part, her words bouncing off the walls. She clenched her fist, staring down at the floor.

Neekay turned to look at Aretta before sighing and lifting herself up on the table with the dead body and crossing her legs as she placed her hand on the dead woman's hip, patting it. "It seems my daughter's situation has you more tense than I expected. But fine, since you seem so insistent, I'll answer your question. In war they teach you there's only two ways to be in battle, live in constant fear, which keeps you on edge and can lead to fatal mistakes. Or you can bury that fear and cope with it later in private—often with a bottle of wine or with a lover's arms around you. Preferably both."

Aware of how she must look after a moment of silence with Warbird staring at her, she then turned away; her head directed at the floor. "I'm... I'm sorry, I shouldn't have yelled. It's not my place to question you."

"Oh, and now you're back to being timid and submissive. You really know how to run the gambit on personalities. My poor daughter must be at her wits' end with you," said the Warbird before placing a finger to her lip in mock thought. "Although she does enjoy complicated puzzles. Another trait she must have gotten from her father."

Aretta sucked in her lip, clenching the clothing at her side, not saying anything.

The Warbird lowered herself back down to the floor, allowing the body to fall back flat on the table. "Goodness, I wonder if I was like this as a child." She then stepped towards the exit. "Come along, girl."

"Ma`am... I thought you wanted to examine the body?"

"I did, and I have a pretty good idea of what happened. There're a few questions left, but I won't find those answer here."

Holding the door open for her, Aretta stepped over into the next cavern. The air was fresher here, leading outside.

"Why have a tunnel here?"

"Purely for appearances. When people watch a body go

into a house, they might want to follow. You watch a body going down a dark cavern, where you'd need a torch to guide you, then they'll be less likely to enter.

"Why would someone chase a dead body?" asked Aretta as she reached the steps that lead above ground. "I don't understand."

"If you ever meet the mortician, then I'm sure he'd be happy to answer.

Aretta stepped outside into the sidelight with squinted eyes. The fresh air was very much appreciated as she found herself in a court square with trimmed hedge bushes and a fountain in the middle. Ahead, she could see guards standing by a gate that led to the outside.

There was some confusion as, through the gate, they could see a large amount of people moving in a hurry.

"Well, that's odd," said the Warbird tilting her head in curiosity.

"What's happening?" asked Aretta to one of the guards as she stepped towards the gate. The guards shrugged their shoulders. Then, spotting a child, Aretta reached out to her, grabbing her by the arm. "Child, why is everyone in such a hurry?"

"Don't know? They say something exciting is happening in the town square. Some think maybe it's the assassins. They could've been caught." Confused, Aretta turned back to her. "Should we go and see?"

"I suppose we'll have to," she said, turning to the guard. "Let us out."

"Yes, ma'am."

The gate opened, and they both began following the crowd. Through the streets, they both went until they finally reached the town square. And there Aretta saw a horrible sight. Both the town guard commander and his lieutenant went strung up by their necks and hung from a tower.

"How?" asked Aretta. "I mean, we just saw him."

The Warbird took a deep breath. "I see that I have

forgotten one of the key rules I learned during the war."

"What?" asked Aretta. "What are you talking about? What rule?"

The Warbird's eyes lowered as she stared at the old man. "Never make friends."

The soldiers that had followed the crowd stood beneath their fallen captain and lieutenant, removing their hats and placing them over their chest.

"What's that on his chest? The cuts, the spell out the word 'Slag.' What's that mean?"

"It means traitor," she said, her tone low and harsh. "During the war, it was what the soldiers' called deserters or anyone who defected to the other side."

"What? But why would they carve it on..."

"They meant it as a message... for me."

Suddenly, as if in response to their thoughts. The old man began to convulse as he coughed up blood.

"Don't just stand there," screamed the Warbird to the soldiers as she stepped forward and began slapping them on the chest. "Cut him down before he's hung."

***

Hours later, Aretta and the Warbird were at the home of the commander sitting on a couch. They were there for some hours before the doctor opened the door and stepped out.

"He's awake and can speak but will need to rest soon." He looked around the room before his eyes locked on to the Warbird. "I'm assuming you're the War Hero. He'd like to speak with you."

Aretta was sitting next to her when she felt a pat on the back, signaling for her to stand as well. With the Warbird's rifle clutched to her chest, they both headed into the room where she saw the old commander lying in bed, looking at the ceiling with bandages covering his chest.

"There you are," he said with a hoarse voice as they came and stood at his bedside.

"Seems you're quite the hard man to kill after all," said the Warbird, a smile across her lips.

He chuckled, a small cough covering his laugh. "Despite my best efforts. Here I lay." He said this as sadness took over his eyes. "My lieutenant, I'm told he did fair as well."

"No...," she responded with a sigh. "He's gone."

"Doesn't seem quite right. Old man keeps living, while the young'uns being the one put in the ground."

"I think we both have lived long enough to know isn't anything fair or right about this world. And death doesn't care about what's fair. It comes just as easy as the wind blows and just changes direction just about the same."

With a sigh, the old man nodded. "That daughter of yours. Heard about her run in with the assassin. Must be proud. Seems she takes after her mother."

"I don't think that's a good thing," she replied, shaking her head. "Tell me, how'd it happen? Did the assassin find you or—?"

"We found them. After you and your daughter and that cripple, we couldn't let you keep making us look bad. Thought after the two you found, figured was only one more. Never got reports of more than two when they'd strike. Turns out there were five of them. Weren't prepared for three and them bringing down a building on my men wasn't planned either."

"So, three left?"

"Aye... three."

"And they look like? Three men, all dark hair. Thanks to the lieutenant, one has a gnash on his cheek and the bastard's missing an eye." He glanced at her. "They can't heal from that, can they?"

"No. He shouldn't be able to."

He shook his head. "The town's guards. Out done by two women and a cripple. A shame I'll never live down."

"Well, to be fair. I never had a building dropped on my head. Seems fairly reckless if you ask me."

The man shook his head before staring back up at the ceiling. "Maybe so."

The Warbird patted him on his arm. "I'll leave you to rest, commander."

"Wait," he said, nodding to his rifle at the side of his bed. "I couldn't help but notice that your daughter had that rifle she's holding there when they found her after her run in with those assassins. Take mine. It seems I won't be much use for a while."

She picked up the rifle and gave it a look over. "It's a beautiful weapon. Is this what you used in the war? Seems fancy for a battlefield."

As the woman talk to the commander, Aretta spotted a set of keys on top of the commanders, set aside uniform. *Is that the prison cell keys?* Unbelieving of her luck, she stepped in beside the Warbird, holding her rifle beside the Commanders. "Why does his look different from yours?"

"It's not so different. They're both bolt action, although I suppose his holds more rounds than mine. What is it, eight?"

"Ten."

"And his reloads from a below, rather than a above."

"His has a lot of pretty designs," said Aretta as she turned, slipping a hand behind her back and pocketing the keys. She'd done this in several homes and knew how to hold them so they wouldn't make a sound.

"That because it's ornate," he said. "Given as a gift after the war. It weakens the wood, but I don't expect your daughter to go around using it as a club."

The Warbird smiled at the joke but lowered it back beside him on the bed. "I think my daughter's done fighting for a while. Best you keep it. You never know, you might be back on your feet faster than you know it." She patted him on the arm. "Be well, commander, let's have a drink when all this is over."

He placed a hand over hers and gave her a sincere nod back.

They both left the house and headed back outside. By then, nightfall was settling in, and darkness was beginning to envelop the city.

"What are you going to do now?" asked Aretta.

"Now? Now I'm tired and I wish to see my daughter, so we will head back."

The feeling of relief in Aretta made her feel as if the world had been lifted from her shoulders. The threatening of the magistrate, the dead body, and the other almost dead body of the commander. She once again began to question her involvement in things. *Frovik may have been right. Maybe I should find* Drogal *and try to get others out of this city.* Her finger rubbed across the key in her pocket. *I just need to find him and get Frovik and maybe get out of the city before this bitch gets us all killed.*

The city seemed so lonely at night. The further they got away from the house, the lonelier the streets felt. In the beginning they passed a few nobles, but as they continued their walk, they appeared even more slowly until eventually it was just the Warbird and her. They walked quietly through the night, the mushing sound of the snow beneath their feet the only thing accompanying them. Even when they passed roads near houses, they all seemed empty.

That was until, up ahead, they saw a long figure standing in the snow as if waiting on them. The person just stood there, but Aretta knew it was something bad. Every fiber of her being was beckoning her to run, but it felt as if she had no other option, or perhaps, she knew that being around this War Hero was the safest place she could be.

The Warbird, on the other hand was as confident as the day they met, never broke her stride until she was only a few yards away from the figure. Up close, she could tell it was a man. He removed his hood and instantly she recognized him as the man who had held a blade to her neck that night. He didn't say anything for a moment, he just stared at the two of them.

"My job is to kill you and your two friends," she said, her voice as calm as ever. "I assume they're nearby."

"They are. And while our job wasn't to kill you. We will take pleasure in your death and those that you love." He pointed a finger at Aretta. "That girl, perhaps. We've been watching. She doesn't seem to have the essence. We could kill her now?"

"Maybe. Or maybe you know that this girl standing beside me is the only thing keeping you alive right now. And seeing as your men haven't taken their shot, it seems they know it too."

"There is another girl that we can attack," said the man with a smile.

"Yes, my daughter. She seems to have had quite the run in with one of you. A woman, apparently. Counting the one that tackled me outside of that burning building, I must say that your group is vaster than I would have assumed. A shame, though, really. I would have liked to have spoken with her. But sadly, there's only so much information you can get from a corpse."

"You're correct. But your daughter, she would do well as a replacement. Trained well. No experience. But we can give her that."

The Warbird was quiet for a moment. "You," she pointed a finger to her own face, pulling on her check a little to expose more of her iris. "I see that you still have both your eyes. That's good. I want to ensure you see it clearly when I put a bullet between them."

The man smiled again. "We will look forward to seeing you soon, Warbird." said the man as he walked off toward the corner of a building. "Because right now, you could say it's the only thing we have left to live for."

And just like that, he disappeared behind one of the

buildings, leaving them both alone in the snow.

They stood there for a moment with Aretta not daring to move until the Warbird did so. Then, after what seemed like forever, she took a step and Aretta followed in behind her.

"Alright, they're gone."

"What was that? Are you really going to fight all three of them?"

"Perhaps. I'll probably need to lure them somewhere."

She adjusted the rifle strap on her shoulder, the man's words replaying in her mind. "Wait—what he said. Is that why you've had me carrying your rifle this whole time? So that they'd think I had essence?"

"They most certainly know that my daughter and I have essence. But you? They're uncertain. And I doubt they'd risk giving away their position for an unknown target. They're careful."

Once again, her mind went back to all the times they were together and how she was made to carry her weapon. Even the time when she was sent off to find Ebele. Aretta stopped in the snow; her mind lost in thought. *She didn't want me to bring Ebele her weapon. She just wanted it to be my protection while I was traveling the city alone. She knew even back then that they might have been watching me. She made it seem as if it was three of them by adding me whenever one of them went out.*

"Are you alright?" asked the Warbird, who had turned around and was now standing in front of her, the falling snow sticking to her hair. "We should get back. There's nothing more we can do tonight."

"Huh?" replied Aretta, being brought back to reality. "Ah, yes. Yes, we should."

And with a pat on her back, Aretta walked beside the Warbird, on the snowy path, heading towards the Harsetti manor.

CHAPTER 14

The next day, the Warbird ordered them to stay inside while she herself went out into the city. Ebele was stuck inside of a room with Helheim. Her mother had told the cripple boy to stay with them now since he was involved in the direct murder of one of the assassins. Aretta assisted the two, noticing that, while not speaking, they had grown fond of each other. So much so in fact that they spent their time now playing a board game that had been left in the room by one of the maids.

The game was to complicated for her, but they would play for hours against each other. So far, as much as she could tell, they had tied each other with two wins a piece. She had no idea what each piece meant; but she could see who was winning by the frustration on the loser's face. When someone moved the big horse-looking piece at the center of the board, it usually meant the game was about to be over.

Aretta watched them for a day. By the next day, she was getting annoyed with being trapped inside. "I think I'll head downstairs for a bit to stretch my legs," she said, getting up from her seat where she watched the two. "Would you like for me to bring you both some water on my way back?"

Although her voice had somewhat begun to resurface, Ebele was cautioned against speaking, except sparingly, to prevent further damage to her throat. So instead, she smiled and raised two fingers back to her, and Helheim did the same. Two fingers meant "No," and these two had grown accustomed to speaking in that manner and apparently had developed other simple hand gestures, which Aretta had no idea what they meant.

"Alright," said Aretta, "you two enjoy your game." And she casually left the room, closing the door behind her. *How is she so carefree after almost getting killed? How can she just smile like that? And that boy, he's just going along with it. You'd think he would be mad. I mean, he was shot in the face. Isn't that something to be mad about?* Aretta shook her head as she continued down the hallway. Inside the pocket of her garments, her fingers rubbed against the cell keys that she stole from the commander's house.

I just need to find Drogal, *and then we can get Frovik out of jail. There has to be another way out of this city, and even if there isn't, if I can just get him out, then that bitch won't be able to use him against me.* Down the stairs, she went to a corner room to glance out a window. The Warbird had requested more guards for Harsetti's home as she went out during the day. But watching the yard routes the day before, Aretta knew the rear of the house wasn't as tightly guarded and a few bribes of sweets to the children gave her the information of an opening in the wall covered by bush.

Taking her time, she headed to the washroom and grabbed a bucket filled with water and loose clothing before heading to the washing line. She passed the rear guards, giving them a friendly greeting as she began to hang the clothing. When out of sight, she stepped over to a bush and, just like the children had said, behind the bush was a hole in the wall. *It's not that big, but I suppose to an eight-year-old it's large enough.* She gripped the side and knelt, trying to slide herself through. While the stone wasn't sharp, it did scratch against her skin and clothing before she was finally able to make it to the other side.

Once out, she followed the road near the wall and headed towards the Dread Quarters. As she traveled, she had the oddest feeling. She missed having the comfort of the rifle strapped across her shoulder. She somehow felt lesser without it. Alone, she was more cautious of those she meant on the street, even those dressed in noble clothing. And in her mind, she was hyperaware to look for anyone who was dawning an eye patch.

Not noticing anyone following her, she continued down to the lower dredges of the city until finally she reached the entrance to the Dread Quarters. *Okay, if he's still in the city, he has to be nearby. I just gotta find out where.* Gathering her courage, she stepped inside. This part of the city had always unsettled her. The city guard's protection didn't extend to this place. But she'd done business here before. She knew most of the locals. And as long as she'd follow the rules, then she figured she'd be fine.

The one thing that stood out to her, though, was the stale smell. *Did it always smell this way?* She asked herself as she stepped into the cave of stacked homes and huts. There weren't many people near the entrance, a few familiar faces, but nothing that she needed to take a strong notice of.

The deeper she went into the Dread Quarters, the darker it became, till the point she felt as if she were walking in a cave. Ahead, she could see a small fire in the middle of the street and adjacent to each side, the light coming from people's homes.

They still keep this thing going. She thought as she

approached the fire, placing out her hand for some warmth.

"Now what brings you this far down into the Dread Quarters?" asked a voice from out of the shadows.

"I've got some business down here, looking for Brushwess. He and I have done some business before."

"Must have been some time ago. I don't remember your face."

"Last time my brothers came. But the guards got'em locked up in their jail. So here I am."

"Alright, so what are ya selling?"

"Information."

"And what are ya wanting in return?

"Just information."

"Alright. Stay your ass by the fire."

A little nervous, her knees shook as she gazed around. She could see others in the windows of their homes, some gazing back out at her and others just simply there, their backs to her. *I just have to find him and ask if he knows where Drogal is. Or if he can find him. I know something that could be useful. It's not like he'll—*

"Sissy..." came a low voice from the darkness. "Sissy... that you?"

"Huh," said Aretta, looking around the darkened area for where the sound came from. The voice called to her again, and she turned her head to what looked to be someone under the porch of a wooden shack. She squinted where she saw an arm reach out. It grabbed the dirt and pulled itself closer until she saw her brother's face. "Drogal? What... what are you doing here?"

"I followed you. What about you? You trying to get a meeting with Brushwess? Have you lost your mind? You know what he's like."

"I came looking for you. Where'd you go? Why haven't I seen you in town?"

"You been walking around with that woman who took you? I couldn't risk getting captured like Frovik. You know, they got him locked up in the magistrate's jail."

"I know... I got the key, we can get'em—"

"Hey," said the voice of the man who had left earlier, now coming back. "He'll see you. Come on?"

"Huh? Oh... ahhh," she stepped back. "I think I was mistaken. I don't think I know anything he'd be interested in."

The man shook his head. "You wanted to see em and now you got it. So, either you come in or we drag you in. And woman or not, us dragging ain't gonna be nice."

Aretta grimaced as she looked around and noticed her brother was gone. But in the other shadowed corners, she could see that several new figures had appeared, and they were more than certainly eyeing her. "Okay, yes." She stepped forward. "I just hope your boss is willing to trade is all. I, ahhh... I heard he gets mad when he doesn't like something."

"Then it's your job to make sure he likes what he hears."

The man held the door open for her as she walked past him, stepping into the light of a building. The inside was large, larger than it appeared in the darkness outside. It wasn't that of a big house, instead it just was a large open area. As if a large box had been hastily created with timber. From the ceiling hung lamps that illuminated the room where fine furniture lay empty and spread out to fill the vast space inside.

And at the center was a man, sitting down on a couch, his head tilted back, and arms stretched out over the shoulders of the couch. Nervously, Aretta's eyes shifted from one end of the room to the other, looking for any dangers. But all but for the man at the center, the room was empty. No guards, no guns, just a single man.

"Come girl. I've heard you have something you wish to ask me and will perhaps rid me of my headache."

"Ahh... yes... Are you Brushwess?"

"What do you think?" he said, keeping his head tilted

back and his eyes closed.

What do I do, what do I say? Should I still ask where my brother is? She began to scratch at her shoulder. *No, if he knows he's right outside, he's going to think I was setting him up for something. He might even know about me going to the magistrate's prison.* "Do you know who I am? My brother, he's had us do some work for you."

"Everyone in this city has worked for me in some form or fashion." He reached up and began pinching the bridge of his nose as he squeezed his eyes.

"Are you okay?"

The man sighed, before finally lowering his head and getting a good look at her. "No. I have a pain in my head that has persisted for months and in front of me stands a woman who has yet to tell me why she is here." He clapped his hand together and out of the corner of the room came two women. One holding a tray of what looked like water and the other holding a vial of black powder.

"I... I want you to help me and my brothers get out of the city."

"The one in prison and the one skulking outside?" He shook his head. "No, either way, there's nothing you have that's worth a prison break. And even if you were to sell that body of yours, I doubt you'd fetch the price for such an escapade." He waved a hand at her. "So, tell me what information you think I might want to know."

"What? I can't, you haven't—"

"The price of you seeing me was the information you thought I wanted. You don't have the coin to afford the help of my men."

"Then what about... do you know about the green powder?" she asked before watching an eyebrow raise.

"It's an experimental powder. The last shipment's been lost, but the stuff might as well be dirt, since no one can even enhance it."

"It's not lost. You have it right? You got it stashed away

somewhere. But since you can't use it, you don't know what to do with it. That's why you gave some to Daylon, knowing if he got caught, he wouldn't have the nerve to rat you out."

"And if what you just said was true, then I'd wager that's dangerous information to have. Some might even say that if someone did wander in here with that information, then I might not be able to let them leave." He waved a finger while shaking his head, then pointed that finger at her. "But you're smarter than that. There's another part to the story that you're not telling."

"Daylon, he's planning to sell it out from under you."

Brushwess laughed, "Ain't no way. No way he's that stupid."

This time, a smile came over her own face. "Then how else can you explain me knowing about the powder and that Daylon is selling it for you? Maybe one I'd know about, but both? Seems strange, don't it? Did he report to you that he might have a buyer? Because he found one days ago."

This time, his face twisted, and she could only imagine the thoughts behind it. But then he brought both hands up to his side and, in a grand motion, brought his hands together in a thunderous clap that sounded throughout the open area. Then she heard the door behind her open.

"You need something, boss?" came a man's voice from behind her.

"Our vegetables. Go and make sure no one's tampered with the barrels."

"The vegetables? Ah... right, I'll go look into that," said the man's voice behind her before she heard the door close again.

"Alright," said Brushwess, gesturing to the seat in front of him. "Take a seat. You're at the table until my man comes back. If he's right, you and your brother outside will be escorted out of the city. Not the one in prison, though. The information you gave ain't worth that."

"What? No, it has to be all three of us?"

"Sorry," he said before snapping his fingers as the women who came out earlier poured the powder in the water. They sat it in front of him after stirring it together. Then one woman's eyes began to turn purple, which in turn made the liquid in the glass begin to sparkle purple in resonance. He then took a swig of the sparkling purple water before wiping his lips with the back of his hand and sighing in relief.

"What? Did you... you can drink that?"

"Damn right I can. It's the only thing that can take the edge off." He licked his lips, before lifting up the half drunken glass as the purples radiance inside began fading back to just regular black powder. "Can't find anyone with enough essence to really give me what I need. But that comes with the territory down here."

His revelation gave Aretta an idea she was hesitant to say. *But I must get all three of us out. I'm not leaving him in some prison to rot.* She thought back to the poor boys in the prison stretched out on the wheel. "What about..." She bit her lip, balling up her fist. "What if I knew someone who was strong enough to enhance that green powder? Would that be worth it? I mean, you've never drank that, right?"

"What? You mean that Warbitch you've been hanging around? I doubt that. The power of a person's essence fails the older they get. For her to be able to—"

"Not her... her daughter. I saw her... I mean, I saw what the green powder can do. She's able to do it."

He studied her face for a while. "Maybe you're right. I heard about that run-in she had with those assassins. The Harsetti's manor's been double and triple guarded since then. Ain't way of getting to her."

"You won't have to. She's my friend. She'll come to you if I ask her to come down here with me."

The door opened once again. "Hey boss. One of the containers, it's empty. Ain't no pow... I mean, ain't no vegetables in it."

This time, Aretta leaned forward and poured herself a cup of the still barely glowing liquid before taking it to her lips and swallowing. She did that as a way to show solidarity with him, but it felt slimy and burned as it went down her throat. But she hid it by tilting her head back and looking as if she was savoring it, while inside, she was trying her best not to puke it back up. And when the moment of bile passed, she exhaled and lifted her head back down to look directly into the eyes of Brushwess. "So... do we have a deal?"

He smiled back at her, his teeth bared for her to see. "Well damn. Who knew your brother had such a woman as a sister?" He extended a hand out to her. "Shits not going to be easy. But I'll help ya get your brother out. Won't be the first time we've done a prison break. First, we gotta get past the guards. I have a few that I pay to watch out for trouble coming my way. I can have'em on guard duty. But that half dead commander, he and the magistrate are the only ones with the keys. We could break the lock, but that's gonna be a lot of noise."

"I have the commander's key," said Aretta, slipping her hand into her pocket and placing the key on the table. "I stole it before coming here."

This time she got to see him looking genuinely surprised as he lowered his hand to pick up the key and began assessing it. "Ohhhh, you little bitch," he said, still smiling. "If I knew you had this much talent, I would have taken you for myself years ago."

"I don't think my brothers would have liked that," she said, extending her hand to have the key returned.

"Yeah, well, they would've been dead," he said, still smiling before looking down and examining her hand, now seeming more interested in her than she'd like.

"You want the Warbird's daughter, right? Then I need to go and get started. And you must get ready to break my brother out."

He glanced down at his drink and then back to her

hand, before he slowly lowered the key back into her palm, then calmly folded her fingers over it and took her hand in his. "Tomorrow, I'll have my men ready. Just make sure you are. We're gonna have some fun."

CHAPTER 15

The following day, Ebele awoke to the feeling of something cold on her forehead. She could feel a drop of water as it slid down the side of her face to the top of her ear. Taking a deep breath, she then exhaled as she opened her eyes to be greeted with the sight of her mother removing a cold, wet towel from her forehead. The scene brought a smile to her lips as she gazed up, realize she was safe and being looked after.

"Well, look who's awake," said Neekay, smiling back at her daughter. "It seems that the fever you had has gone."

She stretched her body a bit, brushing the side of Helheim's arm as she did so. Her eyes glanced at him before turning back to her mother and nodding back at him, confused.

"He's fine. Men tend to sleep more peacefully after spending the night in bed with a beautiful woman."

Ebele rolled her eyes.

"Although who would have thought that your first time in bed with a man would be like this?" asked her mother in a playful tone, lowering the rag into a bucket of water.

Ebele's lips curled, and her eyes glanced slightly away.

"Oh, so you and Saro have already gone that far?" Her mother shook her head. "I'm surprised. I mean, I understand not telling your father, but as your mother, I wish you would have told me. That should have a proud bonding moment for—"

Ebele's eyes went wide as she furiously shook two fingers at her mother, while nodding her head back to Helheim.

"Oh, don't worry about him," said her mother, with that annoying curl on her lips. "I was sure to give the maid instructions to place a double dose of sleep medicine in his tea when she made her final rounds. And to not leave until you both drank it up."

Ebele's mind went back to the previous nights. *So that's why the nurse was so armament about having us drinking the tea medicine. I knew something was off, the way she kept on insisting we finish the entire cup.*

"I trust you, dear, but he is still a young man, after all. And I've found that the mind and the penis often do not work in unison." She nodded to where the boy's crotch was, where a particularly large bulge was appearing in the sheets. "And that particular trait of men somehow being fully away and fully asleep is proof of that." She placed a hand up her chin and gestured over to it. "You know, if you ever wanted to have a look and—"

Ebele threw up two fingers again in front of her mother's eyes, her lips still frowning.

Neekay laughed. "Don't worry. I'm just teasing you. But I am shocked, considering how curious you are about everything else."

I'm not that curious. And he wouldn't do that to me. She thought back to how his eyes were so focused on her when she was topless in bed. *Okay, that's different. It's not as if he was fondling me when I had tears in my eyes and snot coming out my nose.*

"Now, according to our annoyingly selfish host, Mrs. Harsetti, you should be able to try to speak today. Those honey and herbs were meant to lower the swelling in your chest. So, give it a go."

Ebele felt a bit nervous about the prospect of speaking. She hadn't even tried in two days, and since she and Helheim were communicating more or less, she hadn't felt the need to speak and risk the chance of more of the pain and burning. But, seeing her mother's face change to a serious appearance, she didn't feel as if she was going to have much say in the matter.

So, for a test, she swallowed some saliva. It felt sensitive, but it didn't have the stinging sensation from days past. So, with a little hesitance, she took another breath and opened her lips. "Onnnnnee, Twooooooo." She blinked in surprise. It was a little raw, but nowhere near as painful as it had previously been.

"Good," said her as she stood up while grabbing the water bucket. "No need to speak so much. I just needed to know that you could. It seems I owe Mrs. Harsetti some gratitude, I'll be sure to—"

"Ah—sas—sinsssssss," she murmured before her mother could take her leave.

"Oh, don't you worry about them. I've been thinking about how to handle the remaining three. You just rest here, and I'll have this taken care of in a day or two."

As her mother opened the door to leave, she could see the partial figure of a guard standing outside of her door.

Guard? Does she think something's going to happen today? She had only left her room once yesterday to use the facilities which were next door, but she didn't notice any extra guards. Curious, she rolled out of bed, moaning from the stiffness in her body before turning back to ensure she hadn't woken Helheim. Just ever so slightly rising from the covers, she tried her best not to focus on his own stiffness.

Her feet felt a little shaky as she placed her arm on the back of her mother's chair for support. *Damn mother and her sleep medicine.* She closed her eyes while standing on shaking legs, waiting for the prickly feeling to subside before she stepped over to the window. Outside, she could see several guards down below, rifles at their side. *Why? This wasn't needed before... wait, is this because of the one we killed? Of course, they would be angry if we killed one of their own. Have they done something? Tried something here? No? If they'd have tried something yesterday, I would have heard gunfire, yelling... something? Is all this just a precaution then?*

Annoyed, she clenched her fist before turning to look at the door. *Dammit, Mother. What aren't you telling me?* She stepped over to the closet and reached for her coat in case she'd have to catch her mother down the street. She then walked to the door and opened in and stepped out into the hallway.

"Hello ma'am, ready for breakfast?" asked a guard that was by the door. "We can accompany you or have it brought to you—" He paused as she saw her holding her coat. "I'm sorry madam, but the Warbird expressed direction for you to not be allowed to leave the house."

What? That's ridiculous? I won't be— Her own thoughts paused when she saw three other guards posted at her door. *Wait... are they only here? And at my window?* A little confused, she stepped back into her room, allowing the door to close behind her. *I don't like this. I don't like not knowing what's going on. Think... Ebele, think. I was right, this has to be because of the assassin we killed. They must be targeting me. But I didn't see them yesterday. So that means something happened or mother found out something. Wait, she said there were three of them left. Does that mean she's had contact with them? How else would she know?*

She tossed her coat over to a chair by the wall as she

began walking back to the bed and began drumming her fingers over the cushion. *Where's Aretta? She's usually here? Did something happen to her? No... mother would have told... I mean, I think she would have.* She then took her hand and started rubbing her face in frustration. *I don't like this. I don't like not knowing. And now they're trying to lock me in here.* She then looked over to the window. *Am I well enough to jump from here if I have to?*

She closed her eyes and began trying to strengthen her muscles. She could still summon her essence, but she could tell that her body was still recovering, and it was much more difficult to hold onto her power than before. It was as if she was trying to clench her fist, but her hand was half-numb. If her concentration waned for just a moment, she'd lose her grip on it.

There was a knock at the door, then a few seconds later it opened, and she saw a maid come in with a hot plate of breakfast food for her and Helheim.

"Here you are, madam," said the maid as she walked over and placed the food on the table by the window. "Food for you and the young man there." She looked over at him. "For when he wakes up."

Ebele nodded but looked at the cup of tea suspiciously. *Should I try to say something to her?* She thought before raising her hand to stop the maid before she left.

"Yes, madam?"

"Gre... Grechannnnnn."

"Oh, your little friend? I haven't seen her since yesterday when she left. Perhaps that's where your mother's gone, to meet her?"

Ebele's lip began to quiver for a moment, but she held her composure and produced a smile before nodding to the maid to dismiss her and watched as she left the room. *She didn't come back. What? Did something happen to her? If it did, doesn't that mean it's my fault? I'm the one who took a liking to her. I have to do something.* She began pacing the room. *I can't just be locked in her when...*

There was a knock at the door again while Ebele had her back turned towards the wall. She moaned in frustration as she heard the door open. *Can I get a moment to think? I don't need anymore...* Once again, her mind stopped as she saw Aretta closing the door behind her.

"Hey, sorry I wasn't here," said Aretta as she stepped into the room. "I just saw the maid, and she said you were—" Her words were paused as Ebele silently walked over to her and wrapped her arms around her. "Hey, is everything..." Aretta stooped speaking as Ebele clutched at the back of her clothing, her breathing muffling a small whimper.

So glad you're okay. So glad. Ebele repeated the words in her mind as her lips moaned the words into the skin of Aretta's neck. A wave of calmness came over her as she felt the girl's hand softly stroking the back of her head.

"I'm sorry. I should have really come back last night. I ahhh. Well... I found my brother, and we spent the night talking and I sorta lost track of time."

Ebele slowly pulled herself away as she opened her eyes again. The world in front of her was a little blurrier than it was before, and she realized she'd teared up at the sight of Aretta. But the skinship was not unappreciated as Aretta reached out a hand, placing them on her cheeks, rubbing her thumbs underneath her eyes to wipe away the tears.

"After what you've been through, I guess it was kind of selfish of me to not come back and make you worry like that." Aretta then nodded over to the bed. "I just assumed with him here keeping you company that you'd hardly even notice I was gone." She then raised a brow at her. "Are you the reason he's sleeping like a baby over there when it's so late in the morning?"

Ebele playfully slapped her on the shoulder. "Mo... Mo... therrrr..." She pitched her fingers together and tilted her head back, pretending as if she were drinking, then placed her palms together pressing them to her check, imitating going to sleep.

Aretta shook her head. "Goodness. "Your mother really is a piece of work. But I guess I shouldn't be surprised after being around her so much over the past few days. Oh! There was a boy named Tannor, who came to visit a day or two ago. Do you know him?"

Ebele nodded her head.

"Well, your mother found him. And less than an hour later he had her rifle pointed at the Magistrate's head."

Ebele's eyes went wide, and she let out a little moan.

"Yes, exactly. That woman's insane," said Aretta before biting her lip. "Hey, what say you and me go for a walk in the city together? I'm sure the fresh air will be good for your throat."

Ebele shook her head before pointing at the door and then shrugged her shoulders.

"I heard about the guards not letting you leave the grounds." She raised a finger with a smile. "But what if I knew a secret way out? Would you be interested?"

Ebele was skeptical as she considered, but seeing the smile on Aretta's face, she nodded her head.

"Good. Who wants to stay locked up in this stuffy old room all the time, anyway? And walking with you is a lot better than going out with your mother," said Aretta as she stepped over to the table by the window and picked up a piece of sausage from the plate the maid had previously set. "Well, since the smell of food hasn't woken him up, and it'd be a shame to let good food go to waste. How bout we have breakfast then?"

Happily, Ebele sat down at the table for breakfast with Aretta. While not speaking unless necessary, they enjoyed their meal together. Although Ebele mostly just slurped a hashed soup. Over the course of the next hour or so, Ebele was able to teach Aretta a few of the basic hand signs she and Helheim had thought up while in the room together.

Aretta pointed out the window at the hole in the wall

near the bush. "The children told me about it. Behind the second bush, there is a hole we can squeeze through. If you stay here when I leave , you will watch me disappear behind it.

Ebele signaled with her hand. *You're leaving again?* Hoping she understood.

"Don't worry, I'll be back tonight or early tomorrow. My brothers in a bit of a situation and I'm helping him get out of it."

Ebele then stood and walked over to her pouch and pulled out several gold coins, holding them out for her, gesturing for her to take them.

"What, oh, no. It's nothing serious. This is just some light work. I'll probably spend a night working in a kitchen with him and we'll be square. Remember, you found me working as a maid before, right? I'm good at this stuff."

Ebele was still a little concerned, but trusted that Aretta knew what she was doing. *She's spent time in this city before and knows the people here, so I should just let it go.*

"Don't worry," said Aretta, perhaps sensing Ebele's apprehension. "I'll be back before you know it. And besides," she turned to Helheim, who was starting to stir from his slumber. "I guess the smell of the food is finally getting to him. I guess your mother was right. Welp!" she said before standing up from the table and plucking the last piece of sausage from the table and popping it in her mouth. "I hope he doesn't mind waiting a bit longer." She smiled as she headed for the door. "I'll tell the maid to bring up another plate. Remember, be ready when I get back."

And before Ebele had a chance to respond with some type of hand signal, Aretta was gone, with the door closing behind her. *She moves so fast. Wait, Am I really going to sneak out?* A smile came to her lips. *It does sound a little fun. But I don't have a rifle. Mother took hers. I can't leave without a weapon. If I was attacked by those assassins, I'd be as good as dead. No, even if I think it'll be fun and I might run into Tannor again, the practical thing would be to stay safe, maybe even plead with Mother to go out with us when she returns. Even if she seems to be more... well, more of herself than usual.*

There was a knock at the door. Then, a moment later, it opened, and a guard stood ahead.

"Madam, is it okay for me to enter?"

Ebele was a bit cautious as she saw another guard standing behind him. And he was holding what looked to be a large box. But she nodded her consent, and the two guards entered the room.

"Hello," madam said the guard as the other guard walked over and placed the box on the table. "Your mother insisted that she didn't wish for it, but the commander thought that you might find it useful for yourself. So, he leaves it with you. If you also do not require it, then just hand it back to the guards in a day or so and it will be returned."

What? Mother didn't wish... what's in it? thought Ebele as the guard unlatched the clamps holding the box together and lifted the hood, exposing a beautiful blue and gold ornate rifle. *Well, this is quite fortuitous.*

***

After exiting the room. Aretta walked down the hall past the guards, turned towards the stairs where her smile immediately left her face. *Argh... why's she gotta be like that? This is why I left the first time. Well, this time it's too bad for her. She's the key to getting my brother out of prison. She shouldn't be so naive. She knows I tried to rob the stupid lord of this manor and she still keeps looking at me with those same stupid and silly eyes.* She gripped the railing as she scratched at her burning throat in frustration. *Agrh, it's that stupid bitch Warbird's fault. We wouldn't be in this mess if not for her.*

She headed down to the first floor, turning and making her way toward the kitchen.

"Are you alright, m'lady?" asked one of the maids. "You

seem as if something troubles your mind."

"No. I'm fine, thank you," said Aretta, rubbing her face in frustration. "When you have a chance, could you bring another plate to Ebele's room? That boy that she is with, would like seconds for his meal."

"Yes. M'lady, of course."

Aretta then walked back outside into the morning sun. *I didn't get much sleep. But it's fine. And there's a chance I might run into that mother of hers.* She shook her head, trying to rid herself of the reason not to do what she knew she needed to do. *Well, I can't change things now. I'm going to free my brother and she's gonna have to see Brushwess. I mean, it's not like he wants to hurt her. Yes, he's hard to deal with on the best day. But he just wants her for that powder stuff. So, she needs to do her little enhancing thing and then we can get out of the city. She might even come with us. Let her mother rot in this damn city.* Aretta's lips furrowed as she bit down on her lip. *Of course, she's not going to leave her mother. And I bet if I went to her and said we can all escape the city together, she'd still insist on killing those damn assassins. Oh, look at me, I'm the big bad Warbird. Fuck that. Get yourself killed. What kind of woman drags her kid into a mess like this?*

Again, she waited for the guards to disappear around the corner. Then, she stepped over by the bush near the wall. But this time, she turned back and saw Ebele watching her from the window. The sight of her there made Aretta feel as if someone were squeezing her heart. She felt heavy and disgusted with herself. But she made herself smile and wave back at her, before vanishing into the wall and squeezing herself through to the other side.

"Okay," she said to herself while pulling out the commander's key from her pocket. "It's gonna work... it has to." Trying to convince herself, she began making her way through town. Still early in the morning, the streets weren't yet filled with nobles, but it was getting to be around that time. The further she went, the more people she saw leaving their houses. Her heart felt as if it was drumming in her chest the closer she got to her destination. Eventually, her feet would stop in front of a stable where two men were shoveling hay.

"What took you?" asked one of the men when she arrived. "Boss said we gotta get this done fast and done right. Can't have you making mistakes."

"I had my own things to take care of. But I'm here now, so how will we do this?"

The man lifted a corner of the hay onto the wagon, where there was a small compartment drop for her to slide into. "Get in. We'll get you inside. Then on our way out, we replace you with him and walk on out just the way we came in."

Nervously, her leg shook as she looked at the men.

"Look, either you're in or you're out. I ain't standing around waiting—"

"I'm in, okay.... I'm in," she said as she climbed on the wagon and laid down in the hidden compartment and watched as the last pieces of sunlight vanished with the closing of the trapdoor on her. She heard them above as they shifted more hay over the door, and soon she felt the wagon lurch forward. In the darkness, every little noise stood out—the grunting of the men pulling the wagon, the squeaking of the metal beneath her as the wheels creaked and shifted with each bump in the road. *Don't worry, Frovik. I'm coming. And soon we're going to get out of this city.*

The carriage ride was uncomfortable and cramped, but she endured as it made its way through the city. Then, after several turns and random chatter from the world outside, she felt it halt.

"Hey, we've brought this week's supply," said one of the men from earlier.

"Alright, hold on," came the voice of someone who she assumed to be one of the guards. There was a click sound and the sound of metal scraping. "Alright, go on over to the troughs."

The wagon lurched again, and she felt it lumber forward after the man grunted. It wasn't long after that when she heard the sound of hay shifting and the door to the secret compartment opened. She grit her teeth as the sunlight hit her face. She wasn't there long, but the instant change stung at her eyes.

Squinting, she looked around and found herself inside the castle grounds. To her left, high stone walls and to the right, horses that were tied to a small stable.

"Alright," said the man, nodding to a door ahead that lowered into the wall. "Our man inside should have left that open for you. The guards rotate every twenty minutes or so. They'll expect us to be gone before the rotation. We ain't got enough hay to take so long that it don't look suspicious. Now go and bring him back."

Understanding the importance of time, Aretta hopped off the wagon and headed across the ground and down the small stairs towards the door. Pressing her fingers on the wood, she pushed forward. There was a slight resistance at first, but with a squeak, it slowly moved forward, exposing the darkness ahead. And with one final look at her escorts, she turned and disappeared inside, closing the door behind her. Ahead, through the sliver of another door, she could see the shine of the torch that she was told would be waiting for her.

If I had essence, I'd be able to make my own torch. I'd at have something.

Her lungs were still feeling raw, but here she'd do her best to control any coughing fits she might have. So, with gritted teeth and a rub of her throat, she placed her hand on the wall and let it guide her forward into the tunnel. The floor was cold and murky with small puddles that she would never even pay much attention to in any other circumstance.

There were a few squeaks for the rodents that lurked

somewhere nearby. Or at least she thought before she felt something run over her leg, its fur brushing up against her ankle. She instinctively felt the urge to scream, but with her burning throat and the current surrounding, she knew that was not a wise choice.

Come on... come on, don't think about it. Her skin crawling, she stepped closer to the door ahead. Reaching it, she tried peeking through the cracks in the wood. Ahead were the steps that she and the Warbird had come down before. That meant that the door ahead led to the dungeon where Frovik was.

Peaking around as best she could, she didn't hear or see anyone else, so she slid her hand over the door, searching for the handle.

And when she found it, she slowly pulled it open. In the moist air down there, it was impossible for the metal hinges to not squeak, but she was patient and opened it just enough for her to slide through. Once inside the hall, she stepped to the other side and reached for the torch. But before she could reach it, there was another squeak, but this one loud and sharp.

She turned to see a guard, off in the corner, hidden by half shadows. He was asleep in a chair to the side of the stairs. She froze, her fingers just shy of the torch. *What do I do? No one is supposed to be here.* She thought about the knife in her boot. *Even if I did, what would happen when they find him if—.*

The man lurched his head back with a hiccup as a bottle he had in his folded arms fell out and landed on the floor with a sharp clink. The man didn't react at all, and just continued to slumber in his chair.

She took a deep breath and took the torch from its mount and headed in, pushing the door open to the prison. Stepping inside, she closed it behind her. *I refuse to be here any longer than I have to.* "Frovik. You here?" She whispered into the dark. "Frovik."

"Sissy? That you again?"

There was a slight pause in the dark. The sound of movement, a shuffling, and then ahead she saw her brother extend his hand out of the cage. "I'm here."

Quickly, Aretta came over, grabbing her brother by the hand to look in his face. "I'm here to get you out. Here, hold this." She placed the torch in his hand to hold.

"What? No, you'll get in trouble. You can't—"

"Shut up. It's too late, and we don't have much time. So, either you come with me, or we both get stuck here."

Frovik's face had a pained expression as Aretta fiddled with the key. Accepting the situation, he began looking around. "I swear you never listen to us."

"Yeah, well…" she continued, trying to get the key to turn, but it was jamming halfway in the turn. "Come on, you stupid piece of shi—" It finally clicked, and the gate unlatched, becoming loose. She then took back the torch and swung it open.

Once free, they embraced each other, with Frovik grabbing both sides of her face with a smile. "You're the most stubborn girl I've ever met. If we get out of this, I swear I'm naming my first child after you."

She laughed and patted him on the shoulder. "Like any woman would ever willingly touch you."

"That's what the monies for," he said while looking around. "Now, how'll we get out of here?"

"We're going back this way," she said, nodding back the way she came. "I've got some people who'll get you out."

"People? Where's Daylon?"

"He's in the city. Hiding out in the back of Eulon's Tavern. You'll meet him there. Outside, are Brushwess's men. They got a carriage and—"

"Brushwess. Ahh, nahh. Don't tell me you're in bed with him. Remember what happened the last time we did a deal for—"

"I know. Look, alright… I… know." She pressed the

temple of her head against his. "Can we please not argue about this now? When we're out, then we'll talk, okay?"

Frovik sighed. "Alright. You're in charge. So, lead the way."

"Okay, this way," she said, leading him back towards the door and peaking in to make sure the guard was still asleep. Her brother was slow because of his leg. But he bore with the pain, trying not to create much of a sound. "Go straight across the hall to the next tunnel, okay? I'll come behind when you do."

With a nod of his head, he gnashed his teeth and slid in through the door, slowly dragging his leg across the opening. He eyed the half snoring guard in the shadow of the room as he made it to the next door. Sliding through, he entered the tunnel. Once there and inside, he waved for Aretta to come forward.

"Hey, Drebbie!" came a guard's voice from upstairs. "You down there?"

Both Aretta and Froviks eyes went wide.

Aretta quickly found a nearby puddle and soaked the torch in it, extinguishing the flame. Quickly entering the room, she placed it on the mount, then hurried to the door and slid through the opening and as cautiously as she could.

When Frovik went towards the other door. She stopped him and pulled him back. "Wait."

They waited in the darkness, their eyes peeking into the darkness of the door as the footsteps from upstairs echoed off the walls of the room ahead. And with each step, the glow of a torch illuminated the room until the figure holding it finally appeared. It was a guard who, before he even reached the final steps, noticed his coworker sleeping in the corner next to the stairs.

"Get up, you bum," said the guard with the torch as he kicked the other man in the shin.

"Huh, wha," said the sleeping man, being awoken from his slumber. "What's going on? Halt! I'ma...I'ma guard."

"You idiot. What are you doing down here?" asked the guard with the torch as he stepped forward, noticing the door was somewhat open.

Shit, I thought I locked it back. No…. no, please not now.

"Huh? Oh?" replied the guard in his stupor. "What, going on?"

"Why are you down here? You're supposed to be upstairs?"

The half-conscious guard placed his arm over his eyes, trying to avoid the light from the torch. "I… I was just resting. You left, figure. I… you know, watch it for you."

"I see," said the guard as he looked towards the open door suspiciously. Then he walked towards her. And as he did, his foot hit the key, making it slide across the floor, clinking against the wall.

Shit. What do I do?

The guard leaned down, picking up the key and then looked to the open door. He then immediately turned around to the door where Aretta and Frovik were.

If we run, he's gonna hear us. If he comes in here, the torch light will give us away.

Her heart pounded in her chest as the guard stared at the door. It felt as if their eyes were meeting. He closed the door to the prison and locked it, before turning back and stepping towards them. He then turned and kicked at the still slovenly guard.

"Get yourself together and get upstairs."

"Alright… alright," said the other guard as he stumbled to the side of the steps and waddled his way upwards. "I… was just trying to… get some rest."

When he had left, the man turned back and looked at the door, before holding up the key and slipping it into his pocket. "You're sloppy. Brushwess, ain't paying me to clean up after you."

The shock of his words was nothing when compared to the immediate relief that washed over her. This was probably the guard Brushwess had to leave the previous torch for her.

Not wanting to waste any more time, she grabbed hold of Frovik's arm and led him immediately towards the other end of the tunnel. She didn't care about the splashing sound from the surrounding puddles anymore. *Please still be there. Please still be there.* She could tell that her brother was having trouble keeping up, but he would have to suffer through it because she didn't feel time was on their side.

They both pressed against the side of the door with Aretta, sliding it open just enough to peek outside with squinted eyes. Blurry at first, she saw the men heading back to her with an empty wagon. She then stepped outside, so that they could see her but stayed close to the wall.

"We were going to leave the both of you if you hadn't come out," said the man, visibly annoyed. "The guard came to check on us after taking so long. I came earlier, but you weren't here."

"We had a problem, okay," she said before turning around. "Frovik, come on."

Her brother came out, visibly hobbling in pain as they opened the compartment. And with a grunt, Aretta helped him into the compartment and realized it wasn't big enough for both of them. She then checked the other side of the wagon, but there was no compartment, and there was no hay to hide under.

"Where do I hide?"

"What? You gotta find your own way out. Our orders were to get you in and to get him out. How you do that is up to you?"

"What?" said Frovik. "You can't—"

"It's fine... it's fine," said Aretta, calming her brother down and lowering him into the compartment. "I know another way out."

"Sissy!" he said in a stern voice. "I'm not gonna—"

"You know me. I always find a way right. This'll be no

different. You go on ahead. I'll meet you alright?"

He looked at Aretta for a moment and then clenched his teeth before lying down in the compartment. "You better come. Be out soon or I swear—"

"I know. I know," said Aretta as she closed the compartment on him. "I'll be right behind you, okay?" She then patted the wood above him and nodded to her escorts, who then turned away, pulling the wagon forward, and turned the corner, leaving her alone.

When they finally were out of sight, Aretta looked around her surroundings. *I can try going back into the tunnel. Maybe even get that guard to help.* But then she remembered the guards' words about cleaning up her messes and thought better.

Unsure what to do next, she decided to walk near the side of the wall to the corner where she saw a bucket of clothing. Atop it were some maid's attire along with guard uniforms hanging from lines to dry in the sun.

Without hesitation, she stepped over, ensuring that no one was around. There was a singular guard, but his back was turned. Quickly, she snatched down a maid's garb and shuffled herself back around the corner. There she stripped down to her undergarments in the mid-day sun, and dawned the clothing, pulling it over her shoulders. She even snatched a maid's bonnet to cover her hair. Her shoes weren't much better than anything a maid would wear, so she was sure that no one would notice such a thing.

Her bundle of worn clothes wrapped and tucked her arm, she stepped back around the corner and saw that the previous guard was now gone. Seizing the opportunity, she walked forward over to a wash bucket and soaked her clothing inside as she squatted down on her knees.

On the side of the magistrate's building, there was a clear view through the windows. She was patient, even though she wished to make a run for it through the manor's halls and let them believe that their maid had just went mad. But that would go badly if they decided to have a head count, and questions would arise when they found that they have one less prisoner than the day before.

Maybe through the gate where the haymaster had come. But what excuse would a maid have to leave through the side entrance? That might be suspicious. Looking around, there was only a small green field for drying clothes at the side of the manor. The open door seemed as if it was beckoning her and seeing no other real option, she lifted the bucket of wet clothes under her arm, and headed towards the door.

Once under the patio, she saw a guard coming her way and stepped to the side with a lowered head so that he might pass.

"Humm? Where's the previous maid?"

"Sir?"

"The other maid, the one who was here before you. Where is she?"

"I'm sorry. I didn't realize. I only came because I ran out of buckets for the wash and found one out in the yard. Is there something you need? I'd be willing to fetch it for you?"

"No. You may go. But if you see Esmerelda... no, never mind, you may go."

"Yes, m'lord," she said, peaking at the man, then hurrying inside the building. His face seemed somewhat familiar, but she didn't have time to place it. She had been inside before, so maybe then when she had come with the Warbird at her side, but then she had other things on her mind.

Now alone and in a room she had never seen. She realized how well the magistrate lived. The floor was a cold granite in tiles that stretched even into the hall. *This is much better than even when I sneak into other nobles' homes. If I were to just grab anything, how much would...* she shook her head. *No, no time. I need to get out. I'd rather walk on wooden floors forever than be caught here, right now.*

Taking her eyes off the shiny trinkets that adorned the

table and walls, she peaked out of the room and saw several other maids cleaning and scrubbing the walls and floors. Taking a chance, she stepped out and guessed where the front of the manor would be and headed in that direction. She didn't make it far before someone called out.

"Hey, you!" came a female voice. "Where do you think you're going?"

Aretta froze, too scared to turn to the voice. "Madam?"

"I sent off for more water and you walked right past me. Come here and set that down?"

Aretta turned around and saw an older maid wearing a similar outfit to the rest of the maids. Nervously, stepped over to the woman and held out the bucket of water.

"Don't hand it to me. Place it on the floor and take the empty—" The woman's words paused when she saw Aretta's face. "Who are you? You're not one of mine."

"Madam... I ahh, well."

"Must be one of Esmeralda's," she said, shaking her head. "I swear, that woman needs to inform me of her new hires. Rather than just running into them doing random chores. What's your name, child?"

"Ah! Gre... Silvan, m'lady."

"Well, Silvan. Leave that bucket here and pick up the empty one and follow me. There's work to be done before the magistrates' guest arrives." The maid then turned and began walking towards the steps.

Confused, but not wanting to draw attention to herself, she did as the woman bid, dropping her bucket with her clothing. Then she picked up the empty one and followed behind her.

"Where are you from, child? I assume Esmeralda picked you up off the street like she did the last one."

"I'm from the lower part of town, m'lady."

"Yes, another charity case. Alright tell me what you're good at?"

"I ahh... I can clean and cook. I worked as a bed maid

before?"

Aretta raised a brow as she glanced back at the woman. "And by bed maid, I'm assuming you mean folded sheets and not serviced the master of the house?"

"Oh... ah, yes ma`am. I would clean his chamber when he and the lady were out."

"Good, that's something, at least. I won't have your support at the dinner table as you clearly lack the proper etiquette for fine dining. But the floors upstairs have yet to be done. Let's have you start there. We can sort through the rest later."

Up the stairs, they arrived at the second floor, where she saw several other maids dusting the walls and ornaments.

"Ladies," said the woman. "Esmeralda picked up another one."

"Another? This is the second one in the last two days," said another maid.

"Yes. Well, it seems that with the preparations needing to be done quickly and with us being shorthanded, apparently anyone will serve as a maid in the magistrate's manor for the next few days." She shook her head before patting Aretta on the back. "Go on then. This is who you will be working with today. Try to keep up and you'll earn your pay for the day like everyone else."

The woman then turned and left, heading back downstairs and leaving Aretta at the mercy of the interested eyes from the other maids.

"You can help me, since I don't have a partner yet," said one of the maids while walking over and handing Aretta a mop. "I hope you have a strong back."

"Ahhh, sure," said Aretta, taking the mop and allowing herself to be led by the maids. For once, she was grateful for her lowborn heritage. She knew how to fit in here. To acclimate to the chatter of maids. She presented herself as such on many occasions and stole what she could a day or perhaps even weeks later when she'd gained enough trust.

"So, where are you from?" asked the maid as she mopped the floor beside her.

"I'm from up north, but my father brought me to this city. He thought he could make it big here, since this city is supposed to do a lot of trade." Aretta dunked her mop in the bucket before splashing it down on the floor and began scrubbing. "But seeing as I'm here. You might say his plans didn't happen?"

The girl laughed along with a few others that were nearby as Aretta heard their giggles.

"Many of us can say something about the same for ourselves. Family, money, or coming here with a lover." She turned her head upwards, closed her eyes with a smile, putting on a showy accent. "He'll work in the powder rooms, and we'll work as maids until we finally make it big." She then rolled her eyes. "Unfortunately, the only thing big is the load of crap we have to put up with."

"You've been doing this a long time?"

"Long enough to know what's what. Sometimes even before the 'what' shows up."

"Speaking of the 'what'. Do you know why the lord is hiring so many new maids? The lady who brought me here seemed awfully upset about it."

"Don't mind her. She just doesn't like having to look after so many maids. Before, I heard there were only a dozen maids that have been here for years. Now they've doubled that in the last few days. So, she keeps us away from her favorites?"

Aretta looked around at the half-dozen or so maids around her. "So, all of you are new as well?"

"This is my third day. Apparently, they are having some fancy pants come visit. And he'll be here soon. So, we're to make the place presentable for them."

Presentable? It's a castle. How much more presentable can you get than a damned castle? "I see." Confused by the statement, she decided to keep working. Her mind was still thinking about the empty prison cell below them. *If they're leaving today, then maybe it'll be best to leave with them. Nothing to be looked at if a dozen maids leave at the same time. I just hope Frovik won't do anything stupid.*

Deciding this was the best idea, she continued her work for the next set of hours until the sun was set low in the sky.

"Alright girls," said the head maid from before. "You're done for the day. Meet downstairs for your pay."

With her back arched, and her hands on her hips, she took a deep breath. *Now I remember why I don't stick around as a maid for long. I'd gladly choose thievery over worn out and tired.*

She followed the other girls downstairs where she, along with the rest, stood in a line waiting for the day's pay. *A little extra money will be good when we get out of the city.*

"Silvan and Hershire come over here please," said the same head maid from before as she stood at the door of an open room.

"Yes, madam," said the girl who she assumed to be Hershire as she and Aretta walked over.

Shit! Aretta looked at the door. *If I ran out now, there's no way I'd get far. Did they find the empty cell?* "Ahh, yes, madam."

"Since both of you are new, step inside, please. You'll be paid afterwards."

The girls stepped past the head maid into the room, where Aretta saw two guards and another woman sitting down at a table. She seemed somewhat familiar, but she couldn't place the face. *Have I stolen something from her before?* As both girls went and stood in front of the woman at the desk, Aretta couldn't help but feel as if the woman were staring at her rather intently. But past that, there was a large amount of smoke outside of the window behind her. It even looked from her view that it came from the back of her neck. Which didn't help her anxiety about the situation.

"Ladies," said the head maid. "We seem to have an issue. You see, we are one maid over what was scheduled for today. It was supposedly twenty-two, according to our ledger, but we seem to have twenty-three. And seeing as you two are the only new maids, we think one of you might be able to help us with that."

"What?" said the maid beside Aretta. "Does that mean we won't be getting paid? Oh, please miss, my family really needs this money."

"Yes," said Aretta, following along with the girl. "You can't send us home with no pay."

"Calm down, girls. That is not what we are saying," said the head maid before turning to the woman at the desk. "Esmeralda. What say you?"

Esmerelda? The one the guard asked me about.

"I remember that one," said Esmeralda, pointing a finger at the girl beside Aretta. "Her. I remember her. I met her in the market and thought she had a good look about her." She then pointed towards Aretta. "This one, though. I've never met her."

"I see," said the head maid, pointing a finger at the girl. "You may go. Receive your payment with the rest."

Confused, the girl looked around the room, and then to Aretta with worry in her eyes. Then nodded to everyone and hurried out of the room.

"So that just leaves you," said Esmeralda, narrowing her eyes at Aretta, the smoke now even thicker behind her. "Who are you?"

"Madam?"

"She said her name was Silvan," said the other head maid. "Although now I'm not so sure."

Aretta's chest grew tight as her eyes went to the two guards on either side of the room. *I'm fucked. I'm so fucked. But if they don't know about the prison break and just think I'm here for the money, then maybe it won't be so bad.*

"Spit it out, girl. And if we get any hint of a lie. I'll have the guards here throw you in jail for a week. We don't take kindly to someone sneaking into the magistrate's manor for money."

A week. Shit. Should I just say I'm with that bitch of a Warbird? No, they'd probably just hold me here until they went and got her. Ohhh, I bet she'd look so smug, too. Fuck! Think, I have to... Suddenly as she stared at the woman named Esmeralda in front of her. A feeling began to come over her. *I think I remember her from somewhere. That's the woman the guard was looking for earlier.* She looked again, spotting the guard from earlier. *Wait. I remember him too. Where? The Tavern, she was the drunk lady complaining.*

"Guards," said Esmeralda. "If you would be so kind as to escort our little fake maid to the prison. I have a feeling she's going to be—"

"Wait!" said Aretta. "I... well, I didn't want to say it before. But it was you, madam. You invited me to come just a day or so ago?"

"What?" responded Esmerelda. "I would've remembered if—"

"You were drunk. Down in one of the bars of Low Town. You were angry about... well, you were angry about a man."

"Preposterous," said the head maid. "There's no way she'd be caught dead in some bar in Low Town."

"It's not. I was working the tables that night for Mr. Harper. He was helping me out and all since he knew my mom. Well, after a few more rounds, you told me how you were sick of the magistrate and his rush for some maids. And that—"

"That's enough," said Esmeralda. Placing a hand on her face as she shook her head, the black smoke now covering most of the window behind her. "You may go now. Pick up your money on the way out. Guards, ensure that she is paid."

"Esmeralda!" said the head maid in a scandalous tone. "Surely, you didn't."

"We needed more girls. Why else would I be down there? Surely, not over some man," said Esmerelda, as her eyes seemed to purposely avoid looking at anyone.

But Aretta could see the disgust on the face of the guard who asked about her earlier, his eyes lingering on her as they left the room. *Guess that explains why he was looking for her. She has another man in Low Town, perhaps. Either way, that's none of my business. Let them sort it out while I get myself out of here as fast as possible.*

Aretta gladly took her pay, which wasn't much. But anything would help as she and her brothers made plans to leave the city.

The guards opened the door for her, and she expected to be hit by a rush of fresh air and the feeling of freedom. She instead was greeted by a darkened black sky with a fire roaring in the distance. The smell of burning wood pierced her nose.

Below, she could see the townspeople rushing towards a corner a safe distance away. Their chatter and panic even reaching her ears above them. She stared at it for a moment, along with the guards beside her. Somehow, she had a feeling that the fire was not a good sign of things to come. And perhaps so did the guards, but they were there to guard the magistrate's building.

Her senses getting the better of her, she headed down the stairs and into the street, following the crowd over to where the building was burning. And then, as if to confirm her suspicions, she heard the whispers from the crowd.

"It's the Warbird, she's in there," said one of the women nearby.

These whispers were followed by the sound of gunfire. Then the crackle of the flames as a large piece of wood fell from the building to the ground below.

She hated to admit it, but she started to feel worried. *Where is she? You better not die in there, you crazy bitch, and leave Ebele by herself.* The fire roared louder. *Come on... come on. Where are—*

More sounds of gunfire came from the building, but then suddenly one of the windows near the flames exploded as a body was ejected from it with such force that it rolled across the street, hitting a pole on the opposite side. From where she was, she could see that it was a man.

He coughed and gasped from breath as he doubled over in pain in the snow. He clawed his hand into the frost covered ground, trying to pull himself forward. But ahead, from the same window, Aretta saw the Warbird, leaning over the edge. Her hand gripped the side of the building as her hair fluttered in the wind and flames. She didn't even look real. Her clothing half burned, and blood dripping down the side of her face into one of her eyes. The look in her eyes was one she'd never seen before. Not even during that night with the other assassins. It was of determination. She appeared like a ravager and made Aretta feel a fear she didn't even know she had.

With a non-to-amused look on her face, she leaped from the window, flying through the air as if something out of a legend, before plummeting down, landing knee first onto the back of the assassin who had fallen into the snow. Aretta winced. She couldn't see the man's face, but just from how his feet and neck lurched upward upon impact, she imagined it to be a pain she never wanted to experience.

Reaching down, the Warbird grabbed the man by the hair, pulling his head back even further. It seemed like she was trying to rip it from his body. She couldn't hear what she was saying to him, but she could imagine just by the wicked grin that ran across her lips.

The nighttime visage seemed to bring about more snow that caught the wind, sending a chilling down her spine even with the heat from the flaming house. But through the snowflakes ahead, she saw a man with a rifle perched on the edge of a roof. And she somehow knew exactly who the barrel was aimed at.

Before she could even call out, the boom from the rifle thundered. And to her surprise, the Warbird had already raised an arm as the snow kicked up beside her where the bullet was deflected. Quickly, she then sat atop the man, holding a blade to his neck and positioning herself behind him, putting him in the rifleman's way. *How good is this woman? Can she do that to every...*

Then from the corner of her eye, from behind the Warbird, she noticed a blonde-haired woman in a tunic moving through the crowd. When she reached the open, Aretta saw the sheen from a blade in her hand and before she could even realize it, she screamed.

"Warbird! Behind you!" The words left her mouth in a shout, and she felt the burning sensation she'd tried to keep down, now on its way to her throat. She scratched at her neck as she started coughing uncontrollably. The pain caused her eyes to burn and water as she looked ahead, fearful for the Warbird.

But her warning was received as the Warbird turned to her side, just enough to deflect the blade away as the woman ran straight into her, tackling her as they both went rolling over the snow-covered ground. She saw the man that was previously held hostage by her, now with a face filled with snow, getting up. But she also realized the Warbird's rifle was right next to him.

Her body again moved on instinct, and she ran forward into the snow, diving and snatching the rifle away from the man as she did so. He shook his head, removing the snow from his face and hair. Then he stared at Aretta, a frost-covered beard and eyebrows failing to mask his anger.

Shit, shit, shit. What do I do? She pointed the rifle at the man. "Stay back or I swear, I'll—" Then came the thunder, the rifle she had glowed red for only a moment before her shoulder lurched back and the weapon went flying out of her hand. She found herself looking up at the sky, the pure white crystals falling around her and the sound of ringing in her ears. The world itself was muffled. Everything sounded muted when compared to the ringing in her ears. *Did I get shot? Am I dying? Why did I jump out to... it doesn't matter.*

My brothers are safe, that's good enough for...

"Get up," came a muffled yet familiar voice. Then, obstructing the view of her smoke-filled white garden in the sky, came a bloody faced Warbird with that same grin on her lips that she hated so much. She could see half her teeth, from the curl on her cheek. "Get up."

The Warbird reached down, grabbing Aretta by the collar of her outfit and pulling her up to a sitting position. "Not bad," she said before turning her head to look behind her.

Aretta, while a little blurry, followed her gaze. Over by the side of another home was the man she prevented from grabbing the rifle. He was now slumped up against the wall and missing a substantial side of her neck. Aretta's eyes went wide as the pain from her shoulder came to her, along with the realization of what happened. "Did... did I..." Her voice was still horse from the yelling.

"Yes, you did. Well, technically I did, and you just pointed. But it was a good aim."

Aretta looked around nervously, remembering the other assassin girl and then at the rooftop for the man with the rifle.

"Both gone. The woman was a surprise. I didn't figure there'd be another one. And we got lucky with the one on the roof. I saw him fiddling with his rifle before he disappeared. Probably jammed on him." She then slid an arm under Aretta and lifted her up. "Come on, let's get back and have that shoulder looked at."

Parting through the crowd, they got quite a few confused and even scared looks from the townspeople. The walk back to Harsetti's manor was horrible. Not only because of the pain in her shoulder, but also because of who her company was. No matter how she thought of it. She truly disliked this woman. Her attitude, her voice, her smug existence. *All of it. I hate everything about you. Why! Why did I even call out? Now look at me. All of this is still because of you.*

When they returned, Ebele was visibly worried as they entered her room.

"What.... Mother, you're bleeding. What happened, no... don't tell me you went after those assassins again."

Ebele's panicked voice was something else that she didn't want to hear. But unlike the Warbird, she felt that she just didn't like the worried look on the girl's face. Especially if it was turned towards her. Either way, Ebele took Aretta from her mother and escorted her over to the bed.

"Helheim!" said Ebele, turning her finger to the boy. "Turn around."

Aretta was a little surprised and curious why she didn't just ask him to leave. But she was tired and just followed along and let Ebele disrobed her and inspect her shoulder. "Is it bad, mother?"

"Humm," said the Warbird as she placed her thumb over the bruise and Aretta felt the sting as she pressed hard. "Bruised, but it doesn't seem to be dislocated."

"What happened? And why were you back wearing that maid's outfit?"

Aretta grimaced. "I ahhh... I figured that the assassins... well, they might not notice me if I was wearing a maid's garb. I mean, there are tons of maids that walk the city, right?"

"Yes, I suppose that was one way of thinking," said the Warbird as she walked over, grabbing a cloth from a nearby desk to wipe at the blood on her face. "But your friend here... she managed to kill one of the assassins."

"What!" said Ebele, her eyes wide as she stared at Aretta. "How? You don't even have the essence?"

"She didn't need to. She just needed to point the rifle in the right direction. But this can work to our advantage."

"What? How? What do you mean?" asked Ebele as she reached over and grabbed one of her nightgowns of the back of a chair, helping Aretta slide into it.

"Recently, they were so sure about Aretta not having the essence. But now... now they will believe it's three against two?"

"What? Three? I thought you said Aretta killed one."

"There was another woman, apparently."

Ebele shook her head before turning to her mother. "What about you? Your face is still bleeding."

"A cut at the top of my eye. Our essence works wonders for deflecting bullets, not so much blades. I let him get a bit too close and this was the price."

"Mother, while I am always one for new experiences. Don't you think we've done enough?"

"Enough? My daughter, we have killed four of them. Do you really believe that the two or how many of them left remaining are just going to let us go in peace? I know I never taught you this, and perhaps I should have. In war, peace is never achieved until one side is dead. Imagine if we did leave, you'd have to live the rest of your life paranoid about an assassin in every corner. Do you want that for yourself or, better yet, for your father?"

The thought of her father gave her room for pause. While gifted with the essence, he was a researcher and never found a passion for rifles outside of their use of powder. She couldn't imagine him even mastering his essence enough to deflect a bullet, let alone fend off a blade attack. "I see your point."

"Good, then you girls stay here tonight," she pointed to Helheim, who was still sitting in a corner with his back facing them. "He can stay and keep you both company since he's already proven himself capable enough and clearly not on their side."

"Wait! Please tell me you're not going back out there alone."

"No. I think I'm going to get bandaged up and get some sleep.

"Ah... wait, I'll help you," said Aretta, sliding her way out of bed.

"What are you doing?" said Ebele. "You're hurt. Let one

318

of the maids—"

"No, I… I want to do it," she said as she winced, trying to rotate her shoulder, before walking in behind the Warbird, who just raised a brow at the girl before turning back towards the door.

"Fine, come along then. I'll return her to you after we've finished."

Ebele appeared as if she wanted to protest but held her tongue as Aretta and her mother left the room together.

CHAPTER 16

"Are you sure about this?" Ebele asked. They both were dressed in maid's garb as she followed behind Aretta, sneaking their way along the wall of the Harsetti's manor. "I mean, shouldn't we have told someone? I mean, Helheim is going to be worried."

"We tried waking him, remember?" Aretta slid behind the brush into the hole in the wall. "He's the one who decided to drink that weird tea you said the maid brought."

"I tried to warn him about it. But he'd already gulped it down while I had my back turned. Exactly. So, how were you planning to wake him up?"

"I'm still worried," said Ebele, pushing through the wall behind her.

"You have that rifle in that case, right? And plus were dressed like servants. I would have never been noticed yesterday if not for your mother being... well... being your mother." Aretta took Ebele by the arm and pulled her free from the wall. "Besides, you were all for it when I told you I saw someone drinking powder."

"I'm just saying, this clothing wasn't made for essence users. It may be hard for me to channel into this rifle if something happens." She slid her hand down her gown, trying to unruffle the fabric. "And of course, I was interested in someone drinking essence powder. Who wouldn't be after hearing that?"

"Who wouldn't... Anyone. Literally, anyone else wouldn't be. In fact, only you would be."

"You just don't understand. Aren't you curious about what consuming essence powder might do?"

"Oh, I know what it'd do," said Aretta, while reaching up and rubbing at her neck. "It makes your eyes and throat burn and leaves you coughing for days."

"Huh, wait... is that why you've been coughing so much? Noooo, you didn't."

"Yes, I did. And I have no idea why anyone would want to do it on purpose."

"Hummm. An essence user doing it is one thing. But you, how are you not... Was he... hummm, I wonder if it's an acquired taste?"

"I don't know if I've ever told you this. But you're weird."

"Say's the woman who drank essence enhanced powder."

"I... fine, maybe you have a point."

They continued down into the lower parts of the city with Ebele clutching at her new rifle, running her finger over the engravings along the side. "It feels weird using a weapon other than Mothers. Actually, can you tell me about the fight you and Mother had with the assassins in the city the other day?"

"Ahh, I guess so. What about it?"

"I mean. You said Mother ignited the gun herself. How?"

"How? How would I know? She just did it... wait, does that mean you can't?"

"I don't know. I didn't even know that was possible."

"How are you 'that' woman's daughter and you don't even know what you can do?"

"Hey, I always focused on marksmanship, not fancy tricks. Maybe she thought it wasn't necessary. Mother always has her reasons for stuff?" A little annoyed, her eyes glowed red as she tried focusing her essence into the rifle casings, but the only thing she managed to do was infuse the wik. *Okay, now I'm curious. What else can you do, Mother?*

Thoughts of the applications of powder went through her mind as she and Aretta traveled down through Low Town together. Eventually they reached the entrance to the Dread Quarters, where Ebele paused.

"I thought you said to never go in here?"

"You're not supposed to. But today we have permission, so we'll be fine."

"Are you sure?"

"Don't worry. You have that rifle."

"No, I have a rifle that I've never fired before. I've inspected it, but that's not the same thing."

"Don't worry. Brushwess, the guy who drinks the powder is the one who runs this place, and he wants to meet you," said Aretta as she stepped into the Dread Quarters.

"What! Brushwess?" replied Ebele as she nervously followed Aretta. "Didn't you say he was hard to deal with?"

"Did I?" asked Aretta with a frown, then a dismissive wave of the hand. "Well, he's... he's not that bad. I'm sure I wasn't being serious then."

Aretta words hardly convinced Ebele, but still she followed. While the rest of Low Town didn't look like much. In compassion to the Dread Quarters it was a breath of fresh air. Here the buildings looked rotted, and the ground was mushy. Since no sun came in here, water settled in puddles from where the rain would leak through the wooden houses above. It was a man-made cave and if something caught fire, she wondered how fast it would burn.

322

The two pit fires at the side of the entrance caught her attention. And to her amazement as she entered the Dread Quarters, she noticed that it was warm inside even though there wasn't any sunlight to be had here. *Amazing. I wonder how they have the system organized. The powder houses send heat to all the homes, and everyone adjusts their temperature accordingly. But here, the entire area stays at one single temperature. That's why the front is blocked off with a small opening. Whereas outside the system runs through multiples of houses. Here operates as if it is just one gigantic home.*

While still nervous, her mind began thinking of ways that a system of that nature operated. Outside in the streets, there were a few people dressed in rags moving from place to place on whatever activity that had. She even noticed a few children. *If they were homeless, how long would they survive in the cold? How does a place like this even come about? Who thinks of it? Who constructs it?*

Deeper into the Dread Quarters they went until they reached the end where, in the flames, she could see that the wall of the city and there were several men and women standing outside of shanty homes, eyeing them as they approached.

"Well, look who's here. We thought you'd gotten captured since you didn't show," said a man. "Then we caught wind of what you and that war hero had done in the city." He nodded to Ebele. "That the one you've been babysitting?"

"She's the one he wanted to see. Where's my brother?"

"He's inside," said the man with a smile.

Aretta frowned. "Take me to him."

Ebele felt eerie watching the conversation between the two. Especially now with all eyes on them. There were so many faces concealed by the darkness that she wasn't sure she could count them all. And the feeling didn't alleviate when the man ahead opened the door for them. Once opened, it was as if the light from inside was trying to escape into the darkened area where they were. But with a curiosity about the man who consumed powder and a need to support her friend, she followed Aretta into the building.

Inside, what she saw she could only be described as a random mashup of wood. Edges came in and out as the lumber stacked on top of itself to create a large open spaced building. From the ceiling hung circular chandeliers of crude design, where flames danced upon their candle tips, casting a sharp shadow down over the room.

Ahead of them, amongst the sea of randomly thrown-out furniture, she saw a boy tied down to a chair.

"Frovik!" yelped Aretta as she hurried over to him, removing the gag from his mouth. "Are you okay?"

He coughed. "I'm fine. Are you alright? I heard about you and those assassins fighting in the city."

"I'm fine. Why are you..."

"Welcome back," came a voice from the side of the room.

Ebele turned to see a man stepping in from a corner of one of the jagged walls of the room, then leaning against it before chewing on a piece of fruit.

"Brushwess!" said Aretta. "What is this?"

"Don't worry. No foul play on my part," said the man, handing a key to one of his female companions, as she began walking over to Aretta. "It was for his own good. The fool was planning to head back to the magistrate building after you didn't return." He shrugged. "I told him that a woman willing to sneak into a dungeon surely had a way of getting out on her own. If you ask me, I think I have more faith in you than he does."

"No one asked you," said Aretta with a scowl as she took the key, and unlocked the binding around her brother. The chains rattled on the floor around his feet. Helping her brother up to his feet, she began to lead him over toward the door where Ebele stood.

"Uh-uhhh," said the Brushwess, wagging a finger as he walked over and took a seat on one of the couches at the center of the room. "We had a deal. I've done my part. Now you have to uphold yours." His two servant girls then walked over, placing a tray of some liquid, a crystal mug, and some powder.

"So, you really drink powdered water infused with essence?" asked Ebele as she stepped past Aretta and over to Brushwess.

"It's the only thing that clears the mind, young lady, and I've been told that you have a whole lotta essence to spare. So, I'm hoping you really get me to new level of clarity."

"Okay," said Ebele, nodding her head. "I can enhance it. But I'm not responsible for anything that happens afterwards."

Brushwess smiled. "We're only responsible for ourselves." He flicked his finger and one of his women reached for the tray. The other took the crystal glass and took a spoonful of powder, dumping it inside as the first woman poured in the liquid to fill the glass to a quarter. Taking the glass, Brushwess swirled it around in his hand, allowing them to mix before extending it toward Ebele. "Give it a go."

Ebele stared at the glass for a moment, watching the sparkling white crystals clump together while the smaller ones dissolved to the point it would hold any essence. *I guess he's testing me. It's not a high grade of powder, so I guess he's seeing if I can enhance what's left while it's floating and whooshing about.* Ebele smiled. *Okay, I'll play this game if I can set the results.*

Taking in a breath, she tried summoning her essence. She could somewhat feel it, but in her maid's clothing, it was harder to connect to. The feeling was frustrating, so she clenched her teeth and tried harder.

"Something wrong, young missy," said Brushwess, sliding to the side to get another look at her. "Shouldn't be so hard from what I've heard about you."

"Just give me a moment. I need to focus more." Her

stomach tight, she breathed through her teeth until, finally, she felt the essence well up inside of her. Gathering hold, she then forced it ahead toward the area of the glass. It didn't take long for the first sparkle of red to appear in the water. Then another and then several more, until more than a dozen had appeared.

"Wooo! Nice," said Brushwess, inspecting the glass. "I figured you'd wait till it stopped. Okay then, let's see what you got." He took the glass to his lips and gulped it down, a small amount of red liquid sliding from the corner of his mouth and down his chin.

He exhaled as if in ecstasy before bringing the cup down to his side. His head tilted back as his eyelids fluttered. Mouth open, he exhaled a red mist before his body jolted, his neck tensing so much that she could see the veins beneath. Another jolt of his body as watched a crack in the glass from his tightening grip. "Yeahhhhhh!" He said with a long droll before lowering his head to look at her. "You're... stronger than most. I'll give you that. Ohhhhhhhhh! And it's clean."

Clean? What does that mean? Thought Ebele, before noticing that his eyes were glowing the same color as hers. *Is that a thing? Is that my essence in his eyes or his own essence responding to mine? Ahhh, so many questions, but something is telling me that I shouldn't linger in a place like this.* She then stood to leave. "I take it you're satisfied?"

"Oh, no," said Brushwess as he turned his head to stretch his neck. "That was just the test to see if your friend there knew what she was talking about. But now," he reached into his vest, pulling out a small pouch. "Now, it's time to see if you really can give me something I've never had." Out of his vest, he pulled out a small bag tied with a string. Unloosening it, he then upturned the bag on the tray, and out came a large amount of green powder, spreading like sand from an hourglass.

Ebele stared at it for a moment, remembering the

incident at Harsetti's manor. "I don't think you know how dangerous that is."

"Dangerous?" asked Brushwess with a smile as he placed a finger to his temple. "I think you are underestimating what dangerous means. We robbed an imperial transport for this stuff. So, you can imagine our frustration when we find out can't no one even use it." He then pointed that same finger at Ebele. "But you... you don't seem to have that problem."

Is there a way out without having that man explode in front of me? She began looking around the room but quickly came to the realization that there was nothing of much value to be found. Just wood and old furniture. *And even if I did, what are the chances of this place and all of the buildings outside going up in flames like kindling?*

"Your eyes are wondering," said Brushwess with a sigh. "Allow me to bring you some clarity. If you don't do as I say, neither you nor your friends there will leave this room alive."

Damn. she thought as her eyes focused back on him. *Fine, if he wants to die so badly. But what about his men outside? It's not like they are going to let us out if he dies here.* "Sorry, I was just thinking that if you die because of this stuff. I don't want your people to blame me for it. Can you give us any assurances?"

"Assurances. Oh yes, of course. If you don't do it. You will all die. If you do, then you all will at least have a chance of living. How's that sound?"

Ebele frowned. *Okay? There, I guess we're going to try to fight our way out. Maybe he'll blow a hole in the wall, and we can use it to escape.* "Fine. But pour it into a glass first. I want it separated from the rest of the pile. Otherwise, it could be dangerous... well, more dangerous than I'd prefer." *I need to minimize the damage to just him. So, a smaller amount should do.* She shook her head. *How did I go from killing a woman in a building to now preparing to watch this poor bastard explode himself?*

Brushwess smiled before reaching for the pitcher and pouring the glass till it was half empty. Then, grabbing a handful of the green powder, he held it over the glass, letting it slowly drain down. The liquid twisted into a light shade of green as it swirled.

What Ebele didn't like were the large dark green clumps that were forming as it circulated in the glass.

She took a deep breath. *Okay then.* She looked back at the worried face of Aretta and her brother, and then back to the swirling liquid. *I guess I'm doing this.* And with an exhale, she summoned up the essence again. Still having a hold of it from before, she focused it forward. The powder inside was easy enough to lock onto. But the infusion was still as hard as she remembered, harder even, now that she wasn't assisted by augmented clothing. She felt as if it had its own barrier.

Why does it have to be so hard to push into? She leaned forward, placing her hands on the desk as she stared into the glass, trying to enhance her focus. Biting her lip as she inched closer, her eyes glowing intensely until finally she felt it. She pierced it and she could feel it begin to resonate with her essence. The glass sparkled in a golden light, which slowly intensified until it had a powerful glow. "Ahhh!" she grunted before bringing her hand up over her eyes, rubbing her palms over her eyelids. Looking for any relief from the strain, she sat back down on the couch, pointing a finger at the sparking glass.

"There. Is that good enough?"

"Well damn. You fucking pulled it off," said Brushwess as he swirled the glass in hand, watching as the light reflected off the crystal, shining on his face. "Seems to have done a number on you to do it tough."

"Of course it did. It's like there's some kind of shield protecting it." After blinking a few times to clear her vision, she saw that unlike before, the powder wasn't clumping together. Instead, it stayed separated as it circled the glass over and over. *That must be because of the liquid. Is that just regular water?* She squinted her eyes again, trying to blink away the migraine that was surely coming.

"Well then," said Brushwess with the unmistakable look of excitement in his eyes. "Let's see where this takes us, aye?" Then, placing the glass to his lips, he turned it up and swallowed until the liquid was gone. The only remnant, a drop of fluid on the lip that was soon brushed away by his forearm.

Ebele wanted to speak, but she began to find herself enthralled by watching him, waiting for a reaction. And she wouldn't have to wait long as just seconds after drinking it, he began coughing and beating his chest with his fist. His eyes opened wide; she could clearly see a golden hue inside of the blackness of his pupils. The veins of his neck protruded as he tried to contain whatever was happening and, with an exhale, she could see the heat leaving his mouth once again. But this time the smoke was golden.

"Ohhhhhhh, that's... new," he said as he tensed his body, his arms locking in place and his chest protruding after taking a deep breath.

What is happening? thought Ebele, not even realizing that she was once again leaning over the table, studying Brushwess's reaction. *Is he not going to explode? My essence, I can feel it... changing? No... absorbing? Vanishing?* Her hand was outstretched as she found its way to the side of his face.

"Hey, you can't—" said one of the women as she grabbed a hold of Ebele's arm, just for Ebele to push her off and send her flying back, sliding against the floor before crashing into the leg of a table. An action that made the other girl step back out of fear.

As Brushwess still convulsed on the couch, Ebele found herself climbing over the table and mounting him. Sitting atop him, she pulled his head back and began staring into his eyes. There she could see the golden flicker slowly glowing dimmer in the blackness of his iris. *Where's it going? What's happening to it? It feels as if... wait; I wonder if...*

Taking in a deep breath of her own, she began summoning the essence from inside herself before casting it out while staring directly into Brushwess's eyes. *It's there. I can feel it.* Brushwess convulsed harder under her as his mouth went agape. But Ebele could see the golden flame in his eyes reignite as she forced her essence into him. A smile came over her own face upon seeing it. *He's accepting it. What is this? I wonder what else...*

"Ebele!" screamed of Aretta.

"Huh!" said Ebele, coming back to her senses. She turned around to see Aretta holding her sleeve, trying to pull her back.

"What are you doing?"

"What?" asked Ebele before looking at Brushwess and realizing that she was on top of him as he gasped for air. "What? What happened?"

"What happened? That's what I want to—"

"Ahhhhh!" yelled Brushwess as he leaped up, sending Ebele tumbling back on the table, spilling the drink and powder before falling to the floor.

In a small daze, Aretta pulled Ebele up to her feet and watched as a very active Brushwess began stomping back and forth on the floor.

"What was that? Wooooo! I ain't never felt nothing like that?"

"Boss?" said the woman who wasn't flung across the room. "You, okay?"

"Okay? I'm better than okay." He reached up and began rubbing his face. "I'm... so... much... better than okay. I'm everything. Every... fucking... thing?" He turned back to Ebele. "Ohhhh, you's a special fucking bitch, ain't ya? I don't know what that was, but I know I ain't never felt anything close to it."

"Then that's it, right? You got what you wanted. So, we're clear."

"Oh yeah, me and you… We're clear."

"Good. Then we're out of here. Tell your men—"

"Nahh, I said you're clear. You and your family. I'll get you all out of the city. But that one…" He pointed towards Ebele. "She's gonna stay here for a while."

"You can't be serious. You know who her mother—"

"Aye, I do," said Brushwess, high stepping as if he was stretching, and stomped over, standing before them. "And she's busy with them assassins. Don't worry, she'll get her daughter back with no harm done. But ain't no way I'm letting this special goose out of here after pulling a stunt like that." He raised his hand in the air before leaning in, closer to both girls, their faces only inches apart as he stared into Ebele's eyes. "What you say, sweetheart? You got enough in you for another go?"

Suddenly, a thunderous blast sounded through the open area. Still a bit dazed, Ebele closed her eyes at the sound as it startled her already dazed mind. But when she opened them, she was surprised to see a bullet hovering in the air between Brushwess's fingers. And to her surprise, from where it was, she could see that it was aimed at her.

"Oh, you half-dead fuckers," said Brushwess. "You dare try to take my new toy."

"You protected…" said Ebele in surprised; until she realized what he called her. "Toy! Wait… half-dead? What's that mean?"

"Ebele!" said Aretta, pulling her away. "It's time to go."

"Oh… yes," said Ebele, before turning back to Brushwess. "Look, even if I wanted to. I can't. Enhancing that powder drains me, and I probably won't be able to do it again for another day or so. She didn't know if that was true, but she certainly did feel drained. Can you provide us safety back out of here until then?"

Brushwess stared at Ebele's face, as another shot ran out and Brushwess' shield deflected it. He then turned back to the one of the women in the room. "Hey, grab my rifle and alert the men that our contract with those assassins is over, and if they see them, to hunt them down and bring them to me."

It was less than a minute later before Ebele was ushered back out into the darkness of the Dread Quarters. But by now, she could hear gunshots ringing out above her head.

"Boss," said another man, running up to him.

Brushwess smiled. "I see you boys have already started without me. But the hunt—"

"It ain't us, boss," said the man, catching his breath. "It's someone else." More gunshots rang out as pieces of the roof above them exploded. "It's someone else. The assassin and them is up there fighting?"

Ebele looked up and instantly knew who it was. "Mother."

That revelation was, of course, followed by the scent of smoke, and that's when they all saw the fire in one of the windows.

"Fuck," said Brushwess. "Get the men to all grab themselves some buckets. We gotta put that out before it spreads."

"What about the assassins?"

"Fuck'em," he said a scowl. "The fire has to come first, then we can hunt those bastards down if that damn Warbird doesn't get to 'em first." He turned back to Ebele. "And you. Get the fuck out. Just remember, we ain't done."

Ebele clutched at the rifle in her hand as she looked at the fire in the window, hearing the continued gunfire, which was now followed up by the sound of men's screams.

"Tell the men to keep their distance from those two," said Brushwess. "The water. Get the water. We'll just hope they kill themselves." He then ran off into one of the huts, followed by his men.

"Don't you dare think it," said Aretta, looking over past her brother. "Your mother will be fine. We have to worry about that other assassin if they're not already up there."

"But—"

"Didn't you just say you were feeling weak after doing whatever the hell you were doing?"

Ebele frowned but had to admit that she did indeed still feel drained; the effects of enhancing that weird powder, not to mention whatever that was with Brushwess. So, with restraint and a bit lip. She and Aretta pressed forward while supporting Frovik's weight from his bad leg, heading for the exit.

Dammit. Why now? Why must she always do everything alone? Did she follow me down here, or did she follow the assassin? Is she fighting one or is she fighting more? Dammit, Mother.

The entrance back into Old Town seemed ever darker through blurry and tired eyes, but ahead they could see the opening, as if a piercing beacon in the darkness. Behind them, the sounds of screams and gunshots pushed them forward. *Almost there. Mother will be fine. She's always fine.*

Reaching the exit, they stepped outside in the still earning morning light. The snow sat over the ground, covering the city.

"Come on," said Aretta, turning to lead them up the street. But along with the morning sun, another sound of thunder greeted them, and Ebele felt her leg give out as her arm slipped from under her. Then the next thing she knew, she was face down in the snow with a pain surging through her ankle.

Through the pain, she heard Aretta scream her name and before she knew it; she felt herself being dragged through the snow as several more thunder sounds came ringing in her ear. She had no idea where the sounds were coming from. She just instinctually closed her eyes and enhanced her shields as much as she could.

Every hit that came near her, she could feel. Near the head, near the shoulder, then near the stomach. She could hear the bullets flying past her, either hitting snow or some nearby wood. It only stopped when Aretta released her, and she opened her eyes to see a trail of crimson along the powdery snow leading to her.

"Ebele... Ebele, are you alright?"

"I... I think so," she said as Frovik placed the rifle in her arms. "Where... where are they?"

"The rooftop ahead, I think," said Frovik. I think I saw a puff of smoke coming from there. "They shouldn't be able to see us from here."

"What do we do?" asked Aretta. "Should we run?"

"No... they... they were probably waiting for us or Mother to come out. Who knows who followed here."

"You think... you think they'd come after us?"

"Me and Aretta.... Probably yeah."

"Shit," said Aretta. "Ah, ahhhh, Frovik, you have to get out of here."

"What! There's no way."

"It's us they are after. Maybe you can find Drogal. But you can't stay here. We don't have whatever they have. We can't just get shot and be okay. Your leg's still messed up. What if they catch you?"

"Me? What about you? Sissy, I'm not—"

"Please, Frovik. We'll be fine. If you're not here, we can hide out until her mother comes out. She's the war hero, remember? If we can hide long enough, she'll save us. But we can't do that when it's the three of us."

"Argggh! Why are you so... fine." He stood up. "But I swear, you better not die on me. Not after all this."

Aretta smiled and then turned to Ebele. "He can't really run. So, are you able?"

"Yeah? It just grazed my side. Mother taught me to at least have my essence around my body at all times. I guess I see why now," she said as she placed her hand to her side, feeling where the bullet grazed her. *That damned powder drained me. I'm not as strong as I should be. But better to pierce the skin than pierce the body.*

"Okay. So, what do we do?"

"We...." she stood up with a grunt, sliding her back

against the wall for leverage. "We draw them away, while your brother goes in the opposite direction." She smiled back at Aretta. "Simple, right? And we try not to die."

"I feel like that's all I've been doing since I met you?"

"Good. I think I can I say the same about you," she looked towards Frovik. "You Ready?"

"Just keep my sister alive."

"I promise that's all I want to do right now." She took a deep breath and slowly exhaled, summoning her essence as best as she could. "Go!" she said, before stepping around the corner. Aretta stayed near and looked around as best she could for the assassin. But their wait wasn't long before Ebele spotted her target. With eyes of crimson, she squeezed the trigger and, as if simultaneously, twin sounds of thunder boomed through the area.

She felt his blast hit the essence around her, being deflected as she maneuvered to the other side of the street. But she herself knew her shots were on point. One after another, shot after shot, from that small dot in the distance. While not sure of all the skills that having essence gave. She was certain of her skills with a rifle. Each bullet would be hitting its mark, and she knew that that alone would be a drain on their essence more than a few shots in different places.

And to her satisfaction, as she laid down fire, she saw the assassin buckle and lower their head to remove themselves from the onslaught.

"Okay, here... here," said Ebele, as they entered an alley-way to escape the sight of the assassin. It felt as if her leg was burning. She could feel the blood running down it from her wound from earlier.

Fuck! Why am I even here? I don't even know who these people are? They're just strangers who started shooting at us. Why are we even trying to kill each other? She tried to peek her head around the corner, only for the side of the wall where her head was to explode as the assassin fired off another round at her.

"Ahhh!" yelled Ebele, as dust splattered over her face. While her essence would divert the bullet, it did nothing for the debris that it caused. "Oh, you son of a useless cow!" she yelled before stepping out and aiming her rifle again. Another shot, causing the assassin to hide behind the beams of the tower.

But even behind cover, Ebele did not stop firing. Instead, she increased the drain on her essence, striking the wooden beam adjacent to where the assassin was hiding. Again, she fired, till the wood started shattering, splinters of it being torn off until she saw the head of the tower being to wane. The assassin must have realized what was happening but was stuck in the tower. He didn't have many options.

That was until the support holding up the tower began to buckle. With a smile, she watched the assassin leap as the bell came crashing down where he was. From under its own weight, the tower imploded upon itself.

The assassin hit the roof, rolling down the side before plunging a dagger into the roof to halt their fall. And this gave Ebele the opening she needed. Breathing heavily and almost completely drained, she waited for the moment when his momentum halted. And when it came, she aimed for the head, pulling the trigger, and heard the most soul dampening sound of a click. She had been so focused on the target that she didn't count the rounds left in her rifle. She had gone empty.

She cursed as her lips began to tremble in rage. As she watched the assassin rise back up to their feet and look down over at her. There their eyes focused on each other. He still held his rifle, and she still held hers, but they, unlike her, most likely, still had ammo.

For a moment out there in the cold, she truly wanted to curse her luck in the world. Here with the snowflakes falling down around her, the steam of her breath matching the beating of her heart. Her blood loss was causing fatigue to set in much faster than normal. Match that to her already expended essence usage, and the world was slowly growing still and dim.

The world isn't fair. She thought to herself as she lowered her rifle. *I guess you were right again, mother.*

But the world would not stand still forever and then, just as quickly as it paused, it began to move again. Slowly at first, she saw the assassin above her lift their gun.

Summoning what will she could, she turned back into the alley, grabbing Aretta by the arm, and began running as the corner of the alley shattered into pieces as the thunder of a rifle fire rang out.

"I'm out. We have to run."

"Out? What do you—" her words were cut short as glass shattered above their heads from a nearby window. "Don't you have more?"

"I... I didn't think to bring more, okay?"

"That's all you do is think. How could you forget now?"

"It was early. I'm slow in the—" Out the corner of her eyes as she cleared the alley, she saw something high above on a rooftop and swung Aretta around behind her as a rain of bullets poured down, pelting the surrounding snow as Ebele tried her best to hold on to what little essence she had left. Each impact was getting harder to deflect. As with each shot, she was being driven backwards until finally, with a final shot she went tumbling backwards over Aretta. Perhaps surprised by her fumbling over in the snow, the assassin's next shot missed.

She heard the shot, but she never felt the impact, which was good. Because the shot that sent her tumbling over forced her to lose any essence shield she had left. She shuttered in the snow, rolling on top of Aretta to shield her. She tried once again on hands and knees to summon what essence she could to deflect another barrage. But there was nothing, only the white snow clenched in her hands. Between the pain in her leg and the exhaustion, she couldn't feel her essence at all.

No. come on... please... something. Let me have something.

Frustrated, she pounded her hand down beside Aretta's head, and with fear and clenched teeth, she turned her head to get a look at the man who had outdone her. And almost as if to add insult to injury, she witnessed the assassin standing on top of the rooftop reloading his weapon.

Of course, they have extra bullets. Thought Ebele as she struggled to her feet, grabbing Aretta by the arm to make another run for it. But there, above him, she saw something appear behind the assassin. It was a person. *The other assassin.* She feared at first till she recognized the shirt tucked into overalls. *Tannor? No! What are you doing, you idiot?*

Ebele stepped forward; her arms stretched out wide with rifle in hand, standing as if trying to show she was protecting Aretta. Which she was, but also to drawing in the assassin's gaze and focus. *Oh, what am I doing? I'm going to get him killed.* The thoughts of regret already filling her mind, but at the moment she couldn't think of any other options.

The assassin took aim and Ebele closed her eyes. *By the Maker's Kin and the Graces, please keep us safe.* She prayed in anticipation of another rain of bullets. But while there was a shot, she didn't feel the impact. Instead, she opened her eyes to see Tannor struggling with the assassin, grabbing his rifle. They shuffled around on the roof before the assassin lifted the rifle, elbowing Tannor in the face, making him lose his grip and go stumbling back.

Ebele's heart skipped a beat as the assassin lowered the rifle to take aim at him. But with the roof on a slant, Tannor rolled back toward the assassin. And with such a short distance, he lifted himself back on his feet and lunged forward. Not for the rifle, but instead he wrapped his arms around the assassin's waist. And with a loud yell, he lifted him up and began running down the side of the roof. At the edge, he jumped with the assassin in his grasp as they both went flying through the air.

The scene looked surreal, the boy in overalls seeming as if to be gliding through the snow-filled sky with a man clad in black on his shoulders. But no matter how slow a moment seems to move in one's mind, the inevitable always proceeds. They both crashed against the wall of the building on the opposite side of the street, falling onto the awning above a set of steps leading to a front door. Their crash was so hard that they fell independently of each other to either side of the steps below, with the assassin landing in the middle of the street. His hood and cloak were now torn free and now hanging from the corner of the awning, blowing in the wind as if it was a black ghost in the snow.

On the ground, on his hands and knees, the assassin couched before stumbling back up to his feet. He wore a sleeveless vest, his arms tattooed in spiral designs. From the rooftop, she hadn't noticed, but here on the ground, when compared to Tannor, he was huge.

Situated, he started to gather in his surroundings as a nearby dazed Tannor was clutching at his side. The reason was because underneath him; she saw the metal of a rifle. Even after the fall, he had held on to it after wrestling it from the large man.

A swift kick from the assassin to Tannor's side removed him from the weapon and sent him rolling over the snow, crashing against the wall of the building. Before she could realize what she was doing, Ebele found herself in the air, leaping off the side of the steps. With the rifle reversed in her hand, she swung it like a club above her head. The man blocked the butt end of her rifle.

When she landed, he pushed forward, sending her sliding back in the snow. With the little space he had, he raised his rifle, pointing it at her head, but Ebele had already leapt back at him, her hand on the rifle's barrel, pushing it away as the thunder crackled through the air around her. She felt the vibration piercing her hand, going up her arm and into her neck. But she ignored it all as she held the barrel end of the captain's rifle in her other hand and once again swung it at the assassin's head.

This time, it connected with the side of his face, sending him spinning around as the barrel of his rifle slipped from his hand. Ebele swung again, but he regained his senses, blocking her blow with the side of his arm. Before she had the chance to respond, he stepped into her momentum, kneeing her in the stomach. Ebele's eyes went wide as she was lifted off her feet with the blow, bent over the man's knee as the breath left her body.

Never had she felt a pain in her stomach this heavy. That was until the follow up strike to the back to the back on her neck came immediately afterwards and she went rolling off his knee and down face first into the muck. Her body shook as she grabbed a handful of snow, trying to regain her footing and retaliate. But each blow from this mammoth of a man shook her system from the outside in. She knew another blow would come before she could get up, but she pushed forward anyway.

Then before another blow could come, the shadow of something passed by her. There was the sound of a girl screaming. And when she looked up, she saw a frantic Aretta in front of her, a small blade in her hand, swinging wildly. An unskilled blade is just as sharp as a skilled one, and the assassin made sure to dodge the panicking woman in front of him. But after the third uncoordinated swipe. He just simply reached out, grabbing her by the wrist, then buried his other fist into her face.

One hit was all it took for Aretta to go limp in the man's arm, her knees buckling as the knife went falling from her hand, towards the snow.

But catching it on the way down was Ebele, as she stepped in low to the ground, slashing it upward towards the man's chest. She wasn't thinking anymore, her eyes glowing with a wild heat she couldn't comprehend. Not strategy, she just knew that every fiber of her being was telling her to hurt this man. The moment she saw Aretta stop moving, she found herself unable to control her own body's movement.

The first swing caught him off guard as it pierced his clothing, forcing him to drop Aretta and step back. She did pierce the skin of his chest, but the cut was shallow. She then followed up with a lunge, which he sidestepped. Trying to rebound to face him, her only reward was a fist to the side of her face. Rattled, she took the blow; her face sliding from his knuckles to his wrist and then up his arm as she gnashed her teeth, swinging the blade towards his face.

This time, the blade dug into his cheek as he twisted his face, trying to dodge. He then stepped back, away from Aretta's body; his face now finally showing an emotion of anger.

Ebele's own face was bruised, and she could see the steam from her breath as she hunched over, one hand protectively over Aretta's body and the other holding a blade, pointed at him, ready to attack. He was bigger, stronger, and probably faster than her at this point. But she didn't care. She'd never been in a fight like this and had no idea what the right way to do anything was. All she knew was that she was angry and that he was the reason why.

The rage inside kept her conscious even though her body felt as if it was screaming at her. Heavy breathed and with the world growing dimmer by the second, she lunged at him again, blade aimed at his throat. He in response, swiped down hard on her wrist in a chopping motion. The impact forced her hand open and sent the blade flying to the side as she went crashing into his large body. There, before she knew what had happened, she found his arms wrapped around her, lifting her into the air.

The realization hit quickly as she found herself trapped in his arms as he began to squeeze. It felt as if her body was being crushed. Her legs started to fold backwards as she placed her hands at each side of his face, digging her thumbs into his eyes. He gritted his own teeth and squeezed harder. She, in turn lurched back into his grasp and took as much of a breath as she could, before swinging her neck forward and sinking her teeth down into his neck.

The combination of couched out eyes and a bitten neck forced a gargle of pain as he tried stepping back with her in his arms. But he tripped, and they both went falling into the snow, where he finally released her, gripping the hair at the back of her head to pull her bloodied mouth away from his neck. He then punched her again so hard that she rolled off of him back onto the snow.

Aretta, having regained consciousness, peered through bloodied eyes, seeing that he had tripped, and gripped onto his leg as he flailed.

Another sight, in the snow, was the assassin's rifle, and the memory of her battle with the previous assassin came rushing back into her mind. So, before the assassin could regain his footing, she reached out, grabbing his weapon. Then, attaching herself to his back, she placed the core of rifle atop his neck and began to pull as hard as she could.

He rolled over, crushing her into the snow before reaching up and grabbing the middle of the rifle, trying to free it from his neck. From side to side, he rolled while trying to escape, pushing up on the rifle, trying to prevent suffocating. He was strong, stronger than her, and she was losing. She could feel the rifle begin to buckle, the splintering of the wood sounding over their moans and heavy breathing. Her fingers raw with the desperation to not let him free, she gripped harder; she pulled harder; using everything she had.

Then it happened. With a snap, the stock of the rifle shattered; metal and wood splinters bursting free as he gasped for air.

"Noooo!" she yelled in a panic as she released the rifle's

remains and wrapped her legs around his side and reached up, swinging her arm under his chin, and began trying to choke him again. But with her head within reach, he began punching at her head over and over. Each punch impacted her so much she could feel her teeth rattle. But she held on, squeezing as hard as she could, even as he took a hand full of her hair and began to pull.

She prayed for strength; any essence she had left she exhausted as she lay crushed under his weight. She tried to fight on, but she couldn't think of anything else to do. So, she did the only thing she could, just hold on as long as she could as he battered and pulled on her.

But then, while he still held her hair, the battering to the side of her face stopped. She heard a grunt and managed to open one eye, barely able to see a battered Tannor holding on to the man's arm so that he couldn't move.

There, under the snow while Aretta held the man's leg and Tannor clasped onto his arm, Ebele seized the opportunity and lurched back with whatever strength she could, trying her best to choke the large man. He flailed even more, his gargled moans defiant of them all.

Then he began to slow, his grip on Ebele's hair loosening as his body twitched, becoming still. But Ebele kept her teeth gnashed, still squeezing, only releasing it when she could no longer feel the pounding of his heart on her chest.

And there, all three of them lay covering one large man as white crystals danced around them in a field of cold powder. With the threat of violence gone, the people who ran into their homes earlier were now stepping out of their doors, and Ebele rested her hand down in the snow, her arms stretched out as they all came surrounding them.

CHAPTER 17

Aretta sat in a pretty green dress, a solemn look on her face as she stared at her own reflection in the mirror. In front of her knelt a maid, a skin powder kit in her hand, to touch up the bruises on her face. She remembered little about the day before. There was a struggle and some punching involved. But then she remembered being kicked in the face while she held onto the leg of an overly large man. The next thing she knew, she was back in the Harsetti's home.

A stinging sensation under her eye, she turned her face as the maid tried to apply make-up to the side of her face. The feeling only heightened as the door to the room opened, and she saw the Warbitch enter.

"Now, now," said the maid. "Miss, you must let me cover that. I'm sure you don't want to be—"

"No. She looks fine," said Neekay, walking up and

leaning against the wall beside the mirror. "The dark marks under her eye lends an air of betrayal that I think suits her." She then turned to the maid. "Leave us."

"Ah, yes ma`am," said the maid as she placed the skin powder kit on the table and left the room, closing the door behind her.

"Have you come to laugh at me?" asked Aretta, looking up at her jailer.

"Why would I laugh?" said Neekay. "Do you not like the dress?" she said before sliding a foot between Aretta's legs and lifting her dress just enough to reveal the shackles around her ankles. "And I think the jewelry is fitting for someone who broke into the magistrate's building, freed a prisoner, and then offered up my own daughter to the king of Old Town."

Aretta sucked in her cheek with a frown as she turned back to face the mirror. "So, what now? Am I just your slave now? Why do you have me dressed in this?"

"Our mission here is done. We just have to meet with the magistrate before we go. Figured you might as well look the part," said Neekay before walking over to the door and opening it for her. "Come on. Out we go."

Aretta stared at the door outside into the hallway for a moment before closing her eyes with a sigh. Then, resigning herself to her fate, she stood up, the slight jingle of the chains at her ankles drifting into her ears. *Let's just get this over with.* She bit her lip in frustration, trying to swallow her pride. *I'm too tired to care about whatever this woman has planned anymore.*

She stepped out into the hall and the first thing she noticed was the absence of the guards that were at the door before. *I guess that means no more assassins.* She then followed behind the Warbitch.

Heading to the hall, she turned on the balcony where below she saw Mr. and Mrs. Harsetti with the children and Ebele. The lady of the house had a smile on her face as she fluffed the frills on Ebele's dress.

"Really Darlene," said the Warbird as she came down the steps. "I think that's the first smile you've managed since we've arrived. I never thought anyone would be so enthralled with our departure."

"Then clearly you do not know yourself," said Mrs. Harsetti as she rubbed Ebele's cheek. "But this one is welcome to visit whenever she pleases. If only to give her a reprieve from the influence of an at best 'questionable' mother. And besides, the children seem to like her."

"Allow me to walk you all to your carriage," said Mr. Harsetti.

And with several half-hearted farewells, Aretta and the group were escorted outside. There, in front of the manor, she saw the most ornate carriage she'd ever seen. It was white with gold trim and was even pulled by white horses. Amongst the snowy ground, it seemed like something out of the stories that parents told their children. The ones filled with magical flying animals and miniature people with wings.

"The magistrate seems to be trying to impress us," said the Warbird as they walked over to the carriage.

"I imagine this is the least he can do after what you've done for this city," said Mr. Harsetti as they reached the carriage. "Give my greetings to the Magistrate on your way out, will you? And I wish you the best too, of course."

Neekay placed a hand on his shoulder and smiled. "Goodbye, Harsetti. I wish you health. Oh, and do try to keep your penis out of the maids you bring home in the future. No need to have your lust scaring the children who might stumble in on you."

Mr. Harsetti's eyes went wide. But he quickly regained his composure and nodded his head. "I'll remember that advice."

"See that you do, and I thank you for the use of your home. I'll be sure to have the magistrate reimburse you for the damage."

They all gathered in the carriage, and with a snap of the reins by their chauffeur, they were off. The inside of the carriage was just as amazing as the outside. Beautiful white seats that felt softer than anybody that she'd even slept in. And on the wall were little gold lines that circled and spread through the entire interior.

"Aretta," said Ebele, reaching upward to her face. "You didn't let the maid cover your bruises?"

She shirked away from Ebele's touch. "Stop it, it still hurts. And you're no better with those scars on your face. I can see it under your makeup." The carriage apparently hit a small hole outside that caused the girls to bump into each other, the heads doing a soft tap together. "Owe. You were too close."

"You're the one who leaned in pointing your—" said Ebele before her eyes glanced down towards the floor. Then back towards the Warbird. "Mother!"

Aretta looked down, realizing that their head bump and subsequent reflex to lift her leg from the pain caused the chains around her ankles to show.

"Do not Mother me. She broke our contract. This is her punishment.

"She saved my life."

"After putting your life in danger, and lest we not forget, offering you to the king of Old Town in exchange for her brother."

"She did not. I just had to enhance his—"

"Ebele, stop," said Aretta, reaching over and placing a hand on hers.

"What? But—"

"She's right... your mother's right. The plan... the plan was to give you to him and for me and my brother to escape. I... I just figured nothing'd happen to you since you're like a noble and stuff." She lowered her head, not wanting to look her in the eye. And then, in a meek tone, she spoke. "I didn't change my mind until after I had already taken you to him."

Ebele balled her lip before shaking her head and once again turning to her mother. "Well, I don't like it. If she wants to go. We should just take off the chains and let her do what she wants."

"I'm sure you do think such easy thoughts," said her mother with a smile. "But unfortunately for you. It's not your decision to make. She owes me a debt and I intend to see that she pays it."

The carriage slowed to a stop, rattling as the driver dismounted and opened the door. They all stepped out, and to Aretta's surprise, she saw what seemed to be the entire town's guards standing in front of her. And ahead, were a set of men and women in white and gold, holding similar rifles while looking overly serious.

"What is all this?" asked Ebele as she looked around, confused.

"It seems someone important has finally arrived," said the Warbird as she began ascending the steps and waving for the girls to follow along. Up the steps they went to the slow applause of the town's guard, before reaching the top where she saw an older man in white and gold standing waiting for them.

"Greetings, Warbird," said the older man as they approached.

"Greetings Commander."

"I arrive here, and the first thing I am greeted with is a tale of how not only you, but your daughter, have apparently taken out a group of assassins. I see the years and child rearing have not dulled your skills."

"I will admit, the years have been kind to me," she said with a smile. "What about yourself? I heard that you were appointed as a king's guard. Are you enjoying the court affairs and political scheming? Did he order you to bring us to him?"

The old man sighed. "No, unfortunately, your

information is slightly off. While I do protect the royal family, I am, in fact... not a king's guard."

"No, he is not," came a feminine voice from a shadowy corner as a woman appeared, stepping forward to stand by the commander. "He is, in fact, a Queen's Guard." She tapped her finger on the shoulder of the man.

"Hello... Cete," said her mother with a shake of her head, but a smirk on her lips.

She raised a finger. "Uh uhhh. It's Queen... Cete. You should know. It was you who put me in the position."

The Warbird smirked with a nod of her head. "Queen... Cete. Do you want me to bow and kiss your feet now?"

"Just the Queen will do for now," she said as she stepped forward, till she was just inches away from her, looking her up and down. "I see you've been busy. Your essence is pouring out all over you. Must have been an exciting fight."

"Must you play these games?" asked Neekay with a roll of the eyes and a sigh. "Clearly you—"

Aretta could have sworn she felt the world change as she saw the Queen reach up and grab the Warbird by the collar of her shirt, pull her forward, and place her lips on hers. But apparently, she wasn't alone, because as she looked around to see if she was in fact hallucinating, she saw the same expression of shock on Ebele's face.

The sight of their lips pressed hard onto each other was amazing. Not only did the Warbird let it happen, but she seemed to be responding to it. Not to mention the sight of the Queen cupping a breast in her hand as she did so.

Then, after their moment had passed, the Queen removed herself from the Warbird lips, letting go of her ruffled collar then patting it to smooth it back on. "Ohhhh." She smiled. "It has been a while, hasn't it?"

"Yes," said the Warbird with a similar smile. "Although, I think it's been longer for you than it has for me."

"Well, I might just say that is because of you." She placed a finger on the Warbird's chest. "You became quite stingy with your affections after you found that husband of yours." Apparently satisfied, the Queen's eyes wandered over the group, seemingly finding something of interest in Ebele. So much so that she had to look twice. "Oh my. She really is another you at that age." The Queen stepped to the side of the Warbird, staring at Ebele so hard that Aretta thought she might see an encore of the previous moment, just with the daughter.

"Ah... hello... your highness," said Ebele, a hint of fear in her voice.

"Hello child. Has anyone told you how much like your mother you appear?"

"Ah, yes ma`am. I was recently told that by someone who claims to be my great auntie."

"Claimed?" said the Queen with a curious look. "Do you often get strangers claiming to be your relatives?"

"She's talking about Analyse Prydwen," her mother chimed in.

"Oh," said the Queen before realization came to her eyes and she resumed her smile, turning back to the Warbird. "Really? Are you so out of sorts with your family that you'd deny your daughter that?"

"And do you think you're the one to lecture me on family?"

The Queen laughed. "Yes, I imagine you're right."

Neekay stepped beside the Queen and turned to Aretta and Ebele. "Girls, this is Queen Cete. We, like Mrs. Harsetti, all attended school together."

"Harsetti?" asked the Queen, looking confused.

"Darlene."

"Oh, yes, right. I supposed even she could convince someone to marry her."

"Girls," said the Warbird, making a face acknowledging the comment. "The Queen is what you might call an essence eater?"

Apparently noticing the confusion on her face, the

Queen clarified. "It just means that I am able to consume another person's essence and use it in any way I see fit."

"I've read about that," said Ebele. "Is that how you consume essence? By kissing?"

"Oh… yes, it can be done that way, amongst many others. Although I suppose kissing is one of the easiest." She then patted Neekay on the shoulder. "Now, if you don't mind. I would like to speak with your mother about something."

"Oh, yes. That's fine."

"Do not worry, dear," said Neekay, as she nodded down the steps. "I'm sure you will have other things to occupy your attention."

Ebele turned to see Tannor and Helhiem down at the bottom of the steps being held up by the guards. Holding the sides of her skirt, she hurried down the steps to greet them. Aretta just stood there for a moment, not knowing if she should follow Ebele or her mother.

"Go on," said the Warbird. "Just remember, you are not allowed to leave her side. I doubt you'd want every city guard here looking for you."

Aretta frowned as the Warbird followed the Queen inside the magistrates' building. But with a sigh began descending the steps, taking her time, and heading over to be with Ebele. She walked slowly, minding the chains around her ankles, imagining that a fall would be quite bad.

Ebele was smiling and laughing with the two boys.

"Does this mean you'll be leaving the city now?" asked Tannor.

"Yes, I think we will be leaving tomorrow and heading home. I think we're too late for the Ballasade Tournament. I mean, I was supposed to enter, but with everything that's happened. I'll be happy to just go home and sleep in my own bed. What will you two do?"

"I think I'll be leaving this city," said Tannor, with a smile. "After pointing a rifle at the magistrate's head. I don't think it would be wise to stay." He gave her a suggestive look. "I don't suppose you know of a place that might be available. Perhaps one with a girl about your height and with a smile similar to yours? Also, it'd help if she enjoyed kissing while hanging out of a window."

"You mean when someone surprises her with a kiss? And who's to say that she liked it?"

"Perhaps she needs to try again. Just to make sure."

Ebele rolled her eyes with a shake of the head before turning to Helheim. "And what about you... Oh, wait, your photograph machine. The Queen is here. I bet if I asked Mother, you'd probably be able to take a picture."

"Really?" asked Helheim. "If it's not too much trouble." He lifted his case. "I did bring it, after all."

Suddenly, there was a commotion down the road. Aretta turned to see the guards parting and allowing another carriage through. Atop it were two men, and one was waving. Aretta squinted her eyes as she looked at the man who had the reins. *Where do I know him from?* Then she remembered the weird moment when she first met Ebele and the man who had been her attendant. *It's him. He's returned. Then who's—*

"Father!" shouted Ebele with a grin as she bounced up and down, waving back at him. The carriage finally stopped, and the man dismounted, giving Ebele a grand hug that lifted her off her feet and into his arms.

"I'm so glad you're safe. We've ridden day and night to get here." He looked around. "Where's your mother?"

"Up there," said Ebele, pointing to the top of the steps. "Apparently she is talking to the Queen about something."

"The Queen is here?" he, asked as a slight grimace came over his face.

"Why? Does the Queen have an issue with you? She seemed to be fond of Mother... I think."

"Well... it's a long story, dear. No need for boring tales now."

The door to the carriage opened, and out stepped a

young man who smiled at Ebele. "Hello there."

Ebele grinned from ear to ear at the sight of the young man as he walked over to her and leaned down, placing the temple of his head against hers. She, in kind, responded by leaning up and kissing him.

"Ahem," said her father, in a cough.

Ebele then pulled herself away from the young man, stepping to the side of him and with her cheeks heightened by a smile she couldn't seem to rid herself of. "Sorry. Ah… everyone." She pointed to her father. "This is my father." She gestured to the boy beside her. "And this is my finance, Saro."

Saro then extended his hand to the three of them, bowing and kissing the hand of Aretta. She could see why Ebele was enthralled by the young man. He was a broadly made boy and easily over a foot taller than Ebele. Tannor looked to be in shock as he shook the young man's hand. Whether from the kiss or the sight of him, she wasn't sure. Although Helheim now had a mischievous grin on his face, his chest jerking as he tried to hold in his apparent laughter. With the scar on his face still healing, she imagined it hurt quite a bit to laugh.

***

The Queen escorted Neekay into the magistrate's building and into a lavishly decorated room. At the center were two couches and between them a tea set and glass cups.

"Take a seat, Neekay," said the Queen as she herself sat down. "Would you like something to drink? It's a blend that we grow in the capital. I think you will enjoy the flavor."

"Thank you," said Neekay, taking a seat opposite the Queen and crossing her legs. "What is it that you wish to speak about?"

The Queen poured herself and Neekay glass. "Go on. Give it a try. I think that bitter information should be swallowed with something sweet."

Neekay looked at the Queen for a moment before reaching forward and grabbing the cup hand and lifting it to her lips. "Fine, but first, tell me about the green powder your husband seems to be so interested in."

"I see. I assume it was too much to hope that you hadn't fallen on that information. But given that one of the researchers is your family. I guess it was just hopeful thinking on my part." The Queen waved her hand dismissively. "But no matter. We've found a more potent form of powder, and it seems that only a select few can make use of it. And given your ability, I'm sure that you were."

"I haven't tried. I was too busy focusing on other things."

"Really? That is surprising. Well, either way, my husband is apparently determined to find people who can harness its power."

"Your husband? Are you sure it's not yourself? For an essence eater such as yourself, I imagine the prospect of having a horde of high-class soliders within arm's length might sound highly enticing."

"Humph. As if I would feast upon a gathering of bumpkins from who knows where. I have more control than that."

"That didn't seem to stop you when it came to me."

"Please, given our history together, it just so happens to make your essence taste sweeter." She bit a finger, looking her over. "I wouldn't mind another more intimate taste if you're willing."

"Oh, you're asking my permission this time? There's a rare occurrence."

"Well, you are married now. I figure it's the least I can do. But let's progress, shall we? Unless there's something else you wish to ask?"

"There is the matter of the assassin that my daughter managed to subdue. He's in the dungeon, I assume. I'm curious about what you wish to do with him. He should be waking up soon."

"Oh. him. He woke some time ago. Apparently, after losing to your daughter and her little friends, he's lost the will to live. We'd interrogated him, of course, but it ended up proving to be useless, so we just pierced his neck and gave him what he wanted. A merciful end for the remnants of the war."

"Remnants. The same could be said of us."

"Yes. Although less atrophied than most." She placed her hand under her chin. "Anything else?"

Neekay swirled the teacup beneath her nose, embracing the aroma. "No, that's it. You are free to continue."

"Good. First, I would officially like to thank you for handling this mess with the assassins. The king had his interests on the matter ever since he'd read the reports."

"Interests? Is that what you call leaving a city to wallow in death from the comfort of a castle?"

"Not so much as you would think. A few of our agents infiltrated the city before you arrived. But after your arrival, I gave word for them to hold off on any activity and allow you full dominance. I do remember how you hated being interrupted when you're working. Or answering to anyone, for that matter." She took a sip of tea. "The Warbird doesn't exactly prefer cages, unless it's the ones she makes for herself. Speaking of which. How is married life? We never get to talk about our prospective husbands."

Neekay sighed. "You're never going to let that go, are you?"

"Oh dear, I've long since accepted it. I just enjoy reminding you of the situation you placed me in." She shook her head with a sigh. "While being Queen has its benefits, one can hardly say that it is ideal. So much responsibility. Children, spies, assassins, holding royal court, nobles to be placated or killed. It can all get to be so tedious."

Neekay took a sip of her own tea. "I seem to remember you being very good at navigating most of those things."

"Yes, well. Then that leads me to the reason I've come. The spies in the city have reported that it wasn't just you who performed the murder of the assassins. Your daughter also participated. And judging by the scars on her face, I'd supposed that intel to be true."

"She played a part, yes. But in matters of war, she is unrefined. She doesn't have my vision for it."

"Be that as it may. My husband seems to have taken an interest." She leaned forward. "The same interest he'd taken in you all those years ago."

Her tongue rolled around the side of her jaw, as she stared at the Queen for a moment. "I'm not letting him near my daughter to sire any bastards."

The Queen smiled. "No, not him. His sons. They are all around her age. Sixteen. Seventeen. And how old is yours? Seventeen also, I believe?"

"She's engaged."

The Queen laughed. "You and I both know that's no cover for her to hide behind. While running off and marrying that researcher did wonders for your freedom and my social status, it would seem that the consequences of our selfishness has now fallen to our children." The Queen placed her tea back down on the table and folded her hands on her lap, looking her directly in her eyes. "I did try to convince him to forgo this decision, but he simply will not budge on the matter. Your progeny will be attending school come the summer, along with his other sons, and subsequently, the tournament. No longer can you hide her in your home. Whether she has your gift or not, we shall see."

Neekay was quiet for a moment before taking in a long sip of the tea. "Fine. But if I remember correctly, every student is allowed to have a servant come along with them. Has that changed?"

"No, it's still allowed. Although very few actually do as the servant also has to be around the age of..." The Queen smiled. "The other one that was with her who also had the bruises. I see. You always were good at planning ahead."

***

A little while later, Ebele greeted her mother as she walked out of the Magistrate's office with the Queen.

"Look at you, dear," said her mother as she approached her father. "Were you trying to come in valiantly and save your damsel of a wife?"

"It was something of that matter, yes. Surely you didn't expect me to just wait while you and our daughter were apparently trapped in a city with shadowy assassins."

Neekay kissed her husband, wrapping her arms around his waist, before turning to Saro. "And I suppose you thought you would be the second hero and swoop in to save my daughter."

"Yes, ma'am. That was the plan. I even brought an extra rifle after hearing you only had yours."

The Warbird reached over, pinching the cheek of Saro with a smile. "Good boy, I'm glad to see you've turned out so well."

"Hello Arlan," said the Queen. "It's so good to see you again."

"Yes," said her father, with a smile and a bow. "It's very wonderful that you've come to this city. After the turmoil it has just endured. I think it will do wonders for its people to know that their Queen cares so much for them."

The queen laughed. "You really have turned into a well-spoken man, haven't you?"

"Excuse me," said Helheim as he approached the Queen. "Hello, your highness. I was wondering if you would give me the honor of a photo. My friends here will be leaving soon, and I wish to give it to them. Oh, and of course if you like, I will have one for yourself as well."

The Queen stared at Helheim for a moment and then looked down at his luggage case. "I see. I suppose that shouldn't be a problem."

Together, in front of the steps to the magistrate's building, they all gathered around to stand before Helheim as he covered himself with the cloth. From behind it, he held up a small tray with powder atop.

"Ebele, if you would be so kind."

And with a glow of her eyes, there was a flash as they all smiled.

Afterwards they all said their goodbyes, Ebele, Aretta, her mother, and father all entered the wagon, with her fiancé taking a seat outside at the head of the carriage with Kayin.

"Well," said her father. "It sounds as if you've had a new experience. Although I'd prefer our daughter not to be involved in wars and murder. How are you, Ebele? Are you well?"

Ebele pondered the question for a moment. *Am I okay? I mean, I think I am. I've never had to fight for my life before. Or see someone killed before.* She thought back to her fit of crying in the room with Helheim. *Well, I certainly wasn't okay then.* "I... I don't know, father. I think I'm doing as well as could be expected. But I'm sure when we get home, I will have a lot of questions for you."

"Really? Such as?"

"Well, like having family members I wasn't aware of or how certain people are able to drink powder enhanced by essence."

"Our daughter managed to get herself involved with someone who was essence addicted," her mother chimed in. "A self-proclaimed king of a shantytown in the city's lower depths."

"That doesn't sound safe," he said to his wife before turning back to Ebele. "I guess it's too late to ask that you stay away from those types. But essence addiction wasn't something that would have ever come up back home in Tymit. We address those issues fairly quickly. And besides, only those who have essence can even drink it and survive. Otherwise, they'd die from poisoning since their body wouldn't be able to process it."

Ebele's eyes went wide as she turned towards Aretta, whose face carried a similar look of shock.

"Hummm," moaned her mother with a smile as she stared at Aretta. "I must have forgotten that bit of information." She then turned to her husband and wrapped an arm around his, leaning in to give him another kiss on the cheek. "Thank you, dear. You seem to have just given me something to occupy my time with."

Epilogue

The following day, the Queen exited the Magistrate's manor, followed by the Magistrate himself. There was a crowd of people ahead that stood to see her off. Her adoring subjects waved and she raised a hand in kind. At the head of the crowd, she noticed an older one-eyed man holding a cane to support his hobbled leg. The sight of his leg made her smile a bit.

"Thank you for the visit, your highness and please give the king my well wishes."

"Do not worry, Magistrate. We do not blame you for the incident with the powder being exposed. If anything, because of your shortsightedness in involving the Warbird, you may have presented the royal family with a solution to a problem that has been plaguing us for quite some time."

"I... I don't understand how. But I'm very glad to have been of use to you."

"As well you should be. We will be sending a convoy to retrieve the final load of Sillian Powder in the coming weeks. Please be sure not to lose it this time."

"Yes, Your highness."

"Good," said the Queen as she reached the bottom steps. There her guards stood waiting, with one holding the door open for her. She stepped inside and took a seat. "And Magistrate, you do have a child at the academy, do you not?"

"Ah yes, ma`am. My daughter attends the academy. Her mother and I are both very proud. She has achieved full marks since she's arrived."

"Full marks? That is quite the achievement." She signaled for the door to be closed. "Be well, Magistrate."

And with the shout from one of the guards, the horse stomped forward, pulling the Queen's carriage down the city street. Eventually, she would make her way towards the gates where the carriage would stop. The door opened, and Helheim would poke his head inside.

"Hello, mother."

"I was wondering where you'd gotten off to."

Helheim stepped inside and took a seat opposite the Queen, placing his photograph luggage on the floor and his cane over his lap. "I had, to say goodbye to a friend."

"Yes, well, tell me. What was that the other day? Did you not wish to reveal yourself to the Warbird?"

"Not so much that. I just assumed it would be less of a hassle to keep up the ruse, rather than answer all the questions that would have come had I admitted who I was."

"I see," said the Queens as she looked him over and shook her head as the carriage started moving again. "How is your leg?"

"Still as annoyingly half-functioning as it ever was," he said as he rubbed his knee. "Using my essence to dull the pain has gotten less taxing over the years, and the focus is I need is hard to maintain."

"Well, we'll have a doctor look you over when we return

to the capital."

He placed a hand on the bandage at his check. "As well as this?"

"The leg, yes. The face, depending on the severity, perhaps not. You're a prince and I think it would do your reputation some good to hold a scar you received while in the line of duty. Think of it," she said with a raise of the hand as if weaving a thin line through the air. "A crippled boy, fighting off the onslaught of assassins with the legendary Warbird herself. Deficient as he may be, he couldn't stand to see his people suffer." She smiled. "I do believe you will be thought of in the light of, perhaps, a young, gallant knight."

"Except that I have two healthy older brothers, and I doubt father would ever choose me over them to succeed him."

"You'd be surprised. I have spoken to your father about your accomplishments in this city. He seemed impressed and wished to hear the story from your own lips."

Helheim sighed. "I really do wish I shared your wishful thinking when it comes to father, mother. He gives my brothers rifles and horses, and what does he give me? A photograph machine, that was itself, an unwanted gift from a lesser noble."

"Do not worry," said his mother as she reached over, patting her son on his crippled leg. "The expectation of your brothers might serve as a hindrance for them, whereas your hindrance may serve as a benefit for you in the end." She gave him a warm, motherly smile. "The game is played in multiple fashions, my child."

Teddy Baire

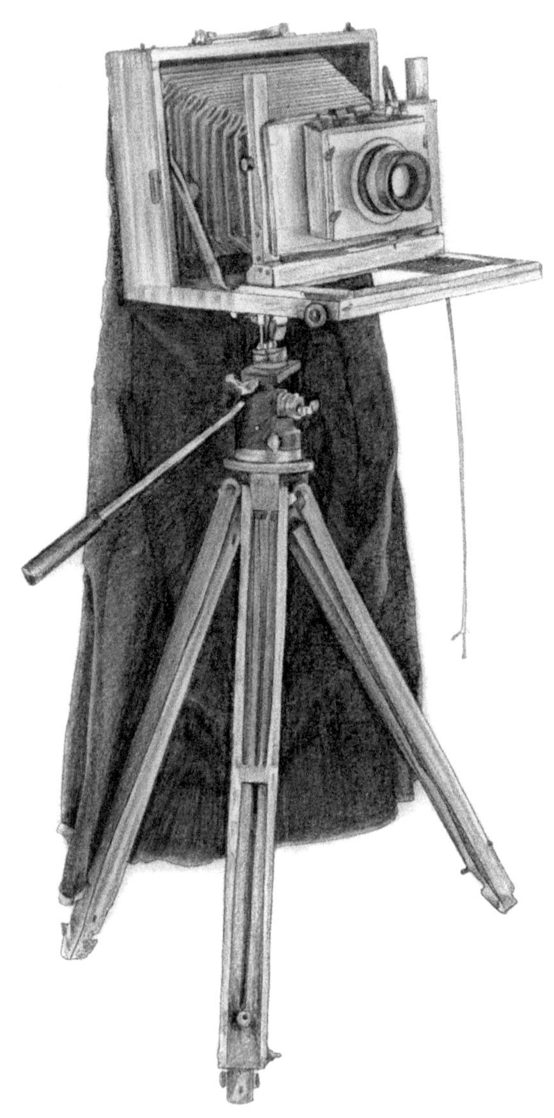

Thank you for reading

Gunpowder Dolls

This is book #7 in the Teddy Baire 10 book project. We hope that you have enjoyed this novel.

And if you are interested in Teddy Baire's 10 book project. Please visit the web site.
www.teddybaire.com
and see what other novels have been written.